THE
DAY AFTER
OBLIVION

**Pinnacle Thrillers
by TIM WASHBURN**

The Day After Oblivion

Cataclysm

Powerless

THE
DAY AFTER
OBLIVION

TIM WASHBURN

PINNACLE BOOKS
Kensington Publishing Corp.
www.kensingtonbooks.com

PINNACLE BOOKS are published by

Kensington Publishing Corp.
119 West 40th Street
New York, NY 10018

All Kensington titles, imprints, and distributed lines are available at special quantity discounts for bulk purchases for sales promotions, premiums, fund-raising, educational, or institutional use. Special book excerpts or customized printings can also be created to fit specific needs. For details, write or phone the office of the Kensington sales manager: Kensington Publishing Corp., 119 West 40th Street, New York, NY 10018, attn: Sales Department; phone 1-800-221-2647.

This book is a work of fiction. Names, characters, businesses, organizations, places, events, and incidents either are the product of the author's imagination or are used fictitiously. Any resemblance to actual persons, living or dead, events, or locales is entirely coincidental.

PINNACLE BOOKS and the Pinnacle logo are Reg. U.S. Pat. & TM Off.

ISBN-13: 978-0-7860-4250-0
ISBN-10: 0-7860-4250-8

First printing: February 2018

10 9 8 7 6 5 4 3 2 1

Printed in the United States of America

First electronic edition: February 2018

ISBN-13: 978-0-7860-4251-7
ISBN-10: 0-7860-4251-6

To

Keira Eve Chandler

and

Camdyn Adalynn Snider,

the first of the next generation.

PRESENT DAY

CHAPTER 1

As the group from this morning's intelligence briefing filters out of the Oval Office, President Thomas Aldridge arches his back, trying to alleviate the pain that has taken up residence along his lower spine. The world's escalating problems are reflected in the length of the briefings, this one lasting more than an hour. Not only are they dealing with the usual problems—North Korea, Syria, Putin—but a growing trend that's threatening every major computer system, both civilian and government: hacking. And it's gone well beyond a few private e-mails leaked to the press.

The Russian and Chinese governments have hacked their way onto the nation's power grids and there's a growing concern it's only the tip of the iceberg. Aldridge knows from his daily briefings that the United States bears some responsibility for the enemy's computer infiltrations. The computer jocks at the National Security Agency (NSA) were the first to burrow into the power grid computer code in both China and Russia, as well as in many other countries. Aldridge can live with a power grid détente. It's the constant worry about infiltrations into the country's most sensitive networks that keep him up at night.

Aldridge sighs and arches his back a final time before walking over to his desk. A tall man, it doesn't take him long to cover the distance. He circles behind the desk and drops into his seat, reaching for his smartphone. Rail thin, Aldridge runs five miles on the treadmill every morning before most people are out of bed. And at fifty-six, he has the usual aches and pains but he's remarkably healthy for a man who has spent the past three years lugging around the mountain of problems that come with his office. He slips on his reading glasses and pulls up the favorites list on his phone. He sends a text to his son Jacob, a high school senior, about his first-hour calculus test.

The fact that President Aldridge has a smartphone is a long-simmering issue between him and the Secret Service. The battle raged until Inauguration Day, when the service relented and presented him with a phone that had been specially programmed by the computer whizzes at the NSA. Now the phone is always within reach no matter where he is in the world.

With his son struggling through calculus most of the semester, Aldridge wants to be a supportive parent. He glances up at his chief of staff. "What's next on the agenda, Isabella?"

Chief of Staff Isabella Alvarez consults her iPad. "You're meeting with a Girl Scout troop here in the Oval at ten."

Aldridge groans as his phone chimes, signaling a message. He taps the screen and chuckles. "Is it bad my son doesn't have a clue about how well he did on his test?"

"I'm sure he did fine," Isabella says. "Calculus was definitely not my subject. I think you either get it or you don't. Unfortunately I never did." Alvarez, forty-three, has the dark complexion and raven black hair of her Mexican ancestors, but her azure eyes are a gift from her Caucasian father.

The President thumbs out a reply, but before he can hit send, the phone powers off and begins to reboot. When the screen lights, a tingle of dread races down his spine. "What the hell?"

"What's wrong, sir?" Isabella asks, striding across the room.

The President turns the phone her way. On the screen are three words—*VENGEANCE IS OURS*. The white letters are in stark contrast to the scarlet background.

"I thought your phone was supposed to be unhackable," Isabella says.

"You and me both. See if you can get in touch—"

"Mr. President," his secretary says over the intercom, "I have an urgent call from General Vickers on line one."

The President picks up the phone and pushes the flashing button. "Earl, I think my phone's been hacked."

There's a slight pause on the other end of the line. "That's the least of our problems, sir. Both the NSA and DOD networks have been infiltrated."

"By whom?"

"Unknown, sir. It appears our system is frozen. All the monitors in our office are displaying a single message."

CHAPTER 2

U.S. Cyber Command
Fort George G. Meade, Maryland

General Earl T. Vickers, director of the NSA and U.S. Cyber Command, disconnects the secure line to the President and immediately mashes another button. "Colonel, I want the best computer operators we have in my office forthwith."

"Military or civilian, sir?" the colonel asks.

"Colonel, I don't care if they're from Mars. Send me the best we have." The general replaces the handset, stands, and begins pacing the perimeter of his office while his mind clicks through the list of probable suspects.

Located approximately forty miles northwest of the White House on the edge of Fort Meade, the National Security Agency occupies a sprawling office complex dominated by two large buildings sheathed in dark glass. The black glass creates a mysterious aura, befitting the secret work that goes on inside.

Created in 2009, USCYBERCOM started at the back of the pack and remains in catch-up mode as they attempt to thwart the daily assaults on the nation's defense networks. The man charged with the mission, Vickers, is a four-star who rocketed up the army ranks. A broad-shouldered man of average height whose salt-and-pepper hair is cut high and tight, Vickers has two advanced degrees from an Ivy League university. Unfortunately, neither is computer related, and the general is also playing catch-up, learning on the fly.

Vickers stops pacing when there's a knock at his door. "Enter," he shouts. That's the other thing about Vickers—he's not big on gatekeepers. If you want to see him, you knock and enter, if so instructed.

The door opens revealing a woman, early thirties, dressed in ripped jeans, flip-flops, and a T-shirt—all in black. Standing beside her is a man, approximately the same age, tall and broad, outfitted in khakis, a blue blazer, and a button-down shirt. Vickers waves a hand at the two chairs fronting his desk and works his way back to his chair. The woman saunters over, plops down, and crosses her leg, letting a flip-flop dangle from the edge of her big toe. The man straightens his blazer and sits, his posture ramrod straight.

Once both guests are seated, General Vickers drops into his chair finds it hard to draw his gaze from the silver hoop dangling from woman's left nostril. "You two are my computer experts?"

"Let me guess—you were expecting a couple of good old boys?" the woman says.

If the general has learned anything since taking command, it's that it takes all types to make a world, especially when it comes to computer programmers. He smiles. "I don't care what's between your legs, young lady, if you can get the job done. Names?"

The woman leans forward and grabs a foam football from the general's desk. "I'm Alyx Reed." She jabs a thumb toward the man seated next to her. "He can speak for himself."

"Sir, I'm Zane Miller, working for the National Security Agency."

Alyx leans back and begins squeezing the football. "Some shitstorm, huh?"

"How could our systems be hacked?"

"Anything powered by a computer can be hacked." Alyx tosses the ball in the air and catches it.

"The NSANet isn't connected to the Internet. It's a closed system."

"Intelligence operators all across the world have access to the system," Alyx says, tossing the football in the air again. "The system may be air-gapped from the World Wide Web, but there are other access points."

"Zane, are you thinking this could be an insider?"

Before he can answer, Alyx says, "The name Edward Snowden ring any bells?"

General Vickers scowls at Alyx, before turning to Zane. "Mr. Miller—insider, or have we been hacked by an outside group?"

"Unknown, at this time, sir. It's going to take some time to decipher *how* they hacked the systems and we're a long, long way from knowing who. But, sir, a more troubling problem presents itself."

"What's that?" Vickers asks. Alyx tosses the football to Vickers, who catches it one-handed.

"Good catch," Alyx says. "If they're on the NSA and DOD networks, you can bet your ass they've infiltrated most everything else."

Vickers leans forward in his chair. "Such as?"

"Sir, whoever they are," Zane answers, "they've probably spent years probing our networks, searching for weaknesses. Once they found a way in, they most likely spent many more months mapping our systems."

Alyx uncrosses her legs and leans forward in her chair. "What Zane is trying to say is that they've got us by the balls."

"But who?" Vickers asks.

"Won't know until we know," Alyx replies.

The intercom buzzes and the general's aide says, "Sir, Ms. Alvarez is on line one."

Vickers stabs the button and puts the phone to his ear. "Yes, ma'am?" He listens for a moment before hanging up the phone. "You two go to work. Set up in one of the video conference rooms in case I need you." He scribbles something on a piece of paper and slides it across the desk. "That phone number will reach me anywhere in the world, twenty-four/seven. I've been summoned to the White House."

CHAPTER 3

Weatherford, Oklahoma

Gage Larson eases down his driveway, the gravel crunching under the tires and the vast Oklahoma horizon filling the windshield. Weatherford, Oklahoma, is a dot on the map an hour west of Oklahoma City. Once a hotbed of oil drilling activity, the town has returned to a sleepy little hamlet after the price of oil dropped through the floor. Now it's back to plowing fields, baling hay, and rounding up cattle, unless you're lucky enough to land a job with the new boom—wind. Gage is one of the lucky ones. Growing up on a farm, Gage has a lifetime of knowledge when it comes to fixing things.

The Larson family stretches back four generations in Weatherford. Gage's great-great-grandfather homesteaded the original 160 acres after the land was released during the Cheyenne-Arapaho Opening in 1892. Over time the previous Larsons added to the original homestead and today the family farms 1,280 acres, a section two miles square. But Gage and Holly, his wife, wanting something different, bought ten acres and a two-bedroom fixer-upper on the edge of town. Now they can walk to get a gallon of milk instead of having to drive four miles into town.

The highest point in Custer County is not much taller than an average sapling, and the rest is flat farmland that spreads as far as the eye can see. This makes Weatherford the perfect location to harness one of Mother Earth's most abundant resources. The road transitions from gravel to potted pavement and the tires sing along the asphalt. The morning sun is bright, and Gage fumbles around in the seat for his sunglasses. He finds them tangled in the seat belt and pulls them free, plopping them in place. A farmer on his tractor is raking cut hay into furrows to be baled and the sweet aroma of freshly mown grass fills the cab. Nearing his turnoff Gage watches the shadows dancing across the field as the massive blades rotate in the wind and he pulls into the drive and bounces across the cattle guard.

Rounding a bend in the road, he can't help but marvel every time at the sheer size of the machines. The tower stands 260 feet tall and the blades extend another 126 feet beyond the hub, making the overall height 389 feet. In the distance, the towering turbines are lined out in a row that stretches for miles—ninety-eight in all. And Gage's job is to keep them turning. Each turbine is capable of producing 1.5 megawatts of electricity, and the entire wind farm pumps out 147 megawatts, enough to power over ninety thousand homes.

Gage pulls up to the closest turbine and kills the engine. He steps out, grabs his climbing harness from the back, and pulls it on. The newer turbines are outfitted with a small service elevator, but it traverses only a portion of the tower, leaving plenty of climbing to do. He cinches the harness tight and ties a line to his tool-box and a small ice chest and carries everything inside the tower. He wedges himself into the small elevator car and punches the button. It's a tight fit for Gage, who stands six-two and weighs north of 230 pounds. Although heavy, his weight is evenly distributed across his large frame. When the elevator stops, he wiggles out onto a small platform and begins to climb, the ice chest and toolbox dangling beneath him. The higher he goes the narrower the tower becomes. By the time he's reached the opening to the nacelle, or hub housing, he's drenched in sweat. In the August heat it's like climbing through a blast furnace. Gage pulls himself through the hatch carved into the floor and immediately triggers the power doors that open outward away from the guts of the machine.

The view is breathtaking, with visibility stretching for miles. In the far distance, he can just make out the top of the newest skyscraper towering over Oklahoma City. He pulls out his phone and snaps a few pictures to show Holly, his wife, after work. Little does he know the photographs will be the last he takes of ordinary life.

CHAPTER 4

White House Situation Room

President Thomas Aldridge strides into the Situation Room and waves down those rising to their feet. He pulls out his chair at the head of the table and sits. In addition to General Vickers, the others parked around the table include the director of Homeland Security, the chairman of the Joint Chiefs, the director of the CIA, director of National Intelligence, the vice president, and the President's chief of staff, Isabella Alvarez. All are members of the President's National Security Council, with the exception of Alvarez. In addition to the principals, deputies and aides line the perimeter of the room.

"I want to know how the nation's most secure networks were infiltrated and I want to know who's responsible." Aldridge turns his gaze on Vickers. "Earl, how could they have hacked an array of supposedly closed systems?"

"Sir, we're just beginning our investigation. The discovery of the infiltration only came to light when we received the message. It's unacceptable, but finding how and who is going to take some time. With your permission, sir, I'd like to videoconference in two of our top computer experts."

"General, I don't care who you conference in, but I want some damn answers."

Vickers nods to one of the technicians, and the large screen at the front of the room comes to life. On it are two people sitting side by side. "Sir, on the screen are Zane Miller and Alyx Reed, two of the best we have at Cyber Command and the NSA."

President Aldridge turns his attention to the screen, where the names are superimposed under their images. "Mr. Miller, how extensive is the damage?"

"Sir, we're in the very early stages of the investigation, but I believe we should assume they have access to most everything on both the NSA and Department of Defense networks," Zane replies.

Alyx takes advantage of the momentary pause. "This is not a pimple-faced teenager hanging out in his parents' basement. Whoever they are, they've most likely been in these computer systems for months, if not years."

"How did they gain access?" Aldridge asks. "These networks aren't connected to the Internet."

"You need to eliminate the idea of closed networks from your brain," Alyx Reed says. "If something is connected to a computer, it's hackable. Period. End of story. All software code has flaws. They've probably exploited several zero days to penetrate our networks."

"What the hell is a zero day?" Aldridge asks.

"An unknown vulnerability in the software," Zane replies. "I hate to be the bearer of bad news, sir, but it could be months before we discover who the real culprits are, if at all. That said, the sophistication of this infiltration does lead me to believe a nation-state is involved."

"For what purpose?" the President asks. "So they could post a graphic with this 'vengeance is ours' bullshit? That makes no sense. And why now?"

"Probably some type of triggering event or the last piece of the puzzle finally fell into place," Alyx says. "If they've hacked the DOD network, how big a stretch is it to think they've also hacked some of the military weapon systems? We've known for years that our computer systems are vulnerable, but there's so much dysfunction in this town nothing ever gets done. It's only when the shit hits the fan that someone takes notice and decides to do something."

General Vickers bristles at her comment. "Young lady, don't forget who you're talking—"

Aldridge waves a hand, cutting Vickers off. "She has a valid point, Earl. Seems we're always playing catch-up." Aldridge leans forward in his chair and stabs the table with his index finger when he says, "If this country is under attack, I need to know who the culprits are and I need to know today, not months from now. I want every agency with cyber capabilities working to unmask these bastards." Aldridge turns his gaze on Martin Caldwell, secretary of defense. "Marty, get the troops working to discover if any of our weapon systems are compromised."

"That's a tall order. We'll have to scour through millions of lines of computer code and that takes time, sir."

Aldridge sighs and runs a finger around the inside of his shirt collar. "How can we narrow it down? Which systems, if hacked, would do the most damage?"

"Duh," Alyx Reed says from the screen. "The nukes. There're four hundred fifty ICBMs set on hair triggers that are controlled by computer code that was out of date when it was installed. That's where I would start."

"The nukes are secure," Admiral Henry Hill, chairman of the Joint Chiefs, says. "The command and control systems are isolated from any and all outside networks."

"I don't know what it takes to get through to you, Mr. Four Stars," Alyx says, her voice laced with a touch too much disdain. "Anything controlled by computer code is hackable. It could happen with an infected flash drive, a piece of malware that slips through the system, or a careless employee. And that's just off the top of my head. Even here at the NSA, we have tools to gain access to air-gapped networks. You can bet the other side does, too. You need to wipe the thought of unhackable networks from your brain. They do not exist."

"Duly noted, young lady," Admiral Hill replies. "But I stand by my statement—the nukes are secure, Mr. President."

Revved up, Alyx charges in. "Forget the ICBMs for a moment. What about the ballistic missile submarines? Are they secure? Are they unhackable?"

"The nukes are secure," Hill replies, crossing his arms.

President Aldridge shifts uncomfortably in his chair. "Do you know something different, Ms. Reed?"

"As a matter of fact, I do. I think all of those stars on the admiral's shoulders are blinding him to reality. When those submarines surface there's a Windows XP chip on the engine that broadcasts the maintenance schedule back to base. We're talking an operating system that's years out of date and has more holes than a round of Swiss cheese. That XP chip is also connected to the submarine's control systems. And while we're talking about this tiny computer chip on a multibillion-dollar sub, that maintenance data is shared with other contractors via an unclassified network. Does that scare the hell out of you?"

Aldridge stands and leans forward, placing his palms flat on the table. "Admiral Hill, priority one is to determine if any of our nukes are compromised. Assign as many people as you need—hell, assign a battalion or two—but I want an answer before the end of the day. As for the rest of you, find the culprits. General Vickers, develop our options for a cyber counteroffensive. These people are playing in the wrong backyard and the big dog is about to bite back. We'll reconvene in one hour. And to be perfectly clear, I want answers." The President turns and strides from the room, Isabella Alvarez hurrying to catch up.

CHAPTER 5

Zane Miller unclips the microphone and steps around the table to kill the camera and the hot halogen lights. The temperature in the room is edging in on the inferno level and both occupants are perspiring. Alyx unclips her microphone and stands, arching her back as if feline blood was flowing through her veins. Lithe and lean, her movements are fluid. "So how did you get the name Zane?" she asks.

"Really? You just humiliated the chairman of the Joint Chiefs and you want to know about my name?"

"Four Stars is an overconfident asshole who doesn't have a clue. So, Zane?"

Zane shakes his head. "My grandfather and my father were both big Zane Grey fans. I tried to read *Riders of the Purple Sage* and only made it halfway through. Not my taste. So Zane it is." He works his way around the table and takes a seat in front of his laptop. "Back to the matter at hand. Who?"

Alyx bends down for a couple of toe touches before

arching her back again. She walks over to her work-space and sits. "Well, we haven't done much to piss off the Chinese lately, so my money's on Iran, North Korea, or Russia. Could be North Korea and Iran in some type of collaboration. Those jackasses are passionate in their hate for us."

"Could it be ISIS?" Zane asks.

"Too sophisticated for them. Unless they're working in tandem with one of our enemies. But I think that's highly unlikely. Hell, everyone on the planet would love to wipe those ISIS assholes off the map. Even if they are capable, which I find highly unlikely, they're too busy watching for missiles up the ass to organize something like this."

Zane navigates to the NSA gateway and enters his credentials. "I'm going to look for cross talk chatter about the hack. You?"

Alyx rests her long fingers on the computer's keyboard and begins to type. "Look for clues, maybe a partial IP address. Probably a dead end. These people aren't amateurs and I can guarantee you they're spoofing. But, who knows, I might get lucky and find a stray address that slipped through. I think Mr. Big Man is going to be disappointed when his one-hour deadline arrives."

"I'm not sure the President fully understands what's required to find the hackers," Zane says. "Unless . . ."

"Unless whatever surprise they launch points a finger?" Alyx says, leaning back in her chair. "Might be too late then."

"Think they're bluffing?"

"To what end?"

"Maybe hacking our most secure systems is the big payoff. Something they can pound their chests about," Zane says

"Bullshit. Send us a message—and then stand up and give us the finger? I don't buy it. Whoever is responsible has been planning this for years."

Zane wipes the sweat from his forehead. "Meaning they probably have something big in the works."

"Don't worry, Zane. Four Stars says we're safe . . . the conceited asshole. All those weapon computer programs are older than Methuselah."

Zane takes a moment to survey his new partner. Tall at five-eight, Alyx's bottle-black hair is sheered close to the skull on one side while the other half remains long, cascading down to conceal a portion of her face. The shorn hair reveals a left earlobe studded with piercings to match the one in her left nostril. He wonders what the rest of her body would reveal. "You married or have a significant other?"

"No and no. Have a couple of fuck buddies available when needed." Alyx glances up from her keyboard to see the blood rushing to Zane's cheeks. She smiles. "You?"

"Was and no. I spent four years in the army and the marriage was a hastily arranged affair we both thought we wanted. It began to unravel almost as quickly as it began. We were both deployed at alternating times. Probably had something to do with the unraveling."

Alyx straightens in her chair. "Might have something."

"What?"

"Maybe a partial IP address. Three numbers."

Alyx copies the partial address and pastes it into a browser on the NSA's network. She taps her foot, waiting for a response. The odds are long, with only three numbers and over six billion possible number combinations. She groans when the screen fills with nearly a million hits. "There has to be some way to narrow this down," she mumbles out loud.

"Can you exclude locations?" Zane asks. "Focus the search on known IP addresses associated with bad actors?"

"I used fairly narrow search parameters. Or I thought I did." Alyx begins typing. "Let me try something else." Going with her gut, she narrows the search parameters and the list of possibilities is narrowed to a hundred, all clustered in one region. "I can't say with one hundred percent certainty, but I believe the partial IP address resides somewhere around Shaoxing."

"Are you suggesting the Chinese are behind the hack?" Zane asks.

"Not necessarily."

CHAPTER 6

Weatherford

Gage Larson pulls a rag from his back pocket and mops the sweat from his face. Although he's working 260 feet above the ground, what little breeze exists only stirs the stifling heat around. The heat makes his job twice as difficult and exacerbates the fact the equipment is not cooperating. Today he's attempting to replace the brake pads, and every damn bolt he tries to unscrew is being a pain in the ass. Much like the brakes on a car, the braking system is used to slow or completely stop the turbine in times of emergency. Although blade pitch is used to control the turbine's speed, the braking system is the fail-safe to keep the turbine from destroying itself in high winds. Two skinned knuckles into the procedure, he finally breaks the last bolt loose. As he works the ratchet, his mind drifts to Holly.

Married for two years, Holly broke the big news almost eight months ago—she's pregnant. Now she looks like she swallowed a watermelon, and Gage is slowly coming around to the fact that he'll soon be a father.

It's not that Gage doesn't want children—it's more a matter of money. He's making about half of what he made in the oil patch and Holly's paycheck as a teacher barely covers the debt on the new tractor and ten head of cattle they purchased last year. By the end of the month, they're lucky if they have two quarters to rub together. Being able to afford everything raising a child demands is a concern weighing heavily on Gage's mind. He thought about selling some of the cattle or the tractor, but the cattle are moneymakers and the tractor is an essential tool. He sighs. He's going to have to come up with a plan because the baby's coming despite his misgivings.

Gage works the last of the bolts loose and pulls the heavy caliper away from the large steel wheel. The wind sends a blast of brake dust up his nose and he sets the caliper aside and stands to clear his nostrils. In the distance, an AWACS plane is taking off from Tinker Air Force Base in Oklahoma City. The large round radar dome mounted at the rear looks like a foreign appendage, much like a suckerfish on a shark. Gage recalls one of his buddies telling him the jets travel all over the globe, spending days in the air while being refueled by aerial tankers. That same friend also told Gage that Tinker Air Force Base has a big red X on it if something were to ever happen. But that's a worry for another day, Gage thinks—or hopefully never.

Watching the jet climb higher into the azure sky sparks a yearning that he quickly tamps down. While the crew flies off to parts unknown, Gage knows, without a college degree, he'll likely be working similar jobs the rest of his life. He did attend the local college to pick up a certificate that allows him to work on the turbines. And it's not that he lacks intelligence—he's plenty smart. It's just that he finds the classroom boring, especially discussing this theory or that theory without ever accomplishing a meaningful task. Gage is more of a doer. He turns away and pulls a bottle of water from the ice chest and unscrews the cap. After guzzling most of it, he pours the remainder over his head and tosses the empty bottle back into the ice chest and returns to the job.

Working to install the new brake pads, a task he's performed numerous times, his mind drifts again to Holly. She moved to town her junior year of high school, and it took Gage most of the year to convince her to go out on a date. That date stretched into their senior year, but the relationship hit a rocky patch when she left for Norman and the University of Oklahoma. She couldn't understand why Gage didn't want to "better himself"—her words—by getting a college degree. During her sophomore and junior years the relationship withered on the vine. Gage dated around, but spent most of his time moping. The other girls around town weren't like Holly. Not even close. His greatest fear was that she'd find a frat boy and move to the other side of the world. During her senior year, when thoughts turned to life after college, she and Gage would share an occasional dinner when she was back in town. It wasn't until Holly decided to return home to begin her teaching career that the last fragments of the smoldering fire reignited. Two years later they married.

A smile plays across Gage's face as he recalls the honeymoon in Cancún. But the smile quickly fades because thinking about their time frolicking in the sun and bedroom is not going to do anyone a bit of good, especially with Holly eight months pregnant. He knows. He's had his hand slapped more than once. Pushing those thoughts aside, he returns to the task at hand. After replacing the last brake pad, he reattaches the caliper to its mounting on the wheel and ratchets down the bolts. He stands and stretches his back before moving over to the side. In the distance, sunlight dances off the surface of a pond while, closer in, a pair of hawks cut lazy circles in the cloudless sky. Gage enjoys the view, having no clue how quickly it will all change.

CHAPTER 7

North American Aerospace Defense Command (NORAD)
Cheyenne Mountain Air Force Station, Colorado

If it flies in, out, through, or over North American airspace, NORAD tracks it. Tucked inside Cheyenne Mountain on the outskirts of Colorado Springs, the North American Aerospace Defense Command is also responsible for providing early warning of enemy attacks via missile, aircraft, or space vehicles over the United States and Canada. Using an array of sensors scattered around the globe, NORAD can detect a missile launch as soon as the rocket engines fire. Once moved to Peterson Air Force Base in a cost-cutting move, NORAD is back home in Cheyenne Mountain after the military brass decided the highly specialized equipment might be safer surrounded by several thousand feet of granite. So back NORAD went, the mountain acting as a natural shield against a possible electromagnetic pulse.

Carved out of the mountain during the height of the Cold War, the interior campus covers nearly six acres. The information from those thousands of sensors is fed into NORAD's supercomputers and the output is funneled into the Cheyenne Mountain Operations Center, a dimly lit room in the heart of the complex. Inside, large video screens are mounted high on the walls, and the floor space is occupied by U-shaped desks, computer monitors, and staff. Also scattered around the room are enough hardwired phones to open a telephone betting parlor.

Corporal Gary Rutledge, manning the satellite tracker, plucks one of those phones from the console and punches a button. When the call is answered, he says, "Sir, first signs of life from NORAD object three-nine-zero-two-six." He waits for the reply and sits up straighter in his chair. "Yes, sir," he replies before hanging up the phone. The object, a satellite, is of particular interest to those at NORAD.

Within moments, the duty officer, Captain Brice Tremblay, arrives at Rutledge's desk. "What do you have?"

Rutledge clicks on a video clip and turns the monitor for the officer to see.

"A course correction?"

"Appears so, sir," Rutledge replies. "The satellite has been tracking more northwest to southeast."

"And now the track is more north and south?" Tremblay asks.

"Yes, sir. I've extended the track out." Rutledge clicks on another video clip that projects the satellite's new course.

"The next pass brings it right across the central portion of the United States?"

"Yes, sir. Think they've been playing possum the entire time?"

"With them, you never know. What altitude?"

"Around three hundred miles, sir."

"How long to make the next loop?" the duty officer asks.

"Approximately ninety minutes."

"Task every available resource to track the target, Corporal. I want eyes on. I'm going to contact Space Command to see if they've intercepted any communications to or from the satellite. Notify me immediately if there are further changes."

"Will do, sir," Rutledge replies. As Tremblay retreats, Rutledge tags the satellite for easier tracking then searches the databases for any and all information on KMS-4, the latest North Korean satellite to enter Earth's orbit.

CHAPTER 8

President Aldridge and Isabella Alvarez reenter the Situation Room before the one-hour deadline has elapsed. Aldridge takes his usual seat and Isabella slips into a chair at the back of the room. Back on the video screen are Alyx Reed and Zane Miller.

"What do we know?" the President asks. The eyes of those around the table remain downcast. "Damn it, there has to be something." He glances at the screen. "Mr. Miller, Ms. Reed, anything on your end?"

"Sir, the staff here is combing through all of the signals intelligence," Zane says. "As of now, we've yet to find anything even vaguely related to the infiltration. Whoever is behind the hack, they're remaining tight-lipped. The search is ongoing and something may eventually turn up."

President Aldridge sighs and leans back in his chair. "Ms. Reed, any input?"

"I did find a partial IP address. Ran it through our databases and received about ten thousand hits. I narrowed the search to include likely bad actors and ended up with about a hundred hits. Interestingly, several of those were servers located in western China. I'm not sure it means much. They're almost certainly spoofing the attack."

"And by spoofing, you mean?" Aldridge asks.

"They've concealed their real IP addresses by hijacking other servers. That's what I would do."

Aldridge turns his attention to Admiral Hill. "Admiral, where are we with the nuclear weapons?"

"We're working it hard, but, as I said before, a software vulnerability could be a line or two of code out of millions upon millions. The weapon systems are extremely complex. Manpower isn't the problem, sir, it's time."

"Meanwhile, we don't have a clue what's in the works," Aldridge says.

"Kevin, are you picking up any chatter?" Vice President Camila Martinez asks.

The director of the CIA (DCI), Kevin Wilson, shakes his head. A tall, round man with a hairline in rapid retreat, he removes his steel-framed glasses and twirls them by the stem. "We're scanning every scrap of intel and pumping every asset we have for information. It's eerie how quiet it is. But, I don't think the silence can be sustained. I believe that whatever is going to happen will happen quickly. Otherwise, why reveal themselves?"

"Is there anything significant about today's date?" Martinez asks. Fifty-three, the former senator from Texas was a collegiate volleyball player who is still in remarkable shape. "An Islamic holiday? Or something of historical significance?"

"Not that I know of," the DCI says. "But I'm not a

holiday kind of guy. Could be today's the day everything fell into place."

"Hell, we're just speculating," Aldridge snaps. "If we don't have a clue about who the hell it is, we sure as hell can't arrive at a motive. So, do we sit here with our thumbs up—"

The intercom chimes. "Sorry for interrupting, sir," the voice says, "but I have an urgent call for Director Wilson on line four."

Rather than take the call at the table, Wilson stands and works his way to a phone at the back of the room.

"We need contingency plans," Aldridge says. "Both military and cyber. I want to hit these assholes with everything we have in our arsenal."

DCI Wilson returns to the table, his face ashen. He pulls out his chair and sits. "Sir, one of our flight teams has lost control of a drone."

"What do you mean, 'lost control'?" Aldridge asks, the veins visibly pulsing in his forehead.

"They said they've lost all flight capability and the drone is not responding to commands. I hate to say it, sir, but they believe the drone has been hacked."

"What type of drone?" Aldridge asks, his voice tight with anger.

Wilson glances at the video screen then at those assembled in the room before turning back to the President. "The newest one we have, sir."

The President glances away then whips his head back. "What?"

Wilson glances, again, at the screen. "Sir, can we lose the video feed?"

The President clenches his jaw. Only two other people present know what Wilson is referring to. He looks up at the screen and makes a snap decision. "Mr. Miller and Ms. Reed will stay with us, Kevin. They may be able to provide insight on the computer systems used to control the drone."

"But, sir?" Wilson pleads.

"What the hell is going on?" Martinez asks. "Just shoot the damn thing down."

"It's more complicated than that, Camila," the President says. He sags in his chair. "Lay it out, Kevin."

"Sir?" Wilson asks, his face as red as that of a toddler pitching a fit. "This entire project is need-to-know only."

"Well, now they need to know. All of it."

Wilson sighs, throws his hands up, and takes a moment to ponder the best way to present the information while still covering his ass. He takes a deep breath and says, "The drone we are discussing is not a run-of-the-mill drone. Code-named Stalker, the drone is a highly modified MQ-9 Reaper."

"Modified how?" Martinez asks.

Wilson loosens his tie. "The drone is a special DARPA project that's been years in the making. Powered by a small nuclear reactor, the drone can stay aloft indefinitely and cruise at altitudes beyond seventy thousand feet."

"If we're worried about military secrets, just obliterate the damn thing," Martinez says. "It'll be in so many pieces no one could ever reverse engineer it."

Wilson straightens a stack of paper on the table. "We can't, Madam Vice President, because of the drone's armaments."

Martinez leans forward in her chair. "Still, we're not talking about a nuclear warhead," Martinez says, watching both the President and DCI as their gazes drift toward the table. "Oh, Jesus, please tell me we're not."

Wilson takes a sip of water, his hand trembling. "Unfortunately, we are. The drone is armed with two tactical nuclear warheads."

Vice President Martinez tosses her pen onto the table. "What in the hell were you thinking? Seriously? A drone armed with nuclear weapons?"

Admiral Hill finds his voice. "The drone is a last-resort weapon in our fight against ISIS. The weapon would only be deployed under the most extreme circumstances."

"Well, Admiral," Martinez says, her voice filled with venom, "we no longer have control of your *last-resort* weapon." She turns her withering gaze on Wilson. "Where, exactly, did you lose control of this drone?"

Wilson grimaces. "Along the Iraq-Iran border."

CHAPTER 9

Semnan Missile and Space Center
Semnan, Iran

Buried deep underground, two hundred kilometers east of Tehran, is the command and control center of the Islamic Republic's Revolutionary Guard's aerospace division. This morning, the center is fully staffed and everyone is on high alert. Six years in development, the secret plan between Iran and North Korea will be enacted today. Even with the recent easing of sanctions, the Iranian bitterness lingers like a festering wound.

Today the wound pops.

Brigadier General Amir Mohammadi, commander of the aerospace division, is pacing the perimeter of the room. He stops, again, next to Saman Rezaei, the major in charge of communications. On that long-ago day, an e-mail account was established where both countries could communicate by using the draft function and never posting e-mails online.

"No change, sir," Rezaei says. "The satellite will be in position at the appointed time."

General Mohammadi glances at the clock on the far wall. Thirty minutes from execution of the grand plan. Thirty minutes for something to go wrong. Or worse, be discovered before implementation. There are a few things the United States didn't know when negotiating the latest nuclear agreement. The reason Iran was so willing to agree? They already had a fairly substantial stockpile of nuclear warheads. Mohammadi glances at the clock again and resumes his pacing. He stops at the missile launch console. All is in order. Birds are ready to fly. Mohammadi moves down the line, coming to a stop at the drone flight control center. "Where is the drone?"

"We're crossing the Caspian Sea, sir, at an altitude of twenty thousand meters. We will reach Russian airspace very soon."

"And the target?"

"We'll be on target, sir, at the eleven-hundred-hour deadline."

"Detonation altitude?" Mohammadi asks.

"If all goes according to plan, sir, three thousand meters."

"Excellent," the general says. "If antiaircraft fire becomes a problem, you are ordered to detonate."

"Yes, sir," the pilot says.

Mohammadi turns away and circles back to Saman Rezaei's station.

"No new e-mails, sir," Rezaei says. "Sir, have we . . . have we considered . . ."

"Spit it out," the general orders.

"Have we . . . considered . . . the implications . . . of our . . . actions?"

"Of course. Our supreme leader has a precisely detailed plan. Do you prefer to be relieved of your post, Major?"

An image of a firing squad pops into Rezaei's brain. He wipes a bead of perspiration from his forehead. "No, sir."

The general pivots on his heel and kicks his pacing into high gear. After a few moments, he returns to the communication console. "Is the link to the supreme leader open and secure?"

"Yes, sir," the lieutenant answers. "Would you like to speak to him?"

Not wanting to hear, again, what will happen to him and his family if he fails, Mohammadi waves away the request. The supreme leader is buried deep in a bunker beneath Tehran, surrounded by his five wives, a brood of children, and numerous other family members. The bunker is fully staffed and stocked with enough food and clean water to support the leader's family for months. The general's family remains topside and will move into the bunker only if Mohammadi is successful.

He glances at the clock, again—ten minutes and counting.

CHAPTER 10

NORAD

Operated jointly by both the Americans and the Canadians, personnel from both countries rotate through NORAD. Captain Brice Tremblay of the Royal Canadian Air Force is today's duty officer. A quirky man who favors precision, he glances at the clock to watch it click to the top of the hour before pouring his final cup of coffee for the day. Another of his quirks has earned him the nickname Tugger, for his nervous habit of tugging his left earlobe when stressed.

Corporal Gary Rutledge is watching intently as the North Korean satellite passes over eastern Texas. Traveling at 17,000 miles per hour, the satellite covers nearly five miles every second. Moments later the satellite is nearing Kansas City when the image disappears from the screen. "What the hell?" Rutledge mutters.

A second later his muttering is drowned by the shouts of "Detonation!" from a senior airman on the opposite side of the room.

"What type of detonation and where?" Captain Tremblay asks.

"A high atmospheric explosion over Kansas City. Wave signatures suggest it may be nuclear."

"Communications, work the phones. Send an urgent message up the chain of command to alert them of a possible EMP event."

Corporal Rutledge jumps to his feet and races across the room. "Sir, we've lost contact with the North Korean satellite."

Tremblay tugs his left earlobe. "We didn't lose contact. It exploded. Now we need to find out if the satellite—"

"Sir, I have multiple missile launches outbound from Iran," another airman shouts.

"What's multiple?" Tremblay shouts. "Two or twenty, for fuck's sake?"

"At least a dozen, sir."

"Heading?" Tremblay latches on to his left ear and gives the lobe a hard tug.

"Veering west, sir."

"Seal the blast doors until we can figure out what the hell is going on." Tremblay picks up the phone and calls the four-star in command, Air Force General Amy Carlyle. "Ma'am, Captain Tremblay, NORAD." He's in the process of explaining what has occurred when he's interrupted by another shout: "Detonation!"

"Hold one, ma'am." He covers the mouthpiece with his palm. "Where?" Tremblay shouts to the room. His shoulders sag when he hears the location. He takes a deep breath and removes his palm, placing the phone to his ear. "Ma'am, we're tracking another large airburst explosion near Krasnodar, Russia. Could be nuclear in origin." He replaces the handset and begins scanning the room for someone with more embellishments on their collar, and spots Colonel Hal Hooper surging into the room. Tremblay waves a hand to flag him down.

Colonel Hooper, a tall, stout man, bulls his way through the gathering crowd.

"What's the situation, Captain?"

Tremblay begins to explain when his voice is drowned out by shouts of "Missile launch!"

"Where?" Hooper shouts.

"Israel, sir. I count twenty missiles currently outbound," a master sergeant replies.

Hooper glances around at the growing crowd and shouts, "If you don't work in this room, get the hell out. And that's a direct fucking order."

People begin scurrying toward the door as the colonel picks up the phone. Bypassing about ten layers of command structure, he says, "Get me the President."

CHAPTER 11

Weatherford

Gage is finishing up with the brakes when the interior of the hub lights up like a mirror reflecting the sun. The flash of brilliant light is followed by a deep rumble of thunder, and Gage is wondering if he has slipped into another dimension. He glances up to reconfirm what he already knows—there's not a cloud in the sky. He stands, stretches his achy back, and steps over to the side, thinking there must have been some type of explosion. But there's not so much as a puff of smoke on the horizon and no visible signs of anything amiss. When he steps over to the town side of the turbine, his brain registers something different, but he can't pinpoint what it is. Shrugging his shoulders, he returns to work.

After a few minutes, the niggle in the back of his mind pushes its way to the surface. He retraces his steps for another look. Very few automobiles are moving and a good number of them are stopped in places where a person wouldn't normally stop. A couple of pickups are stopped in the middle of the road leading out of town, and two dusty sedans are stalled out in the middle of a busy intersection. Closer in, the farmer who was raking hay is down from his tractor, the hood up over the engine. Gage turns his gaze back toward town and, upon closer examination, discovers the interior of the Quick Stop dark. The owner, an asshole new to town, usually has about a half-dozen signs flashing, but they, too, are dark. Last week there had been a fire at the electrical substation that knocked out power for a couple of hours . . . but that doesn't explain the auto situation, Gage thinks. His mind spins through possible scenarios as he shakes his head and shuffles back to his work area.

Something else he's seen is bothering him, but he can't put his thumb on what it is. He steps over to the ice chest for another bottle of water, and it hits him. The other turbines aren't moving. Turning for another look, his recollection is confirmed—all the turbines are as still as statutes. "Huh," Gage mutters. Digging around in his bag, he grabs his laptop and plugs a cable into the computer of the turbine he's working on and hits the power button and waits for the computer to boot up. And waits. And waits. He punches the power button again, but the whir of the hard drive remains silent. Gage checks to make sure the battery is properly seated and gives the laptop a shake before trying again. Same result. He remembers putting the laptop on the charger before hitting the sack last night so it can't be a dead battery.

Curious now, Gage sets the laptop aside and approaches the rack of computer equipment mounted on the back wall of the nacelle. None of the lights are flashing and Gage can smell burned plastic. A tingle of dread starts at the base of his neck and inches down his spine like a spider. Although Gage didn't finish college, he knows a little about a lot of things. Putting everything together in his mind, there's only one reasonable answer for what's happening. And as improbable as it sounds, it's the only valid explanation—an electromagnetic pulse.

CHAPTER 12

The intercom in the Situation Room chimes. "Mr. President, I have an urgent call from a Colonel Hal Hooper at NORAD."

Aldridge glances at the chairman of the Joint Chiefs, who shrugs. "Don't know him, sir."

Aldridge scowls and picks up the phone. He listens for a few moments, the blood draining from his face. He hangs up the phone with a trembling hand and stares at a spot on the far wall for a moment. Then, in a flat tone, he says, "Punch up the feed from NORAD."

When the screen showing missile trajectories pops into view, everyone in the room gasps.

"In addition to the missile launches you are seeing and the explosion of our drone over Russian soil," Aldridge says, "a nuclear weapon was detonated high over Kansas City that triggered a massive EMP. The explosion was tracked to a North Korean satellite—"

Aldridge is interrupted by the arrival of six Secret Service agents. The lead agent of his personal protection detail, Ed Henry, steps forward. "Sir, we'd like to move you into the bunker and move the vice president to another location."

"Stand down, Ed," Aldridge says. "We need to get a handle on the situation before we even think about relocation."

"But, sir—"

"Ed, I said stand down. That's an order. We'll worry about that stuff later. Right now, this nation and our staunchest ally are under attack."

Ed Henry hesitates for a moment, but finally accedes to the President's wishes and signals the other agents to leave and falls in behind them. Aldridge, his composure returning, begins calling out orders. "Isabella, get the Israeli ambassador on the phone. Camila, work with State on reaching out to the Russians. Explain to them that our drone was hacked and not under our control when it entered their airspace. Admiral Hill, I want a list of military options if this situation spirals out of control." Aldridge turns to the director of homeland security, Nancy Copeland. "Nancy, talk with your folks at Homeland Security. I want some type of damage assessment from the EMP."

Hands start reaching for phones as the vice president and Jim Keating, secretary of state, huddle in a corner of the room talking strategy before reaching out to the Russians.

"Sir, I have the Israeli ambassador on the line," Isabella says.

"Put him on speaker."

Isabella reaches over to a triangular-shaped device on the table and punches a button. "You're on, sir."

The President glances up at the big screen to see

more red lines streaking away from Israel. "Benjamin, what the hell is going on?"

"Sir, my country is currently under attack from Iran. Entirely unprovoked."

"And you are responding with what?" the President asks.

"We are responding in kind, sir."

"With what type of weapons?"

There's a long pause as the room waits for the ambassador's reply.

"Sir, we've launched a flight of twenty intercontinental ballistic missiles."

"Benjamin, you're evading my question, so I'll make my next question succinct. Are the missiles armed with thermonuclear warheads?"

"Yes, sir, they are."

Another collective gasp sounds from those gathered in the room. When the President speaks, his voice is low, urgent, "Ben, patch me through to your prime minister." While waiting for the call to go through, Aldridge strides across the room, stopping near the vice president and secretary of state. "Did you reach out to the Russians?"

"We're strategizing the call, sir," the VP replies.

"Fuck strategy. Make the call." He pivots on his heel and returns to his place at the table as the prime minister of Israel comes on the line.

"Mr. President, we believe the incoming missiles from Iran are nuclear in origin," the prime minister of Israel, Eliana Salomon, says.

"Believe, but don't know for certain?" He picks up a handset and signals Isabella to kill the speaker. "And you fire off a nuclear barrage with no consultation?"

"There wasn't time for consultation, Tom. My country is under attack."

"As is my country, Eliana. We've been hit with some type of EMP device, but are searching for a more measured response."

"This is our measured response," Salomon says.

"How many of those Iranian missiles will actually penetrate your vaunted air defenses?"

"One is too many, Mr. President."

The President pauses his response on the approach of the vice president. He covers the mouthpiece with a palm and Martinez says, "The Russians are refusing to take our call."

"Goddammit," the President mutters. He puts the phone to his ear. "Eliana, please refrain from launching any further attacks until we can get this sorted out. I'll phone you again, within the hour." The President drops the handset in the cradle. "Why are the Russians refusing to take our call?"

Before anyone can answer, three chimes sound through the speakers, and the video screen transitions to a man, surrounded by a wall of computer monitors. His camo fatigues are darkened with sweat and his face is pinched with worry. A name pops onto the screen: *Colonel Hal Hooper, NORAD*. "Mr. President, we are tracking well over two hundred ICBMs that have been launched from mainland Russia. In addition, we are also tracking multiple submarine-based launches along the eastern seaboard."

CHAPTER 13

Off the northwest coast of Russia

Cruising at a depth of 300 feet, the Ohio-class ballistic missile submarine, USS *New York*—SSBN-744
in navy terms—is twenty miles off the northern coast
of Russia and sailing west. Eighty-seven days into
their ninety-day mission, the crew is looking forward
to some R & R at the end of the week. The USS *New
York* is one of fourteen such submarines in the navy
fleet. The subs are silent predators and represent the
third leg of the nation's nuclear triad. Armed with
twenty-four Trident II missiles with nuclear warheads,
the crew can put a missile within a hundred yards of
target from a distance of 7,456 miles.

Although there are only twenty-four missiles aboard
ship, each missile is armed with eight individual warheads that can be independently targeted. The USS
New York operates in near silence and carries the
equivalent of 7,680 Hiroshima-sized nukes on board,
making the sub an apocalyptic piece of military hardware capable of wiping out an entire continent. Although poised to deliver death at a moment's notice,

the submarine and her crew have yet to launch their lethal weapons on live targets.

Captain Rex "Bull" Thompson is the commanding officer. A graduate of the Naval Academy, Thompson is a stocky, broad-shouldered man, hence his nick-name. His salt-and-pepper hair is cut high and tight, and his dark, deep eyes are famous for their penetrating gaze. Seated in an elevated chair in the center of the bridge, he's perusing the personnel schedule when a yeoman from the radio room rushes in and thrusts a piece of paper into the hands of Lieutenant Commander Thomas Quigley.

Quigley reads the message and his lips begin to tremble. He steps over to Captain Thompson, the paper fluttering in his hand. "Captain, we are in receipt of a valid emergency action measure that directs the launch of target package one. Request permission to authenticate?"

"Authenticate the message," Thompson orders. He stands from his chair and steps over to the chart table where he's joined by his executive officer, Commander Carlos Garcia, and other senior officers. Thompson looks up. "Conn, sound the general alarm. Battle stations, missile." As the electronic Klaxon sounds, Thompson turns to Quigley. "Q, is this a drill?"

Quigley looks up, sweat popping on his forehead. "No, sir, I don't believe it is."

"Christ," the captain mutters.

The message is coded with a cypher to insure the order originated from the President. Quigley calls out the code while Garcia authenticates. Once the message is decoded, Garcia exhales a breath and says, "Captain, the message is authentic."

Two of the other senior officers concur, and the captain authorizes missile launch. Quigley and Garcia walk over to a dual-dial safe inserted into the bulkhead and both enter their combinations and pop open the doors to retrieve the launch keys.

Captain Thompson begins barking orders. He calls down to the missile control center, one deck down. "Insert targeting package one." He punches another button on the intercom handset. "Radio room, I want a patch through to USSTRATCOM." He looks toward the helm. "Dive Officer, take us up to one-three-zero."

His commands are repeated, and the sub begins to ascend. Captain Thompson, twenty years into his naval career, is wondering, why now? He calls down to the missile control center again. "How long to insert the targeting package and incorporate the Permissive Action Link?" The PAL is required to arm the warheads.

"A little more than seven minutes, Skipper."

Thompson makes another call to the radio room.

"Radio room, sir. We haven't received any return radio calls, Captain," the radio technician says.

"Run out a communication buoy and try again."

His order is confirmed and Thompson turns to Garcia. "If the comm buoy idea doesn't work, I'm thinking of ordering an emergency blow to make a phone call to USSTRATCOM for confirmation of the orders. Your thoughts?"

"We'd be a sitting duck, sir. And we don't have any idea what the hell is going on topside. If the message has been authenticated, and it has, we should launch the missiles."

Thompson lowers his voice. "We launch these missiles we can kiss our world good-bye."

"It may already be happening, Bull," Garcia says, turning his body so that he can look his captain and friend in the eye. "We have no way of knowing if we are the first strike or a follow-up attack. We've trained for years on this exact scenario and now the order arrives and you have second thoughts?"

"Don't you?"

"I do. But there has to be a valid reason for the President to issue a launch order."

"What about our families, Carlos?"

Garcia hesitates before answering. Then in a faltering voice, says, "They may already be gone, Bull."

The radio room reports the communication buoy deployed and Thompson grabs the phone and pushes the hotline button to the U. S. Strategic Command (USSTRATCOM). He puts the phone to his ear, but the only thing he hears is silence. He hails the radio room. "Is the buoy operational?"

"Affirmative, sir," the yeoman at the radio controls says. "Communication buoy is up and operational."

"What's wrong?" Garcia asks.

"The phone is dead," Thompson says.

"I don't think it's the phone, Bull," Garcia says.

"You think the satellites are toast?"

Garcia nods.

Thompson slowly replaces the phone. "Conn, turn to a heading of two-seven-zero and take us up to periscope depth." As the sub's nose rises at a twenty-degree angle, Thompson looks at Garcia. "I should be able to see part of the Russian mainland. Just a quick peek."

Within moments the sub levels out and the periscope ascends. Thompson steps up to the viewer and swivels the periscope toward the Russian mainland. What he sees makes his blood run cold. His shoulders sag as he slaps the periscope handles up and orders the periscope down. In a subdued voice, he says, "Dive, make our depth one-three-zero," as he walks unsteadily to his chair and sits. When the sub levels off he hails the missile control center. "How long?"

"Two minutes, sir," the weapons officer replies

"Roger, fire when ready."

Garcia approaches. "What did you see?"

"Mushroom clouds all across the horizon." Thompson white-knuckles the arms of his chair as the huge boat shudders with each launch of her twenty-four deadly missiles.

CHAPTER 14

Over Greenland

Melissa Watkins sighs and unbuckles her seat belt, climbing over the other two people sitting in her row. Three hours out of London, their flight is scheduled to land at New York's JFK airport in six hours. Melissa shuffles up the aisle and stops next to the teen who has been a thorn in her side the past eleven days. She grabs the left earlobe of fourteen-year-old Jonathon Taylor and twists, whispering, "I'm not going to tell you again. Keep your hands to yourself." She gives the earlobe another twist to reinforce her words as Jon tries to duck away. She points a finger at him then shuffles back down the aisle and climbs over her fellow passengers, collapsing in her seat.

Melissa is exhausted. A middle schoolteacher from Lubbock, Texas, she supplements her teaching income by chaperoning a group of teenagers as they tour a foreign destination for twelve days in the summer. The organization, Teen World Discovery, offers an international program designed to broaden the minds of middle school students. This year's group numbers seventeen, including Jonathon and another turd-head, Caleb Carson. Their behavior has Melissa questioning whether she'll ever do this again.

Most of the students are from West Texas, as is the second chaperone, Lauren Thomas, who teaches at Plainview Middle School, north of Lubbock. Lauren currently occupies the seat next to Melissa and she leans over and whispers, "Jon again?"

"Yes. I'm ready for that little shithead to be out of my hair. If I have any hair left after this is over."

Lauren chuckles. "I'm tired of looking at all of them. The girls aren't much better. Drama, drama, drama." The two teachers had divided the group, Lauren taking responsibility for the ten girls, while Melissa drew the short straw and ended up with the seven boys.

Melissa kicks at her overstuffed carry-on crammed under the seat in front of her. "Tell me again why we do this?" Melissa is twenty-three, has a pear-shaped body, and is a tad too heavy for her five-foot-three-inch frame. She has an on-and-off boyfriend and the relationship is currently in the off position.

"The money, honey," Lauren says. "Three grand for twelve days is more than we could make working part-time for an entire summer. Plus we get free travel to places we could never afford."

"All of that sounds divine if we could leave the kids behind."

During their trip, they've hiked, bussed, and trained all over the United Kingdom. From London to Glasgow, they toured archaic churches, bustling parks, and historic landmarks, finishing most evenings with a nice dinner. Or what were supposed to be nice dinners. Taking seventeen teenagers to dinner is like herding cats. The first items tossed around the table are the sugar packets, followed by the loosening of the lids on the salt and pepper shakers, and all that is topped off by spitballs shot through straws. Melissa shudders, thinking about it. She flags down a flight attendant and orders a glass of red wine.

If the dinners weren't bad enough, once back at the hotel, Melissa and Lauren were responsible for keeping the students in their assigned rooms. They instituted a strict curfew for 11:00 P.M., but were often up well past midnight to enforce it. No doubt some of the kids are sexually active and the last thing either of them wanted was for a girl to return home knocked up. Melissa pushes those thoughts out of her mind when her wine arrives. She chugs the first glass and orders another.

"How long is our layover in New York?" Lauren asks. Twenty-seven, Lauren is the exact opposite of Melissa. She's long, well proportioned, and has a head of dark wavy hair that brushes the top of her narrow shoulders. Currently unattached, she has her share of suitors, but none have clicked as of yet.

"Two hours, I think. I can't remember what time we're due to arrive in Dallas." Melissa cranes her head over the seat in front of her to see Jon playing hand slap with the boy seated next to him. "Lauren, do you mind switching seats with Jonathon?"

"No, I don't mind. But I wouldn't wish that on my worst enemy. I'll go talk to him."

"Thank you. Maybe we could slip him an Ambien."

"I wish." Lauren pulls herself out of the seat and climbs across the lap of Lindsey Scott, a mousy fifteen-year-old from Lubbock. A clinger, Lindsey hasn't been more than ten feet from Lauren during the entire trip. Lauren shuffles down the aisle and squats down next to Jonathon. "That's enough. If I have to come up here again, I'm calling your father the moment we land. Do you want me to call him?"

Jonathon shakes his head.

"I'm going to be watching you the rest of the flight. Keep your hands to yourself or my first call is to your father. And it won't just be a telephone call, Jonathon. I'll request he fly to New York to pick you up. Think that'll make him happy?"

Jonathon frowns and shakes his head again.

Lauren makes a jabbing motion toward her eyes with two outstretched fingers and points at Jonathon before retreating to her seat.

"How'd it go?" Melissa asks.

"I threatened to call his father. Told him I'd make his dad fly to New York to pick him up."

"Jesus, I hope that doesn't happen. That man's an asshole." Having taught Jonathon last year, Melissa's very familiar with the boy's father. "*Overbearing* doesn't even begin to describe the man. No wonder his son is such a little shit."

Melissa takes a sip of wine and both women settle into their seats. Little do they know their journey is just beginning.

CHAPTER 15

10 Downing Street, London

United Kingdom's prime minister, Blair Hamilton, is reading through the latest in a pile of documents on Britain's exit from the European Union when his phone rings. He turns to look at the phone console, but doesn't see any flashing lights. On the second ring he realizes the call is coming from the special beige phone tucked away in a drawer of his desk—the hotline to the White House. He opens the drawer and picks up the handset. "Hello, Tom," he says as he leans back in his chair and crosses one leg over the other.

President Thomas Aldridge clears his throat and says, "Blair, we have an emergency situa—"

The call drops. "Hello? Tom, can you hear me? Hello?" Hamilton uncrosses his legs and leans forward, tapping the disconnect button then speed dial one. Silence. He hangs up the handset and turns to his office phone, triggering the intercom. "Brenda, please place a call to President Aldridge."

"Yes, sir," his secretary, Brenda Montgomery, says.

While waiting for Brenda to make the call, he tries

the hotline again and gets the same result. "What the bloody hell," he mutters, hanging up the phone again.

Moments later, the intercom chimes. "Sir, I tried to ring the White House, but the call won't go through," Brenda says.

"What do you mean, 'won't go through'?"

"All I hear is silence, sir."

A tingle of worry forms at the nape of Hamilton's neck and begins to inch down his spine. "Try placing a call to our ambassador in D.C."

"Yes, sir," Brenda replies.

Hamilton, feeling like a telemarketer working the phones, picks up his office phone and makes a call to the Director of MI6. "George, is something going on?"

"Yes, sir. You were my next call. It appears that the—"

"Hello? George? George?" Hamilton slams the handset down just as the intercom chimes again.

"Sir, the same thing is happening when I try to call our ambassador."

"Silence?"

"Yes, sir."

Hamilton pushes to his feet. "Keep trying, Brenda." He kills the intercom and steps over to the window, the tingle of worry now a full-on rush. Looking out into the rose garden, he's mentally clicking through reasons for the phone failures when he's blinded by a flash of light that's like a million-watt bulb clicking on. He screams and covers his eyes with his hands. Before the pain can register with his brain, the pressure wave from the detonation of the nuclear weapon collapses the building and the ensuing wall of fire incinerates everything within.

CHAPTER 16

Tokyo

With a population in excess of thirteen million people, Tokyo is brimming with buildings and bodies. One of those bodies is twenty-two-year-old Kayoko Yamamoto, who is currently fighting her way through the ass-to-elbow crowds clogging the sidewalks in central Tokyo's business district. Entering her third year of law school in the fall, Yamamoto is finishing up her summer internship at one of the largest law firms in the city. She slows to a stop at the next intersection, waiting for the light to change.

When she started her internship she was enamored with the beautifully appointed law offices that occupy the fortieth floor of Tokyo's tallest building, Toranomon Hills Mori Tower. But as the summer wore on she came to realize the alluring interior spaces and the lavishly decorated offices were a façade, much like an exquisite piece of shiny fruit with a rotten core. Backstabbing is the sport of choice among both the partners and those who really do the work at the firm—the recent law school graduates working hundred-hour weeks, the interns hoping to land a job upon graduation, and the support staff that churn out an unending trail of paperwork. To say Yamamoto is disillusioned would be an understatement.

The light turns green and Yamamoto steps into the intersection. She hears a squeal of brakes and glances to her left, jumping back to avoid being clipped by a taxi running the red light. If she had any energy she'd flip the bastard off, but she doesn't. In addition to the heavy workload, Yamamoto had spent most of the previous evening arguing with her parents. Her father put his foot down and informed his daughter she would finish law school, regardless of the dismal employment outlook for the flood of law school graduates in recent years. A stern, hard man, her father believes once you start something you must finish. Her mother was sympathetic, but there's no doubt who wears the pants in Yamamoto's family. To make matters worse, her father also controls the family's purse strings and is not hesitant to use the flow of money to bend Yamamoto to his will. Not that she lives in splendor. She shares a shoebox-sized apartment with three other law school students. The living quarters are so tight they have to take turns breathing. She sighs and glances up, adjusting her course as she trudges toward the entrance to her building..

A short, rail-thin woman, Yamamoto is steps from the front doors when the citywide siren sounds. She stops and looks up, then around, but doesn't see anything amiss. She turns around and continues on. The siren doesn't sound frequently, but when it does it usually signals an earthquake has occurred somewhere in Japan. After the Fukushima disaster and ensuing tsunami, city officials are quick on the trigger if there's even a hint that another tsunami could occur. Not that it would really matter to Yamamoto—she's miles inland and safe from any surge of water. She shrugs and follows the flood of people through the revolving door, heading for the bank of elevators.

Yamamoto steps off the elevator on the fortieth floor and stops dead in her tracks. Her coworkers are standing, staring out the windows with their hands clamped over their mouths. A natural response, Yamamoto's hands do the same as she gapes at the mushroom cloud expanding over eastern Tokyo. The building's fire alarm sounds, but people remain rooted in place, peering at the ongoing carnage.

Yamamoto's fear transitions rapidly to anger—who would use such a weapon on her homeland for a *third* time? Her great-grandparents had survived the horrors of Hiroshima and now this? She begins to tremble, a mixture of fear and anger coursing through her body as her mind clicks through the list of possible suspects. But before her brain can settle on an answer, another nuclear device detonates over the city. Yamamoto, blinded by the flash, doesn't see the glass shattering. She does feel the fragments ripping through her body, but only for an instant before she's cremated by the ensuing fireball.

CHAPTER 17

Paris

Americans Clay and Patsy Campbell are in Paris to celebrate thirty years of wedded bliss and to fulfill a promise Clay made to Patsy the day they got hitched: Yes, he would take her to the City of Light. So what if it took him thirty years to do it? They had a family to raise, a house to buy, and jobs to work to pay for everything. Clay grimaces when the man behind him steps on his heel, again. In line for a ride to the top of the Eiffel Tower, Clay is ruing the day he made the promise. "Forty freakin' dollars to take a damn elevator ride," he mutters under his breath.

Patsy whirls around. "Don't you start, Clay. We're on vacation."

Clay grimaces. His idea of the perfect vacation includes a lake, his bass boat, and an ice chest full of Budweiser. Born and raised on a cattle ranch in West Texas, Clay, a tall, broad-shouldered man, took over the ranch at twenty-one after his dad keeled over with a heart attack while branding calves.

Patsy shuffles back a step and puts an arm around

her husband's waist. Slim and petite on that day long ago, Patsy is now thirty pounds heavier, and her short, dark hair is shot through with gray. She gives her husband a squeeze and tiptoes up to whisper in Clay's ear. "I've got a little surprise back at the hotel."

"What is it?" Clay asks. He bends down and gives his wife a peck on the lips.

"If I told you, it wouldn't be a surprise, now, would it?"

"C'mon, give me a hint." He puts his arm around Patsy and lets his hand drift down, lightly stroking her ass.

"I'll just say I made a couple of new purchases before we left?"

Clay arches his brows. "From that store at the mall in Dallas?"

"Maybe." Patsy winks. "I think you're going to like it."

Clay smiles and runs his hand lightly across her ass again. "Is there some leopard print and lace involved?"

Patsy shrugs. "I'm not telling."

"Want to skip this mess and head back to the hotel?"

Patsy shakes her head. "Nope. You better tie it in a knot."

They're next in line and they step into the elevator with a dozen others. Jammed tight as teeth, Clay elbows more standing room, the view of Paris widening as the elevator ascends. Staring at the mass of buildings, Clay figures there's more people in one block than in the whole town of Sweetwater, Texas. He shakes his head at the thought. At the top, they maneuver out of the elevator and onto a crowded platform. Patsy pulls out her phone and starts snapping pictures.

Clay wades through the crowd and steps over to the fence, glancing down at the pigeon shit coating the outer ledge before turning his gaze on the city. A few boats are patrolling the river Seine, and Clay wonders if there're any good fishing spots close by. His thoughts are interrupted when Patsy wedges in next to him. She makes him turn around so she can snap a few photos of them with the city as a backdrop. Clay forces a smile and tells her to hurry up.

An ear-numbing roar rips through the sky, and they whirl around to see a missile plowing into Charles de Gaulle Airport. The ensuing mushroom cloud sends a bolt of fear through everyone atop the tower. People begin screaming and rushing toward the elevators. Patsy is elbowing Clay to run, but he spends a few seconds studying the growing cloud of radioactive debris and glances back at the throng of people waiting for the elevator. Clay reaches out and puts his arm around his wife. "We had a good ride, bab—"

His last words are ripped from his mouth by a massive overhead explosion. The expanding conflagration, created by thermonuclear fusion upon detonation and burning hotter than the surface of the sun, vaporizes Patsy and Clay Campbell milliseconds later.

CHAPTER 18

Dix, Nebraska

The tractor's canopy offers some relief from the sun, but with the temperature pushing a hundred degrees there's no escaping the heat. Cooper Hansen wipes the sweat from his brow with the back of his hand and repositions his ball cap as the old John Deere bounces across the rough terrain. With the start of his senior year only weeks away, Cooper's butt is dragging the ground after a two-hour football practice this morning. Tall at six-three and heavily muscled, Cooper is the starting defensive end on the team that took state last year. He's been getting a few looks from some D-I schools, but he's undecided if he wants to pursue a football career in college. Cooper glances over his shoulder to check the hay rake and makes a minor adjustment with the steering wheel. Seconds later the rake hits a gopher mound and throws up a cloud of dust that clings to Cooper's sweaty face. He curses and pulls a rag from his pocket, making a futile attempt to wipe away the grit.

Most of his cursing is directed at his father, who sits

in secluded, air-conditioned comfort inside the cab of the new tractor they bought this year. His dad is baling the hay Cooper's raking at the other end of the field. The sweet aroma of alfalfa hangs in the still air and, mixed with the hangover Cooper's still nursing, he's slightly nauseous. He mutters another string of curse words as he makes a wide turn around the fenced section of buildings in the middle of the field. Cooper's dad leases this eighty-acre section from Uncle Sam, who erected a couple of low-slung buildings and planted a missile silo in the ground in the early 1960s. The place was a novelty the first twenty times Cooper and his father worked the field, but now it's just another damn obstacle to navigate around.

The main building is manned twenty-four/seven and the only time things get interesting is when there's a shift change, the crews rotating through the bunker buried deep underground. Cooper waves toward the building, having no clue if the man inside is looking in his direction. Someone has put up a basketball goal and painted some lines on the asphalt parking lot, but in all the times Cooper's been out here he has yet to see anyone shooting baskets.

Cooper makes another turn, skirting the silo section of the site. His mind drifts to Leslie Brown, his current love interest. A tall, curvy blonde and captain of the cheerleading squad, their first real date is scheduled for the upcoming weekend. They've messed around some—a few sloppy kisses after more than a few cold beers—but that's been the extent of their relationship. Cooper's hoping for a little more, both physically and emotionally, with a primary emphasis on the physical aspects of the relationship.

Leslie's breasts do a nice job filling her cheer uniform, and Cooper's fantasizing about burying his face right in the middle of them when the hexagonal-shaped silo cover slams open. Cooper nearly pisses his pants and jumps a foot off the seat, all thoughts of Leslie's breasts gone in a heartbeat. Adrenaline floods his system as he struggles to come to grips with what's happening. *Are they running some type of drill? Has there been some type of accident?* The questions bombard his brain as he shifts the tractor to high gear and opens the throttle to the stops, aiming for his father at the other end of the field.

Cooper glances back to see smoke rising from the silo, and his blood runs cold. A siren sounds and is followed seconds later by a tremendous roar. Although the tractor's in high gear, Cooper is only a hundred yards away when fire erupts from inside the silo. He glances over his shoulder again to see the nose of the rocket edging out, smoke and flames erupting skyward.

But what Cooper fails to see is the Russian missile streaking toward earth. Seconds later Cooper and the tractor he's riding on are obliterated when the Russian warhead slams into the launching missile and detonates.

CHAPTER 19

Hollywood, California

Reece Martin puts the megaphone to his lips and starts barking orders. After a shooting schedule that has stretched on for six grueling months, today they are shooting the final scene of a movie that is over budget by miles and two years past due. Set up high in the Hollywood Hills, they're prepping the final scene where one of the leading characters dies in a fiery accident. If only it were real, Martin thinks as he returns to his seat. The two lead characters, a male and a female, have squabbled over the minutest details. Martin is tired of arguing with them, tired of directing them, and tired of looking at them. And screw having a wrap party. If Martin never lays eyes on them again, it'll be too soon.

Martin triggers the megaphone again. "Quiet, goddammit." They've already blown up two cars and are currently working with the third and last. If they don't get a usable take this time, Martin is contemplating having the two lead characters fight a duel in which both die. "It would serve them right," Martin mutters under his breath. He checks with the six cinematographers via radio and takes a deep breath. "Action." He leans forward to watch the developing scene on a video monitor. The sprinklers kick on, drenching the roadway as the car, another brand-spanking-new red Mercedes, comes roaring around a curve. But before the car can crash through the guardrail and sail over the cliff, sending the female lead to a fiery death, the entire crew is startled by a ground-shaking explosion.

Every eye on the set is drawn to the mushroom cloud spreading over downtown Los Angeles. The cinematographers turn their cameras away from the unfolding movie scene, focusing their lenses on the horror below. As the new Mercedes sails off the cliff unrecorded, the crew watches as the destruction expands in an ever-widening circle. Martin looks up to see a passenger jet spiraling out of control and turns away before the plane plows into the ground. Death and destruction are fine on film, but to see it unfold in real life is another matter entirely. Several members of the crew are weeping, others are standing, their mouths agape.

Moments later there's a flash of light that sears the vision of half the crew, but their screams are drowned out by another massive explosion high over the city. As the cameras wink out from the electromagnetic pulse, the pressure wave, traveling at 300 miles per second, slams into the city, crushing everything in its path. Anything left standing is consumed by the following fireball that reaches temperatures of 150 million degrees Fahrenheit.

As the destruction spreads across the city, Martin thinks, for the first time, about their safety. How much radiation they've been exposed to in the last minute and a half. Enough to kill them? "We need to get below-ground," he shouts as he turns a circle, looking for nearby structures. But stuck atop the highest point in the region, their options are few. Martin starts herding the group toward the rental vans, running scenarios through his brain. The Griffith Observatory is a possibility, but from here it's miles away.

When they reach the line of vans, Martin yanks open the door, but that's as far as he gets. In the next instant he and everyone around him are annihilated when a nuclear warhead detonates high above the iconic symbol of American excess—the white, nine letter sign spelling out HOLLYWOOD.

CHAPTER 20

Moscow

A Klaxon sounds throughout the Kremlin yet Alexandra Vasilieva is in no hurry to leave her desk. Someone on the president's staff, usually one of the deputy chiefs, runs an emergency drill every couple of months, but they end up being time wasters and that's one thing Alexandra doesn't have. An administrative assistant to the president, she's hours behind on a video presentation that's due by the end of the day.

"Aren't you coming?" her friend and coworker, Darya Ivanova, asks.

Alexandra glances up from her computer screen. "I don't have time. Do me a favor and call my cell if there's an actual fire."

The two chuckle at the absurdity of the drills that no one in the building takes seriously.

Darya puts two fingers to her lips and tilts her head. "You sure? We could steal a smoke break."

Alexandra pauses, thinking, and changes her mind. She stands and slings her purse over her shoulder. "Screw

it. Five minutes is not going to make much of a difference."

The large room is portioned into cubicles and the two
women fall in at the end of the line as they and their
coworkers exit into the hall. The corridor is streaming
with people, but, like always, no one is in a hurry. Darya
elbows Alexandra in the ribs, nodding toward a tall, attractive man joining the mass of people at the top of
the stairs. "If you're not going to bed Evgeni, I will,"
Darya whispers to her friend. Short and somewhat
chubby, Darya is not particularly picky when it comes
to hooking up with coworkers, both male and female.
Experimentation, she calls it.

"Hands off. We have another date scheduled for this
weekend," Alexandra whispers back. Twenty-four, she
ended a four-year relationship several months ago and
has been slow to rejoin the dating scene. Tall and slim
with a mane of dark hair, she and Evgeni have been out
several times, but haven't yet been intimate. Alexandra
hopes that changes this weekend.

Alexandra and Darya follow the crowd down the
stairs to the first level. That's when Alexandra notices
an immediate difference from all the previous drills.
Heavily armed guards are manning the doors while
other soldiers are directing people to the stairs to the
lower levels. "What do you think's going on?" Alexandra whispers to Darya.

Darya shrugs. "Who knows? But I really need a cigarette."

Alexandra scowls. "Think there's been some type of
terrorist attack?"

Darya shrugs again. "They're not going to tell us
anything. They never do."

They follow the procession down the stairs to the basement. The odor of stewing cabbage drifts from the cafeteria down the hall as another group of soldiers directs them to another set of stairs.

"Shit," Darya says, "They're putting us in the bunker. I've got to have a cigarette before we go in."

"You can't smoke in the building," Alexandra says.

"Watch me." Darya digs through her purse, pulls out a cigarette, and lights up. She gets in one puff before a soldier approaches, pulls the cigarette from her mouth, and grinds it out beneath her boot. Darya glares at the soldier, who smiles and pivots away, on to her next task.

"I told you," Alexandra says. The line to the stairs grinds to a halt and Alexandra and Darya are left standing in a wide corridor that runs the length of the building. Both jump when a loud crash reverberates through the structure. A millisecond later, there's another jarring crash and then another. Alexandra's first thought is it's an earthquake as the hallway fills with dust and debris. People begin screaming and running in every direction as Alexandra grabs Darya and pulls her under a doorframe to an office—Earthquake 101 for a girl who grew up in a seismically active area. Alexandra leans out, peering through the haze to see if a section of the upper floors have collapsed. But what she sees instead is an oblong object piercing the ceiling in an area two floors below the president's office. There is no lettering on the device, but she can see a portion of a flag painted on the surface. One she knows well from working on projects regarding the United States. It's the last thing Alexandra sees before the weapon detonates.

CHAPTER 21

Manhattan

Sean Smith glances at his watch and winces. The damn trains are running late again. Riding the number 2 train from his apartment near Columbia University, Smith's still three stops away from his destination in the Financial District. And he has only fifteen minutes to make a meeting he's worked six months to get. A meeting that could be life-changing for him and his fiancée. The man he's meeting, a venture capitalist, has a mild interest in a start-up Smith founded two years ago. After months of pestering, the man relented and agreed to a face-to-face to allow Smith an opportunity to lay out his grand plan. That plan is on the laptop in his bag—a nicely designed PowerPoint presentation that's concise and thoroughly researched. Smith glances at his watch again and stands, moving closer to the door for a rapid escape.

After two stops, the subway finally pulls into the Wall Street station. Smith taps his foot, waiting for the doors to open as people pile up around him. Beyond the glass, another mass of humanity is waiting to board.

The doors part and Smith steps out, shouldering his way through the crowd. If he can reach the surface quickly, the man's office is only a block away. He hurries to the escalator and edges past the standers, lunging up the steps. Glancing up, his heart stutters when he sees a clearly panicked crowd surging inside. His first thought is it's another terrorist attack and here he is only blocks away from where the original twin towers stood. He's still too far away to see outside so maybe there's hope it's only a random shooter and the cops will quickly eliminate the threat. But then his mind stops and backs up. Are we so used to these random shootings that they're now mundane? He quickly builds a mental wall. Now is not the time to debate that point.

As he gets closer to the exit, he sees a good number of people weeping, some kneeling in prayer. Okay, so maybe not a random shooter, he thinks. Then his mind drifts to the images of a truck plowing through people at a parade. Not likely, he reasons, on the jam-packed streets of New York. But something definitely has these people spooked. Smith finally reaches solid ground and hurries toward the exit, plowing through the onrush of people like a salmon swimming upstream. There's a sound of shattering glass and the crowd in front of him balloons as people push their way inside through the demolished doors. Smith works his way toward the outer edges of the swelling mass, circling back to the exit.

Dripping sweat, his perfectly pressed suit in ruins, Smith bulls his way outside and stands to catch his breath in the center of the street. He looks up, and all thoughts of his meeting, his start-up, and his future evaporate. His mind turns instead to his fiancée as he watches a mushroom cloud expand over the city. Pulling out his iPhone, he unlocks the screen and pulls up a picture of the woman he'll never marry. He's staring at her image when a nuclear warhead detonates in the skies above Wall Street.

AFTER

CHAPTER 22

Weatherford

Other than a few quick trips back to the house for food or quick jaunts outside to heed the call of nature, Gage and Holly have been holed up in the tornado shelter behind the house for the past week. With Holly in her eighth month of pregnancy, Gage makes all the trips to the house, trying to limit Holly's radiation exposure. The power to the house went out just before Armageddon arrived, and they've heard no news and have no idea how widespread the devastation is. For days on end, the skyline to the east has glowed red—a result of the pounding Tinker Air Force Base took. Gage counted at least eight earth-shaking explosions the day it all started.

With a persistent southerly breeze, the wildfires pushed to the north along with most of the radiation. Still, they aren't in the clear. Not by a long shot. Those same breezes are pushing a toxic mix of smoke and ash up out of Texas and, with no tools to measure radiation, Gage can only assume the heavily clouded skies are laced with death.

On the first day, after Gage raced home from working on the wind turbine, he quickly went to work. The sight of missiles streaking through the sky forced him to work at a frenetic pace. Using four of the replacement AC filters for the house, Gage cobbled together a primitive filtration device, which he attached to the air intake vent in the cellar. After that, he scoured the barn for any items they might need, hitting the jackpot when he uncovered a pair of chemical masks that he'd used last spring while spraying for weeds. Next, he attached a garden hose to the little pump in the shallow well out by the vegetable garden and ran it over close to the shelter. Powered by a small windmill, the well is now their primary source for drinking water.

Although flush with a source of fresh water, food is becoming a major concern. Every year, Gage's mother plants an enormous vegetable garden. By season's end, she's canned dozens of jars of various fruits and vegetables, which she distributes out to the extended family. Gage and Holly are down to two jars of canned tomatoes and one jar of plum jelly. A short trip outside to hunt small game is one option, but it's not without risks. Along with Gage's risk of exposure, there's concern the meat might now be tainted.

"Maybe I could run over to Mom and Dad's to see if they have some extra food," Gage says. The hiss of the old kerosene lantern Gage discovered in the barn fills the silence. With five gallons of kerosene in reserve, they try to run the lantern as much as possible to ward off the darkness.

Holly tucks a strand of red hair behind her ear. Although underground, the cellar feels like a hot box, a combination of the August heat, along with the superheated air blowing north from the distant wildfires. "They're all the way on the other side of town. How you going to get there?"

"I bet the old hay truck still runs."

Holly pokes on her protruding womb. "Fine. But, I'm going with." Holly has the pale complexion of redheads the world over, with a splash of freckles across her nose and cheeks. At five-six, she had a curvaceous body with full hips and ample breasts. But that was eight months ago. Today, her ankles and feet are swollen and her once-svelte waistline has swelled to the size of a ripe watermelon.

"Too risky, babe."

"Gage, I'm absolutely miserable. The heat, the pressure on my bladder, the kicking of my ribs . . . I don't know how much more of this I can take." She gently pushes on her belly, trying to get the baby to change positions. At the last ultrasound they relented and both agreed to find out the sex of the baby—a girl. "How long do we have to stay down here? Forever?"

"I think at least until the baby comes."

Holly groans. "I'll wear the mask."

"You can also absorb radiation through the skin, Holly. Be best to wait."

"Pull the truck up next to the cellar and I'll climb in."

Gage ponders her request for a few moments. "I just don't know."

"Please," Holly pleads. "I'd like to check on my parents while we're out."

"We'd be risking even more exposure. The truck will help a little, but most of the floorboards are rusted out."

"I'll wear a poncho and wrap up in damp blankets. Think that'll help?"

"I don't know. Hell, what I know about radiation wouldn't fill a thimble." Gage rakes his hands through his dark hair. "It might work. Maybe for a short period of time."

"Please, Gage? I'm going stir crazy down here."

Gage sighs. "Okay, I'll run to the house and get some ponchos and blankets, then head for the barn to get the truck. Do not open the door until I get back."

Holly gives him a mock salute. "Yes, sir."

Gage slips on one of the respirators, pushes up out of the door, and runs toward the house. Once inside, he heads for the hall closet and grabs the rain ponchos and an armful of blankets. He glances out the window at the barn a hundred yards behind the house and slips on one of the ponchos and drapes a blanket over his shoulders. He sucks in a lungful of air, opens the door, and races toward the barn.

Before the event began in earnest, Gage had herded the cattle up closer to the barn to provide some protection. As he draws closer to the barn, a stench invades the respirator mask. Being winded and gasping for air only adds to his growing nausea, and the stench grows stronger the closer he gets to the barn. The odor is familiar to those growing up on a farm who have dealt with the loss of livestock—the odor of death. When he's close enough to see the corral he finds the source. All of the cattle are dead and the carcasses are buzzing with flies. A bolt of fear nearly seizes his heart. The cattle appear to have been dead for several days, indicating the radiation exposure was more severe than Gage had originally thought.

CHAPTER 23

When NSA personnel were ordered to evacuate to the bunker beneath the building, Alyx Reed and Zane Miller, having insider knowledge of the scope of the attack, made a break for it. They piled into Zane's '67 Chevrolet Camaro and headed west. With the world exploding behind them, they made it as far as Morgantown, West Virginia, before the old car succumbed to Zane's frantic driving. With the sky growing darker by the minute, they sought shelter in one of the campus buildings at West Virginia University. And they weren't the only ones. The main building's basement was crowded with college students and university employees. A raiding party was sent to the cafeteria and the food court and they returned with armloads of canned goods. The first day or two, Zane and Alyx said as little as possible and tried to blend in. But as time wore on and the food dwindled, resentment began to build. Alyx and Zane were singled out as interlopers and, fearing for their lives, slipped away before daybreak.

Before slinking away from campus, Alyx and Zane

made two critical stops. At the ransacked hospital they scored big with two lead-lined smocks from the radiology department. And in the emergency room, they loaded up on surgical masks and gloves. In the doctors' lounge they hit pay dirt again when they found two full boxes of protein bars in one of the doctor's lockers. From there they backtracked across campus and entered the looted bookstore, where they stocked up on rain gear, stadium blankets, flashlights, and backpacks to carry it all in. Weary about pressing their luck, they lingered a few moments longer to gather all of the bottled water they could find.

But, that was nearly a week ago.

Today, battered and bruised, they're limping southeast along Highway 81, trying their best to stay out of sight. Ash rains down from the sky and distant fires dot the horizon. The lead-lined smocks are heavy and hot, and combined with the backpacks and suited up with surgical gloves and masks, it feels like they're walking around in a steel mill in the middle of July. With no way to measure how much radiation is present, they are playing it safe. It's been two days since they had anything to eat and both are beset with gnawing hunger pains. They are down to six protein bars, and both agreed to hold them in reserve for as long as possible. Until the last few days, they relied on the kindness of homeowners along the route for food and water. No longer. They've had shotguns and pistols pointed at them, and were even threatened by a knife-wielding woman dressed in a tattered housecoat.

Zane glances ahead and sees a group of people approaching and nudges Alyx off the road and into the trees. As the other group nears, they see it's two adults, a man and a woman, and two young girls who are plodding along behind them, zombielike. The parents are humping backpacks and the two girls are struggling to keep up. Their faces are covered with a rash of blisters, and Alyx and Zane quietly argue about approaching. They decide no, and let the group pass.

"They'll be dead within the week," Zane whispers.

"Wonder where they're from?"

"Does it matter?"

Alyx scowls, then whispers, "Yeah, it does. Might tell us what's ahead."

Zane pulls the mask down and wipes the sweat from his face. "The same thing that's behind us." Once the group is out of sight, they return to the road. "Tell me again, where we're going?" Zane asks.

"Weatherford, Oklahoma. That's where my parents and sister live. I've told you all of this before. I'm beginning to wonder if the radiation has infiltrated that thick skull of yours."

"Not radiation. Exhaustion. Why don't we find a place to hole up for a while?"

Spotting another group approaching, Alyx grabs Zane by the arm and pulls him off the road. With no weapons at hand, they've played the walk-and-avoid game along the entire route and today they're approaching the outskirts of Bristol, Tennessee. "We can't stay here. We're outsiders."

"Everybody's an outsider," Zane whispers.

"The people wandering the roads, yes. But I can guarantee you there are clans of families up in these mountains. They'd never let us in."

As this group draws closer, Alyx and Zane hunker down a little lower. There are five people in this group—three middle-aged men toting shotguns and two young women, midtwenties, who look as if they've been rode hard and put away wet. The women's wrists are bound and they're being pulled along by ropes tied to their necks.

"Should we try to help them?" Zane whispers.

"With what? Are we going to choke out three armed men with a pair of shoelaces?"

The group halts and the man leading the pack turns in their direction. Zane and Alyx freeze, both hesitant to take a breath. After several heart-pounding moments, the leader whistles and the group trudges onward. Once they've disappeared from sight, Zane and Alyx breathe. "We need to find a weapon," Zane says. "We're sitting ducks out here."

"Well, when we get to a Dick's Sporting Goods, you can buy yourself a gun."

"Funny," Zane says. "Seriously, we should start searching some of the abandoned homes we come across."

Alyx steps out of the tree line and moves up to the road, Zane following behind. She waits for him to draw abreast. "I'm all for finding a weapon, but how are we going to determine if a home is abandoned?"

"I think we'll know it when we see it."

"Maybe, maybe not. Anyway, you'll have plenty of time to find one. By my calculations, we have weeks to go before we reach our destination. And that's if all goes well, which is highly unlikely."

CHAPTER 24

For a week, the group from West Texas has been holed up at the Minneapolis–Saint Paul Airport. And they're not the only ones. The place is jammed with stranded travelers and flight crews who consider themselves fortunate to have survived. Many other travelers weren't so fortunate, with a dozen crash sites visible through the terminal's windows. Lauren Thomas heard their survival had something to do with their flight path and a lot of luck, but she and Melissa Walker aren't feeling especially lucky today. More than a thousand miles from home, they're responsible for seventeen teenagers and no one knows if any of their parents are still alive.

With no power and no water, the terminal building smells like a cesspool. The restaurants and stores were raided the first day, and if it hadn't been for an older airline captain who took charge, the situation could have turned perilous. With the assistance of two police officers who were stationed at the airport, the food was confiscated from the looters and what remains is stored behind a locked door. There is one good thing about the situation—there are no weapons handy because the passengers and crews passed through TSA screeners at their original departure cities.

Lauren glances at her watch. "Jonathon, you're about due to start your shift."

Jonathon rolls his eyes. "I don't like working in the bookstore."

"Tough. You're not going to sit around here all day bothering everyone."

Jonathon scowls. "Make someone else take my shift."

"No, sir. Everyone earns their keep."

With drooping shoulders, Jonathon shuffles up the corridor. Melissa, Lauren, and two other stranded teachers converted the terminal bookstore into a lending library. Those who wish to borrow a book or magazine—all the newspapers are pulp, they've been read so many times—must present an ID and provide their location within the terminal. At least it keeps the kids occupied. They played with their electronic devices until they crapped out on the second day. It took them all of about thirty minutes after device death to start moaning about being bored, forcing Melissa and Lauren to find something to occupy their time.

Lauren spots Stan McDowell walking up the corridor. He's the airline pilot who's now ramrodding the show. A tall, broad-shouldered man, he has a head full of gray hair and, today, he's dressed in his uniform slacks and white shirt. Watching him walk, Lauren can still see the traces of his military training. She threads her way through the crowd and meets him. "What have you heard from the city councils?"

"Basically, they're refusing to acknowledge we even exist. They've discontinued any further talks." Using an old airport tug, Stan had sent a stranded attorney to parlay with the city councils of Minneapolis and Saint Paul.

"How can that be? Isn't this airport their property?"

"Yes, but they're more concerned with their constituents than an assemblage of strangers stranded at the airport. To tell you the truth, I'm not sure I wouldn't do the same if I were in their shoes. It's a new world, Lauren."

"How much food do we have left?"

McDowell takes her by the elbow and steers her toward a sparsely populated corner of the terminal. "A day, maybe two, but that information needs to remain confidential."

"Of course," Lauren says. "What happens then?"

"I guess it's everyone for themselves." He leans against the wall. "Tell me again where you and the kids are from?"

"Lubbock, Texas, a long damn way away. What about the airplane we flew in on? Could we refuel it and have you fly us back home?"

"There are several reasons we can't fly the aircraft—one, there is no power to run the pumps to refuel and, even if we could find another way to do it, there are few if any places to land a jet of that size. We were damn lucky to make it here without radios or navigation. Things were dicey getting these planes landed without further incident. But the more pressing issue is whether more bombs are going to be dropped, something we have no way of knowing. The last place I want to be is in the air if that happens." McDowell rakes a hand through his hair. "Know how many airline crashes I saw between here and New York City?"

"How many?"

"I stopped counting at thirty. And every major airport we passed was either bombed to hell or cluttered with crashed aircraft."

Lauren gasps. "But how did this airport survive?"

McDowell bends his leg and props his foot against the wall.

"A lot of luck. Minnesota is one of the few states that lacks a sizable military installation. Now extrapolate what I said about those other airports and expand it to the rest of the country. The Deep South is littered with military installations as are Texas, Oklahoma, and most of the West. Add in the missile silos in the Dakotas and Wyoming and there's a high likelihood a vast portion of this country has been destroyed."

"But there'll still be pockets of people."

"Most likely. Probably even in Lubbock if the wildfires didn't scour the area. But back to your original question, the only option for making it back home to Lubbock is to walk."

"It's over a thousand miles. Do you foresee two teachers and seventeen teenagers ever making it that far? I sure as hell don't."

McDowell ponders her question for a moment. "I'm itching to get out of here, too." He pauses, considering his options. After a few moments, he says, "I'm based out of Dallas and I'll accompany your group to the Texas-Oklahoma border where we can split up and go our separate ways."

"You'd do that?" Lauren asks.

"We're at the end of the line here. Between now and when we leave, have your kids hoard anything that'll hold water. I'm going to see if one of the policemen will let me take one of their shotguns and some ammo."

Lauren steps in to give him a hug. "Thank you. When are we leaving?"

"Tomorrow morning would be best. Are there any atlases in the bookstore?"

"I don't think so, but I'll look. What are we going to do for food?"

"We're going to ration everything left in the storeroom this evening. We'll have to stretch it as far as we can until we can find some game along the way. And, Lauren, I'd prefer you not tell the children before later tonight. Be best if we could sneak away without creating an uproar."

"Of course. I'll tell them later tonight. That'll give them time to pack a few of their things. I assume we want to travel light?"

"Yes—one extra outfit and one additional pair of shoes for everyone. Oh, and a jacket if they have one. Everything else gets left behind. We'll pile our food and water supplies into a couple of empty suitcases."

"Are we tilting at windmills?" Lauren asks.

"We won't know the answer to that until we hit the road."

CHAPTER 25

Saddle Rock, Long Island, New York

The West Shore Hospital is choked with people, and patients are packed six to a room designed for two. Any hopes of patient privacy lasted all of about thirty minutes after the bombs rained down on Manhattan. Tucked into one corner of a room on the third floor is ten-year-old Sophia Dixon. For a week her parents have been by her bedside as the ventilator pumps, breathing life into her small body. Outside when a nuclear bomb airburst over Queens, Sophia is now suffering from radiation burns, and her lungs are scarred from the heat of the blast. And she's just one of the hundreds in this one hospital.

Today, Emma Dixon, her mother, is snuggled up in bed with Sophia, quietly reading *The Hunger Games* while stroking her unconscious daughter's hand. She and her husband started rotating shifts to allow them to spend more time with Tanner, their twelve-year-old son. Their home damaged in the attack, the family has been camping in the basement of the local YMCA. Luckily for most on Long Island, the atmospheric winds pushed most of the toxic radiation north and the firestorms that erupted over Manhattan failed to make a jump across the bay.

Emma's favorite nurse, Latreece, a transplant from Kingston, Jamaica, comes striding into the room, a grim expression on her face. She bypasses the other five patients and makes a beeline for Sophia's bed. "Ms. Dixon, Dr. Bhatia would like a word with you in his office."

Emma slides off the bed and pulls the covers up to Sophia's chin. Tall and thin, Emma's short, dark hair is matted from lying on the bed. "Do you know what he wants to talk to me about?"

Normally chatty, Latreece is now demure, failing to meet Emma's eyes. In fact, Latreece's dark, cherub face doesn't drift much above her shoes "No, ma'am, I truly don't. I do know he's had several other members from other families in and out of his office most of the day."

"I wonder if it's a problem with the insurance? Oh, wait, that can't be it. I don't think they can even process a claim. It's not the backup generators, is it? Or maybe they're going to move her to another floor," Emma says, rambling on to avoid thinking about the upcoming conversation with Sophia's doctor.

Latreece refuses to engage and says, "If you'll follow me, please, I'll take you to his office."

The way the nurse is acting, so out of character, has the hairs standing up at the nape of Emma's neck. She wishes she could call her husband, Brad, but there's not a phone within 4,000 miles that still functions—cell or landline. She wrings her hands as she falls in behind Latreece. They take the stairs down a floor and the nurse leads her to a nondescript office and opens the door, still refusing to meet Emma's gaze. "Have a seat, Ms. Dixon."

"Will you check on Sophia while I'm down here?" Emma asks.

"I will. The doctor will be with you in a moment." Latreece pulls the door closed, leaving Emma alone with her thoughts. Her brain clicks through possible reasons for this meeting and her blood pressure rises with each scenario that plays through her mind. She picks up a magazine six months out of date and immediately places it back on the table. Emma stands and begins to pace. The room is small and after three trips around the perimeter, she stops and leans against the wall.

A blood-curdling wail pierces the silence, startling Emma. She walks over to the outer door and opens it for a peek down the corridor and doesn't see anyone in despair. It's then she hears the deep sobbing coming from within Dr. Bhatia's office. Shortly thereafter a young couple, dazed and bereft with grief, exit, the man carrying most of the woman's weight as she leans into him, hands covering her mouth.

Dr. Bhatia, a short, thin-framed man, steps out of his office. "Ms. Dixon, please come in." He stands aside as Emma enters the office, closing the door behind her. He waves to a pair of chairs fronting his desk. "Please, have a seat." Though the doctor left his homeland, his heavy Indian accent accompanied him to this country.

Emma looks at the chairs and thinks, momentarily, about turning around and leaving. "I'll stand."

The doctor pulls out his chair and sits, crossing one leg over the other. "As you wish." After straightening his tie, he gets to the heart of the matter. "Ms. Dixon, we knew upon admission that Sophia's prognosis was not good. Since her admission date there has been no improvement in her—"

Emma holds up a hand. When she speaks, her voice is filled with venom. "Stop right there, asshole. You are not removing my baby from that ventilator."

Taken aback, Dr. Bhatia is momentarily stunned. "Ms. Dixon, I do not appreciate your language. I understand you are upset, but we must be reasonable about this matter."

"Fuck reason. Sophia is *my* child." She stabs her chest with a thumb. "Mine."

Bhatia uncrosses his legs and leans forward in his chair. "You must understand, Ms. Dixon, the hospital has a very limited supply of critical medical equipment. There are other, more viable, patients in need of ventilators."

"More viable? You summon me to your office without the courtesy of including my husband to discuss the viability of my daughter's life? What kind of monster are you?"

"Time is of the essence, Ms. Dixon. This situation demands difficult decisions. I understand you are devastated by the injuries your daughter sustained, but as a physician, I must do what's in the best interest for *all* the patients under my care."

Emma Dixon reaches for the door handle. "Touch my daughter and it'll be the biggest mistake you ever make. That, you can take to the bank." She pushes through the door and it's not until she's in the stairwell that the dam breaks. Tears are streaming down her cheeks as she slowly ascends the stairs. Wishing deeply for the accompaniment of her husband, she shuffles through the door leading to the third floor, her eyes in a watery haze. Blindly, she staggers down the hall, turning into her daughter's room. She sags to her knees and releases a howl of despair when she discovers her daughter's bed empty. Two large men appear at her side. The men gently lift her to her feet and lead her down the stairs to the main floor, never uttering a word. They usher her outside and before retreating allow her to collapse on a bench in the garden.

CHAPTER 26

Weatherford

Discovering the dead cattle sent Gage Larson scurrying back to the underground tornado shelter. Once he catches his breath he tells Holly what he found.

"The cattle have been dead for a while, Gage," Holly says. "That doesn't mean the radiation is as bad now. Surely, after a week, the wind has dissipated most of it." She stands, fisting her hands on either hip. "I can't spend another moment down here, Gage. I just can't."

"Holly, think of the baby. We don't know what effects the radiation will have on her."

"I'm nearly full-term. We're past all of the major growth milestones." Although they know the sex of the baby, they continue to argue over names. Holly's pushing for Olivia while Gage favors Rachael. Gage has no doubts about who will eventually win this contest, but he's not ready to give in just yet. "I'll go by myself if I have to. Another day or two is not going to make much of a difference. Besides, we're almost out of food and the baby needs protein."

"Where are we going to find protein?"

"Mom and Dad have that generator. I bet the freezer is still running."

"Is it worth the risk, Holly?"

Holly throws her hands up in the air. "Whatever."

Gage grimaces. That word is often a precursor to nothing good. "Okay, Holly, you win." He steps over and wraps most of her up in a hug. Even as big as he is, his arms no longer wrap entirely around his wife. "Stay underground until I get the old truck over here. Wet those blankets while you're waiting. We need all the protection we can get." Gage slips on the poncho, seats the respirator over his nose and mouth, and makes a break for the barn.

The old truck is a '57 Chevy one-ton more covered with rust than paint. What little paint is visible consists of about fifteen shades of green, from dark to light. The truck might be hideous, but it has never failed to start, except for one very cold winter day. He grabs a tape measure and tugs open the door, measuring the width of the cab. Gage wasn't kidding about the floorboards. A rash of weeds have sprung up through the floor, nearly filling the cabin. Once he has the measurement, he finds a piece of leftover sheet metal from a recent roof replacement on the barn and cuts it to size with a hacksaw. Bending the metal one way, then the other, Gage gets it fitted across the floor. He climbs in and twists the key. The old truck fires up, billowing black smoke like a mosquito fogger in the middle of June. While the engine warms, Gage prowls around the barn for items they may need. He grabs some of his work tools and throws them in the back and pulls two winter toboggans from a plastic bin and tosses them on the dash.

Gage follows the toboggans in and backs the truck out of the barn. The grass and weeds stay where they're rooted, slipping under the new metal floor. He pulls around behind the house and parks next to the cellar. The door rises and Holly hurries into the pickup. Gage pulls up close to the front door. "I need to get one more thing before we leave."

Gage pushes out of the truck and hurries into the house. After a few minutes, he returns carrying his shotgun and two boxes of shells, which he parks on the seat between them.

"Expecting a war?" Holly asks.

"To tell the truth, I don't know what to expect. But it's a damn sight better to be prepared. Where first? Your parents' place or mine?"

"Mine are closer. Let's go there first."

"You got it." Gage drops the truck into gear and steers around to the road.

CHAPTER 27

Tennessee

With the debris-filled atmosphere, it's difficult to judge the time. But to Alyx and Zane it feels as if they've been walking for hours. A little farther down the road, Zane grabs her by the elbow and whispers in her ear, "I saw a splash of color way back in the woods. Could be a house."

Exhausted and hungry, Alyx is desperate for food and a comfy place to sit down. "I'm game. But we need to be careful."

Zane nods and glances around to see if anyone is nearby before pulling Alyx off the road. Rather than trekking the dirt road into the woods, they stick to the tree line. The going is tough. Limbs, covered by a dense layer of leaves, lie in wait as trip hazards, and Alyx stumbles twice, skinning the toes on her right foot. To make matters worse, the trees are unevenly spaced and the few openings that do exist are often blocked by patches of briar. The thorns tug at their clothing, making walking damn near impossible. Zane helps Alyx extricate herself from the briars and they take a moment to catch their breath.

"Let's move a little closer to the road," Alyx says.

"What if we're spotted?"

"We'll say *sorry* and get the hell out. I don't have the strength to fight through all that brush."

Zane ponders her request for a moment and looks over at the thick brush on the other side of the dirt road. "Maybe the other side is easier going."

"Does it look easier?" Alyx snaps.

"I suppose you're right. If we can hug the side of the road the trees will offer us a little cover."

Walking along the side of the road, they travel a hundred yards, pause to look around, and continue on another hundred yards.

"Where is this house of yours?" Alyx whispers. "I think we're on the road to nowhere."

"The road has to lead somewhere. And the house being this deep in the woods could be a positive for us."

They each take a sip of water from a water bottle and continue on. A quarter mile in, they catch first sight of the home. Zane leads them back to the tree line and they move closer. The small, square house looks as if it hasn't felt the bristles of a paintbrush since Jimi Hendrix was singing at Woodstock. The yard is filled with an assortment of rusted vehicles, an old washing machine, and something so far gone neither Zane nor Alyx can determine its purpose. A narrow porch runs along the front of the house, and it, too, is overflowing with junk, including a ratty floral couch slumped in the corner, three cats napping upon it.

"I wonder if there're any dogs," Alyx whispers.

"I think they would have smelled us by now. Hell, maybe they ate it."

Alyx punches him in the arm. "What now?"

"We watch for a while. Maybe wait till dark to see if anyone lights a candle."

Alyx steps deeper into the trees, finds a bare spot of ground, spreads out one of the stadium blankets, takes off the heavy smock, and plops down. "Tell me if you see anything."

"Four eyes are better than two," Zane whispers.

"You could watch that house with one eye and not miss a thing. I need to stretch out for a few minutes. My back is killing me."

Zane scowls, but doesn't argue. He moves deeper into the trees, trying to work his way a little closer. He finds a tree stump and sits. His stomach is growling loud enough to be heard if anyone was around to hear it. He tries to push the hunger from his mind and his thoughts drift to his traveling companion. Tall and thin to begin with, Alyx now more closely resembles a scarecrow. The veins and tendons are visible on her arms and neck, and her collarbones stand in stark relief to her muscled shoulders. Even with that, she's still attractive as hell, as far as Zane is concerned. They've gotten along well but there are no hints of a budding romance, at least on Alyx's part, or so Zane thinks. He's not exactly an expert on women, having been single for a number of years.

In his peripheral vision he catches slight movement from the curtain on the far window. He watches intently for a few more minutes, but the curtain remains still. With the number of cats snuggled on the couch on the front porch, there's a high probability there are more inside the house. Zane closes his eyes for a moment to reduce the strain. After a time, he, too, grows weary. He decides to wait until dark and works his way back to Alyx and strips off his smock, joining her on the blanket. She rolls over and spoons against his back. With the physical contact, and despite being exhausted and starving, Zane's little head takes over the thinking department. He moves his hands to his crotch to conceal the tenting of his jeans.

Zane is astonished moments later when Alyx's right hand slips over his side and drifts down to his crotch. She whispers in his ear, "Would you like to put your little friend to use?"

"He's my big friend," Zane says, rolling over to look Alyx in the eyes.

Alyx cackles softly. "Is he now? Truth or dare?"

Zane ponders the question for a moment. "Truth."

Alyx begins to stroke his penis through his jeans. "How many times have we fucked in your mind?"

It doesn't take Zane long to answer. "Too many times to count."

Alyx smiles and leans in for a long, lingering kiss. "I've had similar thoughts, too."

It doesn't take long for them to shed their clothing. Though neither has bathed in a week, the mix of musky odors only adds to the desire, and their lovemaking is intense, passionate, and exhausting.

Alyx rolls over and says, "That was nice."

"I couldn't agree more. We should do this more often."

Alyx laughs. "I could probably be persuaded." Alyx

sits up and removes the hoop from her left nostril, then all of her earrings, and tosses everything into the woods.

"Why did you have all of that stuff to begin with?" Zane asks.

Alyx shrugs and stretches out next to Zane, pulling another blanket over them. "I guess to announce my presence. Know how many female programmers there are?"

"Yeah. Not many."

"Exactly. It's damn hard to get ahead." Alyx sighs. "I guess I wanted to shove my femininity in their faces. Anyway, all that shit's behind me now."

Zane runs a finger across the tattoo above her left breast. "And the butterfly tattoo? Any significance?"

"Nope. That's the result of too many tequila shots when I was in college." She turns to face Zane and snuggles against his chest, draping an arm across his midsection. After several moments of silence, they drift off into an easy, contented sleep. When they wake it's full dark and both quickly dress. "Are we going in?" Alyx asks.

"If there are no signs of life, yes." He clicks on a flashlight and smothers the lens with his palm as they creep closer to the house. The interior is as dark as the outside, with no sign of a candle flicker or any hint of movement. He looks around on the ground and leans in to whisper in Alyx's ear. "Grab that big stick, in case we need a weapon."

Alyx nods and bends to pick up the stick before continuing their approach. When they reach the porch, a cat darts through Zane's legs, momentarily stopping his heart. Zane can feel Alyx trembling beside him as he steps up to the door. He buries the light against his thigh and cups a hand around his face to peer through the window, but it's too dark to see a damn thing. He lets a little of the light from the flashlight eke out and reaches for the door handle, surprised to find it unlocked. Carefully, he twists the knob and nudges the door open. The first thing to greet them is an awful stench. Alyx gags and claps a hand over her mouth as they step farther into the house.

"What's that awful smell?" Alyx whispers in his ear.

"Something dead," Zane whispers. He repositions the flashlight, allowing more light to leak out. They're in the living room. A tattered floral couch, similar to the one on the porch, holds center stage and is flanked by a pair of scarred wooden end tables. At a right angle to the couch sits a broken-down red recliner. Newspapers are stacked on a stained coffee table and a threadbare rug lies underfoot. The only concession to modernity is the fifty-inch television resting on a pair of plastic milk crates. Behind the couch is the kitchen, with a narrow hallway leading to the rest of the house. Imprinting the layout in his mind, Zane kills the light.

Not sensing any threats, he whispers to Alyx to ditch the club and takes her hand, leading her around the couch and down the hallway. Within the confines of the corridor, the stench is gut clenching, and both are gagging. Zane covers the lens and switches on the flashlight. Three doors lead off the hallway, and as luck would have it, all are closed. Zane gags, bends over, and dry heaves. "Screw it," he mutters, shining the flashlight down the hallway. He opens the first door and it's a filthy bathroom, but not the source of the odor. He deduces the other two doors are bedrooms. He approaches the first door on the left and quietly pushes it open to find a bedroom that had been converted into a sewing room. Partially completed quilts drape across every surface. Zane backs out and steps over to the last door and sucks in a deep breath, something he instantly regrets.

Zane twists the knob and nudges the door open. The odor that escapes makes his eyes water as a swarm of flies zip past their heads. Zane aims the flashlight through the door and shines the beam around the room. On the bed, and atop one of the quilts, are two dead people. The bodies are bloated and there are enough flies still left in the room to produce a near-constant hum. Zane steps farther into the room. Most of the skin has sloughed off their faces but the remnants of gray hair suggest the couple was older. Congealed blood covers nearly every inch of the quilt, and, upon closer examination, Zane discovers half of the woman's skull is missing.

"What happened to them?" Alyx says out loud, making Zane jump.

"Murder, suicide, I think." Zane edges around the bed and spots an old revolver on the ground. "Found the gun. Looks like he shot her, then himself."

"Why?"

"Guess they didn't want to spend their last days in a screwed-up world." Zane places the flashlight on top of a broken-down dresser and rolls the edges of the quilt over the dead couple. He leans down and scoops up the pistol and tucks it into his waistband. "Grab one end. We need to get them out of the house."

"Where are we going to put them?"

"Outside. I'll try to bury them in the morning."

Alyx gags as she grasps the edges of the quilt. The couple hadn't been large in life and the corpses are even lighter. Working together, she and Zane scoot down the hallway and out the front door. Alyx backs down the porch steps and they carry the dead couple over to the tree line.

Once back inside, Zane opens every window in the small house and props the front door open for the flies to escape. Alyx is scrounging for candles and finds some, which she lights. "Time to take stock of the situation," she says, opening cabinet doors. After enduring the stench of the dead bodies, the dead refrigerator remains closed.

In a small pantry, Alyx finds a loaf of moldy bread and then gives a small shout of joy when she discovers a good number of canned goods. There are soups, several tins of Spam and Vienna sausages, along with cans of corn, beans, green beans, and snow peas. She passes a can of the sausages to Zane and he pops the top and peels back the lid. He's hungry, but not so hungry to plunge his filthy hands into the container. After opening four drawers, he finds the forks and tosses one on the counter for Alyx and digs in. No, it's not a juicy fillet, but when you haven't eaten for two days it almost tastes like one.

Alyx opens a can of Spam, grabs the fork, and takes a seat on the sofa. Zane polishes off the first can, grabs another, and follows, sagging onto the couch and propping his feet up on the coffee table. The pistol digs into his side and he pulls it out and places it on the table. "We'll do a more thorough search in the morning. But, judging from the age of the house, I wouldn't be surprised to find a root cellar. If we're lucky, it'll be loaded with food."

Alyx finishes her Spam, grabs one of the three remaining bottles of water, and takes a swig before passing it on to Zane. "We have two bottles of water left. Hopefully, we can find a water source around here." Alyx stands and returns to the kitchen for more food and comes back with her own can of Vienna sausages. She spears one and plops it into her mouth before sitting. "How long we going to stay?" she asks around a mouthful of sausage.

"A few days, hopefully." He points to the pistol. "At least we now have a weapon."

CHAPTER 28

Saddle Rock

Emma Dixon has no recollection of how long she's been sitting on the bench in the hospital's rose garden. Dusk has descended and when Emma stirs from her reverie the ember of rage burning in her gut reignites. She struggles to her feet as her brain clicks through the various ways to inflict pain on Dr. Bhatia. "How dare you," she mutters as she shuffles down the street toward the local YMCA. Two blocks down, she cuts over a block, now within in shouting distance of the location.

Her husband, Brad, usually spells her for the night shift to allow her to spend some time with their son, Tanner. As she nears the Y, her husband steps through the front door and approaches. "I was just coming to relieve you," he says.

Emma zombie-walks forward, collapsing against her husband's chest. "They . . . killed . . . her . . . Brad," she says between sobs.

"Who?" he asks, wrapping her in his arms.

"That asshole Bhatia!" she shouts. "He . . . he

called . . . me into his . . . office . . . and when . . . I . . . went . . . back . . . to . . . Sophia's . . . room . . . she . . . was . . . gone." Her sadness veers to anger and she begins pummeling Brad's chest with her fists.

Brad pulls her closer, trapping her flailing arms against his body.

Her flash of anger subsides almost as quickly as it began and the sobs return, racking her body. "Then the bastards . . . escorted me out . . . of the . . . hospital . . . like I was . . . a piece . . . a piece . . . of . . . garbage."

Brad Dixon holds his wife as tears drip down his face, wetting his wife's hair. They sob for several moments and then Brad dries his eyes and says, softly, "Maybe she just slipped away."

Emma wriggles out of his grasp, the anger returning. "No, Brad. She didn't slip away. They killed her."

"Why? What possible motive would they have?"

"For the fucking ventilator." She places her balled fists on her hips. "They need them for other, more *viable*, patients. That's what that asshole Bhatia told me."

Brad, his eyes downcast, says, "We knew the possibilities for Sophia—"

Emma presses in and gives him a hard shove. "Don't you do it. Don't you take up for that son of a bitch." She brushes past her husband and hurries toward the entrance.

"Where are you going?" Brad shouts after her.

She stops and whirls around. "To fix it." She turns back and disappears inside.

It hits Brad then, what she has in mind. He races to the entrance, ducks inside, and hurries down the corridor, taking the steps to the basement two at a time. The place is jammed with people, and Brad plows through the crowd, heading for the tiny space they carved out on the far side of the room. Tanner is propped against the wall, his nose buried in a book. "Did you see your mother?"

Tanner glances up. "Yeah. She grabbed one of the backpacks and said she'd be back in a little while. How's Sophia? Any better?"

Now is not the time to tell him his sister is gone. "Which way did your mother go?"

Tanner waves to the other side of the room. "Up the back stairs. What's going on?"

"I'll explain, later," Brad says, turning away. Hurrying toward the back stairs, a toddler darts in front of him and he's forced to stop as the mother crowds in after the child—precious seconds ticking away. Brad turns sideways, edges past, and hurries for the stairs. At the top, he runs down the corridor and bangs through the outer door. It's dark as hell and it takes a moment for him to get his bearings. He turns, spots the lights of the hospital, and takes off at a sprint. Arriving at the hospital, his breathing is ragged and he holds his side while scanning the area in a desperate search for his wife. Wondering if he arrived first, he loiters near the front entrance for a moment, berating himself for not following the shelter's rules. Seeing no sign of Emma he hurries inside and grabs the first nurse he sees. "Where's Dr. Bhatia's office?"

"All physician offices are on the second floor."

Brad hurries to the elevator and slams his palm against the button.

The nurse shouts at him. "Elevators are for patient transport only."

He resists the urge to shoot her the finger and races toward the stairwell and flings open the door, lunging up the stairway to the next floor. Brad bursts through the door on the second floor and scans the corridor. When he looks left he catches a brief glimpse of his wife entering an office farther down the hall. "Emma!" Brad shouts.

Emma doesn't acknowledge his presence.

Brad takes off at a dead sprint. As he slows to round into the office a gunshot rings out. He pushes into the office to find Dr. Bhatia slumped in his chair, the medical certificates on the wall behind him coated with blood and brain matter. Brad turns to his wife, his pistol grasped firmly in her hand—the same pistol that was supposed to be under lock and key with the authorities back at the YMCA.

"Emma, give me the gun."

His wife appears composed and calm, as if in a trance. She raises the weapon and points it at her husband. "No, Brad. I have one more person to see. Latreece."

"Emma, you can't do this. Please give me the gun. You can't bring Sophia back."

"I can make them pay." Tears spring from the corners of her eyes. "Move, Brad."

"No, Emma. You're going to have—"

Two men charge into the room, guns drawn. They knock Brad to the ground and turn their weapons on his wife.

"No!" Brad shouts, but his words are muffled by an eruption of gunfire. Brad looks up in time to see his wife slump to the floor, her body riddled with bullet wounds.

CHAPTER 29

Weatherford

Gage takes his foot off the gas and lets the old truck coast up to the intersection. It's eerie with no other vehicles on the road. In the distance, Interstate 40 looks more like a parking lot than the cross-country interstate it once was. Dead cars are scattered haphazardly across the asphalt, stopped where they died. Gage wonders about the people who were in them then pushes the thought away, having more than enough problems to worry about. On the opposite corner, the Quick Stop is dark and all the glass is shattered, unwanted items such as antifreeze and motor oil scattered across the parking lot. Gage eases through the intersection and, two blocks farther on, hangs a right to take a drag down Main Street. Holly stares out the window at the devastation, her mouth agape.

Weatherford is a small town and the main drag stretches only four blocks. They pass the ransacked Braum's, a local ice cream store and market. The parking lot is stained with melted ice cream, and cockroaches skitter through the abandoned cardboard containers.

Farther on, several other businesses remain intact. The tag agency and the local insurance office are closed, their plate glass windows still in place. The same can't be said about the bank on the next corner. The brick façade is blackened by fire and the ATM machine is overturned, the doors pried open.

"Why would they break into the bank?" Holly asks. "What are they going to buy?"

"Don't know. My bet is there wasn't any money in there to begin with. Or if it was, it was locked up in the vault. You'd need dynamite to blow that thing open."

At the next intersection, the parking lot of the Walgreens looks like a war zone. Baskets are overturned and the shelving from inside the store is bent and twisted and scattered around the lot. Plastic bags, snagged by the light poles, flutter in the breeze. "I bet there's not a pill left in that store," Gage says. "Let's hope no one gets sick."

"Who did all of this damage, Gage? Surely, not the people we know."

"Probably some from those people stranded on the highway, but I'd bet there were some locals involved. People are desperate. Let's check out the Walmart." Gage steers under the highway bridge and picks up the access road. When he turns into the parking lot, Holly gasps.

"Are those bodies?" She turns to stare at her husband. "There must be twenty or thirty bodies just lying in the parking lot."

Gage throws the old truck into reverse and backs out of the lot, launching a swirl of grit and gravel. He quickly shifts to first, mashes the gas pedal, and hits second gear under the bridge.

"What if some of them are people we know?" Holly asks.

"There's nothing you can do for them now." Gage hits fourth gear and winds up the engine, heading out of town. Holly's parents live north of town on an acreage they bought when they moved to town Holly's junior year of high school. Holly's dad, Henry Reed, is an engineer for a national wind company. He got his start in the wind-blown deserts around Palm Springs where Holly lived until moving to Weatherford.

The ash falling from the sky has lessened, but smoke paints the skies a leaden gray. In the far distance fires continue to rage and probably will for years, or until the next big rainstorm hits. Gage slows the pickup as they near the turnoff leading to Holly's parents. They bump across the cattle guard and he steers up the driveway.

The house, a low, sprawling four-bed ranch, is in immaculate condition. Henry and Holly's mom, Susan, designed it to exacting specifications. The family rented a house in town during the fourteen months it took to construct. Fronting the house is a wide, deep porch, complete with half a dozen rocking chairs. The yard, still retaining most of its deep green shading from the latest fertilization, is devoid of weeds. A giant oak tree, surrounded by a precisely manicured flower bed, shades one side of the yard and is offset by a large metal barn on the other side of the house. The exterior of the home receives a paint job every three years, whether it's needed or not. Gage pulls up close to the front door and kills the engine.

Holly's parents push through the front door before they're out of the truck. "I've been worried sick about you two," Susan Reed says, stepping off the porch. "I tried to get your father to run me over there, but none of our vehicles are running." Susan wraps an arm around her daughter and leads her into the house.

Henry steps off the porch and shakes Gage's hand. "Follow me to the barn. I want to show you something." In his late sixties, Henry Reed is a thin, wiry man with a full head of flowing gray hair that was once red. Steel-framed rectangular glasses are perched on his nose, magnifying his bright blue eyes. Not only is he Gage's father-in-law, but also his mentor and employer. Henry pushes the large sliding door aside and steps inside. Against the far wall is a workbench surrounded by a rack of carefully arranged tools. He leads Gage over to the table and unfurls a set of blueprints.

"I want to tap into one or two of the wind turbines for power," he says.

Gage bends down for a closer look at the modified plans. "How are we going to control the blade pitch?" Blade pitch determines the turbine's speed.

"That's where I'm hung up. Everything else I have figured out. But without a computer to control the pitch, I don't know how we'd keep the turbine from destroying itself."

Gage pulls a stool from beneath the table and sits. "Is it safe to work outside?"

"I believe it is. The radiation decays relatively quickly and we're a good distance from any of the heavily bombed areas. It would be nice to have some dosimeters or a Geiger counter, but we don't."

Gage crosses his arms. "To change the subject for a moment—Holly and I drove by the Walmart. The parking lot was littered with dead bodies. Hear anything about that?"

"Yeah, I did. The sheriff stopped by the house. He's got one of those government surplus military Hummers that's hardened against an EMP. Apparently, right after everything happened, some unsavory characters from up on the highway broke into the store and went straight to the guns. They barricaded themselves inside and shot anyone who tried to enter. I think it went on for a couple of days until the sheriff deployed a couple of snipers up on the highway. They eventually picked off three or four inside the store and the rest made a break for it, sparking a gun battle in the parking lot."

"They just going to leave the bodies out there in the open?" Gage asks.

"None of the county's heavy equipment is operational. There's nothing left to dig a grave with. Especially one big enough to hold all those bodies. I think because the store is situated on the outskirts of town, the sheriff decided to leave them be. No telling what diseases are lurking around that place. I hope you didn't linger in the area."

"Nope, turned around and got the hell out. Any locals killed?"

"I don't know the answer to that question, Gage. I know the area was swamped with stranded people. My guess is most were out-of-towners."

"Huh," Gage says. "Hell of a thing. Never thought I'd see something like that. Especially here." Gage stares at something at the back of the barn for a moment before turning to Henry. "Back to the turbine problem. Instead of using blade pitch to control the speed, why don't we use the braking system? I've got enough spare parts to replace the brake pads several times over. Plus we could scavenge parts from the other turbines if needed."

"Might work," Henry Reed says. "But how are we going to control the braking systems? That was all controlled by the computer."

"I've got a couple of old analog pressure controllers left over from the oil patch. We could hook them into the hydraulics of the braking system. Pressure gets too high, it'll lock the turbines down."

"That might just work."

CHAPTER 30

Off the coast of the United Kingdom

Having shot their wad, the crew of the USS *New York* made a deep and hurried run to the Norwegian Sea. Now, a week later, the sub is meandering off the coast of Great Britain at a depth of 300 feet. Towing the communication buoy, the radio room has tried to contact U.S. Strategic Command (USSTRATCOM), other surface ships, and even other submarines, to no avail. Captain Thompson doesn't know if the radio masts were damaged during the launch, or it they are the only people left on earth. Either way, Thompson has no intention of surfacing to find out. They are slowly working their way toward the U.S. Naval Submarine Base Kings Bay, off the coast of southern Georgia.

The mood aboard ship is melancholy. You don't launch 192 nuclear warheads, each twenty-five times more powerful than the bomb dropped on Hiroshima, and not wonder about the lives lost. Captain Thompson continues to suffer from nightmares that are too graphic and violent to render into words. Weary from lack of sleep and concerned about his family back in Georgia, he stands from his chair and arches his back. When he's finished stretching, he grabs the ship's phone and makes a call. "Dan, can you meet me in the ward-room?" He receives a reply and hangs up the handset.

Thompson appoints an officer of the deck and exits through the hatch. Taking the ladder down one level, he turns toward the bow and enters the officers' ward-room, sagging wearily into a chair. Moments later there's a light knock, and Senior Chief Petty Officer Daniel Ahearn pushes the door open and steps into the room. Of Irish descent, Ahearn, with a headful of shaggy red hair, is a large man for submarine duty. Thompson overlooks Ahearn's nonregulation hair be-cause he's the best damn chef in the navy. It took the captain six months of coaxing and prodding to per-suade the big man to come aboard the boat.

Thompson waves to a chair. "Have a seat, Dan."

Ahearn pulls out a chair and sits.

"What's the food situation look like?" Thompson asks.

"We're running on fumes, sir. I planned for a ninety-day tour and we're already well past that. Are we head-ing for port?"

Thompson takes off his cap and rakes a hand through his hair. "There may not be a port, Dan."

Ahearn rears back in surprise. "What do you mean, no port?"

"This stays between us, but we haven't received so much as a hello since the launch order. We've tried every available method to contact USSTRATCOM and there's been no response. Hell, we've tried to contact other ships and still haven't had any luck. How long can you stretch the food stores?"

"Two days." Ahearn pauses to think. "Might could cut the rations in half and stretch for a couple of more. Anything much beyond that and we'd be facing mutiny. We pride ourselves on serving the best food in the navy, and the crew has grown accustomed to that."

"We're now living in a different time, Dan. For now, make it half rations. I'll deal with the crew."

Ahearn pushes to his feet. "I'll do what I can, Skipper."

"Thanks, Dan. That's all any of us can do."

Ahearn pulls open the door and exits. Thompson stands and makes his way over to one of the ship's computer terminals and pulls up a chart for Great Britain. Thankfully, the shipping lanes in this part of the world have been used for centuries and the charts are accurate to within a foot for sea depths all around Great Britain. Thompson, having docked in England before, knows the country has three naval bases. Using his index finger as a pointer, he traces out the three locations on the monitor. Her Majesty's Naval Base Clyde is the closest to their position, but also the most difficult to navigate. HMNB Blyth is on the other side of the country, on the shores of the North Sea. Farther south, along the southern coast of the country, is HMNB Devonport, providing much easier access. "Devonport it is," Thompson mutters. He flags the location on the map and picks up the phone. "Carlos, set a new course." He relays the coordinates. "Keep her slow and silent."

"Where are we headed?"

"Her Majesty's Naval Base Devonport," Thompson replies.

"Think it's still there?"

"Don't know. Won't know until we get there."

CHAPTER 31

When the terminal quiets down for the evening, Lauren and Melissa gather up the kids and herd them toward the bookstore. The last shift ended fifteen minutes ago and three of the students are working via flashlight to put the place back in order. Once all of the students are inside, Melissa grabs the hook, pulls down the rolling metal screen, and twists the lock. Lauren takes the flashlight from Lindsey Scott and covers most of the lens with her palm. "Kids, have a seat on the floor," Lauren whispers.

Once the kids are settled, Melissa steps into the wash of light. "We're leaving in the morning."

Her statement is met with a chorus of moans.

"We don't have any choice. The last of the food was passed out this evening."

"Where are we going?" one of the girls asks. She's beyond the cone of light but Melissa can tell from her voice it's Hannah Hatcher, daughter of Alexander and Meg Hatcher, one of the wealthiest families in Lubbock.

"We're going home," Lauren says.

"How?" Hannah asks.

"We're walking."

Hannah scoffs. "You're joking. We have zero chance of walking home."

"There are no other alternatives. We stay here, we starve to death."

"I don't care. I'm staying," Hannah says. "You two aren't my parents and you can't tell me what to do."

Melissa sighs. "You're wrong, Hannah. You are all under our care until you're returned home to your parents. You will do what we say, when we say."

There's an audible huff from the rear of the group.

"Now, moving on," Melissa says, "I want you to round up all the empty water bottles you can on the way back to our area of the terminal. You will pull out one extra set of clothes, one pair of extra shoes, and a jacket if you have one."

"What about everything else?" Caleb Carson asks. "I'm not leaving without my iPad."

Melissa shakes her head. "Your electronic devices stay behind, as does everything else in your luggage. We'll consolidate all the clothing and shoes into a couple of the better suitcases. Food and water will go into two additional suitcases. If you have a backpack and would like to take it, you may. But keep in mind, no one else is going to carry it for you."

"This is stupid," Hannah says.

"That's enough, Hannah. I don't want to hear another word from you. Is that clear?"

A mumbled "whatever" is Hannah's response.

"We are going to do all of this without attracting any attention to our activities. Pull out the items you wish to take and we'll pack everything in the morning. Once we leave this store, there will be no mention of our leaving. Is that understood?"

The kids acknowledge Melissa with a few scattered nods.

"We are starting a dangerous journey, but if we stick together we can make it. Remember, no talking about what we're doing. The plan is to be out of the terminal building before dawn."

"Hey, what's going on in there?" a man shouts from beyond the locked screen.

Before either Melissa or Lauren can answer, Hannah shouts, "They're kidnapping us!"

Melissa steps across the seated students and feels for Hannah's mouth, clamping down hard and whispering into Hannah's ear, "Don't say another word. Is that clear?"

Hannah nods, but Melissa's hand remains clamped over the girl's mouth.

"We're playing a game," Lauren says.

"What's she talking about kidnapping?" the man asks, peering through the metal grille.

"It's all part of the game," Lauren says. She removes her palm from the light and points the beam at the man's face. "Now kindly move along."

The man peers through his splayed hand, trying to see beyond the light. "Funny game, sounds like to me."

"It is fun, isn't it, guys?" Lauren asks.

A few of the children answer in the affirmative.

Lauren waves the beam down the corridor. "Please move along, sir. We're just trying to break the monotony."

"That I can understand," the man says before shuffling down the corridor.

Melissa removes her hand from Hannah's mouth and leans in, whispering, "Try that again and I'll leave your ass here. Do you understand?"

Hannah nods and Melissa pushes to her feet and walks over to raise the screen. The students pile out in twos and threes and Lauren hands the flashlight to one of the students. Melissa pulls the door down and locks it, leaving the key in the lock.

"She's going to be trouble," Melissa whispers to Lauren.

"I'll talk to her. Let's just get through tonight and tomorrow morning."

Once they return to Gate 15, their small piece of territory, Lauren masks the flashlight with one of her sheer blouses and lays it on the floor. There's just enough light to see without it leaking much beyond the group. Pleased with the lighting results, Lauren is horrified when a dozen opening zippers pierce the silence. She and Melissa quietly work through the group telling the students to be slow and methodical with the zippers. A one-time occurrence is explainable, but if it happens again, it might raise a few eyebrows. Once the kids have finished and settled down for the night, Lauren kills the light, and she and Melissa lie down and stretch out on the floor. After several moments of silence Melissa searches the dark for her friend's hand. "Are we doing the right thing?" she whispers.

Lauren gives her hand a squeeze and whispers her reply: "It's the only option we have."

CHAPTER 32

L auren startles awake when a hand grips her shoulder. Momentarily disoriented, a red light clicks on and she looks up to see Stan McDowell kneeling beside her. "It's time," he whispers. Still discombobulated, Lauren whispers, "Why's the light red?"

"It's a flashlight we keep in the cockpit—never mind, I'll explain later. We're out of here in five."

Lauren rolls over and wakes Melissa. Lauren clicks on her muted flashlight and together they fill the two suitcases with the kids' clothing and shoes. The food and water were packed last night, and they lift those suitcases up onto their wheels. Melissa and Lauren work through the sleeping teenagers, waking them up, a finger to their lips to enforce the silence.

McDowell returns with his own suitcase and a shotgun slung over his shoulder. He pulls Melissa and Lauren close. "I don't know if they're watching the main entrances and exits, but we're going out the back way." He leads the way over to the jetway of Gate 15 and unlocks the door, holding it open while the rest of the group passes. He steps through, eases the door closed, and relocks it.

It's chilly and many of the kids are shivering. McDowell squeezes through the pack and leads them to the door where cabin baggage is checked. He pushes the door open and holds up his red flashlight, lighting the stairway. Once everyone has descended, he herds the group away from the terminal. McDowell stops and turns, trying to get his bearings. He had spent most of the week imprinting a map of the airport and surrounding area in his mind. He knows that at the far end of the facility, near runway one-seven, a construction project had been under way and a portion of the perimeter fencing is missing. But trying to locate the exact area in the dark is difficult. He clicks the red-lensed flashlight on every few minutes to keep the group together. The children are quiet—the only noise is the scrape of shoes and suitcase wheels on the tarmac.

After several minutes of walking across the taxiways, McDowell leads them to a national shipper's warehouse situated on the other side of runway one-two. They traverse the length of the building and McDowell calls the group to a halt. "Let's take a short break. Grab a couple sips of water if you need it." McDowell clicks the red flashlight on and places it on the ground in the center of the group to allow them some light. Some of the kids stretch out on the pavement, trying to absorb the residual heat left in the asphalt.

"How far is it to Texas?" one of the girls, Amanda Brooks, asks. Fifteen, with long blond hair, Amanda hit puberty early and she's much farther down the path in the breast department compared to the other girls—

a fact that elicits some unkind comments on occasion making Amanda very self-conscious.

"It doesn't matter," Lauren says. "We're taking this one day at a time. We get there when we get there. Worrying about the distance is wasted energy."

Amanda cocks her head, thinking about the answer. "Okay. But it's a long way, right?"

Melissa sighs. "Yes." She can't tell the kids how far it is because she doesn't know. Stan had estimated the distance at a thousand miles plus, meaning if they average twenty miles a day the trip could take about two months. Tell that to a teenager who thinks a week is a long time and you risk mutiny before even beginning.

Stan leans down to retrieve the flashlight. "Everyone ready?"

There are a few groans but the teens scramble to their feet. McDowell leads them around the corner of the building and they cross the final runway. Dawn is breaking on the horizon as the group clears the perimeter fence. Across the street is a series of looted stores, including Home Depot and Target. Now on the main road, McDowell leads them south. He's been to Minneapolis more times than he can count. If they can jog west to Interstate 35, one of the few highways to bisect the country from north to south, it's a straight shot to Dallas and beyond.

At East 77th Street, McDowell leads the group west. Two miles farther on they hit I-35. An hour and a half later they're in Bloomington. There are other people traversing the highway, mostly families who look at the large group and shake their heads. McDowell calls another halt and, while the kids rest under the watchful eye of Melissa and Lauren, McDowell searches through a looted grocery store for any items left behind. He returns ten minutes later, empty-handed. "There's nothing edible left," he whispers to Melissa.

She nods and prods the students to their feet. If they stretch it, the food they have might last a couple of days, but that's not a very encouraging thought when facing a journey that could last for months. Melissa falls in behind the kids as they trudge down the highway. They shuffle past dead cars, some empty, some not. The first few incidents when they encounter the dead are fraught with hysteria, but that, too, fades as the miles pile up. Eventually, the children learn to quit looking.

An hour later they pass over the Minnesota River and enter Burnsville. They pass another Home Depot, a ransacked strip mall that was once brimming with people as they shopped for electronics, shoes, or office supplies, and another looted Target. McDowell tells the group to continue on as he ducks into the Target. This time he bypasses the food section entirely and walks straight to the sporting goods area and finds what he's searching for. He grabs a plastic bag and loads it with fishing gear before grabbing a handful of fishing poles. He hurries from the store and catches up with the group farther down the highway. He distributes the fishing poles to some of the kids and crams the gear into his suitcase. Minnesota is known as the Land of 10,000 Lakes. No reason not to supplement their diet with a few fish along the way.

CHAPTER 33

West Virginia

After sleeping on the floor—neither had a hankering for sleeping on the blood-soaked bed—Zane and Alyx stir awake with the first light of the day. With the smoke in the atmosphere, the sun hasn't made much of an appearance since the madness began. But still, the sun's rays do brighten the world. Zane rolls over, stands up, and begins searching the kitchen. Alyx, raking her fingers through her hair, walks into the kitchen. "I'm going outside to pee. I'll look around for a cellar."

"Sounds like a plan," Zane says, pulling open drawers. In one he finds more ammunition for the pistol, which he sets aside. Opening the bottom drawer, he finds two boxes of shotgun shells. "Pay dirt," he mutters. He exits the kitchen and slips down the hallway, turning into the first bedroom. He rummages through the closet, checks behind the doors, and comes up empty. Stepping back out into the hallway, he inhales two deep breaths and opens the door to the second bedroom.

With the windows open, the odor has diminished somewhat, but still lingers and probably will for weeks. The mattress cover is stained with bodily fluids and the flies are busy at work. He debates moving the mattress outside, but he's eager to find the shotgun. After checking behind the doors, he wades into the over-flowing closet. The man had been relegated to one tiny corner, the rest is jammed with dresses, shoes, and handbags—all cheaply made items, by the look of them. Behind a hanging rod jammed with dresses, he finds the shotgun. He pulls it out and carries it into the kitchen for a closer look.

The gun is an ancient double-barrel and he cracks the breech open. Although old, the shotgun has been well cared for, the barrel covered by a thin layer of oil. Which seems strange when Zane considers how far back it was tucked in the closet. Most people with weapons prefer them close at hand. But around here people most likely slept with their doors unlocked, much like the door to this house, Zane reasons. He shrugs and sights down the inside of the barrel and finds it smooth and clean. He lowers the weapon and steps over to the counter, where he slides in two shells and closes the breech. He glances out the window to see Alyx racing around the side of the house.

She eases the door open and hurries across the carpeted floor, coming to a stop next to Zane, whispering, "Someone's coming down the road."

"How many?"

"I saw three. Two men and a woman."

Zane holds up the shotgun. "They don't know this house doesn't belong to us."

"What if there are more?"

He steps over to the coffee table to retrieve the pistol. He quickly reloads the two spent cartridges and tries to hand the pistol to Alyx. She holds her palms against her chest. "I don't know how to shoot that thing."

"It's easy. It's a double-action revolver. All you have to do is pull the trigger." He glances up to look through the window. "I'd really like you to cover me from inside the house."

"Why don't we take what food we can find and just leave?" Alyx whispers.

Zane steps closer to the window and peeks outside. He turns back to Alyx. "It's too late. Pick up the gun." He cocks the shotgun and steps out on the porch as the three people round the bend in the road. Luckily for Zane they're all bunched up. They stop when they spot the shotgun aimed at their midsections. "Turn around and keep walking," Zane says.

One of the men breaks from the group, taking two steps forward.

"Come any closer and I'll blow a hole in your midsection large enough for your friends to put a hand through."

The man, with long, stringy hair and a full beard, stops. A small smile forms on his lips, sending a chill down Zane's spine. "That ain't no way to treat your fellow man. All we want is a little food."

"We don't have any food. Now get the hell out of here."

The man jabs a finger in the air. "I'll remember your face. Maybe we'll meet up down the road." He winks then turns and walks away, the other two following.

The shotgun never wavers in Zane's hand. He tracks their progress until they disappear from sight. With the shotgun still braced against his shoulder, he backs his way toward the door. "Alyx, we'll go with your plan. Gather up all the food you can find."

Inside, Alyx scurries around the kitchen, throwing canned goods into her backpack. Once the pantry is cleaned out, she picks the revolver up and looks at it. After a moment of indecision, she tucks it into the waistband of her jeans and stuffs the pistol ammunition into the backpack. Slinging it over her shoulder, she makes her way to the door. "What about the smocks?" she whispers through the door.

"Leave them. We should be safe from radiation now. And I need to be able to maneuver."

"Should we wait? Let them put some distance between us?"

Zane lowers the shotgun and steps through the door. "I don't know, Alyx. My gut is telling me they're not going anywhere. They could sit out there and wait us out for days." Zane appears calm and collected, but inside, his heart is hammering. "Did you see a water well when you were out?"

"Yeah, but it's attached to an electric pump."

"No telling how deep the well is. It could take forever to pull the pipe and slip a bucket down there. And we're now out of time." Zane moves into the kitchen and takes a peek out the back door. "We could be walking into a firefight if we go out front." He spots an old ramshackle barn about two hundred yards behind the house.

"What did you see while you were outside?"

"Mostly more junk. But there's an old barn out there."

"I'm looking at it. Did you see any trails leading away from it? A way out?"

"If there are trails or tire tracks, they're overgrown."

Zane strides across the room and takes a position near the front window while his brain clicks through possible scenarios. Although Zane spent four years in the army and served one tour in Iraq, he has never been involved in close-quarters combat, other than a few training sessions with dummy bullets. Mostly he worked computers in the intelligence section, but even now the shotgun feels comfortable in his hands. He longs for a pump shotgun that can be loaded with six shells. But it is what it is. He returns to the counter and shoves a handful of shells into his pocket before putting the remaining ammo into his backpack "If we stay here they could burn us out. I like our chances outside. But we're not going to be stupid about it. We're going out the back door to the barn. We'll stay low, keeping the house between the road and us. You'll go first and I'll follow a moment later. Sound like a plan?"

"What if there's not another way out once we get there?"

"Then we're moving through the tree line, back to the main road."

Alyx groans.

Zane tightens the straps of her backpack and leans down and kisses her. "Only options we have. Ready?"

Alyx nods and follows Zane to the back door. Zane slings his backpack over his shoulder and cinches down the straps. It's heavy with all the canned goods stuffed inside, but it's either grin and bear it or leave the food behind. He eases the door open far enough for them to slip through and gently closes it. He moves

Alyx around to the front, allowing him the ability to shoot behind them. He taps her on the shoulder and Alyx takes off like a rabbit. And that's when he realizes his first mistake—the canned goods are loud in the silence as they clatter around in her backpack. He winces and follows a moment later as they race toward the barn. The grass is hip high, making running difficult. A shot rings out behind them and Zane stops and drops to a knee, the shotgun coming up. He fires both barrels toward the far side of the house, where the shot had come from and pops the breech to reload. He glances behind him to see Alyx disappearing inside the barn.

Zane takes a deep breath and lunges to his feet, racing for the safety of the barn. The footing is treacherous in the high grass, but Zane does his best to zigzag before finally reaching the door. He ducks inside, his breath coming in ragged gasps. He grabs Alyx by the arm and leads her toward the back of the barn. "We . . . have . . . to keep . . . moving. Don't . . . know . . . how many there . . . are."

At the back door, Zane pauses for two quick breaths before sliding the door open just far enough to look out. A line of scrub oaks runs from east to west about fifty feet behind the barn. "Okay, here's what we are going to do. You still have the revolver?"

Alyx reaches for the gun tucked into the waist of her jeans, but her hand comes away empty. Her shoulders slump and a moan of despair escapes her lips. Zane tilts her chin up. "It doesn't matter. We've still have the shotgun. We'll move on to plan B."

Alyx's eyes are shimmering with tears. "I'm sorry, Zane. I should have put the pistol in the backpack."

"Water under the bridge, Alyx." Zane pauses to

think for a minute. "Okay. This is what we're going to do. Give me ten seconds to get back to the front then take off for the trees. I'll wait a few minutes and follow. I'll be watching for a signal from you if you spot anyone coming up behind me. Just wave a hand and I'll know to turn around. Ready?"

Alyx nods.

"Count to ten and take off." Zane hurries back to the front of the barn. He eases the door open a sliver and squats down, the shotgun braced against his shoulder. Zane focuses his attention on the back of the house, but occasionally scans the field between the two structures. After several moments of watching and waiting, he spots movement out of the corner of his left eye. Zane pulls more shells from his pocket and places them on the dirt floor beside him. He's determined to end this now. Otherwise, they'll be looking over their shoulders for days to come.

Scanning the field from left to right again, he spots the high grass moving unnaturally on the right side. One left and one right, about thirty yards apart. Zane hopes it's only the two, or he's going to have to do some pretty slick reloading. He takes two deep, calming breaths and waits, thinking how quickly life has changed. A week ago his hands were tickling the keys of his laptop and today his hands are grasping a shotgun, waiting to kill another human being. It's hard for Zane to wrap his mind around. A grunt on the left pulls him back to the present.

Like a covey of quail, the man on the left flushes from the high grass, hurrying for safety at the side of the barn, not knowing that Zane is crouching down by the door. Zane allows the man to draw closer before

unloading the left barrel of the shotgun. The double-
aught shot hits the man in the chest and he drops like
someone had tripped him. Zane doesn't need a second
look to know the man is dead. He immediately shifts
his focus to the right. The man on that side is up and
firing a pistol at Zane's position. It's the smiling man.
The bullets kick up dirt just in front of Zane and he
hunkers down, waiting. When the man is less than ten
feet away, he unloads the other barrel. It hits the man
center mass and blows a section of the man's rib cage
away, creating a red mist that floats in the air. With the
man still falling, Zane quickly reloads and waits.

After several minutes, and no other sign of movement, Zane slips back inside the barn and eases the
door closed. He strides toward the back and, on the
way, discovers a door he hadn't seen before. He steps
over and pulls it open. "I'll be damned," he mutters before hurrying to the rear door and waving Alyx back in.

She shoots him an angry glare, but wades back
through the brush and arrives back at the barn. "I thought
we were going out that way?"

Neither makes mention of what just occurred.
"Change of plans," Zane says. "Follow me." He leads
her back to the recently discovered door and swings it
open.

Alyx steps inside. "What makes you think it runs?"

"We didn't see any other vehicles in the yard, other
than those junkers up on blocks. This has to be their
everyday vehicle." Zane steps over and cracks the door
open. "Keys are in it." *It* is a 1976 Chevy half-ton
pickup, painted harvest gold with a strip of lighter yellow running horizontally through the middle of the
body.

"It's more rust than truck," Alyx says.

"I don't care." Zane slides across the tattered seat and clicks the key over a notch and discovers the truck has a half tank of fuel. "Alyx, look around for a gas can." He twists the key all the way and the old pickup fires to life. Leaving it running, he jumps out to help in the search. He finds an old water hose and cuts off a few feet, tossing it into the bed as Alyx returns with a five-gallon gas can. From her lack of strain, he knows it's empty. "Toss it in the bed. We'll siphon gas from some of the dead cars along the road." Zane takes a quick look around for other items they may need and scores when he discovers a partial case of bottled water near the back doors of the garage area.

He swings the doors open and snatches up the shot-gun, returning to the front of the barn for another look. There is no further movement—the two dead men a deterrent against another approach. Zane hurries back to the truck and jumps behind the wheel. "I'm going hit the driveway pretty fast. We still don't know how many people are around that bend."

Alyx searches for the seat belt and finds a frayed fragment, the rest probably cut out years ago. Zane backs out of the barn and drops the old truck into gear. He shoots across the pasture and veers around the house. When he hits the dirt road, he floors it. When they reach the bend in the road, they discover a group of fifteen to twenty people who scramble to get out of the way. Before they can react, Zane blows by them. He slows to make the turn onto the main road then feeds the big V-8 more gas.

CHAPTER 34

Saddle Rock

After a long, tearful night, Brad and Tanner Dixon are up early at the YMCA. Tanner, who lost his sister and his mother on the same afternoon, had spent most of the evening asking *why*. Brad, also still dazed, had few answers. After much discussion, they both decided it was time to leave their temporary shelter. Brad walks across the floor and puts his wife's things into the donation box before returning to retrieve his backpack. Tanner grabs his stuff and the two ascend the stairs, stepping outside.

The sun is a hazy smudge on the horizon as they strike out down the road, headed back to their damaged house. Not to live, but to retrieve a few items and all the remaining food. They turn right on Middle Neck Road, surprised at the number of people out and about. The area is fairly secluded and it appears the town hasn't yet been inundated by the unwanted. Nevertheless, Brad and Tanner avoid direct eye contact.

At the corner, the CVS has been plundered, with garbage and abandoned shopping carts littering the parking lot. When they reach the next intersection they discover the sushi restaurant ransacked and, across the street, all the glass is shattered at the local art gallery. Tanner sidles up next to his father. "Why would they break into the art gallery?" Those are the first words of the morning from Tanner. Brad will hear an occasional sniffle from his son and each instance breaks another piece from Brad's heart. No twelve-year-old should be suffering the grief that Tanner is now dealing with.

"Who knows? Let's get off the main thoroughfare." They take a left at the next residential street and the damage to the homes escalates with each block as they near Long Island Sound. Across the bay is the Bronx, which was leveled by an airburst nuclear detonation on the first day. The day Sophia was injured. Saddle Rock avoided the fires, but the pressure wave from the blast caused considerable damage.

A vice president at a Manhattan bank, Brad had scheduled this week off for family time. At six-two, Brad has been carrying an extra twenty pounds on his thin frame of late, despite regular visits to the gym. Now the pounds are melting off with very little effort. They cross to the other side of the street to avoid a downed tree, Brad thinking how lucky he is for not being in Manhattan on the day it happened. Or how lucky he was. The luck ran out yesterday, and thoughts of his wife and daughter crowd into his mind. A tear forms and drifts down Brad's cheek—he, too, has a mountain of grief to work through. He wipes away the tear as they continue pressing forward. At Vista Drive, they make a right, now only a block from their home. The two-story house on the corner is listing badly while the house across the street shows little evidence of damage. Leaves and limbs lie scattered across the lawns and an uprooted pine tree blocks the road.

Two houses farther on they turn up the driveway to their home, a white two-story Federal-style house. The shutters Emma had insisted on hanging are catawampus, and all the glass at the front of the house is blown out. A section of the roof is gone and the large pine tree between their house and the neighbors' caved in the roof on the east side of the house. With a balance of $450,000 remaining on the mortgage, the house will never be repaired—nor be paid off. Brad and Tanner step through one of the broken windows and Brad says, "Gather up what you want to take with you. Pack an assortment of clothes; both warm- and cool-weather stuff. I'd like to be out of here fairly quickly."

Tanner nods and climbs the stairs to his room. First stop for Brad is the master bedroom. He pauses at the doorway, suddenly nauseous. The sight of the bed he shared with his wife for nearly fourteen years almost brings him to his knees. He grabs the doorframe for support as tears well up. In a watery haze, he shuffles toward the bed and sits. After several minutes of sobbing, Brad wipes his cheeks dry and stands, shuffling into the master closet. Turning his focus to what lies ahead, he picks out several articles of clothing, a pair of sandals, a pair of hiking boots, and underwear, tossing everything on the bed. From the back of the closet he retrieves an old lever-action .30-.30 rifle that once belonged to his father. Brad hasn't shot it in years, but he does have a couple boxes of ammunition, which he pulls down from the top shelf of the closet. Placing the rifle and ammo next to his other items, he kneels and pulls a suitcase from under the bed. After loading everything but the rifle, Brad grabs a backpack from the closet and enters the bathroom to retrieve a few items.

He exits the master and enters the kitchen. He opens a cabinet door and pulls out the baskets of meds that Emma had organized. After spending a moment trying to predict what meds they'll need in the future, he shrugs and dumps the entire contents into his backpack. He pulls down another basket and adds bandages, gauze, alcohol, and hydrogen peroxide to the backpack.

Next he ventures out to the garage. The sight of his daughter's bicycle threatens another shower of tears, but he pauses, inhales a series of deep calming breaths, and tries to shake it off. For a week they knew Sophia's prognosis wasn't good, allowing the family some time to come to grips with what might happen. But still, her loss hurts like hell.

With his emotions in check, Brad ignores the two cars parked inside and steps beyond them to grab the wheelbarrow. He loads it up with a tackle box full of fishing gear, grabs his bag of tools from the work-bench, and discovers a case of small green propane bottles he'd bought on sale last year. It all goes into the wheelbarrow, and Brad steers it inside and adds his suitcase and backpack, before stopping in front of the pantry. All the canned goods get tossed in the wheel-barrow as well as a few remaining bottles of wine. Pausing, Brad debates grabbing the five thousand in cash he keeps in the safe, but disregards the notion. The money isn't worth the paper it's printed on. He opens a box of cartridges and feeds several into the rifle's magazine and carries it out to the front porch where he takes a seat on a rocker, waiting for Tanner.

A few minutes later his son appears, wheeling a suitcase behind him. He's wearing a heavy backpack that Brad knows is filled with books. "Put all your stuff in the wheelbarrow and we'll take off." Brad pushes to his feet and returns inside, grabbing the wheelbarrow and pushing it out the front door. They now must trek all the way to the other side of the island to reach their destination. They spend a moment discussing whether to search the surrounding houses for food and decide against it. Brad steers the wheelbarrow down the driveway and into the street.

Two houses down, their neighbor Don Mathis meanders out of his home. "Where you going, Brad?" Mathis is thin and has the ruddy complexion of an alcoholic, which he is. He's also an asshole.

Brad continues walking. The last thing he needs now is a tagalong. "Hitting the road, Don. Don't see any reason to stay here."

Mathis follows them down the street. "Where you going? And where are Sophia and Emma?"

Brad winces at the names of his wife and daughter. "Don't know where we're going, Don." Brad picks up his pace, eager to get away from their nosy neighbor.

"But what about your wife and daughter?"

Brad stops, puts the wheelbarrow down, and turns. "They're dead. Now leave us the hell alone." Brad turns, picks up the wheelbarrow, and continues down the road, Tanner loping along beside him.

Once they're a block away, Brad slows his pace. They walk for four grueling hours before reaching their destination.

The Cedar Creek Marina is located on the south side of Long Island and fronts Island Creek, with access to South Oyster Bay. Brad steers the wheelbarrow up to the locked gate and parks it. His hands are cramping and he struggles to open the combination lock. After several attempts, he dials the correct combination and springs the lock, opening the gate to the docks. His palms blistered, he grimaces when he grabs the wheelbarrow handles again. He grits his teeth and steers it through the gate and down the dock. At the next intersection, they hang a left then a right and traverse another hundred yards to their new home, the *EmmaSophia*, a thirty-seven-foot Dufour Gib'Sea sailboat.

In anticipation of taking the boat out sometime this week while on vacation, Brad had filled the 120-gallon freshwater tank, the fuel tank, and had stocked up on groceries. His father, when he died of a heart attack at fifty-seven, left his older boat to his son and, when Brad made a little extra money, he traded up in model years. The *EmmaSophia*, a 2002 model, is capable of sailing the open seas. For now the plan is to sail south along the coast to see what they find.

After stowing all of their gear, Brad inserts the key into the ignition. Outfitted with a twenty-four-horsepower diesel engine, he has no idea if the engine will start. It appeared the EMP was hit-or-miss for some electronic devices, and Brad's praying for a miss. He twists the key and the engine purrs to life. But it's not all good news. None of the delicate electronics will power up. That means no navigation, fish finder, and more important, no radio. Brad shrugs off the bad news. They can always sail within sight of mainland and use the old mechanical compass to navigate. He asks Tanner to free and stow the dock lines before dropping the engine into gear. They motor down Island Creek, cut through the outer banks at Lookout Point, and venture into the North Atlantic Ocean.

CHAPTER 35

Weatherford

Gage awakens to the aroma of frying bacon and fresh-brewed coffee and his mouth is watering before he can get untangled from the covers. He and Holly made the decision last night to stay with her parents until the baby arrives. One reason is that Gage couldn't pry Holly away from the air conditioner. With a generator and a thousand-gallon propane tank, Holly's parents have been running the generator enough to keep the freezer frozen and the house cool. Gage rolls over, kisses his still-sleeping wife on the cheek, and climbs out of bed. The generator also powers the pump for the water well and the propane fires the water heater. Gage steps into the bathroom and flips on the shower. They didn't make it to Gage's parents' yesterday and that's on the agenda for today.

After the water warms, Gage steps in for his first shower in over a week. Not wanting to be gluttonous, he keeps the shower under three minutes and steps out to dry off. He's wishing they had thought to bring fresh clothes as he tugs on his dirty jeans. Instead of putting on the stinky shirt, he slips into the master and borrows a T-shirt from Henry. Fitting Gage's broad shoulders inside of a size large T-shirt is difficult, but with some pulling and stretching he accomplishes the task. The end result is that Gage looks as if he's been squeezed into a sausage casing.

When he steps back into the guest bedroom, Holly is waking.

"Is that bacon I smell?" she asks.

"Yep. And coffee, too." Gage holds his hand to help Holly out of bed. "There's hot water for a shower."

Holly, ravenous, says, "The shower can wait. I want food. Oh, by the way, nice shirt. Could you not find a smaller size?"

Gage chuckles as she waddles down the hall toward the kitchen. He slips on his socks and boots and joins Holly. Henry and Susan are both up, sitting at the granite-topped breakfast bar, a mug of coffee in hand.

"We have eggs, bacon, and coffee," Susan says. "No toast, though. Bread ran out a couple of days ago. We've eaten. The rest is for you two."

"I think I can manage without toast," Gage says, heaping the food onto his plate. He places it on the counter and walks across the kitchen to pour coffee for himself and Holly, whose plate looks as if it could use some sideboards. Gage passes his wife a cup of coffee and sits.

"How much food do you have left?" Holly asks.

"We have enough," Henry says. "I had a steer butchered a couple of weeks ago. We're having steaks for dinner."

Knowing this is not the end of the food, Holly savors every bite as she forks in eggs and chomps on a piece of bacon. Gage wolfs down a mouthful of egg and washes it down with a sip of steaming coffee. "Did you hear anything from Alyx before all of this started?"

"She sent me a text message about thirty minutes before it all started," Susan says. "Said she and one of her coworkers, a Zane somebody, had made it away from Fort Meade and were headed west. If anyone can find her way home, it's Alyx. It's just going to take her some time." Alyx was already in college when Holly and her parents moved to town.

Gage, knowing the odds are long for Alyx, holds his tongue and continues to eat. He and Alyx have a strained relationship. Of course the fact that Alyx believed Holly was marrying beneath her might have something to do with the strain. But single and thirty-four, Alyx doesn't have a lot of ground to stand on when it comes to relationships. Despite their disagreements, Gage is hoping like hell Alyx does make it home.

"Gage, did you give any more thoughts to the wind turbine idea?" Henry asks.

Gage finishes chewing the food in his mouth and takes another sip of coffee. "I think the only way it'll work is to manually set the pitch angle and lock the blades down. We'll use the braking system to control speed. And if it looks like the wind is getting up, one of us will have to climb up and lock her down."

Henry stands and retreats to his office, returning with a piece of paper, which he hands to Gage. The paper is filled with small, precisely drawn mathematical equations.

"Henry, I might as well be reading Chinese. Help me out here," Gage says, passing the paper back to his father-in-law.

"We'll set the angle of the blades to a medium pitch angle. Can you free up the yaw control, so the turbine will turn with the wind?"

"Yeah," Gage says. "We'll have to keep an eye on the cables running down the tower. Otherwise, they'll be a tangled mess. How are you going to step up the voltage?"

"I have a couple of transformers in the barn that have never been put into service. They should be fine."

Gage polishes off the last of his eggs. "When are we starting?"

"Today?" Henry says.

Gage carries his empty plate over to the sink. "Works for me. But I'd like to go say hi to my parents before we get started."

"That'll work," Henry says. "I could probably use some more time to refine the design."

Susan rolls her eyes. "Holly, you staying with me or going with Gage?"

She glances up at her husband. "Can you wait for me to take a shower?"

"Absolutely. We should probably run by the house and grab some more clothes."

"Why? You looking forward to a shirt that'll actually allow you to breathe?"

Susan and Henry laugh as Holly carries her plate to the sink. She runs her hand across her husband's shoulders as she waddles down the hall.

CHAPTER 36

Off the coast of the United Kingdom

After running all night, the USS *New York* is closing in on Her Majesty's Naval Base Devonport. Sailing submerged along the English Channel, they'll have to navigate around the point at Plymouth and travel inland to reach the naval base—all without the aid of GPS. Luckily, the onboard computer and the sub's internal navigation systems are still working. During the night the submarine occasionally ascended to periscope depth to plot their course via celestial navigation. But now, entering the area where navigation is critical and with daylight waiting to greet them, the sub has slowed to a crawl, relying on passive sonar to work their way around the obstacles.

The executive officer, Commander Carlos Garcia, returns from the mess to join in the navigation fun.

"What do you think, Carlos? Periscope depth?" Thompson asks.

"The question is whether there's anything flying, but I guess we're not going to know that until we look."

"I concur," Captain Thompson says. "Q, take us up to periscope depth."

"Aye, Aye, Skipper," the dive officer, Lieutenant Commander Thomas Quigley, replies.

The nose of the boat tilts upward and everyone on the bridge leans forward to maintain balance. The submariners pride themselves on their ability to lean with the angle of the deck without grabbing for something to hold on to. After several moments of leaning, the boat levels out and the dive officer reports the sub is at periscope depth. "Periscope up," Thompson orders. He steps over and catches the handles as the scope slides up through the deck. He positions his eyes in the eyecups and walks a circle before coming to a stop. What he sees sends a chill down his spine. The area is dotted with giant craters, and wildfires are still raging in the distance. Her Majesty's Naval Base Devonport no longer exists. His shoulders slump as he steps away to allow Garcia a look.

Garcia takes a peek and his head sags as he raises the handles of the periscope, aware that everyone in the room is watching them.

"Sonar, depth?" the Captain asks.

"One-five-zero feet, Skipper," the sonar tech, Mike Adams, replies.

"Conn, lower periscope. Q, take us down to seventy-five feet. Mr. Patterson, make our course one-nine-zero. All ahead, two-thirds." The captain glances at Garcia then nods toward the far corner of the cramped control room. They huddle together and lower their voices. "What options do we have?" Thompson asks.

"We could be in Bermuda in six days," Garcia says.

"We don't have six days of food remaining. Hell, we don't have two days of food left."

"What if we cut to quarter rations?"

"That might stretch it out to three or four days. A hungry crew could be a dangerous crew. What about the Azores? We could make that in a day and half."

"That's Portuguese territory, Bull. Might be pretty hostile to a ship sailing under the Stars and Stripes. At least Bermuda is UK territory."

"I don't think we can make it in six days, Carlos."

Garcia grinds his forehead against the palm of his hand. "I don't know, Bull. Are we going to pull up to the Azores and beg for food? We sure as hell don't have much cash on board and the Amexes in our wallets are worthless." He ends the grinding and turns to look at his captain and friend. "I think we need to level with the crew. Tell them what's going on."

"What does that buy us?"

"Understanding? They know something's up, Bull. And if we keep plotting courses for places where we never surface, they're going to wonder if we've lost our minds. A crew left to wonder is also dangerous. I think we have to tell them."

Thompson rubs the whiskers on his chin. "What exactly am I supposed to tell them? That life as they know it is gone? And what would make them believe me?" The two men ponder those questions as the submarine continues to descend.

Thompson snaps his fingers. "I've got an idea." He strides back to his position on the bridge. "All stop. Q, takes us back up to periscope depth."

As the submarine makes another ascent, Thompson grabs a microphone from overhead and, before triggering the transmit button, orders, "Conn, sound the general alarm." He allows the alarm to sound for several seconds before ordering it off. He places the microphone to his lips. "All crew members, this is the captain speaking. As you may have guessed by now, we were not the only ones who launched our nuclear weapons. We were hoping to resupply at one of the British naval bases, but are unsuccessful. You will see why on the shipboard monitors momentarily. I want all of you to know we are working diligently to find supplies. The next few days are going to test your patience. And that goes for everyone on the boat, myself included. I promise you as captain, we'll work through the issues, and hopefully do it quickly." As the boat levels off, Thompson orders the periscope up and puts the radio back to his lips. "The video feed will be up in a moment. As a point of reference, we are currently positioned just south of Plymouth, England."

The captain replaces the handset and walks over to the periscope, triggering the video camera. He leans forward to peer through the lens and dials in the strongest power and turns the scope toward the mainland. The graphic images of the destruction are broadcast throughout the boat. Submarines depend on silence to maintain their stealthiness, but at this moment, the boat is as quiet as Thompson has ever heard it. After a little more than two minutes he orders the periscope down and issues a dive order. "Mr. Patterson, set a course for the Azores. All ahead, two-thirds."

The helmsman repeats the order as Thompson walks over to his XO. "Too heavy?"

"Right on point, Bull. At least they have an idea what it looks like topside. So Azores, huh?"

"It's on the way, and it won't cost us anything to take a look."

Chapter 37

Near Knoxville, Tennessee

Other than dodging around expired automobiles, Zane and Alyx are making good progress in Old Goldie. Now they're approaching Knoxville, hoping to pick up I-40 west. Zane exits the highway they're on and steers into the parking lot of a plundered convenience store situated near a run-down residential area. With the shotgun in hand, he exits the truck and steps through the shattered door in search of a map. The inside of the store looks like a herd of bulls stampeded through. The cash register is busted into a thousand pieces and all the shelving is overturned. Not only is the store in shambles, there's also a foul odor that smells like spoiled milk and rotten meat. With a hand covering his nose and mouth, Zane approaches the front counter and comes up empty in his search for a map. Cursing, he glances behind the counter and discovers a partial source for the stench—a body. The body is bloated and a puddle of organic matter has oozed onto the floor, attracting a horde of flies. Zane gags and hurries from the store.

When he steps outside, he sees a dozen people converging on their location. Zane hurries to the pickup and climbs in, handing the shotgun to Alyx before shifting the truck into gear and making a wide turn back toward the road. "You might have to shoot. You okay with that?"

Looking at the growing crowd, Alyx nods. The nearest person, a male, comes to a halt in the middle of the road about fifty yards away. Zane spots the pistol in his hand and stomps the gas, aiming the nose of the truck down the centerline. He doesn't want to hit the man and risk damaging the truck, but more people are converging onto the road and he may not have a choice.

He scans the area ahead for options and comes up blank. "They picked the wrong guy, if they want to play chicken," Zane mutters. Now only twenty yards away, the man raises his arm and fires before diving out of the way. The man misjudges his timing and the side mirror hits him in the face, sending him head over ass, the pistol skittering away. Zane keeps the accelerator to the floor and, with only seconds to spare, the center portion of the group collapses, with people fleeing in all directions. Zane sideswipes a woman, who spins around and face-plants on the pavement, but he never lets up on the accelerator as gunshots ring out behind them.

Once clear of the people, Zane slows the pickup to a more normal speed. "That was an operational error on my part," Zane says. "From now on, if either of us leaves the pickup the other will stand guard with the shotgun."

"I agree. Damn, that was creepy. Was all of that an effort to steal the pickup?" Alyx asks.

"I have no idea. Maybe they thought we had a stash of food. Whatever it was, it damn near cost us our lives." He steers up the ramp to I-75, the highway they've been traveling on.

As they draw closer to Knoxville, the landscape begins to change. Fires have scoured the ground and, when they reach a high ridge in the road, they discover downtown Knoxville no longer exists. "Why the hell would they bomb Knoxville?"

"Not Knoxville. They nuked the Oak Ridge National Laboratory and the Oak Ridge Reservation."

"Where are, or where were, they located?"

"Just west of Knoxville. I did some computer work at the Oak Ridge Reservation several years ago."

"What kind of work did they do?"

"If I told you, I'd have to kill you."

Zane scowls.

"The lab did nuclear weapons research and Y-12, a portion of the Oak Ridge Reservation, did nuclear weapons production work. It was considered a National Security Complex and was part of the National Nuclear Security Administration."

"Now it makes sense," Zane says. "There's no telling how many nukes they dropped on this place." Now traveling on an elevated section of the highway, Zane looks up and stomps on the brake. The old truck shimmies and shakes as the back wheels lock up, sending Alyx face-first into the dash. The truck goes into a slide and Zane tries to steer in that direction to keep it under control. He glances over to see Alyx slumped on the floor, blood pouring from the lower half of her face. He pumps the brake pedal and, finally, the truck skids to a stop. He slams the gearshift into park and reaches for Alyx, helping her back onto the seat. "Where are you hurt?"

"Nose," she mumbles.

He pulls his shirt off, then his T-shirt, and uses it to apply pressure to Alyx's nose, trying to stem the flow of blood.

She pushes his hands away and grabs the shirt, using her own hands to apply pressure. "Thanks . . . for . . . the . . . warning."

"I'm sorry. I didn't see it in time."

Alyx lifts her head to gaze out the windshield. "Oh shit."

"Oh shit is right." In front of them the highway is gone. Jagged pieces of concrete jut out into nothingness, the ground forty feet below them.

Alyx removes the shirt and gently touches her nose. The blood flow appears to be slowing. "I think it's broken."

"I think you're probably right."

Alyx shoots him a nasty glare and puts the shirt back to her nose. "This shirt stinks."

"At least you can smell it."

Alyx shows him her middle finger. Zane opens his door and steps out, his heart still hammering. They missed certain death by ten feet. He walks up to the edge and looks down. A nest of charred cars rests on the remains of the collapsed roadway. He turns and retreats back to the truck. "How's the nose?"

"I'll live." She wads up the shirt and throws it at Zane. She opens the glove box in search of a napkin and finds a small package of travel tissues. After ripping it open, she wads up a couple of tissues and gently pushes them into her nostrils. When she speaks her voice sounds funny. "I should have thought of it sooner. We need to skirt the entire area. We're probably sitting in the middle of a huge hot zone."

Zane drops the truck in gear and turns around.

"We should have gone back into that house for the lead smocks," Alyx says.

Zane slows the truck to a stop. "Water under the bridge. How large of an area do we need to avoid?"

"Large. Miles large."

"Means backtracking."

"No, it means staying alive."

"I remember seeing an exit for a highway leading west about fifteen miles back. That far enough?"

Alyx rips a small piece from the tissue in her nose and tosses it out the window. The tissue drifts away, moving toward the rear of the truck. "Should be. Wind's blowing from the north."

Zane releases the brake and eases down on the gas pedal, wishing he had a map.

CHAPTER 38

Along the coast of New Jersey

With the sails up, the *EmmaSophia* is moving along at a good clip. Brad Dixon is surprised by two things—the number of boats and the number of bloated human bodies bobbing along the surface of the water. Many are charred beyond recognition, but a few leave Brad wondering about the cause of death. A nuclear bomb is designed for one thing—mass casualties. Not only does it kill with the initial burst, but it also kills months later via radiation poisoning. Brad spots a shark fin slicing through the water and turns away, not wanting to witness the shark feasting. For now they are keeping their distance from the other boats and the rifle remains within easy reach. They are sailing about two miles off the coast of Long Beach, New Jersey. Tents line the beach and smoke from the campfires drifts along the breeze. Brad wonders what they'll do come winter. He glances over at Tanner, who is curled up on the front bench, staring at the water. Brad keeps trying to get him to open up, but Tanner remains silent.

Brad glances behind for a quick scan of the surrounding area and turns back. Then does a double take. It's the same small Sunfish sailboat he had seen earlier. Thirteen feet long, the small boat is overloaded with the four adults sitting around the cockpit and holding on to the mast. He grabs the binoculars for a closer look. The four appear to be two couples, probably in their midtwenties. Two suitcases are piled up in the middle of the small seating area. Brad refocuses the binocs on the boat itself. Up near the bow, above the waterline, is a sticker that he can't quite make out. He fiddles with the focus, trying to sharpen the image. He can see the word *Brigantine* and that's all he needs to see. The boat was stolen from the Brigantine Beach Club, a time-share place on the South Jersey shore. Brad lowers the binoculars and hands them to Tanner. "Keep an eye on that little Sunfish. Please."

Tanner nods.

After clicking through the images in his brain, Brad realizes the boat has been following them since daybreak. Could be an ominous sign, or simply a coincidence. But Brad's betting it's not a coincidence. After all, which boat would someone rather have—a thirty-seven-footer with room below for a family of four, or a thirteen-footer with no room at all? Brad turns the wheel and the mainsail boom swings across the deck, temporarily luffing the canvas. He trims the main and the boat picks up speed as Brad steers the *Emma-Sophia* farther out to sea. He glances back and, sure enough, the Sunfish is turning to follow. So much for it being a coincidence. Brad moves the rifle closer.

Tanner is, at least, engaged with the binoculars. He's zoomed in on the beach, and Brad's hoping he's checking out hot chicks—anything to take Tanner's mind off what happened yesterday. Brad tugs on the rope to tighten the mainsail and the boat picks up speed. He hasn't yet unfurled the jib, relying on the larger canvas for now. Brad glances back to see the Sunfish still following in their wake. The *Emma-Sophia* is gaining distance, but that'll change when they drop anchor at dusk.

Tanner turns the binocs on the boat following them. "Dad, I don't think they know what they're doing. There's too much slack on the mainsail."

"I agree. The sail has been that way the entire time. I think they took the boat from the beach at Brigantine, hoping to sail—"

"Dad! Their boat overturned. They're in the water."

Brad eases the mainsail and the boat coasts to a stop.

"Dad, you have to turn around."

"And do what, Tanner? Allow them onto our boat?"

"I don't know. Take them back to shore, or something."

"What if they don't want to go back to shore?"

"Dad, they'll never get that boat upright again." Tanner moves to the back of the boat, his eyes still glued to the binoculars.

Brad ponders the situation. If they're good swimmers they can swim back to shore. It would be a difficult task, certainly, but doable. At present, the group is probably two miles from shore, a forty-five-minute swim, maybe.

"Dad, they don't look like they're very good swimmers. They're doing a lot of thrashing around."

Well shit. Now what? Brad didn't invite them to follow along. And there's little doubt the group has dubious intentions.

"What are you waiting for, Dad?"

Brad starts the engine and angrily spins the wheel. "We'll get them on board, Tanner. But I want you to take the helm. We'll take them to the closest dock."

"Why am I driving the boat?"

"Because I'm going to be covering them with the rifle."

"Why?"

"That's just the way things are going to work." If Tanner hadn't lost his mother and sister yesterday, Brad would have sailed on. He steers the boat toward the swimmers and eases back on the throttle. "Help them into the boat and then take the wheel, Tanner." Brad picks up the rifle and levers a shell into the chamber, moving toward the bow for a wider field of fire. He fits the stock against his shoulder and waits.

Tanner helps the first waterlogged swimmer aboard. She's a thin knock-kneed woman, but younger than Brad thought. She looks to be in her late teens and she's in desperate need of an orthodontist. He waves the barrel toward the backseat and she timidly complies. The second person that comes aboard is also female. But this one doesn't need any work. She's a very attractive, tall young woman, probably early twenties. She gets the same treatment from Brad, but her reaction is very different. She gives him an ugly snarl before sitting. As of yet, no one has said a word.

The next person to board is a male. He's tall and thin as a rail. "Thanks for saving us."

"You're welcome," Brad says, the gun never wavering from the man's chest. "Have a seat with your friends."

The last person aboard is a large, broad-shouldered man. The man is a bear and he appears older than the rest of the crew, maybe late twenties.

"Why are you holding the rifle on us?" the man asks.

"Because I don't know you. Why were you following us?"

"We weren't following you. We were just sailing." He ends the comment with a snide smile then says, "Hell of a greeting."

"I could have left you in the water," Brad says.

"Yeah, you could have. But you didn't. Lucky for us, huh."

Brad's brain is churning through a string of bad scenarios. He makes a snap decision and steps forward, the gun centered on the last man aboard. "I've changed my mind. Take a swim."

"What?"

"What are you doing, Dad?"

"Quiet, Tanner. I'm not going to tell you again. Get your ass back in the water. You're a big boy. You can swim back to the shore."

"And what happens if I don't get in the water?" the man asks, crossing his arms.

"You're going in the water. You can do it alive, or we can roll you in after I shoot you. This rifle is loaded with .30-.30 cartridges. Ever see what that does to a man? It'll blow a hole in you big enough to see daylight. Now get your ass in the water."

The man remains where he is.

Brad cocks the hammer. "I'm not going to do any of that count-to-three bullshit. This is your last chance."

The man shoots Brad the finger and steps toward the back of the boat. He turns. "You better hope I never see you again."

"Jump in," Brad says.

The man hesitates again, and Brad fires the rifle. The shock of the blast startles everyone on deck. Brad quickly levers another round and cocks the hammer. He didn't shoot the man, but he came damn close. "Consider that a warning shot."

This time the man doesn't hesitate, jumping in headfirst.

"Tanner, drive the boat."

Tanner is rattled by the series of events. He's as still as a sculpture.

"Tanner, take the helm."

After another moment, Tanner comes to life and, with trembling hands, takes the wheel. He eases the throttle forward and turns for shore. There are no pleasant conversations. The attractive young woman glares at Brad all the way to the dock. Near the shore, Tanner is struggling to get the boat parked next to the dock.

"Idle the throttle, Tanner. This is close enough." Brad steps toward the stern, the rifle tight against his shoulder. "You three, off the boat." The three reluctantly stand and, one after another, jump into the water. Brad steps to the back rail, tracking their retreat down the barrel of the rifle.

"Take us out of here, Tanner."

Tanner reverses the boat and after he's clear of the

dock, turns the wheel starboard and gooses the throttle. Once they're clear, Brad lowers the rifle.

"Would you have shot that guy?" Tanner shouts above the wind noise.

Brad nods. "Yeah, I would have. Last week maybe not, but today, yes."

CHAPTER 39

Weatherford

Holly exits the bedroom after showering and dressing and Gage helps her into the truck. He slides behind the wheel and steers down the drive, hanging a right on Caddo Road. Soon after they were married and had purchased the land, Gage started work restoring the two-bedroom rancher that was in desperate need of repair. Slowly, he has made the home livable after reframing portions of the house, patching the roof, and remodeling the one and only bathroom. The kitchen is next on the to-do list, but Gage is wondering if the kitchen will ever get done.

The sweet odor of alfalfa fills the cabin as they roll past one of the fields. Gage slows to make the turn onto their road and, after traveling a short distance, pulls into the gravel drive and eases the truck up next to the house. "Do you want to take some of the baby stuff over to your parents'?" Gage asks.

"Let's hold off. I still have a month to go."

Gage steps around to the other side to help his wife

out of the truck. With her pushing and him pulling, she makes it out and waddles toward the front door. As she's ascending the steps, she stops midstride and doubles over in pain, fighting for breath.

"You okay, Holly?" Gage asks, concern etched on his face.

Holly sucks in a lungful of air. "Just give me a sec."

"Are you having more contractions?"

"Yes."

"Hard contractions?"

"Are you a fucking doctor?" she snaps.

Gage has learned over the past few months when to speak and when not to speak. He unlocks the front door and slips inside, taking up position at the edge of the front window. Holly is still breathing hard, her hands pushing on her swollen womb. Over the past month the contractions have come and gone in a matter of minutes and Gage is hoping these also subside. It's not like he can rush her to the hospital. Hell, for that matter, he can't take her to the obstetrician, either. They're all out of business. Gage makes a mental note to find out where Holly's doctor lives. After one final deep breath, Holly shuffles toward the front door as Gage makes a beeline for the bedroom.

He removes two suitcases from beneath the bed and begins adding clothes to one of them. Holly wobbles down the hall and takes a seat on the end of the bed. Not knowing if it's safe to speak, Gage holds his tongue and returns to the closet. He grabs a couple pair of jeans, a handful of T-shirts, underwear, and socks, tossing everything into his suitcase. His wife remains seated on the bed. Gage steps around the bed and kneels in front of his wife. "Are you okay, babe?"

"I think so. Those were the hardest contractions I've felt. Sorry for snapping at you."

Gage smiles. "And all the other times, too?"

"You put a bowling ball in your stomach and see how you feel. My ankles are swollen, my back hurts, and she keeps kicking me in the ribs."

"How many children did you say you wanted?"

Holly shows him her middle finger and tries to push up off the bed. Gage stands and helps her up. She leans into him and gives him a kiss before toddling toward the closet. "How long are we going to be staying at my parents'?"

Gage thinks of the hot water and the stocked freezer. "As long as you want. Or until they kick us out."

Ninety-five percent of the clothes in Holly's closet no longer fit. She grabs some sweatpants, the rest of Gage's T-shirts, and dumps them into the empty suitcase. She returns to the closet for her oversized bras and panties, looking wistfully at her satiny negligees. Most of her shoes also no longer fit, so she opts for flip-flops and two pairs of slip-on house shoes. She looks at a pair of tennis shoes, but the thought of trying to tie the laces makes the decision for her. She tosses the remainder of her items into the suitcase and lumbers down the hall to the bathroom to retrieve the rest of her essentials.

Gage changes into fresh clothes before following her into the restroom to grab his toothbrush and deodorant. "I'm going to drive out to the barn to get more of my work tools and a couple of other items. You about ready to head out?"

"I'm almost finished in here then I need to change. I'll be ready when you get back."

Gage disappears down the hallway as Holly packs the last of her creams and lotions into an overnight case. After stepping back in the bedroom, she peels off her dirty clothes. Pushing her panties down, she steps out of them. When she bends to pick them up she discovers the panties are soaked with blood.

CHAPTER 40

Burnsville, Minnesota

The pace is slowing as the children tire. By McDowell's estimation they've covered almost eight miles. At this pace they'll be lucky to cover twelve miles before dark. He curses under his breath and leads the group off the highway and into a copse of trees surrounding a small lake. "We'll rest for a while. Hold off eating until later."

"I'm hungry," Jonathon Taylor whines.

His words elicit a round of similar comments from the other students.

McDowell mutters another string of curse words and kneels down beside the suitcase containing their food supplies. He pulls out two small bags of trail mix and hands them out. "Save some for the next person. That's all we can spare for now."

His comment is met with groans, which he ignores. "I'm going to fish for a little bit if anyone else wants to fish."

Six of the boys stand and an argument breaks out

over who gets to fish, Jonathon the only one not to enter the fray. McDowell looks to Melissa for help.

Melissa gathers up the four fishing poles and hands one to McDowell before facing the teens. "We are not fishing for fun. We're fishing for food. The six of you will take turns, but I want the most experienced to fish first. Who has fished before?"

All six raise their hands and Melissa sighs. She casts a wary eye at Caleb Carson. "Caleb, when have you fished?"

"My dad and I fish all the time."

Melissa knows that's not true because he was a student in her class last year. Caleb lives with his mother and rarely, if ever, sees his father. At this point in time hurt feelings are way down the list of Melissa's concerns. "You'll have to wait your turn."

Caleb puffs up to protest and Melissa cuts him off with a look only a teacher can give. She hands the three remaining poles out randomly and the boys follow McDowell down to the water. He hands them each a lure and ties a plastic worm onto his line. The boys tie on their own bait and two of the lures go skittering out into the lake on the first cast. McDowell sighs. "That's it for you guys. Sorry."

After twenty minutes of fishing and no bites, McDowell calls a halt. Using a pair of fingernail clippers swiped from a store at the airport, he cuts the remaining two lures from the lines and places them back in the sack and heads back to the group. As he nears, he spots Jonathon playing with the shotgun. He hurries forward, drops the fishing pole, and yanks the gun from the boy's hands. "You do not touch this weapon. Ever," McDowell shouts.

As Jonathon's bottom lip begins to quiver, McDowell looks at the rest of the group. "This shotgun is for our protection. Without it we're defenseless. Does everyone understand that?"

The kids nod and Melissa steps over and says in a low voice, "I'm sorry, Stan, I should have kept a closer watch on everyone."

"It's not your fault. They need to take some responsibility for their actions." He looks down at the ground and packs the dirt back into a gopher hole with his boot, trying to regain his composure. He looks up at Melissa. "Hell, they're just kids." He turns to Jonathon. "I won't apologize, young man, but you have to understand the situation we're in."

Jonathon wipes a tear from the corner of his eye and turns away.

"Damn it," McDowell mutters. After stuffing the remaining lures into his suitcase, he stands, slings the shotgun over his shoulder, and walks over to the suitcase containing their cache of water. He zips it open to count the bottles. There are thirty full water bottles left and a dozen empties. He grabs three bottles and hands them out. "Take a few sips and pass it on."

Once everyone has had a sip, he dumps the empties back into the suitcase and zips it up. "Time to go," he says. He leads the group out of the woods and up the highway embankment and turns south. As the group plods forward, McDowell drifts to the back of the pack to talk to Lauren and Melissa.

An hour later they get their first real taste of life on the road.

In the distance, McDowell spots three men headed their way, rifles slung over their shoulders, and they're pushing a couple of shopping carts. McDowell unslings the shotgun, jacks a shell in the chamber, and moves to the front of the pack, carrying the weapon low against his leg. He glances over his shoulder and waves a hand toward the left side of the road. The group meanders that way, hugging the outside shoulder.

When the three men are within ten yards, they stop and McDowell calls a halt. The three men appear to be in their late forties and all are missing teeth.

"Where you headed?" the man in front asks.

"South. You?" McDowell asks.

"The Twin Cities. Where y'all from?"

"Here and there."

The man smiles and surveys the group before turning back to McDowell. "You in a tradin' mood?"

"Maybe. What do you have?" McDowell asks.

"We've got some deer jerky." The man looks over the group again and points, saying, "I'll trade you some for the young blonde."

Hannah Hatcher shrieks. She's the blonde under discussion.

McDowell waves a hand to quiet her. "Trading's now off the table. You best move along."

The man shrugs. "Hey, at least I asked. They'll be some that won't. What about one of them young boys? We're not too picky."

McDowell braces the shotgun against his shoulder. "Move along."

The man smiles again and nods. "I don't know where you're going, mister, but ain't no way you're all gonna make it."

"I said, move along," McDowell says, his voice low and laced with menace.

"See you down the road. Maybe," the man says before turning and continuing on, the other two falling in behind him.

CHAPTER 41

Weatherford

Gage carries the two suitcases out to the truck and helps Holly climb in. He swings the truck around and pulls back onto the road. His parents' big spread is west of town. The 1,280 acres are planted mostly in soybeans and winter wheat, but Gage's father, Raymond, runs a few head of cattle. Even with modern technology, it's hard work and the fickle nature of the weather often determines whether the year is a boom or bust. And now the modern technology is gone. The high-dollar tractors his father owns rely almost exclusively on computer technology, and Gage doubts either will run anytime soon.

After traveling several miles west, Gage slows and makes a right down a dirt road. The county calls it a gravel road, but it's more dirt than gravel and the tires kick up a whirlwind of red dust behind them. The dust has been a constant complaint of Gage's mother for as long as he can remember. That's the reason Gage refused to look at any property that was situated on a dirt road.

Gage's older brother, Garrett, now does most of the farming. He and his wife, Juliet, built a three-bedroom house about two hundred yards from their parents' house. Six months after they moved in they welcomed their first child, Emma, and three years later Emma's sister, Elizabeth. With a third girl soon to join the mix, who will farm the land for the next generation remains to be seen. If there's any farming to be done, that is. Gage slows and pulls into the long, winding drive leading to his childhood home. One large, old oak tree shades the front yard, the remaining trees cleared to make room for the crops. A picnic table is situated next to the massive tree trunk and a tire swing hangs from one of the tree's gnarled limbs. Gage coasts the pickup to a stop, kills the engine, and steps out to help Holly.

Gage gets the feeling that something is wrong as soon as his boots hit the ground. Usually, his mother is there to greet them at the front door, but the door remains closed, the interior dark.

"Where's your mom?" Holly asks.

"I don't know. Something's going on. I can feel it in my gut." Gage pulls the screen door open and nudges the front door open to reveal the living room. Gage stops in his tracks, stunned. The bed from upstairs is sitting in the middle of the room and lying atop the bed is his father, and his mother is sitting in a chair nearby. Most of Raymond Larson's hair is gone and he looks severely emaciated. He doesn't appear to be conscious. Gage finds his feet and shuffles into the room. "What's going on, Mom?"

With effort, his mother, Ginny, pushes out of the chair and walks quietly across the hardwood flooring, nudging them back outside. Ginny walks over to the table and sits and Holly joins her. Gage, still stunned, leans against the tree.

"I had no way to reach you, Gage. The phones quit working and none of the farm trucks are running."

"Was he outside when it started?" Gage asks.

"Not when it started, but within an hour or two. I begged him not to go outside, but he was determined to get the cattle up and into the barn. He was only outside for a little while." Ginny pauses and dabs a tissue at the corner of her eye. "By day three, his hair was coming out in clumps. Garrett and Juliet came over and moved the bed downstairs for me."

A tear breaks the surface tension and drifts down Gage's cheek.

"How long has he been unconscious?" Holly asks, tenderly.

"He still has some lucid moments. They're fewer and further between as the days pass. I don't know how large of a radiation dose he received, but it must have been substantial."

"And the cattle?" Gage asks.

Ginny glances up at her youngest son, tears shimmering in her eyes. "I checked on them about four days after and they were already dead."

A lengthy silence descends upon the trio, each with their own interpretation of possible outcomes, none of them good. After several moments, Gage asks, "Garrett, Juliet, and the girls?"

"They're all fine. Your brother walks up here a couple times a day to check on him. And me, too, I suppose."

Gage pushes off the tree. "I'm going to sit with him a spell. Holly, you okay?"

Holly doesn't know the answer to that question. With the bloody panties, and now this, it's like an avalanche of dreadful happenings. "Go sit with your dad, Gage. I may walk down and see Juliet and the girls."

Gage nods, palms his cheek dry, and returns to the house. The chair his mother had been sitting in is still warm. He scoots it around where he can reach his father's hand. "I know we don't ever hardly say it, Dad." Gage pauses as the dam breaks and a river of tears flows down his cheeks. "It's only . . . three . . . words, yet between . . . us it was always . . . one"—Gage expels a shaky breath—"one of the most . . . difficult . . . things to say. So I'll . . . say . . . it . . . now. I love . . . you." Gage sobs as he grasps his father's hand with both of his. "I love you, Dad." After several moments of sobbing, Gage dries his eyes and stands, bending down to kiss his unconscious father on the forehead. "I love you so much." Bleary-eyed, Gage makes his way to the door. This time his mother is there to greet him. She leans into him and Gage wraps his mother in an embrace.

CHAPTER 42

Oak Ridge, Tennessee

Backtracking around the Oak Ridge area, Zane and Alyx top a ridge and finally get a look at the surrounding area. Both gasp.

"It looks like Mars. There's not a twig of grass left standing," Zane says. "What was the thought process behind this madness?"

Alyx finds her voice. "That's the problem. There wasn't any thought process. Just sheer madness, plain and simple. I hope those responsible were wiped from the face of the earth."

"Think Washington, D.C., is still standing?" Zane asks.

"Not a chance."

"What do you think happened to General Vickers?"

"I don't want to think about what happened to any of them. I just hope they had time to lob some nukes at the asswipes who did this."

They drive another fifteen miles before finding a road that cuts back west. Now along the Kentucky-

Tennessee border, Zane steers the pickup west through the Daniel Boone National Forest. The road is a winding two-lane dotted with run-down houses every couple of miles. The area is lousy with small creeks, and at the next bridge, Zane slows. "Think the water's safe to drink? I'd like to save the bottled water until we really need it."

"What?" Alyx says. "Are you a hoarder? We have plenty of water for now."

"Okay, smartass, exactly how long is it going to take us to get where we're going?"

"I have no idea. Surely not more than a few days."

A few miles farther on, they pass a church, then another church, and finally a third church, all of differing denominations. "People like their churches around here," Zane says. "They're bunched so closely together you could visit all three on a Sunday morning and not break a sweat." A mile down the road a sign welcomes them to Pine Knot, Kentucky. As they enter the outskirts of town, they pass two more churches, both of indeterminate faith. "There can't be enough people in this small town to fill all of these churches."

"People and their ideologies," Alyx says. "They all think they're going to the same place, with each thinking their path is the only way." Alyx pulls the shotgun onto her lap and points the barrel out the side window. "All of these churches are making me nervous."

Zane laughs. "Why?"

"They must be doing something to repent for on Sundays."

The pass an auto parts store, a local pizza place, and a Dairy Cheer—all ransacked.

Alyx cocks both barrels. "I'm not picking up a good vibe from this place, Zane. Can we skirt this little downtown area?"

Zane glances to his left. "I don't see very many side streets. Might be best to stick to the main road."

"Do it quickly, then. People are moving toward the road." Alyx turns in her seat and braces the stock of the shotgun against her shoulder, the barrel pointed out the side window.

"I see them." Zane spots a sign announcing a north–south highway ahead. "Coming up on a highway. Need to take that south."

"Fine, just don't stop the truck."

Zane presses down on the accelerator as more people spill out of the downtown buildings. "Why are they blocking the road?" Zane shouts over the wind noise.

Alyx repositions herself in the seat to improve her line of fire. "I told you I was getting a bad vibe about this place."

"Hold on. I think I spotted a way out."

Alyx braces a foot against the dash as they zoom past a funeral home. Planted on the front lawn are several oversized crosses, each draped with a dead body. A sign hung around one of the victims reads: LOOTER.

"Why couldn't they just shoot them?" Alyx asks.

The group of people is growing as Zane keeps the gas pedal nailed to the floor. At the last instant, Zane cuts the wheel to the left and they shoot down a diagonal road that T-bones at Highway 27. He slows enough to keep the truck on four wheels, whips a left turn, and stomps on the accelerator. "What the hell was that?"

Alyx pulls the shotgun in, lowers the hammers, and

turns in her seat. "That's what you call crazy. Think those were their fellow townspeople staked to the crosses?"

"Hell if I know. I'm just glad it's not us." Zane releases the breath he didn't realize he was holding. "That takes *Deliverance* to an entirely new level. The only thing missing was an inbred boy picking a banjo."

"I bet he was there somewhere." Alyx rubs her arms and shudders, the shotgun still nestled in her lap.

CHAPTER 43

Lakeville, Minnesota

As the light fades, a slow drizzle begins. Not knowing the current atmospheric conditions, or how much radioactive material remains, Stan McDowell is eager to find an indoor structure for the group to bed down in. The temps are probably in the midfifties and most of the kids are shivering. Up ahead he spies an office building and hurries ahead of the group for a look. According to a placard out front, the place is some type of sign-manufacturing company. He stops and looks around. The office building fronts a large construction yard filled with all manner of equipment. A newer pickup is parked in the lot out front, but the place has a vacant feel to it.

McDowell walks into the equipment yard to check out the barns. The place is littered with trucks of various sizes—and not just one or two but dozens and, off to the right, is a group of semitrailers lined out in a row. The two large barns are open-air structures offering little shelter from the elements. The rest of the yard is a hodgepodge of metal poles, metal signs, and other sharp objects that won't blend well with a group of teenagers. He hurries back to the office and kicks out the glass in the front door. He reaches through and turns the lock, pushing the frame open. He clicks on his flashlight and walks deeper into the building. A fine layer of dust coats the desktops, suggesting no one has been here since the whole mess started. The building is fairly large, containing three offices, a kitchen, and a reception area with a couch and three chairs positioned around a desk. As far as accommodations go it's nothing special, but it is dry. He steps back outside and waves the group in. They're only a hundred yards away and the students break into a run with Melissa and Lauren bringing up the rear at a slow jog.

Once everyone is inside, the first thing to hit McDowell is the odor. Teenagers exude a certain funk—probably something to do with the raging hormones—and that's now mixed with the smell of damp clothes that haven't been washed in a week. In the close confines, McDowell is suddenly nauseous. Melissa and Lauren don't seem bothered by it, their immunity probably built up over years in the classroom, McDowell thinks. He steps back outside for some fresh air and turns to look through the glassless door. "If you need to go to the bathroom, do it before it starts raining harder. I saw some toilet paper in the bathroom in the back. Make sure you go out a ways before doing your business."

The girls step out as a pack and turn one way, while the boys file out and turn the other way, each group with a roll of toilet paper. McDowell steps back into the office. "Was that man serious back there?" Lauren asks.

McDowell rubs his chin. "Yes, and we're only about

fifteen miles from where we started. We have a tall order if we're going to keep the kids safe. Conditions are only going to get worse, and that guy was right, most won't be asking."

Lauren shivers. "I wish we had more weapons."

"Ever fire a gun, Lauren?" McDowell asks.

"I grew up in West Texas. Of course I've fired a gun."

"Let me ask the question another way. Ever fired a weapon when someone was shooting back?"

"Of course not. But how hard can it be? You just point and shoot."

McDowell wipes his damp forehead with his sleeve. "I served twenty years in the Air Force. Believe me when I tell you there's a big difference."

"Still, I'd feel safer if Melissa and I were armed."

"We'll keep an eye out for other weapons as we proceed. That sound reasonable?"

"Yes. Thank you."

The girls come back in a clump, followed closely by the boys.

"I'm going to see if I can get a fire started out behind the building," McDowell says. "Will you take an inventory of items here in the office? Food or utensils would be great."

"Will do," Melissa replies.

McDowell pulls the lighter he'd scored from a restaurant back at the terminal from his suitcase and steps into the closest office to rummage through the drawers. The only thing he finds of use in the first desk is an eight-pack of double-A batteries. After slipping two into his pocket to replace the batteries in his flashlight, he moves on to the next office and finds several pair of scissors and a small pocketknife. He leaves the items on top of the desk and grabs a handful of old newspapers and steps out the back door.

McDowell pulls out his flashlight and rotates the lens to clear and clicks on the light. Made by Gerber, the flashlight lens can be rotated to four different colors, perfect in the cockpit of an airplane for preserving night vision. He fans the beam around the yard and spots a wooden pallet in the closest barn. Using an iron pole, he frees the boards and carries them to the back of the office building and starts to work on the fire. He wads up a few sheets of newspaper and places them under the pile, firing the lighter. The paper catches and he rips the remaining newspaper into long strips, feeding them into the fire. The wood begins to smoke and finally ignites. He lays on more boards and steps back into the building.

The kids are sprawled on the floor and Melissa and Lauren are rummaging through the cabinets and remaining desk. McDowell calls them to the back office. "The fire's lit and should be ready to go in about fifteen minutes. Let's start with the gallon of baked beans and see how far that gets us. You guys have any luck?"

"We found about a dozen coffee mugs which we can use to serve food. The biggest find is two five-gallon jugs of water we found stashed in a closet. I guess they had one of those water dispensers. I can't believe no one came back and got it."

"They still might," McDowell says.

Lauren brushes her damp hair out of her face. "I'll shred some of the remaining beef jerky and add it to the beans. We need all the protein we can get."

"Sounds good. I'm going to poke around outside and see what I can find."

Outside, McDowell adds another board to the fire and walks out into the yard, clicking on his flashlight. Comprising what looks to be about ten acres, the muddy field is jammed with equipment. Most of the sign-making part of the business is off to the north so McDowell veers south and walks along a row of storage containers. He spots two that pique his interest— two jobsite trailers that are ubiquitous at building sites the world over. He grabs a piece of scrap iron and pries open the door to the first. The trailer is outfitted with two offices, one for the receptionist or secretary and another at the back that would be reserved for the foreman or jobsite manager. Against the far wall is a section of floor-to-ceiling cabinets. The first one is full of grimy paper, probably permits or invoices. McDowell hits a gold mine when he opens the second door. It's stocked with canned goods, a mixture of soup and chili, and a cooking pot. Two moldy bags of bread and reams of copier paper are all he finds behind the third door.

McDowell climbs down and grabs a pair of five-gallon buckets up next to another trailer. They're full of nuts and bolts, which he dumps on the ground. He returns to the trailer and loads up the food. There's too much for the two buckets, but a return trip is no big deal. He places the buckets by the door and riffles through the first desk and finds what you'd expect to find—pencils, pens, paper, staplers, and, in the top drawer, a tube of red lipstick. He works his way around the desk and starts in on the second office. In the bottom right-hand drawer, behind a stack of files, he finds a handgun. He pulls it out and places it on the desk. He's not surprised to find a weapon. Construction workers come and go on a daily basis and many don't part on friendly terms. He opens the top drawer and finds a box of .45 caliber ammunition. He places the box beside the weapon.

McDowell puts his flashlight on the desk and picks up the pistol. It's a Glock 21, and he pops the magazine and finds the clip full. He reinserts the magazine and stuffs the gun into his waistband and drops the ammo in his front pocket. The situation is going to require some thought. Not that he thinks Lauren incapable, but in the hands of a teenage boy the consequences could be disastrous. He grabs the two five-gallon buckets and steps out, pushing the door closed. He makes his way back to the building, his mind spinning through the pros and cons of having another weapon in play.

CHAPTER 44

Lakeville

Twenty people sleeping in a confined space is noisier than you might imagine. Mix in the snores and the coughs and McDowell is having little trouble staying awake. The teenagers opted for the two back offices, and Melissa and Lauren are racked out on the sofa. One of the teachers emits a whistling snore on each exhale, but in the dark, McDowell doesn't know which one. The faint whistling is soothing, until it isn't. Divorced from his wife, he's lived alone for the past eight years and his body is more attuned to silence at night. Sitting in the cheap chair at the reception desk, he's having trouble getting comfortable. Every time he moves the chair squeaks, so he's trying to limit his movements, a difficult task in a chair that feels like you're sitting on a two-by-six. He readjusts the Glock in his lap and leans back in the chair.

Even though it's noisy, there's a certain rhythm that develops over time. Enough so that McDowell's eyelids grow heavier every passing minute. His head is rocking against his chest when he hears a noise different from all the others. He slowly lowers his feet to the ground and the chair squeals in protest. It sounds loud in the room, but maybe not loud enough to be heard outside. He freezes and turns his ear toward the door, listens, and hears the sound again. It sounds like a boot scraping on gravel.

McDowell braces his hands on the desk and pulls himself carefully out of the chair. After tucking the Glock under his belt, he grabs the shotgun and walks quietly to the door for a peek outside. He'd plugged the bottom piece of broken glass with one of the signs and had left the top open for a situation such as this. His night vision is exceptional, but he'd need X-ray vision to see anything beyond his nose in this lightless world. He focuses his mind on other senses and hears another scrape. Not enough to identify a location. Then he hears a faint whisper of words, which drift from the direction of the main road. Regardless of who they are, they're here.

Feeling his way toward the sofa, he bends down and feels around for Lauren's long hair. When he finds it, he nudges her shoulder and places a hand over her mouth. She gives a violent shake of her head when she wakes. McDowell puts his mouth to her ear and whispers, "It's me. Someone's outside. Hold out your hand."

Still disoriented, Lauren holds out her hand and McDowell finds it and puts the Glock in her palm. With his mouth still against her ear, he says, "Just pull the trigger if they get past me. Can't let them inside."

He feels her head nodding.

"Wait for the all clear."

Another nod.

McDowell gives her neck a squeeze and stands, using the wall as a guide toward the back door. If he was calling the shots, he'd have someone watching the back door, but he has no idea if he's facing one or ten, or if they have any tactical knowledge. Slowly and silently, he racks a shell into the chamber of the shotgun. If it's more than six, he's going to be in a world of hurt. He debates going back for more shells, but decides against it, time now being the most important variable. McDowell feels along the trigger guard to make sure the safety is off and eases the back door open and slips through, easing the door closed behind him.

The fence to the construction yard is about thirty yards behind the office. He turns his head to the left and listens. The clock ticking in his head is urging him forward, but he takes a deep breath to slow his heart rate. The one thing that hinders him is also the very thing that protects him—the absolute darkness. After hearing nothing, he stands and feels his way to the corner of the building.

He pauses again, to listen. Hearing nothing, he presses forward, using the exterior wall as a guide. He tries to remember if this side of the building is landscaped, and can't. Careful with his steps, he works his way toward the front. At the midway point he feel something with his shoe. He reaches down to feel around and assumes the rectangular piece of metal is part of the guttering system and steps over. At the front corner he squats down to listen. He can hear the faint whisper of voices. Sounds like two people, at least. McDowell turns his head and cups a hand around his left ear. From the whispers, he pinpoints their location to a group of pine trees a hundred feet away. McDowell stands, but maintains his position.

The word *jammed* floats across the darkness and McDowell tucks the shotgun tight to his shoulder. A smothered flashlight clicks on in the distance and in the faint wash of light he recognizes two of the men they encountered earlier in the day. Now he has a number. He holds his fire, not wanting to announce his presence until locating the third man. The light clicks off and, after a moment, McDowell works his way to the abandoned truck parked out front. From here, he has a 180-degree field of fire, with the building behind him. He rests his left forearm on the truck's hood and places the stock of the shotgun against his shoulder, waiting.

Although the night is cool, a bead of perspiration pops on his forehead and trickles down his nose. He ignores the sweat and focuses on the task at hand. The waiting is hard. At this point he just wants it over and he works to tamp down his growing impatience. Finally, he hears a boot scrape off to the left and he now knows the location of all three men.

The wait drags on.

After several moments, he hears a grunt from the front. McDowell swings the barrel that way, and waits. Unwanted, images pop into his mind of what the three men might do to the group of young girls. He quickly pushes the thoughts from his mind and sharpens his focus.

He hears footsteps, this time boots on asphalt. McDowell tucks the shotgun tight to his shoulder and caresses the trigger with his index finger. Now he can hear the nervous breathing of the two men approaching from the front. McDowell estimates the distance at fifteen feet. He nudges the barrel to the left and pulls the trigger.

Flame leaps from the barrel, lighting the two men like a photographer's flash. The one on the left falls face forward as McDowell jacks another shell, eases the barrel to the right, and fires again. The second man drops where he's standing as screams erupt from the students inside the building behind him. A rifle fires from the left and McDowell feels the bullet whiz past his ear. He scoots around the nose of the pickup, putting the truck between him and the shooter.

"Donnie?" the man on the left shouts.

McDowell eases the barrel a smidge to the left.

"John?" the man shouts again.

McDowell centers the shotgun on the voice and pulls the trigger. The flash of gunpowder lights the night as the double-aught buckshot fans out at a speed of over a thousand feet per second. McDowell jacks another shell and waits. After what feels like an hour, but in reality is only a few moments, McDowell steps out from behind the truck, the shotgun up and ready. Slowly, he works his way toward the third man. He knows for certain the two men in front are dead. Not so with the third.

He steps lightly across the gravel road leading to the yard, his ears searching for sounds. He makes his way to where he thinks the third man might be and pauses, listening. After several moments, McDowell reaches into his pocket for his flashlight and clicks it on. The third man is lying by the sign, his face and upper torso pockmarked from the heavy shot. Blood is already pooling around the man's upper body. If he's not dead now, he will be shortly.

McDowell grabs the man's rifle and turns back for the building. When he reaches the front door, he calls softly to Lauren and waits for the all clear before opening the door and stepping through. He fans the flashlight around the room to see the students huddled in a group, holding hands. Lauren and Melissa are holding each other, both trembling.

McDowell walks over and takes the pistol from Lauren. "It's over."

CHAPTER 45

Near Memphis, Tennessee

Taking turns behind the wheel, Alyx and Zane drove most of the night, only stopping for three hours of sleep deep in a wooded forest. They have now traversed most of Tennessee with Memphis, tight to the border with Arkansas, the last major city to pass through. Zane, now driving, pulls up to a newer Ford F-250 and puts the transmission in park. "Let's just hope this truck has some gas in the tank. We're running on fumes." Zane climbs out and grabs the hose from the bed, looking over the Ford to make sure it's not one of the more popular diesel models. Luckily for them, it's not.

Alyx steps out, the double-barrel shotgun riding across her shoulder, and moves to the front of the truck.

"Don't shoot me," Zane says as he pops the fuel door and crams the hose down the filler neck of the Ford.

"I might shoot you if you don't hurry up."

Zane blows out a deep breath and puts the other end of the hose to his mouth. He gives two good sucks and lowers the hose to see if the fuel will siphon out. He's rewarded with a small dribble that flows for a second before stopping. This seems to be a common theme with him. He still hasn't gotten the hang of stealing gas and, worse, now the hose will taste like gasoline. He wipes the end with his hand and sticks it back in his mouth. After three sucks, he gets a mouthful of gas and spits and sputters as he sticks the hose into Goldie's tank. He wipes his mouth as the fuel transfers. "See anyone?"

"Not yet. But I don't want to wait around here forever. We've seen a lot of people walking along the highway."

"Can't rush gravity. Want me to take over the shotgun?"

"I will if I see someone approaching."

Zane pulls the hose back to make sure the gas is still flowing. "We might get lucky and get a full tank off of this beast."

"Couple of people coming up from the east."

"Do they look threatening?"

"Don't know yet. Come and get the shotgun, Zane."

Zane steps over and takes the shotgun from Alyx. "Extra shells?"

"On the pickup seat."

Zane steps over closer to the passenger side of the truck, in case he needs to reload. When the two people are close enough to see, Zane relaxes and lowers his weapon. The duo is a pair of older women. Age is difficult to estimate because their faces are blistered beyond recognition and the skin on their arms is black and peeling. With their gaze focused forward, they're walking side by side, as if part of a zombie army.

When they pull abreast, they stop and the one closest to Zane turns her head. Her head movement triggers images from *The Exorcist* in Zane's mind. "Sir, may we have a ride?"

"I'm sorry. We have a policy of no riders."

The woman nods and begins walking, the other in lockstep with her. Once they're out of earshot, Alyx steps closer to Zane. "What would it have hurt to give them a ride?"

"To where? They'll be dead inside of two days. Besides, even they don't know where they're going. They're just putting one foot in front of the other."

Alyx shudders and wraps her arms around herself. "Can we go?"

Zane peers through the side window to check the gas gauge. "Another couple of minutes. Tank's almost full."

Alyx steps closer and wraps her arms around Zane. "How are we going to survive this shitty new world?"

Zane tilts her face back and kisses her. "One day at a time. That's all we can do."

A clap of thunder rolls across the landscape, spurring Zane into action. He yanks the hose from both tanks and tosses it into the back of their truck and quickly screws on the gas cap. "Hop in the truck, Alyx."

"What's the rush?"

"I don't think we want to be outside if it starts raining."

"Fallout?"

"Exactly." A nearby lightning strike hits and is followed seconds later by a loud clap of thunder. Zane hurries around the pickup and climbs behind the wheel, reaching for the window crank. "Roll up your window, Alyx." Once his window is secure, Zane drops the truck into gear and gooses the gas.

"Wouldn't most of the fallout already have settled out?" Alyx asks.

"There's still plenty left in the atmosphere, and this is the first rain we've seen." There's another crack of thunder and the skies open up. Zane switches on the wipers and the tired rubber blades squeak and stutter across the glass. A quarter mile farther on, they pass the two women. They appear to be oblivious to the rain as they continue marching forward, the rain dripping from their scalded faces. The ash that's been on the roadway for more than a week makes the road slippery, forcing Zane to slow.

When they reach the outskirts of Memphis, Zane steers toward the south loop, skirting around downtown. The slick roads and the large number of dead automobiles on the highway make the going slow. After an hour, the highway they're on links back to Interstate 40 and they motor on.

"On a normal day, we'd be able to make Weatherford in about seven hours," Alyx says.

Zane glances over at her. "That's out the window. How many times have you traveled this highway?"

"Enough times I could probably drive it blindfolded."

"Why? Just for the hell of it?"

"No, smartass. I went to school at Vanderbilt in Nashville. I had just started my first year of college when my parents made the move to Weatherford. I lucked out and missed most of the culture shock Holly had to deal with."

The rain tapers to a fine mist and Zane kills the squeaking wipers

"Where did you grow up?" Zane asks.

"Palm Springs. My dad got his start in the wind industry out there."

"I haven't been to Weatherford but I've been to my fair share of small towns. Must have been a hell of a change for your sister."

"It was. She called me, crying, almost every day the first month. Then the calls began to taper off. She loves it there now."

Zane turns back to the road, shoots his arm out to shield Alyx, and slams on the brakes. The truck comes to a stop a hundred yards from a roadblock. Dead autos have been wedged into place and, behind them, a group of people armed with rifles.

"Why did they put up a roadblock?" Zane asks.

"To keep outsiders from coming in and using up all the resources."

"But this is a federal highway. What gives them the right?"

"The guns they're carrying."

"We'll have to find another way around."

"That's going to be more difficult than you think," Alyx says.

"Why?"

"Because there's two miles of Mississippi River between where we are and where we want to be."

CHAPTER 46

Off the coast of São Miguel Island, Azores

Situated in the middle of the North Atlantic Ocean is the nine-island chain known as the Azores, an autonomous region of Portugal. Volcanic in origin, the islands are isolated—the nearest neighbor is six hundred miles south, and the coast of Portugal lies a thousand miles to the east. After running throughout the night, the USS *New York* is now two miles south of São Miguel Island, drifting along at two knots at a depth of 150 feet.

The crew is hungry. The last two meals have been soup with most of the alleged ingredients undetectable. After four hours of sleep, Captain Thompson is back on the bridge. He logs in to the computer and pulls up the navigational chart for the island. "Sonar, are you hearing anything?"

"Negative, Skipper," Petty Officer Adams replies.

The captain is itching to ascend to periscope depth for a quick look. But even submerged under fifty feet of water, the silhouette of the six-hundred-foot-long sub is readily identifiable from any lofted position, including aboard an enemy ship. But desperate times call for desperate measures. "Q, take us up to periscope depth."

Dive Officer Quigley verbally confirms the order as the XO, Carlos Garcia, joins the captain near the periscope. As the boat levels off, periscope one ascends from the floor. Thompson grabs the handles and positions his face in the eyecups and walks a 360-degree circle to get his bearings. He slows and positions the periscope on the docks of Ponta Delgada, a southern port city on the island. He dials up the magnification and his shoulders sag as he mumbles, "We can't buy a damn break."

"What is it, Bull?" Garcia asks.

Thompson steps away to allow Garcia a look. "You worried about the docked Portuguese Navy frigate?" Garcia turns from the scope to glance at Thompson. "Her radar's not turning. Looks as if she's mothballed."

"Looks can be deceiving." Thompson steps close to Garcia and lowers his voice. "We're a sitting duck if we surface and that ship is active."

"I don't think we have a choice, Bull. We need food."

Garcia returns to the scope. "It doesn't appear the island has sustained any damage. Hell, there are people walking along the coastline. I think they docked the ship and said to hell with it."

Garcia steps away and Thompson returns to the periscope and dials up the magnification, the frigate now looming large in his field of view. He triggers a button to activate the video camera. "Conn, put periscope view on the video screen."

"Aye, aye, Skipper," a petty officer manning the communication desk, replies.

Thompson moves away from the scope, and he and Garcia step toward the monitor. "They could be out of fuel," Garcia says. "I'm not seeing any smoke from the stacks, either."

Thompson turns to the Adams at the sonar station. "Hearing any engine noise?"

"Negative, sir. Quiet as a mouse."

"I'm not seeing any activity aboard ship," Thompson says, pointing to the screen.

"Want to try hailing the ship?" Garcia asks.

"We do that and we give away our position," Thompson says.

"I'd rather let them know we're coming than to sail in unannounced." Garcia runs a hand across the stubble on his chin. "It's decision time, Bull."

The captain ponders the situation for a few moments and finds no easy answers. They'll have to reveal their presence at some point if they're hoping to resupply, but not knowing who's playing on what side compounds the problem. Thompson makes a decision. "Conn, down periscope. Comms, release the communication buoy. Q, take us down to a hundred feet." As the periscope slides down, Thompson glances at Garcia. "That will provide us some measure of concealment." The two lean backward as the sub dives to the designated depth. Once the submarine levels off the captain orders the ensign manning the radio station to hail the Portuguese frigate.

After several unsuccessful attempts to contact the docked ship, Thompson and Garcia discuss the next steps. "I believe the Portuguese ship is unoccupied,"

Garcia says. "I say we move a little closer, surface, and aim for the dock."

Thompson, using his index finger, wipes the sweat from his forehead. "Even if that frigate is empty, they'll be a passel of Portuguese sailors on the island."

"Yes, but they're not going to be hanging around the docks, are they?"

"They could be if the ship is being repaired."

Garcia shrugs and steps over to the monitor, replaying the video from the periscope camera. "I'm not seeing any sailors."

"Okay, Carlos, you win. We'll dock, but the crew will remain aboard. Put together a security team of ten to man the deck and limit the number of rifles to every other sailor. I don't want it to appear as if we're invading their island."

"The crew's not going to be happy about not going ashore."

"We'll assess the situation when we see what type of reception we receive. If we decide on giving them a little R and R we'll do it in shifts. I want the boat operational at all times."

"How are we going to purchase supplies? There might be a couple thousand dollars if the crew pitched in all of their cash."

"I'll figure something out. But let's not count our chickens just yet." Thompson turns back to the helm. "Q, bring us back up to periscope depth. Mr. Patterson, come to a heading of one-five degrees. All ahead, one-third"

The captain's orders are repeated and the boat begins ascending again. "Do you want the security team topside as soon as we surface?" Garcia asks.

"You bet your ass, I do."

CHAPTER 47

Lakeville

Stan McDowell is up just as the faint smudge of the sun breaks on the horizon. The students finally fell asleep after the shoot-out, the girls in one office and the boys in the other. Melissa, Lauren, and McDowell took turns standing guard, switching places on the sofa throughout the remainder of the night. But McDowell never could get comfortable and slept with one eye open. He pulls on his boots and, rather than traipse around inside in the dark, exits through the front door. He avoids looking at the bodies and circles around back. A light drizzle continues to fall as he eases the back door open and grabs a handful of keys from a pegboard screwed to the wall. He clicks on his flashlight and places it in his mouth as he scans the tags attached to the individual keys, but he can't decipher the lettering system used to designate which key goes to which truck.

He removes the light from his mouth, stirs the coals to get the fire going, and ventures into the equipment yard. There are six trucks parked up next to the fence and another dozen parked helter-skelter around the lot. They're all the same type—cab-over sixteen-foot flatbeds, probably in the four-ton range, with staked beds, meaning the back is enclosed by a set of rails. McDowell approaches the first truck and pulls on the door handle. It squeaks open, revealing a mud-splattered floorboard and two captain seats separated by the engine cowling. He tries the first set of keys with no luck. On his sixth attempt, he finds the correct key but the truck fails to turn over. He climbs out and continues down the line.

The problem is all the trucks are of recent vintage and thus more susceptible to an EMP. The prevailing wisdom is that anything electronic dies after an EMP, but that isn't necessarily true. During a stint at Global Strike Command while in the Air Force, McDowell actively participated in various scenarios on the effects of an electromagnetic pulse. Whether a device, or car, or anything based on electronics is affected by an EMP is based on numerous factors, two of which are the altitude of the detonation and the wire length of the device. The power grids were the first to go, but smaller devices that have a shorter run of electrical wires often survive. McDowell is hoping that's the case for at least one of the trucks.

Wearily, he climbs into the cab of another truck. He quit counting after ten and that was a while ago. The good thing is the pile of keys is much smaller. This truck appears to be older than the others, the vinyl seats are split and the dash is veined with cracks. After several attempts he finds the correct key. He pauses, says a quick prayer to someone, somewhere, and twists the key. The starter groans and he pumps the gas pedal.

Finally, the engine coughs to life, spewing a stream of black smoke into the slate-colored sky. McDowell raises his fist and shouts, "Hell, yeah." As the engine warms, he steps down and makes his way over to the sign shop.

He searches the nearest building for fuel containers and finds a pair of five-gallon diesel jugs stashed in the corner of the barn. He pulls them out and continues his search. Stepping around behind the barn, he spots a large fuel tank perched atop a pair of latticed legs and threads through the piles of junk for a look. He lifts the pump handle and sniffs the spout—diesel. He hurries back to the truck and drives it over next to the tank. After topping off the truck's tank, he fills the two containers. That might buy them three or four hundred miles, but not a thousand. He looks around the tank and finds an eight-foot section of four-inch hose buried in the weeds. The original metal collars are still intact and he tosses it all into the back. Used to fill the large tank from a tanker truck, the hose could prove invaluable down the road. Prowling around some more, he's trying to figure out what else they may need. He bends down to check for a spare under the bed and finds the slot is empty. They'll need a spare for sure. After all, it's not like he can call AAA. He returns to the office building and rousts a few of the boys outside to help.

By the time they've finished, they've accumulated two spare tires, four more fuel containers, a large tarp to shield the bed from the elements, nearly a dozen flashlights, and two cases of double-A batteries. McDowell drives the truck up to the back door of the building and climbs out. Most of the group is outside, drinking soup from the coffee cups, and he grabs a cup and ladles in some soup.

Once the boys finish, they lay the area rug from the reception area across the bed and load on the old sofa. The girls pack away the utensils and load the two five-gallon jugs of water, along with the luggage. The six diesel containers get lashed to the outside rails with a roll of found rope, as does the four-inch tanker hose. McDowell debates going back to check the other job-site trailer, but he's feeling exposed now that daylight is in full bloom. When no one is looking, he sneaks into the cab and locks the pistol and ammo in the glove box. It's not much of a lock, but it could keep the kids out, especially if they don't know it's there. McDowell hustles back to the barn and retrieves the bucket of tools he'd put together. The kids pile in back, and Lauren and Melissa play rock-paper-scissors to see who gets the first shift in the back with the kids. Lauren loses, and she climbs into the back. McDowell secures the back rail section and climbs into the cab. He cuts a wide berth around the bodies and points the truck south.

CHAPTER 48

After a brief visit with his brother and his family, Gage spent another hour with his unconscious father before he and Holly returned to her parents'. Gage had been solemn all evening and waited until he and his wife climbed into bed before seeking solace. Cuddled in each other's arms, or as cuddled as you can be when one of you is eight months pregnant, Gage talked about life with his father, and Holly dried the tears on his cheeks. Eventually the well ran dry and they both fell asleep.

This morning, finishing up the last of the eggs and the bacon, the group lingers around the breakfast table. "Gage," Henry says, "if you want to spend some time with your father we can put off working on the wind turbines for a few days."

Gage takes a sip of coffee, pondering. After a long moment, he places the mug back on the table. "I appreciate it, Henry, but I need to be doing something. He won't know whether I'm there or not and Garrett's just down the way if Mom needs anything. Besides, the propane isn't going to last forever." Gage stands, carries his plate to the sink, and returns to give Holly a kiss on the cheek. "Are you feeling a little better this morning?"

"Yeah, I am. We'll see how the day goes."

"Why? What happened?" Susan Reed asks, a tinge of alarm in her voice.

"I've had several series of contractions over the last week or so." Holly makes no mention of the blood-soaked panties.

"I think that's fairly common this late into the pregnancy," Susan says. "I remember having some contractions when I was pregnant with Alyx."

Gage places a hand on Holly's shoulder. "Babe, do you know where Dr. Samia lives?"

"I think out in that new addition. I don't know the specific address," Holly says.

"I do," Susan says. "They moved in next door to the Johnsons."

"Why?" Holly asks.

"In case anything happens. Think she'd mind us making a house call?"

"She better not mind," Susan says, butting in. "Not when my first grandchild's almost here."

Holly glares at her mother before looking up at Gage. "I think she'd be okay with us dropping by, Gage. But I don't want to wear out our welcome. I'm fine for now."

"Still, I hate to leave you two stranded," Gage says. "Susan, would you mind running us out to the jobsite? That way you'll have the pickup in case you need it."

"Gage, I'm not due for another month," Holly says.

Susan pushes back from the table and stands. "I like

that idea, Gage. I'll come and get you both before dark."

"Sounds good," Gage says.

"We need to load a couple of items out at the barn before we're ready to go," Henry says.

"Okay. Give me a shout when you're ready," Susan says, carrying her and Holly's plates to the sink.

Gage and Henry exit the house and climb into the pickup for the short drive to the barn. Henry glances at the shotgun riding between them. "Expecting trouble?"

"Nope. Just being prepared." At the barn, Gage swings around and backs the truck up next to the large sliding door. "What are we getting here?"

"One of the unused step-up transformers."

"We're not going to be able to load that by hand, Henry."

Henry pulls the door open and steps inside, Gage following behind. "We don't have to," Henry says, waving an arm toward the transformer already loaded on a large trailer. "We'll park the trailer up next to the tower."

"What makes you think the rest of the grid is operational?"

"I don't. If we can get just a portion of the grid going I'd be happy."

"Especially if it's the power lines running to this house."

"Of course. It's unlikely we'll be able to power the entire town, but if we can get power to a few houses that's better than nothing."

"Unless you're one of those not receiving power." Gage walks over and puts a foot up on the side of the trailer. "I don't know, Henry. We could be setting ourselves up for a war."

"Admittedly, I haven't thought about all of the societal concerns, but if we have the knowledge and the ability to do it, why not? Maybe we could tie in one of the schools so the other people in town could benefit. At the very least we could get some wells pumping water. Isn't clean water worth it?"

"I'm not saying it's not worth it. I'm just suggesting we need to be careful about how we do this."

"Let's see if getting the turbines working is feasible before we worry about all the other stuff. If you'll back the old truck in, I'll hook up the trailer."

Gage climbs into the cab and, following Henry's directions, backs up to the trailer. Henry attaches the trailer and takes his seat on the passenger side. The old truck is riding low in the ass end when they pull out of the barn. They stop at the house to pick up Susan, and Gage takes it slow down the driveway, the truck struggling with the weight of the trailer and transformer.

"Which turbine do you want to try first?" Gage asks.

"The one closest to the house," Henry replies. "Plus, it was one of the turbines off-line when things went sideways."

CHAPTER 49

Along the coast of Maryland

Brad and Tanner sailed until dusk, reaching a point just north of Ocean City, Maryland, before dropping anchor a mile from shore. Both rattled from the events earlier in the day, they had cut a wide swath around other boats all day. Brad wakes when the sun breaks on the horizon, still exhausted after standing guard through the night. He throws off the blanket and stands and stretches. Off to the west, the horizon is smudged with smoke, and in the distance flames are visible as the firestorm, started days ago, rages on. With no one left to fight the fires, the only natural firebreak is the edge of the ocean.

As the crow flies, Ocean City is only a hundred miles from Washington, D.C. The area to the west must have been hammered, evidenced by the significant increase in the number of dead bodies, both human and animal, in the water. Having washed down the Potomac, they are now drifting along with the current. But bodies aren't the only problem. The water is brimming with all sorts of debris, including shattered lumber, sections of ripped-apart houses, and unmanned boats on a voyage to nowhere. It looks as if a tsunami had hit. Life would be so much easier if that's all that had occurred, Brad thinks, shielding his eyes against the rising sun and scanning the water. More than a dozen boats are anchored within a three-mile circle with many other boats motoring along in the deeper water. A good number of the boats passing by are motorboats and Brad wonders what will happen when they run out of fuel.

Brad unstraps one of the fishing poles from the top of the cabin. Ideally, he would prefer to fish with live bait, but unless he catches some, live bait is not an option. He ties on an artificially scented lure and casts it into the water. Far from an expert fisherman, he has no idea if it's the correct bait or not, but all he can do is try. After reeling up the slack, he allows the bait to drift to the bottom before slowly reeling it in. After fifteen minutes of fishing and no bites, he moves to the starboard side and recasts.

He feels something bump the other side of the boat, but thinking it's a piece of debris he fishes on. Then he feels another bump, this one accompanied by a grunt. Brad whirls around to see two hands latching on to the swim platform. He drops the rod and grabs the rifle as a large man pulls himself out of the water and pushes to his feet. Brad cocks the hammer, turns, and fires from the hip. He hits the man in the shoulder and a spray of blood coats the white vinyl seats. The man howls with rage and staggers forward, now only four feet away. Brad levers another shell, seats the stock to his shoulder, and fires again, hitting the man center mass. Blood and bone splatter across the boat and the man crumples to the deck.

Tanner rushes up the stairs, shaking. "Tanner, go back below," Brad shouts as he steps to the stern, scanning the water for more swimmers. Feeling a sharp stick to his bare foot, Brad glances down to discover he's standing on a piece of the man's bone and flicks the fragment into the water. After several more moments of scanning and not spotting any more threats, Brad lowers the rifle and props it against the wheel. For the first time, he looks at the man he killed. The man is big, probably close to six-two and well over two hundred pounds. Facedown, Brad can't obtain an accurate estimate of the man's age, but the full head of dark hair suggests he's fairly young. Trembling from the adrenaline dump, Brad feels zero remorse the man won't ever reach retirement age.

Now the question is, how to get the body off the boat? Brad grabs a foot and attempts to pull with little result. He plants his feet, takes a deep breath, and tries again, moving the body only a few inches. Brad doesn't want to involve Tanner in this mess, so he steps back to ponder another approach. While he's pondering he makes another scan of the water. They really need to move farther out to sea. Screw it, he thinks, walking over to the hatch and shouting down into the cabin. "Tanner, I really need your help."

Tanner haltingly climbs up to the deck, his eyes as big as dinner plates. He takes one glance at the bloodied boat and begins to shake again. "Who was he, Dad?"

"No idea. I need your help to move him."

Tanner is staring at the blood pooling on the deck. "What . . . what are we . . . going to . . . do with . . . him?"

"Roll him into the water. About the only choice we

have." Brad looks up at his son, whose face is now the shade of the whitecaps breaking in the distance. "If you'll just help me with that, I'll clean up the rest of this mess."

"O . . . kay."

Brad moves behind the body. "I think if we both grab a foot we can drag him over to the stern."

Trying to avoid the pool of blood, Tanner tiptoes across the deck. He hesitates for only a moment before reaching down to grab a foot. Working together they drag the body to the back of the boat then move around to the body's other side and, with grunts of exertion, push it into the water. They stand and Brad wipes the sweat from his brow. "Son, if you'll set up there on the top of the cabin and keep an eye on the water, I'll finish up."

Tanner nods and tiptoes back across the deck, taking a seat near the mast. Brad lifts one of the seats and retrieves a bucket. He dips it into the water and splashes it across the deck. After twenty-one more dunks and splashes, the deck and seats are free of blood. Brad grabs a rag to wipe the seats down then grabs the rod and reels in the line. "Tanner, pull up the anchor. We're getting the hell out of here."

After the anchor is aboard, Brad fires up the engine and motors out to deeper water before unfurling the mainsail. With the bow pointed south, the sail catches the wind and the *EmmaSophia* cuts through the water.

CHAPTER 50

Near Ponta Delgada, São Miguel Island, Azores

At the half-mile mark from the docks at Ponta Delgada, the USS *New York* rises to the surface. The assembled security team waits near the main hatch for the order to go topside while Thompson and Garcia survey the harbor using both periscopes. The security team is armed with M16 rifles, and each man has a semiautomatic pistol strapped into the holster at his waist. They are also outfitted with a safety harness they'll clip on to a line that will be deployed along the length of the sub.

Designed to perform flawlessly beneath the water, the nuclear submarine tends to wallow on the surface and, with no tug to offer assistance, getting to the dock will be a dicey proposition. Captain Thompson steps away from the periscope and snaps a microphone from the overhead bulkhead. "This is the captain. Security team, deploy." The security team members climb the ladder of the main hatch, one at a time, the first providing covering fire if needed. "Carlos, you have the deck. I'm going topside."

"Unarmed?" Carlos asks.

"There'll be plenty of guns on deck." Thompson slips on a harness, grabs a set of high-power binoculars, and climbs up the narrow set of ladders inside the sail. At the top he opens the hatch and climbs out onto the bridge. After ninety-some days below the surface, the fresh air is a welcome relief. What is not a welcome relief is the reminder of what happened. Confined inside the sub, thoughts of what might be happening topside take a backseat to the tasks at hand. But up here, the smoke and debris in the atmosphere blot most of the sun's strength and Thompson feels a pang of regret for their role in the cause. He puts the binoculars to his eyes and scans the shoreline. Although there are a lot of pointed fingers, no one seems to be moving with any urgency. Thompson glasses the Portuguese frigate and finds it empty.

Now six hundred yards from the docks, Thompson picks up a radio handset to play the role of navigator, while keeping a close eye on the shoreline. He relays course corrections and speed changes to the helm as the six-hundred-foot behemoth closes in on the docks. "All stop," he orders via the radio. "Send a helmsman up to the bridge. Might make things easier. And send up the tenders. I see some lines lying on the dock."

After making his way up the sail, the helmsman takes the wheel and the submarine resumes forward progress. Thompson lifts the binoculars to study the dock area and the surrounding shoreline again. After a worldwide nuclear war, life on the island appears mundane. The captain triggers the microphone. "Carlos, who's the big kahuna on the island?"

After a delay of a few minutes, Garcia answers. "Ponta Delgado is the seat of government for the Azores and I assume the president has an office somewhere in the city."

"Is there any other information in the computer?"

"I've looked, Bull. I can't find any more about who or where and I can't exactly call the State Department. I guess we're winging it."

"Let's just hope he's a winging-it kind of guy. Anyone on board speak Portuguese?"

"I'll peruse the personnel records, but I highly doubt it."

"What are the chances we have a consulate in the city?" Thompson asks.

"Hadn't thought of that. We should have some information if we do. I'll check."

"We're about two hundred yards from the dock. Check fast."

The submarine slows to a crawl as the boat moves closer to the dock. On the surface the USS *New York* drafts thirty-eight feet, compared to a ship like the Portuguese frigate, which probably drafts twenty. The captain is hoping the charts are accurate and sediment hasn't built up over the years. As the submarine inches closer to the dock, three officious-looking men appear at the entrance and begin striding down the pier. Thompson raises the binoculars to his eyes for a closer inspection. Two are dressed in some type of official uniform, the third is dressed in camouflage fatigues and a beret, common among the Portuguese Navy. Thompson zeros in on the navy man. Although he's unfamiliar with Portuguese insignia, the epaulets on his uniform suggest he's some type of officer. All appear to be unarmed. Thompson lowers the field glasses to make sure none of his security people are tracking the men's progress with a rifle barrel. Wouldn't do to shoot a government minister of the host country before even docking.

Two young seamen make a nimble jump across to the dock and ready the lines. The helmsman puts the engines in neutral and the submarine slowly coasts up to the pier. "Well done, Ensign Taylor. You're a hell of a boat driver," Thompson tells the young man at the controls before disappearing down the ladder. He makes his way over to the main hatch, calling for Garcia to join him. "We probably should have put on our dress uniforms."

"A little late for that," Garcia replies. "I think they'll forgive our rudeness, considering the situation. And I checked, there is a U.S. consulate in Ponta Delgada."

Thompson nods and starts climbing. On deck he orders a gangway be brought across from the dock. The security personnel form a loose perimeter around their captain and XO as they navigate their way down the long black deck. The trio of uniforms is now about fifty yards away and one of them is waving his hand, and not in greeting. "Hold up," Thompson shouts to his men working the gangway. In a lower voice, he says, "Security team, fan out along the deck." He turns to Garcia and says in a low voice, "What do you think that's about?"

"Well, they're not rolling out a red carpet, that's for damn sure. And from their grim expressions they don't appear to be in a cordial mood, either."

"Any Portuguese speakers on board?" Thompson asks.

"Negative."

The trio, eyeballing the security detail, stops when

they're twenty feet from the sub. The hand-waver speaks first, using broken English. "You not welcome here. Leave."

"All we want to do is resupply," Thompson says.

"We not have supplies. Leave."

"We are NATO allies. I would expect your cooperation."

"No NATO now."

"We're still bound by a signed treaty."

"No more."

"I would like a word with someone at the United States Consulate."

"No more consulate. I order you to leave."

"May I have a word with the gentleman from the Portuguese Navy?"

The three men are all shaking their heads. "No speaking. You leave."

Thompson's face turns a deep shade of crimson and the veins in his forehead are visibly throbbing. "Or what?" His words spark the security team into action. Those with rifles are now pointing them at the three men.

The waver raises his arm and flicks his hand. The sound of loud footfalls reverberates along the pier as a group of Portuguese sailors march toward the submarine, their rifles at the ready. Thompson estimates the number at fifty or more, but regardless of the actual number, his small security force is seriously outgunned. And it's way too late to summon more men. "Tenders, free the dock lines and board the boat. Security team, lower your weapons and return inside."

Disgruntled, the security team makes their way to the main hatch. The only two now left on deck are Thompson and Garcia. "Thank you for your hospitality," Thompson says, his middle finger extended. He glances up at the helmsman. "Reverse engines, Ensign Taylor." He and Garcia make their way toward the hatch. Captain Thompson is the last man down the ladder. When his feet hit the deck he orders, "Sound the general alarm—battle stations, torpedo. Conn, recall Ensign Taylor and secure the hatches." He walks over to the attack center and orders tubes one and two loaded.

"Conn, periscopes up."

The two periscopes slide up from the floor and Thompson takes one and Garcia the other as the boat continues to retreat from the dock. Thompson turns the periscope to focus on the group on the dock "You bastards," he mutters. "Q, tell me when we're deep enough to dive."

"Aye, aye, Skipper," the dive officer, Lieutenant Commander Quigley, replies.

Thompson is calm on the exterior, but inside the anger is raging. And the farther the submarine retreats, the more his anger builds. "So much for human compassion, Carlos."

"Yep. You thinking what I'm thinking?"

"Affirmative."

After a few more minutes, Quigley reports the water depth at 225 feet.

"Thank you, Q. Take us down to periscope depth."

"Dive, dive, dive," Quigley says, as a shipwide horn sounds and the submarine slips beneath the surface.

Thompson dials up the strength on the periscope. "Those assholes going to stand there all day, Carlos?"

"I think they want to make sure we're leaving."

"Well, I've got a parting gift for them." He turns toward the attack center. "Mr. White, torpedoes loaded and armed?"

"Yes, sir," replies Weapons Officer David White.

"You have the target?"

"Yes, sir."

Thompson rotates the periscope to the Portuguese frigate. "Fire tubes one and two."

"Roger, firing tubes one and two." The ship shudders as the two torpedoes are propelled out of their tubes.

"Fish away. Eight hundred yards to target," White says.

"Roger," Thompson says.

The two Mark-48 Mod-7 torpedoes clock in at nearly 3,700 pounds each, 650 pounds of which are the high-explosive warhead. Traveling at sixty-three miles per hour, the torpedo can cut a ship in half.

"Four hundred yards to target," White says.

"Are you worried about collateral damage?" Garcia asks.

"Hell no. They made their bed," Thompson says. "If we're lucky those three might catch some shrapnel."

"I don't know about shrapnel, but I'll guar-an-damn-tee you they're gonna piss their pants."

Thompson smiles. "Carlos, trigger your periscope camera and keep it focused on those three. I'll trigger mine and lock it on the frigate." Once the cameras are activated, Thompson orders the feeds broadcast over the shipwide video system via split screen.

"Two hundred yards to target," White says.

"If we're lucky they'll still have some heavy weapons on board," Thompson says. "Be nice to detonate their payload."

"One hundred yards to target." And seconds later White announces: "Contact."

A cheer erupts on the bridge and echoes of the same can be heard throughout the boat.

"Direct hit," Thompson says, peering at the video screen. He glances at Garcia. "Cut that sucker in half." The shockwave from the blast washes across the hull as Thompson and Garcia high-five. "Periscopes down," Thompson orders. "Q, takes us down to two-zero-zero. Mr. Patterson, plot a course for Bermuda."

"Aye, aye, Skipper," the navigator, Mike Patterson, replies.

CHAPTER 51

Weatherford

After a grueling ten-minute climb, Henry and Gage reach the hub of the wind turbine. Gage cranks open the nacelle's doors and the breeze offers a brief respite. They take a few minutes to catch their breath as Gage peers over the side, spotting the Reed residence a couple of miles away. He tries tracing the power grid wires from here to there, but loses track in a tangle of wires at the distribution station.

"This turbine *was* off-line when the EMP struck, correct?" Henry asks.

"Yes. I was planning to do some maintenance on it the following day."

"That might have saved our bacon." Henry pulls out his portable oscilloscope and begins checking electrical circuits. Gage threads one of the two ropes he carried up into the pulley system and hoists his toolbox up the tower and begins working to put the analog pressure gauge on the brake's hydraulic system.

Gage glances up at the sky. "How long is this haze going to hang around, Henry?"

Henry pauses his work to look up. "Years, most likely. And it'll play havoc on the global climate."

"How's that?"

"Ever hear of a nuclear winter?"

"Yes. A plunge in temperatures?"

"Exactly, and that plunge will have far-reaching effects. The decrease in global temps will wipe out growing seasons all across the planet. Not for a year or two, it could be a decade or longer. People like us, those that survived, will endure a famine of unimaginable proportions. Add in the deaths of millions of feeder cattle, hogs, chickens, and turkeys, and we could be looking at the end of life as we know it."

"So why are we going to the effort to produce electricity if it's all for nothing?" Gage asks.

"Because if we get a couple of these turbines working we could grow some crops under the grow lights I have stashed in the barn. And there should be pockets of wildlife that survived. I'm determined my first grandchild, along with my children and you, Gage, will survive. But our only hope is to get some of the turbines producing electricity."

Henry returns to his task, checking the circuits in the power inverter. The inverter converts the power generated by the turbine from direct current (DC) to alternating current (AC), which is the type of electricity supplied to homes and businesses. With the oscilloscope, Henry uses probes to check the continuity of the various circuit boards. After an hour of probing, he pauses to stretch his back. "Gage, hold off on any more modifications. We may be in better shape than I thought."

"How many dead circuit boards did you find?"

"Just three so far. If you'll hoist my electronics case up, I have some spares to replace the damaged ones."

Gage steps over to the pulley system and threads in the second rope. Henry's bag weighs significantly less than Gage's tools and it doesn't take him long to bring them up. Once the case is on deck, the two break to eat lunch, which consists of pieces of thick-sliced ham from the Reed freezer and a hunk of cheddar cheese.

"Do you remember if there were any other turbines off-line on doomsday?" Henry asks between bites of ham.

"Just the one I was working on."

"Which one?"

"Turbine twenty-three."

"Damn, that's a mile away. I was hoping to find two together so we could link them."

Gage cuts off a slice of cheddar cheese, pops it into his mouth, and savors the tangy taste. "This cheese is good. How much do you have left?"

Henry nods toward the ice chest. "That's the last of it."

Gage cuts another smaller sliver and allows it to linger on his tongue before chewing. "Are you thinking the turbines that were up and running are toast?"

"Probably so. You told me they all stopped turning shortly after the first EMP. We'll check a few of them later, but I'd be very surprised if any of the electrical circuits survived."

Gage takes a sip of water. "So do you have this all figured out now?"

"I think so. On paper it works, and I see no reason it won't in reality. All we can do is try."

CHAPTER 52

Memphis

Zane exits off of I-40 in downtown Memphis and picks up 2nd Street going south, searching for a convenience store. Amazingly, most of downtown Memphis remains intact. Other than the damage caused by the looters, most of the structures are upright, and even the famous Peabody Hotel looks as if it could open for business—if they had running water, a working sewer system, and electricity. Zane and Alyx stop at the intersection of Beale Street. The well-known road is covered with trash and there's a faint odor of soured beer that still lingers. There are some people out, but few are paying any attention to the truck.

Zane spots a plundered 7-Eleven and steers the truck into the parking lot. "I wished the damn cell phones worked. Looking for a map is a pain in the ass."

"We only have one more state to cross from here. And I could drive most of it blindfolded."

"Can you tell me where the nearest river crossing is?"

"That I can't do. Never had any trouble on the freeway."

"There you go." Zane pushes open the door and steps out as Alyx climbs down with the shotgun.

Alyx pinches her nose. "What's that smell?"

"Death." Zane pulls his shirt up to cover his nose and steps through the shattered door. Zane counts four bodies before he stops counting. The store is thick with flies and the floor's surface appears to be moving from all of the maggots. Zane spots a rack of maps on the front counter and reaches across to grab one, trying to avoid wading any farther into the store. He latches on to a map and freezes in place when he hears the throaty rumble of a dog's growl. With his body still, Zane slowly turns his head to sees a pit bull three feet away. The dog's face is dyed red, no doubt from gorging on the bodies over the past week. The dog's hackles are raised and he looks ready to pounce. Zane's eyes dart to the window, hoping Alyx is looking his way, but she's not. She's standing near the rear of the truck, her gaze focused outward on the surrounding neighborhood. For the first time, he curses Alyx for losing the pistol.

Zane, as slowly and as carefully as possible, makes a quarter turn to face the dog. With wide, heavily muscled shoulders, the dog is sixty pounds of nothing but muscle and bone. Moving only his eyes, Zane searches the front of the store for some type of weapon. Unless he's going to fend the dog off with a week-old magazine, Zane's out of luck. "C'mon, Alyx," he mutters. Zane changes tactics. He slowly extends his hand, palm down and says. "Easy, boy."

He's rewarded with a deep, throaty growl. The dog lunges forward a step, bloody drool dripping from his mouth. The overwhelming majority of people will tell you to never run from a dog, but Zeke is quickly running out of options. He takes two tiny shuffle steps toward the door, the dog tracking his every move. "Easy, boy." Zane shuffles a little closer to the door. "Everything's all right. I'm not going to hurt you."

The dog snarls, his sharp teeth exposed.

Zane throws the map at the dog before ducking through the door. "Shoot," he shouts as the dog charges out of the store. The dog, unbelievably quick for his size, is on Zane before he's taken a second step. Alyx wheels around the back of the pickup with a horrified look on her face. That's all Zane can see before the dog latches on to his lower leg and drags him to the ground. Zane kicks with his free leg, his boot thudding into the dog's head, but the dog's powerful jaws remain clasped to his leg. Zane rolls onto his back, still kicking, trying to cover his face with his arms in case the dog lunges forward. He hears a crunch and suddenly the pressure on his leg releases. He scrambles away as Alyx hits the dog again with the butt of the shotgun. "Shoot it," he shouts.

Alyx reverses the shotgun and tucks the stock tight to her shoulder.

"Shoot," Zane shouts.

Alyx begins to quiver and she lowers the gun. Zane hobbles over, takes the shotgun from her hands, and shoots the pit bull in the head. Zane glances around to see if the shot has attracted any attention as he pushes Alyx toward the pickup. "Get in. We need to get the hell out of here."

Still dazed, Alyx clambers aboard as Zane tenderly slides behind the wheel. He drops the truck into gear and they roar out of the lot. He doesn't stop until they've passed the city limit sign. He climbs out of the truck, pushes off his shoe, and pulls up his pant leg. His sock is soaked with blood and a large patch of skin is dangling from his calf.

Alyx kneels down for a closer look. "You need stitches."

"I'll make an appointment with my doctor." Zane strips off his outer shirt, then his T-shirt, still stained from Alyx's bloody nose, and hands it to her. "Bind it as best you can, for now."

"Maybe we can find a doctor in town."

"Not likely. Just bind it up." Zane grimaces as Alyx tightens the T-shirt against his calf. "We'll find a needle and some thread and you can sew it up."

Alyx stands. "I can't sew."

"I'll teach you. Let's circle back to that store near the interstate and see if we can find one of those emergency sewing kits."

"You need antibiotics, too."

"One step at a time," Zane says, stepping into his blood-filled shoe.

CHAPTER 53

Near Hog Island, Virginia

The going gets more difficult the closer Brad and Tanner get to the mouth of the Chesapeake Bay. Unlike the West Coast, where the current moves from north to south, here the Gulf Stream current moves from south to north, pulling the warmer water and humid air out of the Caribbean. That same current is now pushing north a raft of debris that is miles wide.

And it's not just the debris that's a problem. The stench emanating from the pile is nauseating—it smells like equal parts rotting flesh, raw sewage, and a restaurant Dumpster seven days in the sun, and the worst part is it's inescapable. Brad and Tanner are wearing strips from an old T-shirt across their faces to keep the smell from imbedding permanently in their sinuses. To the west, where Washington, D.C., once resided, smoke lingers from the continuing wildfires. From Brad's vantage point, the land is scorched for as far as he can see, and the once-visible Washington Monument is a now a gap on the horizon. Brad turns away and trims the sails, steering behind a larger power-boat as if it were an icebreaker.

Across the water to the south, it doesn't appear that Virginia fared much better than the nation's capital. The Hampton Roads area is nothing but smoldering ruins. Naval Station Norfolk, the world's largest naval station, which also houses the largest concentration of U.S. Navy forces, is absolutely obliterated. Brad had sailed this way several years ago and he's astounded at the destruction. Several immense ships, which appear to have been making their getaway, are listing badly at the mouth of the harbor, abandoned and left to find their own watery grave. The fractured deck of an air-craft carrier points skyward, the black tarmac now a runway to nowhere. Most of the wrecks are still smol-dering, and Brad can't begin to fathom how many lives were lost. With God knows what littering the sea floor near the harbor, Brad diverts from behind the power-boat and heads out to deeper water.

Tanner comes topside to stretch his legs. He scans the surrounding area before turning to his father, his eyes wide. "Dad, do you think *any* of our warships sur-vived?"

Brad ponders the question for a moment. Surely those ships at sea had some measure of protection, simply because they would be hard to find, especially if the low-orbit satellites were out of operation shortly after it all began. "Yeah, I do, Tanner. I don't believe they could have targeted every ship in the U.S. Navy. Then you have the submarines, which are damn near impossible to detect on a good day. So, yes, I believe there are some remaining warships."

"Where are they?"

"That's the sixty-four-thousand-dollar question. Maybe they're marshaling their forces before sailing back stateside. Or it could be they're remaining out at sea to avoid detection."

Tanner takes a seat on the back bench. "Do you think there are any bombs left?"

"I sure as hell hope not, but I wouldn't be surprised if there were. I don't know what's left to bomb or what the point would be. You can't destroy what's already been destroyed." Brad sighs. "Unfortunately, there's a lot we don't know and may never know."

Tanner falls silent for several minutes, his gaze focused on something in the distance. He turns to look at his father. "What happened to their bodies?"

Brad, scanning for debris, takes a moment to collect his thoughts. After several moments of silence, he turns to face his son. "Your mother and Sophia?"

"Yeah."

"They'll be buried, son. I know there's no closure for either of us." Brad's mind is clicking through explanations, something that might help alleviate his son's pain, and comes up empty. "Maybe someday we'll be able to have a memorial service for both of them. But, truthfully, Tanner, I don't know what the future holds. We may never make it back home." He wants to tell Tanner that millions of other families are dealing with the same issue, but decides against it. The statement won't help Tanner overcome *his* grief. "I guess all we can do is persevere." Brad reaches up and wipes a tear from the corner of his eye.

"Did Mom shoot that doctor?"

Brad struggles with the right answer. *Maybe. I don't really know. I didn't see what happened. Tell my son his mother was a murderer?* "Your mother wasn't thinking, only acting. But to answer your question frankly, son, yeah, she did."

"Because he killed Sophia?"

Can life get any more complicated? "Yes."

Brad glances at his son. Tanner nods and appears to withdraw deeper within himself. "I'm sorry, son. I wished we could go back in time to change everything. But we can't. Your mother was doing what she thought needed to be done. I couldn't stop her and I don't think anyone could have stopped her. It is what it is. All we can do now is move forward. You understand that, don't you, Tanner?"

Tanner pushes up out of the seat. "Yeah, I understand." He wipes the tears from his cheeks. "Can I take the wheel for a while?"

Brad stands and wraps his arms around Tanner. "I'd love for you to take the wheel, son."

CHAPTER 54

Owatonna, Minnesota

Traveling via a truck is better than walking, but it's still slow as McDowell carefully maneuvers around dead automobiles without jostling those in the back. He pulls the truck over to the shoulder to work his way around a jam. As far as towns go, Owatonna isn't very large. They pass a collection of stores that pop up in many small communities—a local drug store, a True Value hardware store, and a local coffee shop, along with the requisite number of churches. With most of the state's population centered around the cities of Minneapolis–Saint Paul, Rochester, and Duluth, the towns along I-35 are spaced miles apart with nothing but farmland and lakes between them.

They make their way through Owatonna, and Mc-Dowell pulls the truck over to allow those in back a chance to stretch their legs. He steps out of the cab, slings the shotgun over his shoulder, and walks around to stretch his own legs, his eyes constantly scanning for threats. They continue to pass people walking along the highway and many have tried to flag them down. McDowell never taps the brakes. He steps off the highway and heads into the tall grass before unzipping to drain his bladder. Across a barbwire fence, a field of dried cornstalks rustles in the breeze. And that's when it hits him—the immensity of the problems they'll face in the future. Not only is food in short supply now, the prospects for any improvement are grim and the unharvested cornfield is a cold reminder. He zips up and returns to the truck, disheartened.

Once everyone has had a chance to answer the call of nature, they load back into the truck. Lauren is now riding shotgun, and at some point she and Melissa are going to have to learn how to drive a stick shift or all the driving's going to be on McDowell's shoulders. He glances at the gas gauge and shifts into first, steering down the center of the highway. He looks over at Lauren. "How much do you know about the aftereffects of a nuclear war?"

"Not as much as I wish I knew now. I did read Cormac McCarthy's *The Road*. It's pretty grim."

"I made it about halfway through the novel and put it down. I grew up at a time when we practiced bomb drills in school. Like the desks were going to offer any resistance to a nuclear attack. The teachers should have just told us to bend over and kiss our ass good-bye."

Lauren smiles. "So that was it, huh? Crawl under the desks?"

"Yes, and all the rooms were surrounded by glass, not these school bunkers they build nowadays. We wouldn't have had a chance." McDowell slows to steer around a semi. "I did a two-year stint at Global Strike Command. We ran every imaginable scenario. If our missiles cleared their silos, and Russia's did the same, the number of dead might be north of three billion from the initial attack."

Lauren pauses to let the numbers sink in. "And after the attack?"

McDowell glances at Lauren. "Not good. The results of one scenario predicted that half of the remaining population would die in the first year."

"Half?" Lauren asks, her eyes going wide.

"Yes. And another half won't survive the second year. What was the world population before this mess started?"

"Somewhere in the neighborhood of seven billion." Lauren pauses to do the math in her head. "Oh my God, that means that as many as six billion people will be dead by year two. Is that really possible?"

"We won't ever know for sure, but a variety of scenarios we ran predicted similar results."

Lauren turns to stare out the side window. After several moments of silence, she turns to look at McDowell. "Why did it happen, Stan?"

"Don't know. Could have been a simple mistake that started everything, or maybe someone hacked a system they weren't supposed to hack."

"I thought all of those networks were secure."

"Nothing is secure. If something is operated by a computer, it's vulnerable whether connected to the Internet or not. Secure networks do not exist."

"I read something about the Chinese and Russians being on our power grids," Lauren says.

"They are, or were, but we infiltrated their systems, too. No one is innocent in any of this."

Lauren reaches forward and cranks the passenger window down a smidge. "How do we survive?"

"We take it day by day and do the best we can. There'll be a bunch of people die off over the next month or two from radiation poisoning. Sad, but it means fewer mouths to feed."

Lauren turns to stare at him. "That's rather cold, isn't it?"

McDowell shrugs. "There's absolutely nothing that can be done to help them now."

She turns to stare out the side window for the next mile. Eventually, she turns back to McDowell. "I haven't seen many birds or other wildlife. You'd think this place would be littered with deer."

"Most of them are probably dead from radiation poisoning, either by direct exposure or by eating contaminated food. Hopefully, a few pockets of wildlife survived, but it could take years to repopulate. And that's if someone doesn't kill any that are left. If that happens, we'll either have to find a way to fish the oceans or face extermination."

A tear leaks out of the corner of Lauren's eye. "If the prognosis is really that grim, what are we doing?"

"The only thing we can do. Surviving."

CHAPTER 55

Memphis

Zane is working overtime to keep the pain at bay. He and Alyx switched positions and Alyx is now behind the wheel as they cruise back through town in search of medical supplies. The going slows as they near the downtown area. Ahead, three lanes of abandoned cars are waiting for a stoplight that won't be functioning again anytime soon. Alyx detours down a neighborhood street to avoid the clogged intersection. Even a week ago the neighborhood would have been considered seedy, and it's even more so today. Several of the homes have been torched, and Zane stops counting dead bodies after six.

"Can we get out of this neighborhood, please?" Zane asks.

"I'm trying."

"Where the hell are we going, anyway?"

"There's a complex of hospitals near the interstate. Thought we'd check it out." At the next intersection, Alyx turns onto a main thoroughfare that cuts through a dilapidated commercial area. They pass a rickety strip mall featuring a massage parlor, a nail care salon, a used furniture store, and a piercing and tattoo place.

"Too bad they're not open," Zane says, pointing toward a piercing shop. "I was thinking about getting my nipples pierced."

"You've already had something pierced today. I think that's enough fun."

Zane grimaces at the mention of his leg. "Party pooper."

Alyx switches hands on the wheel and reaches over to take his hand. "How's the pain?"

"Tolerable. I'm more worried about an infection. And the nightmares to come."

"Nightmares?"

"Yep. A dog bit me when I was seven. A Doberman. Wasn't a terrible bite, just my hand, but, jeez, did I have some nightmares. I'd wake up in a sweat thinking a dog was chasing me. That's why I nearly pissed my pants when I heard that pit bull growl. But his biting days are over." Zane cracks the window open. "It makes me wonder what happens when all of these stray dogs get a taste for humans? Think we'll become a delicacy?"

Alyx shudders. "I sure as hell hope not. Sorry, I couldn't pull the trigger. I knew the dog was no good."

"If you can't shoot a dog, will you be able to shoot a person if we get in a jam?"

"I think if our lives are threatened, I could. It's us or them, right?"

"Exactly. Any hesitation could be fatal for us."

Alyx makes another turn and the growing profusion of medical buildings suggests they're in the right place. "That's why I prefer you handle the shotgun."

She pulls up into the parking lot of what used to be University Hospital. The parking lot is scattered with hospital gowns, hospital beds, and dead bodies. "This is not going to work," she says, turning to exit the lot.

"Drive around a bit. Maybe we'll spot another place. Everything around here has already been ransacked."

Six blocks square, the area is an amalgam of hospitals, physician's offices, and modestly priced hotels that once played host to patients' families. "Wait a minute," Alyx says, "I've been here before."

"Here, where?"

"I've been on this street before. One of my friends from undergrad has an office somewhere around here. I met her a few times for lunch on my way through."

"I don't think a lunch meeting is in the works for today," Zane says.

"No, but her office might have exactly what we need."

"How so?"

"She's an OB doc. And her husband, Christopher, is a pediatrician. They're like the perfect before-and-after team."

Zane chuckles. "I bet they end up working some funky hours. Can you remember where her office is?"

"Somewhere around here. I remember the office was tucked away in the corner of a strip mall." Alyx steers the pickup into a parking lot and drives slowly along the storefronts. Most of the stores are what you'd expect them to be: a uniform shop, a medical supply store, an outpatient therapy center, and, all the way in the back they spot a sign stenciled on the glass:

SARAH MICHAELS OBSTETRICIAN/GYNECOLOGIST. "There it is," Alyx says, easing the truck to a stop.

"The office appears to be intact. I guess prenatal vitamins aren't high on the list of street drugs. Now what? Break the glass and go in?"

"I hate to break in."

"I suppose we could camp out for a week or two in hopes she eventually shows up."

Alyx scowls. "Smartass. Let's drive around back. Maybe the rear door is unlocked." Alyx takes her foot off the brake and eases the truck around the building. There's nothing on the doors to indicate which business they belong to, but if the doors correspond to the configuration of the façade, the last door on the left would belong to Sarah Michaels, MD. Alyx confirms Zane's speculations. "That's her car, there," Alyx says, pointing toward an older red Mercedes convertible.

"Think she's inside?"

"I doubt it. My bet is her car wouldn't start." Alyx pulls up next to the Mercedes and kills the engine. "I guess we can knock to see if she's here."

"And if there's no answer?"

Alyx sighs. "I guess we break in."

Zane cracks the breech on the shotgun to make sure it's loaded before pushing the door open and climbing gingerly from the cab. He hobbles toward the door and Alyx climbs out to meet him. He rattles the doorknob and finds it's locked. Not only is the knob locked, but the steel door is outfitted with dead bolts at the top and bottom of the door. "She store gold in the office?" Zane asks.

Before Alyx can answer, a gunshot shatters the silence and a chip of concrete, a foot above their head, flies into the air. They turn in unison to find a woman crouched in a shooter's stance forty feet away. Zane leans over and places the shotgun on the ground and he and Alyx reach for the sky. "What the hell do you think you're doing?" the woman shouts.

Alyx lowers her arms.

"Hands up, bitch," the woman says, walking slowly forward, the gun never wavering.

"Sarah, it's me, Alyx. Alyx Reed."

Sarah moves closer, the gun steady in her hands. At the ten-foot mark, she takes a long look at Alyx and lowers her weapon, rushing in to give Alyx a hug. "What in the hell are you doing here?"

"We dropped by for lunch," Alyx says, stepping away from the embrace, both women chuckling.

Assuming he's safe, Zane lowers his hands and takes stock of Sarah Michaels. She's lithe and lean and nearly a head shorter than Alyx. Her dark hair is cut in a fashionable bob and, when she turns to face Zane, he's instantly mesmerized by her sea green eyes.

"And who is this handsome man?" Sarah asks. "Another in a long line of boyfriends?"

Alyx playfully slugs her friend in the arm. "Sarah, this is Zane Miller. Boyfriend status yet to be determined."

Sarah holsters her pistol and shakes Zane's hand. "If I wasn't married with two kids, I'd steal you away from Alyx. Lord knows she owes me." Sarah gives his hand a final squeeze and breaks the grasp. Zane bends over to retrieve the shotgun as Sarah digs out her keys. "What *are* you doing here, Alyx?"

"Zane battled a pit bull and lost. His leg needs stitches."

"And if I hadn't happened along?"

"Undecided," Alyx answers, smiling. She quickly changes the subject. "Why are you coming to the office?"

Sarah unlocks the door and removes a small flashlight from her back pocket. "I still see some of my pregnant patients out of my home and I need to restock some supplies." She opens the door and all three enter and Sarah relocks the door.

CHAPTER 56

After a rotating lunch of chicken soup that was 99 percent water, the crew of the USS *New York* is back on station. There have been some grumbles about the food situation, but everyone is aware of what happened at Ponta Delgada. The video of torpedoing the Portuguese frigate played on a loop until Captain Thompson got tired of seeing it. Back on the bridge, the captain is joined by Carlos Garcia. "Think we should deploy the communication buoy, Carlos? See if we can make radio contact with someone?"

"I don't know, Bull. We towed the damn thing for hours on the way to Ponta Delgada and never heard a blip." Garcia glances at his watch. "It'll be dark in a few hours. Might be best to wait till then. You really think we'll make radio contact with someone?"

"Who knows? We can't be the only boat left. Be nice to hook up with a surface ship and take on some supplies. We're still five days from Bermuda and tonight's soup wasn't the most filling meal I've ever had."

"It's generous to call it soup. What happens if we do make contact and it turns out it's a Russian warship?"

"Don't know. We have no idea if we're still at war or even who's left to fight. I didn't pay close attention to the targeting package for our missiles, but I'd have to think Russia was absolutely decimated. Probably the same applies for our country. Maybe it wouldn't be a bad thing to communicate with a Russian ship."

"And what happens if they pinpoint our location and send a torpedo up our ass? I think it's best if we continue to believe we're at war, Bull."

"We need food. We have no idea how much longer we'll be at sea. My bet is there isn't a port left on the East Coast. Hell, the same probably applies to the West Coast, for that matter. And I can guarantee you Pearl Harbor has been obliterated. Our only hope might be docking in the U.S. Virgin Islands if *they* still exist. If that's the case, that'll add two or three days to our journey."

"Are we going for a look-see at Kings Bay?"

"We'll go for a look, but I'm not holding out much hope. That would have been a primary target for sure."

Garcia winces. "Think they bombed Jacksonville?"

Knowing that's where Carlos's wife and children are living, Thompson is hesitant to answer. After several moments of silence, he does. "I bet they hit the naval air station, but I have no idea if they hit the urban parts of the city. The town is protected somewhat by the St. Johns River and might have been spared from the wildfires. As for radiation, it all depends on the wind conditions."

"Many of the crew's families also live in and around

Jacksonville. Think we could take a peek while we're in the area?"

"Absolutely. But we've got a lot of ground to cover before then."

"Karen and the kids still in Savannah?" Garcia asks

"They left for a week at Myrtle Beach two days before we launched our weapons. A last blowout before the twins start their senior year of high school." Thompson pauses, tears glistening in his eyes. After another moment, he blows out a deep breath. "I haven't wanted to think about them, yet I find myself doing just that when my mind is not occupied with submarine matters. I have no idea if they're still alive or, if they are, whether we'll ever see each other—"

"Surface contact, sir," Sonar Technician Adams says. "Bearing two-nine-two degrees, distance thirty-two miles and closing."

Captain Thompson pushes out of his chair. "Conn, all stop." He steps over to sonar control. "Signature?"

"Working on it, sir."

"Q, depth?"

"We're sitting at three hundred eighty feet, Skipper."

"Roger," Thompson says. "Carlos, have wepps load tubes one and two."

As the order to load the tubes with torpedoes is passed on, the captain taps his foot, waiting for the sonar technician to identify the ship.

"Sir, screw signature suggests the ship is a Russian destroyer."

"Goddammit," Thompson mutters under his breath. "Conn, sound a silent general alarm. Battle stations, torpedo."

CHAPTER 57

McDowell eases the truck to a stop straddling the state line of Minnesota and Iowa. McDowell wonders why someone hasn't a built a house here. A person could wake up in Minnesota and walk into Iowa for a cup of coffee from the kitchen. He smiles at the thought as he climbs out of the truck and informs the students it'll be cold lunch, not wanting to take the time to build a fire. A few grumble but he ignores them.

"We're making good time," Melissa says.

McDowell steps away from the back of the truck to get out of earshot from the kids and Melissa follows. "For now. Things will change as we head farther south."

"Why's that?"

"More military installations. There's a big National Guard base just outside of Des Moines. From there things go downhill. I expect most of Nebraska will be a burned-out wasteland. You have the missile silos out West and a large Air Force base to the east that's home to the U.S. Strategic Command. With little but farm country in between, the firestorms most likely scoured most of the state."

"How long until we hit Texas?"

"Unknown. During normal times, a day and a half. Now? I have no idea. We'll have to skirt around Kansas City because of a military base, but once we hit Kansas it should be pretty easy traveling until we get to Oklahoma City."

"So we stretch it to three days. Think that's doable?"

McDowell wipes his brow and sighs. "A day at a time, Melissa. That's all I can say." McDowell turns and walks back to the truck. The students refuse to touch the Spam or Vienna sausages, so he grabs a can of Spam and pops the top. The ensuing aroma almost kills his appetite, but he grabs a fork, wipes it clean on his pant leg, and digs in. As he munches, he walks around the truck to make sure all the tires are holding up. Everything appears fine, and he polishes off the last of his lunch and puts the can in the trash bag the students had brought along. God forbid they should litter. He rounds everyone up and climbs behind the wheel. Melissa retakes the shotgun seat, and McDowell is surprised at his disappointment. He shifts the truck into gear and eases out on the clutch.

After a couple of miles of silence, Melissa says, "Are you okay after last night?"

"Yes."

"How many were there?"

"Three. The same three we met earlier in the day. I guess they circled back to follow us."

"What did they want?"

McDowell glances her way. "What do you think?"

Melissa shudders. "The girls. Or some of the girls."

McDowell nods. They ride in silence for a few more miles. The landscape begins to change the deeper they travel into Iowa, the green giving way to black, the land singed by wildfires. They pass mile after mile of burned fields and the occasional remnants of charred houses, none spaced less than a half a mile apart. They travel past a family camped out in the front yard, the home a pile of bricks beyond.

It's not until they arrive at the outskirts of Clear Lake that the devastation hits home. Clear Lake looks to have been a fairly good-sized town, judging by the number of city streets. That's the only way to judge because not a single structure remains. McDowell slows to veer around a semi and spots a group digging through the ruins of a building next to the highway. Their bodies are coated with soot, their movements lethargic.

"It looks like there are a few survivors," Melissa says.

"Is that a good thing? Their shelters are burned to the ground and there's probably not a speck of food left anywhere in the area. Probably what they're digging for now. I'm shocked they haven't migrated out of the area."

Melissa tucks a strand of hair behind her ear. "Maybe it's not food they're digging for. It could be they're searching for survivors."

"Hadn't thought of that. You could be right, but I would find it hard to believe there are any survivors left alive in that pile of rubble."

"But if it was your child, or your parents, or your siblings, wouldn't you want to know for sure? Wouldn't you want some type of closure? To see with your own eyes the body of your loved one?"

"For how long? At some point you have to let go and move on."

"Yes, you do. Maybe they haven't yet reached that point," Melissa says. "Or, on a grimmer note, they could have been exposed to a high level of radiation and know their days are numbered and are desperate to retrieve their loved ones so they can all be buried together. Many people have a strong desire to be buried next to their family members. Strange, I know, dead is dead, yet you see it at cemeteries the world over."

"If you're correct, these people are what? Digging their own graves? Then what? Hope you die first so your friends have time to put you in the ground?" McDowell shakes his head. "Jesus, what a macabre world we're left with."

CHAPTER 58

Memphis

With his leg stitched up and a shot of penicillin in his left ass cheek, Zane is almost back to normal. Sarah slathers Zane's wound with some antibiotic ointment and peels off her gloves. "I'll put together some supplies for you to take."

"Do you have any expired medicines that we could have?"

Sarah arches her brow. "Why?"

"To barter with. The bridge across the river is barricaded and those meds might be our ticket across."

Sarah removes another key from her pocket and steps out into the hall to unlock a large cabinet. Alyx, the official flashlight holder, follows them into the hall. "These are all the meds I have," Sarah says. "I'd prefer you only take what's expired."

"Will do," Zane replies.

Sarah retreats down the hall and returns with a couple of plastic shopping bags. She sets to work filling them with the supplies she'll need for the next few days, working side by side with Zane while Alyx holds the flashlight.

"Sarah, did I tell you my little sis, Holly, is pregnant?"

"No, you didn't. How far along is she?"

"Eight months. I'm hoping we get home before she gives birth."

"I'll put together a medical care package for her. Lack of meds is going to be one of the most critical issues we'll face going forward." Sarah shakes her head. "I can't believe Holly is married and pregnant. Last time I saw her she was in braces and worried about finding a prom date."

"I know. Scary, huh? The older I get the faster time flies. How old are your kids now?"

"Ethan is six and Ellie is three."

"I haven't seen either of them since right after Ellie was born. Hard to believe she's three."

Zane clears his throat. "I don't mean to change the subject, but how have you avoided the looters?"

"I think the location has something to do with it. And luck. I'd like to take all the supplies to my house but it's too much to carry without attracting attention."

"Your Mercedes is dead?"

"As a doornail."

"We can put everything in the pickup and drive you home," Alyx offers.

Sarah looks at Zane.

"Hey, sounds good to me," Zane says. "That's the least we can do."

"Alyx, there are some empty boxes behind the receptionist's desk. Would you mind grabbing them?"

"Sure. I'm going to leave you two kids in the dark for a moment and I don't want any funny stuff going on."

Sarah laughs and the other two join in. It's the first

time any have laughed in a long time. Still laughing, Alyx saunters down the hall, the flashlight beam dancing across the linoleum. She pushes through the outer door into the waiting room and the laugh dies on her lips. She clicks off the flashlight and slips back through the door. Using the wall as a guide, Alyx shuffles back down the hall. "Zane," she whispers in the dark, "there are three suspicious-looking characters peering through the front window."

"Did they see you?"

"I don't know. But they must have seen the flashlight through the window in the door."

"Where's the shotgun?"

"You left it in the exam room."

"And I left the rest of the shells in the damn truck. Slip me the flashlight and I'll grab the shotgun." They fumble the flashlight from one hand to the other and Zane feels his way back to the room. He clicks on the flashlight, spots the shotgun, and picks it up before killing the light again and shuffling back to the hallway. "Sarah, are you handy with that pistol?" he whispers.

"I'm pretty good with a target."

"Ever killed anything?"

"No. I'm all about saving lives."

"How about we switch weapons?"

"Okay," Sarah says, a tremor in her voice.

Zane clicks on the flashlight and they exchange weapons before Zane kills the light again. "I don't think they can bust through the back door, but keep an eye on it. The main threat will be from the front. I'll handle that. Is the pistol fully loaded?"

"Except for the one shot I took at you two."

"So I have twelve rounds to work with?"

"Correct," Sarah says.

"Okay. Alyx give me your hand."

Alyx reaches over and fumbles for Zane's hand.

"You're in charge of the flashlight. If anyone other than me enters the hallway, light 'em up to give Sarah a target picture. Sarah, all you have to do is point and shoot. In these tight confines, that scattergun will shred anyone attempting to come down the hall. And, most importantly, don't shoot me. Alyx, hit the light for a sec, I want to make sure the shotgun is cocked and ready."

Alyx clicks on the light and smothers the lens with her hand. Zane reaches over to cock the two hammers. "Don't put your finger on the trigger until you see something."

The sound of crashing glass startles them.

"Kill the light," Zane whispers. "And, Sarah, keep a good hand on the gun. She kicks like a mule." Hugging the wall, Zane makes his way toward the waiting room door. He's kicking himself for not scouting the area the moment they arrived. He doesn't know the layout of the reception area, but he also doesn't know if those entering are armed or not. Not that it will make a difference either way, but he would have liked to know what he's facing, especially if they're armed with automatic weapons. Highly unlikely, Zane reasons as he pauses to expel the clutter from his mind. Can't have clutter when entering a gunfight.

As he draws closer to the door he hears whispering from the other side. Two, maybe three, voices, which eases the burden somewhat. Maybe it's just the three Alyx spotted. He'd hate to slip into the room and discover there had been ten more hiding around the side of the building. When Zane reaches the door, he drops to his knees and feels around the jamb to see which way the door swings. He discovers the door swings out—good for him, bad for them. He puts his ear to the door to listen. The whispers are closer and it sounds like the three are all grouped together. Zane takes a deep breath and slowly eases down the door lever. Positioned on his haunches, he slams his shoulder into the door and rolls forward into the lobby and comes up with the gun ready to fire. His targets are silhouetted by the daylight and Zane starts left and works his way right, double tapping each person as fast as the gun will fire. The last person is drawing a gun from his waistband when Zane's shot pierces his forehead. He drops like his strings were cut. Within six seconds it's all over. Zane pushes to his feet. He doesn't need to check to see if the trespassers are dead. The muzzle flashes seared their deaths in his brain.

"Clear," Zane shouts before opening the door. "I'm coming in."

"Okay," Alyx shouts.

"Sarah, is your finger off the trigger?"

"Yes, Zane. I promise."

Zane opens the door and Alyx clicks on the flashlight.

"Alyx, Sarah, grab what you need to grab." He strides down the hall and takes the shotgun from Sarah, uncocking the hammers. "We need to be out of here as quick as we can."

Alyx hurries down the hallway to retrieve the empty boxes, the acrid smell of cordite and the metallic odor of blood filling her nostrils. She avoids looking at the carnage and grabs the boxes, hurrying back to the medicine cabinet. Zane moves back to the front to keep an eye on things, the shotgun at the ready.

When Alyx returns with the boxes, she and Sarah quickly empty the medicine cabinet. "If you'll follow me with the flashlight, I have some syringes and few other things in the two exam rooms I'd like to take."

"I'm right behind you," Alyx says as they duck into the first room. Sarah quickly clears the drawers and moves on to the next room.

"Are we good, Zane?" Alyx asks, following Sarah into the next room.

"For now. But I'd really like to get the hell out of here."

"Two minutes," Sarah says.

Once they've cleared both rooms, Sarah tosses the items into one of the boxes and pauses to think if there's anything else she needs to take. "I think that's everything . . . No, wait. Alyx, follow me, please." They retrace their steps into the first room and Sarah grabs a piece of equipment.

"What's that?"

"A fetal heart monitor." They step back into the hallway and gather up the supplies.

"We're ready, Zane," Alyx says.

Zane steps away and closes the door before striding down the hall. "Okay, this is how this is going to work. Sarah, you'll unlock the door, the bottom dead bolt last. When I give the okay, you'll crab-walk toward me, pulling the door open. I'll have the shotgun up and ready, so I really need you to remain low until you're behind me. I'll step outside and look for threats before waving you out. Alyx, you're driving. You have the keys, correct?"

Alyx digs in her pocket and extracts the keys. "Yes."

"Put the boxes in the back. When you get the truck started, back out and straighten it up. I'll climb in the back and you hit the gas. Sound like a plan?"

Alyx and Sarah answer in the affirmative. "Okay, Sarah, unlock the top two locks."

Sarah clicks the two top locks open and squats down for the bottom lock. Zane moves forward, places the shotgun to his shoulder, and sights down the barrel and cocks the hammers. "Okay, Sarah."

Sarah moves fast and the door swings open. Zane limps outside, the shotgun braced tight, his head on a swivel. He takes a quick glance around, turns back to his starting point, and makes a slower scan. His internal threat meter isn't pinging, but he doesn't rush his visual sweep. He lifts a hand and waves the women forward. They burst out of the door and hurry for the truck, their arms laden with supplies. They quickly place the boxes into the bed of the truck and climb into the cab.

Zane catches a flash of color in his peripheral vision. He whips around, his finger easing down on the trigger. It's a young girl, no older than ten, standing at the corner of the building. Zane lifts the gun toward the sky and expels a shaky breath. He offers the girl a small wave and hurries over to the truck, his heart hammering. He puts a foot on the bumper, climbs into the truck bed, and holds on to the tailgate as Alyx hits the gas. As they zoom past, the little girl waves, having no idea she was a millisecond away from being killed.

CHAPTER 59

Weatherford

Gage is wondering why everything is always much harder than you ever thought it would be. What should have been a thirty-minute job is now stretching into the third hour. Trying to retrofit the old analog pressure gauge onto the turbine's sophisticated braking system is like trying to put a distributor on a new Cadillac. And Henry's continued probing of the electronics revealed they have more work to do.

Gage wipes his hands with a rag. "Henry, any chance a person could recover from radiation poisoning?"

Henry puts down his tools and turns to look at his son-in-law. "I don't know a whole lot about the topic, but it all depends on the absorbed dose of radiation the person receives."

"How do you know what the radiation dose was?"

Henry closes the lid on his toolbox and sits. "You'd need to have a Geiger counter or a dosimeter at the time of the exposure to know for sure. If those aren't available, exposure levels are usually determined by patient symptoms after the event."

"Which are?" Gage asks.

"Keep in mind, I'm far from an expert, but I've read a few articles on the subject. Initial symptoms would include nausea and vomiting, diarrhea, and at higher doses a severe headache, fever, and probably some cognitive impairment."

"And there's no treatment?"

Henry sighs. "Not in the most severe cases, say, over 800 rad or 8 Gy, I think the new unit of measure is called. At those levels the mortality rate is one hundred percent."

Gage takes a seat on a piece of equipment. "How quickly would a person die at those radiation levels?"

"Gage, I'm not a physician or an expert. I assume we're talking about your father?"

Gage nods.

Henry reaches for a water bottle and takes a sip, delaying. "Gosh, I don't know enough to even venture a guess, Gage."

"But not long, right?"

Henry takes another sip of water. "Probably not. Days, maybe a week or so."

Gage nods again. "'Bout what I figured. I just don't want him to suffer."

Henry pushes to his feet and puts a hand on Gage's shoulder. "Being in a coma is not such a bad thing at this point, Gage." Henry steps over to the computer cabinet and resumes his work.

Gage stands and eases over to the side of the nacelle, looking out over the landscape. He inhales a deep breath, releases it, and sucks in another, holding this one a little longer before blowing it out. Feeling helpless is something new for Gage. Used to working his way through problems, the concerns about the health of Holly and the baby, and the sadness of his father's condition are weighing heavy on his mind. And there's not a damn thing he can do about any of it.

Gage returns to the turbine's braking system and grabs a wrench from his toolbox. Working is about the only thing he can do to keep his mind off his worries. After a short break for lunch, Gage and Henry work through the rest of the afternoon. Finally, Gage puts the finishing touches on his retrofit, but they won't know for sure it's going to work until they free the turbine. As a matter of fact, there're a lot of things they're not going to know until the turbine begins turning. And that's still a day or two away, at best. Gage tosses the wrench into his toolbox and wipes his hands on a rag. The work helped to cloud his mind, muddying his thoughts and feelings. But now that the work is done for the day, the helpless feelings are trying to burrow back into his brain.

Henry steps back from the computer cabinet and looks at the sky. "Susan will probably be here shortly. Are you about finished?"

"Yep. Done about all I can do, until we unleash this beast. You?"

"I've got more work to do. Hopefully I can finish up here by midday tomorrow then start on the step-up transformer."

"How long's that going to take?"

"Don't know. Hopefully not long."

The two tidy up their workspaces and Gage cranks the doors closed before both begin the long climb down.

CHAPTER 60

Now past the mouth of the Chesapeake Bay, the going is easier for the *EmmaSophia*. And the smell is better, too, now that they're past a majority of the dead bodies. Off to the west, Norfolk and Virginia Beach are nothing but craters with wildfires still raging all along the coastline. Tanner is still at the wheel and Brad is trying his hand at fishing again. He's switched tactics, now trolling his artificial lure behind the boat. Brad's learned his lesson from earlier and keeps a close eye on the surrounding water. The mainsail is unfurled and the boat is moving at a leisurely pace.

The Dixons aren't the only ones out fishing. Boats of all types are out on the water, their lines cast out to sea. With no grocery stores, and most of the land animals succumbing to radiation poisoning, life appears to have retreated back to the early days when dinner came from the sea. Brad and Tanner's food stores are in pretty good shape, but won't stay that way for long. They have less than fifty gallons of fresh water left in the tank, and it's a constant worry that gnaws at Brad.

He has berated himself more than once for not shelling out the five grand to purchase a reverse osmosis water system. With that they wouldn't have to worry about their freshwater supplies. But who would have thought two weeks ago that freshwater would be a scarce resource? Certainly not Brad. He's hoping that all of the marinas along the Outer Banks haven't been plundered, and they might stumble upon one of the water systems. With his credit cards now worthless, he'd need to come up with something to barter with. Or steal it.

Brad stands and stretches, his fishing lure trailing behind the boat. He'd love to be able to anchor close to shore and swim to land, just so he and Tanner could stretch their legs. He picks up the binoculars and scans the shoreline a mile away. The Outer Banks begin north of the Virginia–North Carolina line and stretch south for miles. A narrow strip of land, the area is separated from the mainland by variously named bays and sounds and this water buffer spared the area from the wildfires that scoured the mainland. Brad continues scanning with the binoculars. The coast is jammed tight as teeth with people, some with tents, but far more are surviving under, or around, hastily cobbled-together shelters.

Brad's brother, Bobby, and his family, lived in the Raleigh-Durham area before moving to Seattle and Brad has spent a fair amount of time in the state. He knows about the large military installations. North Carolina is home to Fort Bragg, the largest military base in the world, and is also the home to the U.S. Special Forces. No doubt that had been target 1-A for the Russian ICBMs. Add in the Marine Corps Base Camp Lejeune, and there's a high probability that most of

North Carolina is nothing but smoldering ruins. Brad runs the numbers in his head. The state is, or was, home to over nine million people. The number of initial deaths must have been staggering, probably well in excess of six million people, Brad guesses by looking at the devastation. And that's probably on the low end of the spectrum. Brad lowers the binoculars and shakes his head. *If that's the death toll for one state, what'll it be for the rest of the country?*

As if reading his father's thoughts, Tanner asks, "Dad, how many people do you think are left?"

Brad sags onto the bench seat. "Who knows? Maybe ten to twenty percent."

"Of what?"

"Of the U.S. population."

"Which is?"

"North of three hundred eighteen million people."

Tanner takes a moment to do the math, the blood draining from his face. "That can't be right, Dad. That would mean over two hundred seventy million people were killed?"

"We may never know the exact numbers, but that's probably in the ballpark. And that's just the United States. Globally, the number will be much higher. And, this is important to remember, Tanner, the death toll will continue to climb as famine sweeps across the globe."

Tanner is silent for a moment, trying to absorb the enormity of the situation. "Why? Why a nuclear war?"

Damn it. First questions about his mother and sister and now this? Is Tanner focusing too much on death? Are we all thinking too much about the past instead of preparing for a harsh future? "I don't know what the instigating event was, but things obviously spiraled quickly out of control. There is no rational answer for what happened, Tanner. And trying to find one is a waste of energy. All we can do is survive."

"What happens when we run out of food?"

Brad sighs. "I don't have all of the answers, Tanner. Hell, I don't even know all of the questions." Brad stands and steps over to his fishing pole. "What I do know is we have an ocean full of fish. Going hungry should be the least of our worries." *Don't ask. Please don't ask,* Brad's brain is screaming.

"We haven't caught a fish yet."

Brad slowly releases his held breath, happy that Tanner didn't ask about the freshwater situation. "Fishing is all about luck and timing. Do you want to give it a try?"

"I suck at fishing."

"You can't suck any more than I do. Hopefully, now that we're past the worst of the debris, the fish will begin to bite. Hey, how many times did we watch those TV shows where the crews go days without catching one of those monster tuna?"

"Those were shows *you* watched, Dad."

"Okay, but those guys fish for a living. Everyone hits a rough patch every now and then."

Tanner shrugs. "I don't really like fish all that much, anyway."

"You just haven't had it cooked the proper way."

"That's what Mom used to say."

A sudden silence descends at the mention of Emma Dixon. Brad rushes to fill the gap. "You just wait until you taste my fish. You're going to love it."

"You have to catch one first, Dad."

CHAPTER 61

North Atlantic

The USS *New York* is momentarily stationary at a depth of 380 feet. The control room is quiet, as is the rest of the submarine. The captain ordered all current maintenance work stopped immediately and the crew remains at battle stations. The last thing they need is a mechanic dropping a wrench against the hull. Underwater, even the smallest sound can travel for miles. And with a Russian warship in the vicinity, the wrench hitting the deck could be a fatal mistake.

Captain Thompson steps over to the sonar station. "Status, Mr. Adams," he asks.

"Ten miles and closing, sir. She's turning thirty knots."

"Bearing?"

"Coming in on our starboard, Skipper. If she holds true to course, she'll pass two miles off our bow."

Thompson turns to Garcia, who is following the Russian ship on the computer. "Think she's hunting or just traversing the seas?"

"They haven't pinged their active sonar. Yet. And

we haven't been topside since Ponta Delgada. I don't think there's any way they know we're here."

"Unless they switch to active sonar." Thompson turns in Adams's direction. "Any way to tell if they're towing a sonar array?"

"I can detect it, Skipper, but I'm not seeing one at present."

"Conn, ahead one-third, hard left rudder."

"Putting some distance between us?" Garcia asks.

"Yes." Thompson walks over to the chart table and pulls up the electronic chart for their current area. Garcia stands and follows. Thompson uses his index finger as a pointer. "We're just west of the Mid-Atlantic Ridge. If we can run for a couple of miles, we can nestle down into the rift valley. Even if they go to active sonar, they'd have a very difficult job of detecting us." Thompson glances up at his XO. "The next question is, do we want to let her pass and come up behind her and fire the torpedoes?"

Garcia rubs the stubble on his chin. "I don't know, Bull. Might be best to let sleeping dogs lie. We don't have a clue if there are other ships in the vicinity. If it's a Russian destroyer, nine times out of ten, she's traveling with a battle group."

"That scenario was true before this clusterfuck began. Battle groups may no longer exist. I want to agree with you, Carlos, but I don't want to be looking over my shoulder for however long we're under way. If we take her out now, that's one last thing to worry about."

"And we could be stirring up a hornet's nest. Let's wait to see how the ship reacts as it gets closer. If she starts acting erratic with course and speed changes then we'll know she's on the hunt. If not, I say let her go."

Thompson allows Garcia's comments to ping around his brain for a few moments. "Okay, we'll play it your way for now." Thompson pivots. "Mr. Patterson, I want to park the boat in the rift valley running along the Mid-Atlantic Ridge. And I want it done quickly."

"Aye, aye, Skipper," the navigator, Mike Patterson, says.

The boat begins to descend as Patterson inserts the new course into the computer.

"Sonar, distance?"

"Seven miles and closing at thirty knots."

"Roger," Thompson says. "She's running awfully fast, Carlos. It's almost like she's in a hurry—"

"Another contact, Skipper," Adams says.

Garcia and Thompson share a surprised look.

"Bearing two-nine-two degrees, thirty-one miles and closing at thirty-five knots, sir."

"Another Russian ship?"

The sonar tech turns and smiles. "Negative, sir. One of ours."

Sailors on the bridge exchange silent high fives.

"I'll be damned," Thompson says. "Carlos, she's not hunting, she's running. Mr. Adams, what type of ship?"

"An Arleigh Burke–class destroyer, sir."

"Son, how certain are you the second contact is a U.S. Navy ship?" Thompson asks.

"One hundred percent, Skipper. If you give me a few minutes I'll probably be able to tell you exactly which one."

"Roger." Thompson glances at Garcia. "What do you think now, Carlos?"

Carlos smiles. "I say we go hunting, sir."

Thompson moves to the middle of the bridge. "Mr. Patterson, belay my last order. Conn, right rudder, thirty degrees. All ahead full." He steps over to the attack center. "Mr. White, mark that Russian destroyer and plot a firing solution. Tubes one and two are loaded. Load three and four."

"Aye, aye, Skipper," Weapons Officer White says.

"Range to target?" Thompson asks.

"Six miles, Skipper," Adams replies.

With a range of twenty-four miles, six miles is cake for the Mark-48 torpedo. But it also allows time for the enemy to evade or destroy the approaching torpedo.

Thompson turns to the attack center. "Mr. White, you have your target?"

"We do, sir," White replies.

"Stand by. We're going to sneak up behind her."

After maneuvering for several minutes, the submarine is now less than a mile behind the enemy ship.

"Fire tubes one and two," Thompson orders.

"Firing tubes one and two, Skipper." And seconds later, White says, "Fish away, fifteen hundred yards and closing."

"Conn, steady as she goes."

With the torpedoes traveling at 63 miles per hour, it's a tense fifty-second wait. "Mr. Adams, any countermeasures from the Russian ship?" Thompson asks

"Negative, sir. Ship's course remains steady."

The bridge grows silent as they await the blast wave from the two torpedoes.

"Contact, torpedoes one and two."

A small cheer erupts on the bridge.

Seconds later the submarine shudders from the blast

wave. Thompson turns to Adams. "Status of the Russian ship?"

"Multiple sonar contacts from debris, Skipper."

"Any other contacts on the screen?"

"None, other than our ship."

"Dive, take us up to periscope depth."

As the sub's nose ascends, Thompson turns and steps over to the communications area to instruct them to use all available means to contact the American destroyer.

As the sub levels off, the captain orders periscope one up and waits for the tube to finish rising. He takes a deep breath, triggers the video camera, and leans in for a look. "We scored a direct hit. The Russian destroyer is listing heavily to port and taking on water. Conn, periscope down."

"Sonar," Thompson says, "any progress in identifying our destroyer?"

"Yes, sir. I ran the screw signature through our onboard computers. She's DDG-79, the USS *Grant*."

Garcia and Thompson high-five. The captain of the USS *Grant* is Wayne Murphy, one of Thompson's classmates at the U.S. Naval Academy.

CHAPTER 62

Story City, Iowa

With no map, McDowell has no idea of the name of the town they're approaching. If there had been a sign welcoming them to such and such, it's gone now, as is the entire town. The trip from Clear Lake to wherever this is had been nothing but scorched earth. The only thing identifiable here is the metal framework of a sign that paints a vivid picture in McDowell's mind—the brightly colored golden arches that can be seen all across the globe. Just seeing the remnants of the sign has his mouth watering for a Quarter Pounder and a large fries.

McDowell eases the truck to a stop in the middle of the highway for a potty break. With no cover, McDowell stays with the boys at the back of the truck while Melissa and Lauren take the girls around front. Everyone is in a solemn mood as they shuffle to their designated areas. A few people are coughing and sputtering and a burnt stench hangs in the air. McDowell can taste the ash residue on his tongue. He unzips his pants and watches a moment as his urine cuts a trail through the ash-covered asphalt.

Lauren asks for the all clear and McDowell confirms the boys are finished and zipped up. She steps to the back of the truck and takes McDowell by the arm, leading him away from the group. "Is this ash or radioactive fallout?"

"A majority of the fallout will have decayed by now, except in the hot zones. This is mostly fire ash."

"That's a small modicum of relief," Lauren says, "but still, we're eating a lot of ash in the back of the truck. The rear tires are kicking it up by the buckets."

"I noticed some of the kids are coughing. We need to fashion some type of masks."

Lauren glances around the barren landscape. "Out of what?"

"We'll cut up the extra clothing. Only choice we have." He and Lauren return to the back of the truck and open the suitcases. McDowell pulls out his uniform jacket and spreads it out on the bed. He removes the scissors from their supply suitcase and, with a small pang of regret, begins to cut. Lauren digs through their suitcase and pulls out her paisley knit top and a long knit dress belonging to someone else. Most of the rest are jeans or shorts, too dense to be of much use. With the other pair of scissors she sets to work.

Melissa steps in to help distribute the strips of material. When she hands a random strip to Hannah, the girl freaks out.

"Who gave you permission to cut up my dress?" she screams.

Melissa sighs. "The clothes are our communal basket. They no longer belong to the individual who donated them."

"Bullshit," Hannah shouts. "That was my dress. Mine!"

Melissa grabs her by the arm and leads her away from the group. "Hannah, we needed the dress to keep from suffocating."

"I don't care. Cut up someone else's dress."

Melissa plants a hand on her hip. "It's done. Get over it."

Hannah rushes in and pushes Melissa. "Do you know how much that dress cost?"

Melissa regains her balance. "Frankly, I don't care."

"Well, I do!" Hannah shouts. "You cut up a thousand-dollar dress for a bunch of rags."

Melissa grabs Hannah by the upper arm and squeezes, pulling the girl closer.

"I don't care if it cost a million dollars. You will tie that piece of precious material around your nose and mouth. Is that understood?"

"I hate you," Hannah mutters.

"Join the crowd. Now, straighten your ass up and act like a young woman." Melissa turns away and continues handing out material as Hannah stomps back to the truck.

Once everyone has their makeshift masks in place, they climb back into the truck. McDowell adds one of the five-gallon cans of diesel to the tank and climbs behind the wheel, Lauren joining him in the cab.

"Has that girl Hannah been this way the entire trip?" McDowell asks.

"You have no idea. I've wanted to strangle her more than once. You'd think the current situation would humble her, at least a little."

McDowell shifts the truck in gear and steers down the road. "It's her defense mechanism. She from a wealthy family?"

"What was your first clue? Yes, her family is one of the wealthiest in Lubbock. And that's saying something with all the oil families in town."

"She an only child?"

"No, she has an older brother. I think he got tangled up with drugs."

"That makes sense. He probably consumed most of the family's emotional resources, leaving Hannah feeling left out."

"You a psychiatrist in addition to being a pilot?"

McDowell chuckles. "No, but when you've lived fifty-six years on this earth you learn a thing or two."

"Did you grow up in Dallas?"

"No, Wichita Falls. We moved to Dallas when I was a sophomore in high school. Talk about culture shock. What about you? Has Lubbock always been home?"

"Yep. Born and raised there. I'm sure there are far more glamorous locations, but home is home, right?"

"You're right. I've not had the pleasure of visiting your hometown."

"*Pleasure* would be a stretch."

Both chuckle. Lauren glances around the decimated landscape. "I just hope I have a home to return to."

"What are the prevailing winds out in Lubbock?"

"Ninety percent of the time, the wind is out of the south. Why?"

"There's not much out there to bomb, militarily wise. Unless they targeted the oil fields in the Permian Basin."

Lauren twists in her seat. "You think they might have?"

"Not knowing which targeting packages were selected, I can't say for sure, but unlikely. Unfortunately, I can't say the same for Dallas."

"Would they have bombed Dallas?"

"Most likely. Even if they didn't, there are enough military installations around the area that the collateral damage would be significant."

"So why are you going back?"

McDowell sighs. "I don't know where else to go."

"You still have family there?" Lauren asks.

"My parents are long gone. My ex still lives in Dallas, but thankfully our children don't."

"How many and where do they live?"

"Two. My son, Matt, is a senior at the University of Colorado in Boulder. I think he went there for the skiing and not the school. My daughter, Charlotte, the oldest, is working on a master's at Stanford."

"Are they safe?"

"I sure as hell hope so. Boulder's a good distance away from the big military bases, and Palo Alto is right on the coast. California was probably hammered, but the coastal breezes would have pushed most of the radiation inland." He pauses. "What about you, any children?" McDowell asks.

"Are you kidding? Teaching middle school is one of the best forms of birth control on the planet." They both share a laugh.

"No Mr. Thomas?"

"Nope. I was in a relationship for a year and a half, but things went downhill when he got transferred to Houston."

McDowell winces. Houston is a huge population center. "Long-distance relationships are difficult."

"Yes, they are," Lauren says. "You never remarried?"

"No. Once was enough for me. I've had a couple of relationships, but it's difficult with the amount of travel I do. Or did, I should say."

"Will things ever return to normal?"

"Not in my lifetime. Hopefully it will during yours."

CHAPTER 63

Memphis

After a few hours at the home of Sarah and Christopher Michaels, Zane is eager to be back on the road. The trip from the clinic proved to be uneventful and Sarah hasn't mentioned anything to her husband about the shoot-out in her waiting room, yet. It might have something to do with the presence of their two young children. Alyx steps over to give Sarah a hug before moving on to Christopher. Zane steps into the void and hugs Sarah before shaking Christopher's hand. Alyx grabs the bag of medical supplies Sarah had prepared, and Zane handles the shotgun. They step out onto the porch and Zane takes a moment to reconnoiter the area.

"Wait a minute," Christopher says before ducking back in the house. He returns a moment later with two cases of powdered infant formula. He hands them to Alyx. "For Holly and the baby. Protect it with your life because that's going to be more valuable than gold."

Alyx leans forward and kisses Christopher on the cheek. "Thank you. I owe you."

Christopher waves a hand. "Just be careful out there."

Not sensing any threats, Zane descends the steps with Alyx following. He waits for her to store the supplies and climb in before sliding behind the wheel. Zane lays the shotgun on the seat and backs out of the drive, his eyes constantly scanning.

"Alyx, will you pull out a ten-day supply of the expired antibiotics?"

Alyx nods and rummages through the bag, pulling out four sample bottles of amoxicillin. "What do you want me to do with the rest of this stuff?"

"Stuff it under the seat. We need the bag to remain hidden." Zane pulls out onto a main thoroughfare and follows the signs for I-40. The next intersection is blocked by expired vehicles, forcing Zane to back-track. After a series of turns and switchbacks, he spots a highway on-ramp and carefully navigates around a clog of cars and pulls onto the highway.

"What's the game plan when we get to the road-block?"

"Are you okay with making the approach while I cover you with the shotgun?"

"And say what?"

"Tell them the truth. We're only passing through their state on our way home."

"And if they refuse?"

"I haven't thought that far ahead. Let's just hope whoever's leading the ragtag army needs some antibiotics."

"Should I offer additional drugs?"

"No, that would tip our hand." Zane slows the truck as they near the roadblock. He eases forward, hoping to get close enough for the shotgun to be effective, but two men armed with rifles step out from behind a tractor-trailer rig. "Damn, we may not get a chance to talk to the main guy."

The two men approach, one on each side of the truck. Zane cranks down his window.

"The bridge is closed," the man says, coming to a stop six feet away, the rifle tight to his shoulder and aimed dead center at Zane's chest.

The other man assumes a similar position on Alyx's side of the truck.

"We're not stopping in Arkansas. We're only trying to make it home to Weatherford, Oklahoma."

"I don't give a shit where you're going. The bridge is closed." The man sweeps his gaze across the inside of the cab and Zane feels a chill race down his spine. He slowly works his hand toward the shotgun lying in the middle of the seat.

"All we want to do is drive across your state," Zane says, his hand lighting on the shotgun. He quietly cocks both barrels.

"I'll say it for the last time—the bridge is closed," the man says. He peers into the cab again. "Unless you're willing to trade for a little pussy."

"The pussy's not mine to trade, but I assure you she's not interested."

The man waves the rifle barrel Alyx's way. "Why don't we let the little lady decide?"

Zane's eyes flick to the rearview mirror to check behind them and he slowly works his hand toward the shifter. "Pussy's off the table. We do have some antibiotics to trade." He carefully bumps the lever to reverse and returns his hand to the shotgun.

"I might need the antibiotics after. She carrying any diseases?"

"Do you want to trade our passing for the antibiotics or not? Or maybe I should speak to the leader of your outfit."

"You're talking to him, and I told you what I wanted. How about you two step out of the truck?"

Zane steals a glance at the other man. He appears relaxed, his rifle pointed toward the ground. Zane quickly paints a mental picture in his head. "We don't want any trouble. We'll find another way to cross."

"See, I've got a problem with that." The man makes the mistake of grabbing his crotch. "I've already got a hard—"

Zane whips the shotgun up and empties both barrels before stomping on the gas. "Duck," he shouts as the front windshield spiders with cracks from a rifle bullet. Zane glances at the rearview and whips the wheel hard to the left. The truck skids and threatens to roll over before the tires find purchase. Zane slams the shifter into drive and floors the accelerator as rifle shots ring out behind them. He ducks low in the seat just before the back window explodes, sending glass fragments across the cab. He whips around a busted truck for cover and keeps the accelerator floored. He hits the first off-ramp they come to and nearly collides with a dead Oldsmobile, swerving at the last second and clipping the car's rear bumper. He's on the verge of losing control of the truck when he stands on the brakes. Now well below the highway, they're out of the line of fire. The truck skids to a stop. Zane is shaking as he eases down on the gas pedal, steering toward a side road. "Alyx, reload the shotgun."

With trembling hands, Alyx feeds two more shells into the chamber and snaps the breech closed. "Now what?"

"I'll figure that out when my nerves settle." Zane takes a long moment to regain his composure then turns to look at Alyx. "That didn't go as planned."

"You think? Thank you, Zane."

"I did kind of speak out of turn. I hope I didn't spoil a romantic moment for you."

"He forgot to bring flowers on the first date."

They share a nervous chuckle and the tension drains from Zane's body. The shaking subsides and Zane shifts in his seat. "Alyx, will you grab the map and find the closest crossing?" After Zane lost the map by throwing it at the pit bull, the Michaels found an old, yellowed map of Tennessee in one of their junk drawers and passed it on to Zane.

Alyx unfolds the map across her lap. "There's a crossing just south of here on Interstate 55."

"It'll be the same there, I bet. What's next?"

Alyx traces her finger along the river. "The next crossing south is Lula, Mississippi, that crosses over to West Helena, Arkansas. It's about thirty miles from here."

"I've had my fill of Arkansans, or Tennesseans, or whoever is responsible for that roadblock. What's the next crossing?" Zane asks.

"We'd have to drive all the way to Greenville, Mississippi."

"That far south is a no-go. Mississippi and Louisiana are littered with military bases. You probably couldn't find an unburned blade of grass in either state."

Alyx returns to the map. "The nearest crossing to the north is about fifty miles away. We'd have to backtrack to Highway 51 and take that north to Interstate 155 and cross over into southern Missouri."

"That's a lot of backtracking, but I think it's our only option." Zane eases up an on-ramp to the highway, heading back the way they came.

CHAPTER 64

North Atlantic

Still at periscope depth, Thompson is in a quandary. The USS *Grant* is ten miles out and the sub's radio crew has failed to make radio contact with the ship. With no way of knowing if the radio problems are on his end, or with the *Grant*, or a systemwide failure, a surprise surfacing could be dicey. With no visual markings on the hull, there's concern the destroyer crew might misidentify the *New York* as an enemy sub. "Sonar, any other contacts, surface or otherwise?"

"Negative, Skipper. Just our destroyer, sir," Sonar Tech Adams, replies. "She's slowed down and is now turning fifteen knots."

"She's using one screw to conserve fuel," Thompson mutters, turning to Garcia. "Think they'll know we're friendly with the Russian warship torpedoed and on the verge of sinking?"

"I don't think we have much choice one way or the other and we have no idea who else is playing in the sandbox. In all reality the *Grant* could have sunk us when we launched the torpedoes."

"Periscope up," Thompson orders. He steps over and catches handles as the scope slides into position. He walks a circle until the destroyer comes into view. He dials up the magnification and studies the approaching ship. With no radio contact, he wants to make damn sure nothing is amiss. The ship is still too distant to distinguish any crew characteristics, but all appears normal. He steps away from the periscope. "Dive, take us to the surface."

The nose of the submarine tilts up as the boat ascends. Sailing at periscope depth it doesn't take long for the immense boat to breaks through the surface. Thompson turns to the quartermaster. "Chief Chambers, send someone topside to run up the flag," Thompson orders. "Conn, send a helmsman up the sail." Once his orders are confirmed, he and Garcia make their way to the forward hatch. After strapping on the life vests, Thompson grabs the binoculars and a handheld radio, and both climb up, stepping out onto the matte black deck. The destroyer is now only three miles away and heading straight for the surfaced sub. Thompson puts the high-power binoculars to his eyes and glasses the bridge area of the ship. The destroyer is still too far away to distinguish much, other than a group of sailors standing watch. Thompson puts the radio to his mouth and triggers the talk button. "Helm, come to a heading of one-three-six degrees. All ahead two-thirds." With both ships now moving toward each other the gap will close quickly.

Thompson takes advantage of being topside by inhaling and exhaling several deep breaths. The briny scent of the sea smells much fresher than the recycled air below. With the Gulf Stream current, the breeze is warm and he can almost feel his skin sucking up the moisture from the humidity. With the destroyer now closer, Thompson returns to his binoculars. He adjusts the focus and zeros in on the bridge. He laughs and hands the binoculars to Garcia. "Murphy has a message for you."

Garcia puts the binoculars to his eyes and starts laughing. Standing on the bridge of the ship, with binoculars to his eyes, is Captain Wayne Murphy, the middle finger of his right hand extended. Garcia returns the salute and hands the binoculars back to the captain. "You know, I don't think I've laughed since this whole mess started."

"None of us have." Thompson radios all stop and they wait for the ominous-looking warship to pull alongside. Several sailors spill out of the front hatch of the sub. They attach cleats to the deck of the sub fore and aft and wait for the *Grant* crew to toss over the ropes. The crew on the destroyer lowers fenders over the rail to keep the two ships from bumping against each other and within moments the two ships are tied together and the destroyer's crew lowers down a gangway as the ship's anchor drops to the bottom of the sea.

Murphy is there to greet Thompson and Garcia and they exchange back-slapping hugs. "You're still as ugly as ever," Thompson says to Murphy.

Murphy, at six-two and a heavily muscled 220 pounds, is the tall, dark, handsome man women swoon over. And swoon they did, all through their academy years. Thompson stopped counting after the first year because he couldn't compete—with the numbers or in the bedroom. Thompson drapes an arm over Murphy's shoulders as they make their way inside.

CHAPTER 65

Des Moines, Iowa

With darkness approaching, McDowell is searching for a place to hole up for the night. The problem—they're still north of Des Moines, and not a single structure remains. He slows the truck when they come to a fork in the highway. The lettering on the overhead signs is blistered and unreadable. It appears one road leads to the city center, while the other swings out to the west. He opts for the western spur, hoping it's a loop around the downtown area. Here, some of the larger concrete structures are still standing, but the insides are hollowed out from the fires. If McDowell remembers correctly, the Iowa National Guard Joint Forces Headquarters had been located on the north side in Des Moines, meaning conditions should improve the farther south they go.

They cross a wide debris-filled river and the landscape begins to change.

"Did the river act as a firebreak?" Lauren asks.

"It played a part, for sure. But mostly it was wind

direction. I've flown into Des Moines several times and we almost always faced a southerly wind."

Intact neighborhoods begin to appear, and McDowell's spirit lifts a notch. Five miles farther on, the road makes a long looping curve to the south. McDowell leans forward to click on the headlights and curses when nothing happens.

"I guess the damn headlights don't work. We need to find someplace to bed down before it gets too dark."

Lauren leans forward in the seat. "I see a sign for a hotel ahead."

"Probably already filled with refugees. We need someplace out of the way. A warehouse, or something similar to the office building we stayed in last night."

Lauren rocks her head from side to side, trying to pop her neck. "Damn, and I was hoping for a bed."

"I doubt you'll find a bed until you get home to Lubbock."

"You sure know how to shoot down a girl's dream. Can we find someplace where we won't be interrupted by a gunfight in the middle of the night?"

"I could do without that, myself." McDowell points to a cluster of buildings on the other side of the roadway. "That look like a school to you?"

"Don't do that to me, please. Besides, the local community is probably using it as a shelter since it's government property."

"Didn't think about that." McDowell continues driving south. They hit an industrial area and he pulls off the highway. Time is of the essence now as the darkness settles in. They drive past a Lowe's and head deeper into the complex, passing a cluster of plundered restaurants and small office buildings. McDowell spots a building off by itself and pulls into the drive. According to the sign, it's some type of financial services company. "This place might well be out of business forever. How's it look?"

"It's fine, if we can get inside."

"We'll get inside—that I can assure you." He pulls the truck around behind the building and noses into a dense pocket of trees and kills the engine. The truck shakes as those in back jump to the ground. McDowell pushes out of the cab and arches his back, trying to stretch out the kinks. The stretching offers little relief and he reaches back inside and grabs the shotgun, slinging it over his shoulder. "Hey, gang," he says in a low voice, "keep the noise to a minimum. Unload the food, water, and utensils only." He eases around to the other side of the truck and unlocks the glove box. After tucking the Glock into his waistband, he grabs the ammo for both weapons and steps over to Lauren. "The back door is steel and set in a metal frame. Keep them back here and I'll unlock it from the inside."

McDowell makes his way around to the front of the building. He clicks on his flashlight and twists the lens to red. The front entry is a pair of glass doors bookended by two large plate glass windows. He turns and shines the light around the landscaped flower bed and finds exactly what he's looking for. McDowell picks up the rock, turns, and tosses the rock at the door on the right. The glass shatters, launching an avalanche of tiny pieces as the tempered glass falls to the pavement. He steps through the frame and pauses to listen. After several moments of silence, he makes his way toward the back of the building, threading his way through a disorganized stockroom to unlock the back door.

While the students unload the truck, McDowell reconnoiters the rest of the building.

Measuring maybe 10,000 square feet, the building contains a handsomely decorated reception area, complete with a comfortable-looking large leather sofa and a pair of overstuffed leather wing chairs—all positioned precisely on an expensive-looking Persian rug and facing a large natural-stone fireplace. McDowell continues down the hall, wondering who would be crazy enough to let this company handle their assets after seeing the opulence of the reception area. The opulence continues as he passes a half a dozen offices, all outfitted like some private Manhattan gentleman's club with expensive furniture and real artwork on the walls. At an intersection of hallways, he finds a modern conference room with seating for thirty. Down the next hall, he discovers where the real work was done. The generous, rectangular room is bisected by a series of cubicles while the perimeter of the room is made up of series of smaller glass-fronted offices. At the end of the hallway is a small break room, complete with a refrigerator and coffeemaker. McDowell returns to the stockroom. Four flashlights are on, lighting the room.

"Stan, may we have a fire?" Lauren asks.

"Let me scout around outside before I answer. In the interim, there's a kitchen down the far hallway. Might see what you can scare up." McDowell eases out the back door. He walks a wide circle around the building. The back of the building butts up to a greenbelt to the south, and to the north and east are more deserted office buildings. Curious to know what's on the other side of the natural buffer, he makes his way through the trees. After a hundred yards, he steps out onto a residential street. The neighborhood is concerning, but with the greenbelt, not a deal breaker. McDowell retraces his steps and returns to a lean-to he spotted on the far side building. Pulling the door open, he finds a stack of firewood and loads up, returning to a secluded area where the building's walls form an inside corner. Sheltered on two sides, the spot is hidden from the main road. McDowell dumps his load of firewood and returns inside.

The one thing an investment business never lacks is paper. After gathering up a handful, he returns to his fire spot. He shreds some paper and lights it. After adding more paper, the fire is ready for the wood. It looks well seasoned and doesn't take long to ignite. McDowell returns to the storeroom. "Fire's going. A couple of rules before we head out: No loud noises and I'll be the one handling the flashlight." He turns to Melissa. "Any luck in the kitchen?"

"We found two dozen cans of food, mostly chili and soup, and a case of bottled water. I think the kids are wanting to sample the chili."

"That sounds really good to me. If you'll dump it all in the big pot, we'll get the party started."

After dinner, and after a nature call, the kids break into groups to bed down for the night. Because of their relative seclusion, and because of the possible side effects from the greasy chili, it's decided the students could go outside in pairs if anyone needs to use the bathroom during the night. McDowell unslings his shotgun and settles into one of the leather wing chairs. Melissa takes the other and Lauren stretches out on the couch. McDowell reaches back and removes the Glock, placing it on a side table in case it's needed during the night. He's hoping like hell it isn't.

CHAPTER 66

Weatherford

It's now full dark and there's still no sign of Susan Reed. Gage's worry meter is redlining as he sits on the trailer. Gage had left his flashlight with his tools, 260 feet up, and now, with the smoke-filled skies obscuring the moon and stars, it's darker than a windowless room with a broken lightbulb. It was daylight when they descended the turbine, and climbing the treacherous tower ladder again, this time in the dark, is something neither he nor Henry is willing to risk. Without aid of a flashlight they start the journey home. The going is slow as they travel down the winding gravel drive, working their way to the main road. Gage peers into darkness, astounded by the total lack of light. The town is only a couple of miles away, yet you wouldn't know it existed if you didn't know for sure it was there. Add in the absence of vehicle headlights and the darkness is absolute. Gage trips over a limb and falls on his ass, losing all sense of direction. He pushes to his feet with no idea which way to go. "Henry?"

"I'm here, Gage," Henry says. "Are you okay?"

"I'm fine. Say something else so I can find you."

"Did I mention how pissed I am at Susan? She knows better than to leave us out here in the dark."

Gage zeros in on his voice and shuffles in that direction, his hands extended, searching for contact. He brushes across the fabric of Henry's shirt and they play handsy until Henry grabs one of Gage's hands. "I've got you, Gage," he says, locking hands with his son-in-law.

"I'm worried something is happening with the baby," Gage says. "That's the only reason Susan didn't show up."

"Gage, you're going to worry yourself sick. Hell, the truck battery could be dead. Or maybe she had a flat or ran out of gas."

It's difficult for Gage to know if Henry actually believes what he's saying without seeing his face. "I put a new battery in last month, and the gas tank was full when we left home."

"Well, it could still be a flat or something else."

"It's the something else that has me worried, Henry."

"Worrying about it is not going to do a damn bit of good. Here, take the other end of my belt. We'll use it to stay together."

Gage reaches, finds the belt, and wraps it around his hand. "Which way is the main road?"

"Good question. I think straight ahead. If we can stay on the gravel we should be in good shape. I didn't pay any attention when we were coming in. How far to the main road?"

"A couple hundred yards."

With no point of reference, they stumble on, hoping they're traveling in the right direction. As if the gods were taking pity on them, a swarm of fireflies move up out of the creek bottom and fly in their direction. You don't really realize how bright they are until you see them in a lightless world. By the hundreds, they keep coming, swarming high in the air, lighting the landscape in an eerie greenish yellow glow. Henry and Gage hurry along the gravel road, trying to imprint the layout ahead in their minds. The light fades moments later as the fireflies take a meandering flight toward the creek.

Henry and Gage walk for several moments and somehow lose contact with the gravel at one of the bends in the road. They keep plodding forward until Henry shouts, "Stop, Gage. We've hit the fence." He curses as he tries to unhook his shirt from the sharp barbs. "We must be close to the road. We'll have to walk along the fence line until we run into the cattle guard." Once untangled, Henry places a finger on the upper wire and slowly walks to the right. With barbs every eight inches or so, the going is slow, and Henry nicks his finger more than once. Shuffle stepping and feeling for obstructions with his boots, Henry moves forward with Gage following closely behind, the belt grasped in his hand. Eventually, Henry comes to an iron post and feels around with his foot to find the cattle guard. Made out of pipe gapped every few inches, the guard is centered over a depression in the road and allows vehicle access without having to fool with a gate. The cattle won't walk across it, but Gage has seen a horse cross one without even a second thought.

They climb atop the cattle guard and cross, walking up a short incline to the paved road. They hang a right and move toward what they believe is the middle of the road and pick up the pace. Unless they run into a stalled car, the asphalt allows for quicker progress. "There's the house," Henry says.

In the distance they can see the lights on at the Reed residence, the only one with the lights burning. With a beacon to lead them and a straight, smooth road before them, they gobble up the distance and turn up the drive after twenty minutes of walking. Gage's old truck is gone, and a tingle of dread races down his spine. They hurry to the house and Henry swings the door open and they step inside. Henry stops just inside the door and Gage runs into the back of him. Peering over Henry's shoulder, Gage spots the reason—a pool of watery blood on the entryway tile.

CHAPTER 67

Hayti, Missouri

Zane and Alyx cross the Mississippi River as the muted sun sinks toward the water. After traveling fifty miles out of the way, they finally found a bridge that wasn't being barricaded. They bounce across the bridge and pick up Highway 412 headed west. Zane glances at the gas gauge and winces. The needle is hovering above empty and they're in the middle of nowhere. With the distance between houses measured in miles, they're surrounded by fields planted with crops that will never be harvested.

Zane glances over at Alyx. "We need fuel. And I could go for something to eat."

"How much gas do we have left?"

"Not enough. How much food do we have?"

Alyx digs through her backpack. "We have three cans of Spam and a sleeve of saltines. And the remaining protein bars. Maybe we can find an abandoned house up ahead."

"I doubt it. These farmers don't like to stray too far from home."

"How would you know? Did you grow up on a farm? Here, you've been in my pants and I don't know a damn thing about your previous life."

Zane glances her way. "The way Sarah talked, it sounds like that might be a common occurrence for you."

There's a pause before Alyx says, "Do you want me to describe, in detail, the number of times and ways I've been fucked?"

Zane's can feel the heat in his cheeks. "No."

"Then don't make statements like that."

They ride in silence the next few miles. Zane occasionally glances her way, but as the darkness deepens, he can no longer gauge her mood by her facial expressions. He leans forward and clicks on the headlights. It's not like Zane is a saint. He can count the number of women he's been with—if he uses both hands. They pass a sign welcoming them to Kennett and hit the town two miles later. The first store they pass is a looted Walmart Supercenter. Zane slows and whips a U-turn, pulling into the store's parking lot. A good number of expired farm trucks dot the lot and Zane cruises through, pulling up next to an old Dodge.

"Will you cover me with the shotgun?"

Alyx grabs the shotgun, pushes open the door, and climbs out in silence. It's nearing full dark, and Zane hurries to siphon the gas. He gets the gas to flow with the first suck and crams the hose into Old Goldie's tank. Zane's exhausted from the adrenaline spikes and ebbs from earlier in the day. His brain is working overtime to tamp down the images of the five people he shot. He's not suffering regret, but it's damn difficult to kill someone and not wonder if they had families, or others who cared very deeply for them. The hose gurgles and he pulls it out of both tanks and tosses it in the bed.

"Good to go, Alyx."

Alyx squats to pee before pulling open the door and climbing into the cab. Zane scoots around the back and retakes his position behind the wheel. He glances Alyx's way even though he can't see her. "I'm sorry, Alyx. That comment was way out of bounds. I was no angel, either."

The silence is made longer by the darkness. Zane sighs, drops the truck in gear, and pulls out of the lot, making a right on 412. The evening is warm and muggy and there's sweat dripping down Zane's back, soaking his shirt. Food isn't their only problem—they're also going to need water soon. They travel in silence for another few miles, before Alyx finally speaks. "I bet you were a real player, weren't you?"

Zane can feel the heat rise in his cheeks again. "I wouldn't say that. But yes, I've had relationships."

"How are those different from mine?"

Zane searches for the right terminology. "Maybe in frequency?"

Alyx sighs in the dark. "Whatever."

Zane knows that's a dangerous word and remains silent as he slows to read a sign: ST. FRANCIS RIVER. They cross the bridge and Zane turns off onto a dirt road leading down to the water. The headlights reflect off the surface of the slowly moving water and Zane pulls deep into a thicket of trees and kills the lights and the engine.

"What are we doing?" Alyx asks in a flat tone.

"I'm wiped out. I'm going to rinse off in the river and sleep for a little while. Unless you want to drive?"

"No," Alyx says before pushing open her door and stepping out.

Zane grabs a flashlight and the shotgun, and climbs out of the truck. Frogs are croaking, filling the night with sound. Zane clicks on his flashlight and shields the lens, picking his way down to the water. He sweeps the beam across the surface, looking for possible dangers, such as tree stumps or other obstacles. Finding none, he clicks off the light, lays down the shotgun, pushes off his shoes, and strips out of his clothes. Carrying his clothes with him, he slides out into the water. He spends a few moments rinsing out his filthy clothing before carrying them back to the bank where he spreads them out to dry. He returns to the water and drifts a little farther out, dunking his head beneath the surface and scrubbing his face. He pops back up and scans the riverbank, searching for Alyx's flashlight. She's not there, or if she is, she's not carrying a flashlight. He drifts along with the current, cursing himself for broaching the subject of Alyx's past. It's none of his damn business and he knows it. Without warning something clamps on to his thigh, and fearing it might be a gator, he shouts and thrashes in the water, trying to push whatever it is away.

Alyx pops up in front of him, laughing. "You're forgiven," she says, climbing into his arms and wrapping her long legs around his torso.

CHAPTER 68

Weatherford

Gage is despondent, refusing to eat the small dinner Henry prepared. His gaze is repeatedly drawn to the foyer, where they discovered the pool of blood that Henry has since cleaned up. Sitting on the edge of the sofa with his face buried in his hands, Gage's mind spins with possibilities—none of them good. They don't know if the blood had been Holly's or if Susan had somehow injured herself. And with no phones or other working automobiles, all they can do is wait. Gage pushes to his feet and paces the living room like a caged lion. Henry emerges from the kitchen with two highball glasses filled to the halfway point with bourbon. He passes one to Gage and sags into his easy chair.

Gage gulps the bourbon in one swallow, the alcohol singeing his throat and landing heavily in his already roiling stomach. He places the empty glass on an end table and continues to pace. He glances at the clock again. It's nearing 11:00 P.M. "Henry, do you know where Holly's doctor lives?"

"I know the neighborhood, Gage. It's across the street from Prairie West Golf Club, but that's a good five miles from here. And we don't know for sure that's where they are." Henry watches as Gage paces to the far end of the room, turns, and retraces his steps. "You're about to wear a hole in my wood floors, Gage."

Gage doesn't even crack a smile as he continues pacing. "First my dad and now this," he mutters.

"Gage we don't know what *this* is. You're letting your imagination get the better of you."

Gage pauses his pacing. "Okay, Henry, what's your theory?"

"I don't have a theory. And all you have are a bunch of suppositions."

"And a pool of blood in the entryway," Gage says with a little too much heat in his voice.

"It could be Holly's water broke and she's now delivering the baby."

"If that's the case why hasn't Susan returned to pick me up? I'm sure Holly would want me there, goddammit."

Henry takes a sip of bourbon, delaying. "I don't know, Gage."

"Exactly. We don't know a damn thing." Gage tires of pacing and sags onto the sofa.

"Maybe Susan is helping with the delivery," Henry offers. "The doctor could probably use an extra pair of hands now that the hospital is closed."

Gage pushes out of the sofa. "I'm going over there."

"You don't know where the doctor lives."

"I'll look for the truck." Gage pauses. "My shotgun is in the truck. Can I borrow one of yours?"

Henry drains his bourbon and stands. "Only if you'll let me go with you."

"No, you stay here in case they come back. I'll take Arapaho Road over to Lyle. You can tell Susan to come pick me up."

"We could just as easily leave a note. Holly is your wife, but she's also my baby girl, Gage. I'm as concerned as you are."

Gage's anger evaporates. "I'm sorry, Henry. I know Holly is important to both of us. If you'll write the note, I'll get the shotgun."

"Grab my deer rifle and a handful of cartridges. I don't have any expectations of trouble, but I'd feel more comfortable if we're both armed."

Gage nods and heads down the hallway to Henry's study. He and Henry, along with Gage's father and brother, used to hunt every year, both birds and deer. But somewhere along the way Gage lost his taste for killing. The same feeling must have passed through the group because none of them have been hunting for several years. But that doesn't mean any of them have parted with their guns. Chalk it up to life in small-town America. Gage enters the four-digit code and spins the wheel, unlocking the gun safe. Of course, with Henry being an engineer, the eight weapons are perfectly ordered by type and caliber, with a couple of handguns precisely arranged on the upper shelf. Gage selects the Kimber SuperAmerica for Henry. A bolt-action rifle, the weapon is chambered for the .308 Winchester cartridge—large enough to stop most anything on four legs and absolutely lethal for any two-legged species. Gage's weapon of choice is a Browning 12-gauge pump shotgun, prized the world over for its close-in stopping power. After grabbing ammo for each from the bottom drawer of the safe, Gage relocks the door and returns to the kitchen. He lays the weapons and ammo on the counter. "Flashlights?"

"In the utility room. I'll grab them if you'll load the guns."

Gage loads the rifle magazine and seats it in place before feeding the double-aught shotgun shells into the shotgun. He puts a handful of shotgun shells in both pockets and lays out extra rifle ammo as Henry, carrying a pair of headband lights, returns from the utility room.

He passes one of the lights to Gage. "They'll allow us to keep our hands free." Henry looks over the weapons on the counter. "Think we need a handgun?"

"If we can't get out of a jam with what we're carrying, a handgun's not going to do us a damn bit of good."

"Agreed. I left the note by the coffeepot. You ready?"

Gage nods and heads toward the front door, his eyes lingering on the spot where the blood was found.

CHAPTER 69

North Atlantic

With their movements cloaked by darkness, most of the crew from the USS *New York* is now aboard the destroyer, enjoying their first real meal in days. They'll rotate with those crew members still on the sub so everyone has the opportunity for chow. After dinner in the officers' mess, Captain Murphy leads Thompson and Garcia to the officers' wardroom. He unlocks a file cabinet and pulls out a bottle of Maker's Mark bourbon, easily identifiable by its distinctive red wax top. Murphy gathers up three coffee mugs and pours an equal measure into each and passes them around.

"Why aren't you with a battle group, Murph?" Thompson asks.

"We were delayed at port waiting on parts. We were on our way to join Carrier Strike Group Two when the world turned to shit."

"When did you leave port?" Garcia asks.

"A week before it all started, and we haven't refueled since. The fuel level is currently at forty percent and I have no idea when or how we'll refuel." Murphy drains his bourbon and pours himself another. "How long have you been out?"

"We're pushing a hundred days right now," Thompson answers. "We're hoping you'll part with some of your food stores."

"What's mine is yours. How long you plan on cruising around in that tin can?"

Thompson chugs his bourbon and pushes his empty cup across the table for a refill. "I don't know the answer to that, Murph. To tell the truth, I don't have a damn clue what to do. Have you heard anything over the radio?"

"Crickets. We've been patrolling around this area hoping to find other friendlies, but so far the only one we've encountered is the Russian destroyer you torpedoed. And if the Aegis system was working properly, I'd have sunk her three days ago. I think the EMPs fried some components."

"Did the Russians try to engage you?" Garcia asks.

"No. Which means he was probably running empty on hardware. Don't know what the hell that means," Murphy says. "I don't know if they've been over here hunting our ships and he shot his wad or what. It's a mystery."

"What are your plans?" Thompson asks.

"I'm hoping we make radio contact with someone up the food chain. They can't all be dead, can they?"

Thompson takes a sip of bourbon, relishing the heat as it travels down his throat. "I don't know, Murph. You would think some of them survived. Maybe all the communication satellites have been destroyed."

"Even the geosync satellites? Hard to believe anyone would target military satellites twenty-two thousand miles out in orbit."

Thompson shrugs. "Hell maybe everyone *is* dead. But you risk running out of fuel waiting for a voice over the radio."

"I won't allow that to happen, Bull."

"Think any naval bases survived?" Garcia asks. "A place where you could refuel?"

Murphy takes a swallow of bourbon. "We made a run by Norfolk and that's a no-go. A dozen ships have been sunk or are in the process of sinking. The entire port facility is gone—wiped off the face of the earth. I assume the same applies to all the other navy facilities, including yours in Kings Bay. From here, if we can't make contact, we're going to make a run for the U.S. Virgin Islands. I'm damn sure not going to sit out here dead in the water."

"And do what once you're there?" Thompson asks.

Murphy shrugs. "I guess we'll dock her and go ashore. Don't know what else to do or where to go." Murphy grows silent and takes a long sip of bourbon. "My wife and three kids . . . were . . . in . . . Norfolk. Same . . . for most of . . . the . . . crew." Murphy chokes up and pauses. After several moments, he continues. "There's nothing . . . left . . . there . . . for any . . . of us."

Thompson stands and moves around the table, taking a seat next to his longtime friend. He leans forward and wraps an arm around Murphy's shoulders. No words are exchanged as Murphy breaks into sobs. After several moments, he sniffles a final time and blows out a long, stuttering breath. The cup trembles when he lifts it to drain the remaining bourbon.

Thompson frees his arm and leans back in his chair. "We'll go with you to the Virgin Islands." He looks to Garcia, who nods. "We'll make our own little convoy. I'd feel a hell of a lot safer with a surface ship to keep an eye on things." Thompson leans forward and places his elbows on the table. "I do have one favor, though."

"Shoot," Murphy says.

Thompson struggles for a way to frame his request, in light of the last few moments. He decides straight on is the only way. "We make a run by Myrtle Beach then run south to Jacksonville. Karen and the kids left for a vacation at Myrtle Beach a week before everything happened. And Carlos's family and most of my crew's families were living in Jacksonville."

"Deal," Murphy says. "We should have enough fuel and it would be nice to know . . ." Murphy pauses, trying to reel in his emotions. After a moment or two of silence, he exhales and says, ". . . that some of our families survived this madness."

CHAPTER 70

Weatherford

Gage or Henry will occasionally light their headlamp to ensure they're not about to crash into a dead auto or to confirm their position on the road. Approaching the third mile of their five-mile trek they have yet to encounter another human, which isn't unusual considering the absolute darkness and the time. The fetid stench of decomposing cattle carcasses greets them when they reach the first section of Marston land. Before hell rained down, Gage's buddy Mitch Marston was one of the largest cattle owners in the county, often running four hundred head or so across his three sections of land. Now the two thousand acres is littered with cattle remains and it will be weeks before the stench fades.

A vehicle turns at the next intersection, the headlights flaring across the road.

"I bet that's them," Henry says.

Gage chambers a shell. "Nope. Headlights are too close to the ground."

"Who do you think it is?"

"I have a hunch and, if it proves correct, I'd rather be standing here with a loaded gun."

Taking the hint, Henry pulls the rifle bolt back and a large .308 cartridge pops into the breech. He slides the bolt home and clicks on the safety. "Let's don't forget why we are out here, Gage."

"I haven't forgotten. I'm desperate to find Holly, but I've got a bad feeling about who might be driving that car."

With their lights extinguished Henry and Gage move over to the side of the road as the automobile drifts closer, the headlights dancing across the blacktop. With enough firepower to stop an elephant, the thought of hiding never enters their minds. The car slows as it nears, and the rumble of the engine is loud in the quiet night.

Gage steps into the middle of the road and clicks on his light. The shotgun is braced across his chest and his index finger is stroking the trigger as the car coasts to a stop. Gage walks to the driver's side and bends down to look in the car. Inside are two men, late twenties or early thirties, with long, greasy hair and scruffy beards. The driver has two tears tattooed near the corner of his left eye, their crude form suggesting an unskilled hand. Jailhouse tats, most likely, Gage thinks. "You're driving Mitch Martson's '68 Mustang GT Fastback and neither of you are Mitch Marston."

"We found the car," the driver says.

Playing in Gage's mind is the arsenal Mitch keeps at his house. A gun nut, Mitch has one of about everything, including an AR-15, a modified Uzi submachine gun, and a fully automatic AK-47. Henry works his way around the back of the car and takes up position on the other side. "Bullshit," Gage says. "That car stays covered in my friend's barn. You didn't find shit. What happened to Mitch?" Gage asks.

"Mitch who?" the driver says. "We don't know no Mitch."

"You're not from around here, are you, pard?" Gage asks.

"Nope, just passing through."

"In this town, we look out for our neighbors. Now, I'll ask again. What happened to the man you stole this car from?"

The driver turns and smiles, his hands buried somewhere in his lap. "Okay, you're right. We took the car out of the barn. But we didn't see this Mitch person you're talking about."

"So, if I let you go, I'll find my friend and his family safe and sound at home? I may have been born at night, but it damn sure wasn't *last* night. Get out of the car. Both of you."

"Or what?" the driver asks.

In one swift motion, Gage pulls the shotgun tight to his shoulder and fires, the double-aught buckshot shredding the front tire. Gage jacks another shell and swings the barrel up, centering it on the driver. "Appears you have a flat. Now get out of the fucking car."

The man nods and pushes the door open. Before the door comes to a stop, the man's arm comes up, the Uzi grasped in his hand. The Uzi barks, sending out a wild spray of bullets as Gage squeezes the trigger. Most of the man's head disappears, coating the interior of the car with a ghoulish mix of blood, bone, and brain matter. Gage takes one large step to the left and brings the shotgun to bear on the second man, who's struggling to get the AK-47 up and in firing position. Gage fires again, the muzzle flash lighting up the inside of the car. The buckshot only has to travel six feet, and when it hits the man's center chest, it drives him back into the seat. The man rebounds forward and slumps in his seat. Gage lowers his weapon and bends over to vomit as Henry walks unsteadily around the back of the car.

Henry clicks on his light. "Are you okay, Gage? Are you hit?"

Gage shakes his head, unable to speak. He vomits again and wipes his mouth with the back of his hand.

"Why didn't you just let them go?" Henry asks.

Gage gags, but the well is dry. He stands and wipes his mouth again. "Couldn't. His shirt is covered with blood."

"You think they killed Mitch?"

"That's the only way they would have ever gotten his Mustang."

"What about the rest of his family?"

"Don't know." Gage gags again and pauses a moment for the urge to pass. "Mitch's house is on the way. Better stop to take a look."

CHAPTER 71

Off the coast of Kitty Hawk, North Carolina

At dusk, Brad and Tanner dropped anchor a mile offshore from Kitty Hawk, North Carolina. Brad was right. Their luck did change and he snagged two medium-sized black sea bass. Now, standing over the propane stove in the ship's galley, the sizzling fish are making Brad's mouth water. Tanner, on deck standing watch, ducks his head inside to inquire when dinner will be ready.

Brad glances up from the stove. "I thought you didn't like fish."

"I didn't think I did, but that smells pretty good."

"Give me another five minutes. Anything going on up there?"

"No. But it's so dark I can't see much of anything."

"Use your ears. Noise travels a long way across water."

"And listen for what?"

Brad turns the fish, crisping the skin. "Splashes or unusual noises that are close by. And don't just focus on the area surrounding the boat. I'm worried about smaller boats approaching us."

"Okay, *Dad*. I got it." Tanner's face disappears from view.

Brad lifts one end of the fish fillet with a spatula to check the crispness. Using a propane lantern to keep from running the generator, he's eager to kill the light. He scoops the fish onto plates, grabs the lantern, and carries everything up the stairs. He passes a plate to Tanner, sets the lantern on the deck, and sits, the light leaking from below providing enough illumination for them to see their food.

Tanner takes a tentative bite, chews, and goes back for more.

"Like it?" Brad asks.

"Yeah, doesn't taste fishy at all."

"I told you, it's all about how it's prepared."

Tanner takes a big bite. "You can cook this again," he mumbles around a mouthful of fish.

Brad polishes off the last of his fish and sets his plate aside. He didn't anchor at this location on a whim. Earlier he saw a sign for a marina at the Oregon Inlet and the entrance to that inlet is now located a mile off their bow. No doubt the marina has been ransacked, but Brad is hoping someone might have left a reverse osmosis water system behind. The only way he'll know for sure is to paddle the kayak to shore and look. But that creates another set of problems. Leaving the *EmmaSophia* unoccupied is off the table, but Brad is wondering if his twelve-year-old son is up to the task of guarding their lifeline. Especially since Tanner has never fired any type of weapon, including a slingshot. After mulling the matter over for a few minutes, Brad decides he's not willing to risk it.

While his mind clicks through other options, Brad grabs the empty plates and steps out to the swim platform. He kneels down to rinse the plates and a hand latches on to his arm. Off-balance, the hand yanks and Brad tumbles into the water. He surfaces, disoriented, searching for the person who had pulled him overboard. He turns back to the boat to see a woman climbing onto the swim platform. With a strong kick, Brad lunges for the back of the boat. He swipes at her foot and misses. She's up now and climbing over the transom, her wet hair plastered to her face. "Tanner, gun," Brad shouts as he scrambles onto the back of the boat. He gets a leg up and his foot slips off, sending him back into the water. He glances up to see his son grappling the woman, the rifle between them.

Brad roars, braces his arms against the boat, and lifts himself out of the water. The deck is slippery and he loses his footing, belly flopping over the transom. He scrambles to his feet as the woman kicks Tanner in the crotch and grabs the rifle. Brad charges and grabs the woman by the waist, tackling her to the deck and crushing the air from her lungs. Brad wrestles the rifle away and stands, his breath coming in ragged gasps. He cocks the hammer and swings the barrel toward the woman cowering on the deck.

"No, Dad," Tanner shouts, hunched over, his hands wrapped around his midsection.

Brad glances at his son. "Why?" he shouts.

"Don't . . . shoot . . . her."

Brad turns back to the woman. "Get up."

"Can't breathe," the woman stutters.

"I don't care. Get your ass up."

The woman rolls onto her stomach and gets up to her knees. With a hand braced on the center console, she pulls herself to a standing position. Brad gets his first look at her. She appears to be in her midthirties, but he can't tell for sure with her long, dark hair covering her face.

The woman pushes the wet hair aside. "Please, I don't have"—she takes a couple of shallow breaths—"anywhere to go."

"Yes, you do. You're going back in the water."

"Please, just listen to me."

"I'm not up for story time." Brad steps left, now behind her. "Move."

The woman shuffles toward the back of the boat. "I fell in with . . . the wrong . . . crowd," the woman says, sobbing.

"That was your mistake," Brad says, nudging her on with the rifle barrel.

"Dad?" Tanner says.

"Quiet, Tanner," Brad says.

The woman climbs unsteadily over the transom.

"Jump in," Brad orders.

The woman wipes the tears from her cheeks before jumping in the water. Brad grabs a flashlight, clicks it on, and steps back to the stern. He shines the light at the woman's face. "Swim," Brad says.

The woman continues to tread water. "I have no place to go."

Brad brings the rifle up. "I don't want to shoot you, but I will. Swim."

Fresh tears are leaking from her eyes. "Shoot me, then. I'm dead either way."

Tanner crosses the deck and places a hand on his father's shoulder. "Don't shoot her, Dad. Let her come aboard. We can drop her off farther down the shore."

Brad turns his head. "The woman tried to steal our boat."

"I wasn't going to steal it," the woman says. She slips beneath the surface and reappears, coughing. "I was . . . looking for a place . . . to hide."

"So you thought you would swim a mile offshore and try to climb aboard a boat? A boat that doesn't belong to you?"

"I wasn't thinking clearly. I was frightened."

"You weren't too frightened to wrestle my son for the gun?"

"I didn't want him to shoot me. Please, I'm not a bad person."

Brad lowers his rifle and turns to his son. "Help her out of the water." He moves toward the front of the cockpit to allow him room to maneuver and keeps the flashlight aimed at the woman as Tanner helps her out of the water. "Take a seat," Brad orders, motioning the rifle barrel toward the backseat.

The woman sits and brushes the hair out of her face. Brad steps a little closer and studies the woman more closely. She's dressed in a tattered skirt and a once-white tunic blouse embroidered with some type of Aztec design along the collar and sleeves. She lifts a hand to block the light. "You're blinding me."

Brad, wanting to bean her with the flashlight, instead lets the beam drift down to her lower half. Her legs are scratched and bruised and her feet are bare, the last remnants of red nail polish on her toes barely visible. "Who are you?" Brad asks.

"My name is Nicole Stevens. I'm from, or was from, Greenville, North Carolina."

"Age and occupation?"

"What is this? An interrogation?" Nicole asks. When Brad doesn't answer, she sighs, then says, "I'm thirty-four and I'm currently employed, or was employed, as an adjunct English instructor at East Carolina University." She tugs on a strand of hair to remove it from her mouth. "Are you going to tell me who you are?"

"Undecided," Brad says. "What kind of trouble are you in? Do we need to be concerned about our safety, now that you've intruded onto our boat?"

"No, I slipped away from him before I entered the water."

"Who's him?"

"Damon, a man I met on the road out of Greenville. Don't know his last name. We were part of a much bigger group initially but that became too unwieldy. And he's the only one who had a weapon." Nicole sighs. "He was as nice as he could be for the first few days."

"And?" Brad asks.

"Not so much since then. He took . . . advantage of me . . . and tried . . ."—a fresh round of tears starts, spilling down her still-damp cheeks—"and he tried to . . . barter me to . . . others . . . to get things he wanted. I ran away before he could."

"Why didn't you go inland?" Brad asks.

"He told me he would kill . . . me if . . . if I tried . . . to run away." She sniffles and wipes her nose with the back of her hand. "And he's . . . very . . . resourceful."

"And where is this Damon now?"

Nicole takes a moment to regain her composure. "Over there in Kitty Hawk. He was trying to woo another woman into our group." Nicole wipes the tears from her eyes. "I slipped away and ran."

"Did he follow you?"

"No."

"How do you know for sure?" Brad asks.

"I didn't see him."

Brad curses under his breath, all thoughts of the reverse osmosis system gone. "Tanner, I'm going to watch our guest. Will you pull the anchor and motor us farther out to sea?"

"Okay." Tanner scrambles across the deck and pulls up the anchor before returning to the helm. He fires up the engine and spins the wheel, aiming for deeper water.

Brad turns back to Nicole. "Do you have a family?"

"I'm divorced."

"No kids?"

"No. We had issues."

Brad mulls that over for a moment. "I'm sorry about your difficulties, but you're leaving the boat at the first dock we come to."

CHAPTER 72

Weatherford

The continuing anxiety over Holly's whereabouts and possible condition crowds into Gage's brain, expelling the horrific images of the shoot-out on the road. Now nearing the Marston residence, he clicks on his headlamp to pinpoint the driveway, and turns the light off. The home is situated a hundred yards beyond the road, and Gage turns into the drive and pauses.

"How do you want to handle this?" Henry asks in a whisper.

"Straight on. I want to know what's going on with Holly. When we get up to the house, I'll shout out for Mitch and we switch on our lights."

"Are we worried about other intruders or, if Mitch is alive, him shooting us?"

"I'm not worried about other intruders. The two I killed had probably just left here. And the odds of Mitch being alive are slim to none. Let's just get this over with." Gage clicks on his headlamp and starts off at a good clip, Henry struggling to keep up. Gage shouts Mitch's name as they approach the house. There is no movement and no reply. A dozen steps later, they find the reason. Mitch is lying in the front yard, his throat slit, the ground around him soaked with blood. Gage grimaces, but continues on, making his way toward the front door. The door is ajar, and Gage nudges it open with the barrel of the shotgun. "Cindy, it's Gage Larson," he says into the dark void beyond. "Cindy?" Nothing. "Josh, Jacey, are you in there?" Josh is six and Jacey is four.

When he receives no answer, Gage turns to Henry and whispers: "You stay here to cover me."

Henry nods.

Gage takes a deep breath and steps through the door. The metallic scent of spilled blood is heavy in the confined space. He scans from left to right, the flashlight beam lighting up the scene. Furniture is overturned, lamps lie broken on the floor, and the cushions on the sofa have been sliced open. The rage builds as Gage walks deeper into the house. He steps into the dining room and nearly collapses to his knees. Cindy is lying nude on the dining room table. Her throat, too, has been cut, but that's not the extent of her injuries. Her breasts are covered with bite marks and blood is still leaking around the broom handle shoved into her vagina. Gage gags, puts a hand over his mouth, and turns away. He spends a moment trying to regain a sliver of composure before shuffling down the hallway.

Knowing he must check on the children, he tamps down the sudden urge to flee. He turns into the first bedroom, the light washing across pink-painted walls. The letters of the alphabet are displayed on a high shelf running around the perimeter of the room, and the bed, covered with a cartoon character comforter, is empty.

Gage steps over to the closet door and eases it open. Jacey is lying on the floor, nude, her throat slit. He moans with despair at the bite marks and the blood pooled around her hips. Turning away, the ember in his gut ignites into a roaring fire. His vision blurry from the tears, Gage eases the door closed and hurries down the hall, opening the door to Josh's room. On the walls are posters of past Oklahoma Sooners football greats, and on the bed, is Josh. In addition to his throat being slashed, Josh has also been gutted. Tears dripping from his cheeks, Gage hurries to the front door and runs from the house, collapsing to his knees in the front yard and burying his face in his hands.

Henry walks over, kneels down, and wraps an arm around Gage's shoulder. The sobbing continues for several moments. That tiny morsel of remorse Gage felt for killing the two men is wiped from his mind. He's now wishing the men had endured a long, agonizing death. He wipes his eyes and pushes to his feet. With no words of what he had found in the house, he lurches down the driveway, Henry following behind. They walk the remaining distance in silence before turning into the doctor's neighborhood.

Walking up and down the neighborhood streets, they're searching for Gage's old pickup. On the third street they find it parked behind a white Volvo, the doors hanging open. Gage quickens his pace and lunges up the steps, wrapping his knuckles on the door. When the door is not immediately opened he makes a fist and pounds on the door.

Henry steps up to the porch, winded. "Easy, Gage, you're going to wake the entire . . . neighborhood."

Gage whirls around, a snarl forming on his lips. But

seeing the empathy on his father-in-law's face drives the anger from his body. Henry knows that what Gage had seen in that house has shaken him to his core. He turns back when the door opens, revealing a man holding a pistol. "I'm Holly's husband and this is her father."

The man lowers his weapon and steps back, allowing them to enter. "Take the hallway to the left. They're in the master bedroom."

Gage nods and props the shotgun against the wall before making his way down the corridor. The far door is ajar and he slowly pushes it open. Holly is on the bed, tears streaming down her cheeks. Susan is sitting next to her, holding her hand. Holly's doctor, Eliana Samia, is standing off to the side, holding something in her arms. Gage's heart drops. "Holly?"

Holly sobs. "I'm sorry, Gage."

Gage hurries to her side, taking her other hand. "We lost the baby?"

Holly sobs again. "No, Olivia's healthy."

Gage exhales a long, deep breath.

"I'm just sad you weren't here for the birth."

The doctor places the swaddled infant on Holly's chest and slips from the room. Gage sags onto the bed, another round of tears leaking from his eyes as he cups his daughter's head in his hand.

CHAPTER 73

Weatherford

The old pickup is a single cab, and the Reeds climb into the back while Holly and the baby join Gage up front. He fires up the truck, clicks on the headlights, and backs out of the drive. "Olivia, huh? I thought we were still deciding."

"Oh, Gage, she looks like an Olivia. Don't you think?"

With no clue what an Olivia is supposed to look like, Gage shifts into first gear and motors out of the neighborhood. Rather than driving past the bloody Mustang, Gage heads straight on the main road. It's two miles out of the way, but Gage doesn't want to recount their trip to the doctor's house.

"Why did you wait so long to come?" Holly asks.

"We didn't know where the hell you were." Gage pauses, checks his tone. "Why didn't you leave a note, honey?"

"Didn't have time. My water broke in the entryway as Mom was helping me to the truck. I guess we sort of panicked."

"How long were you in labor?"

"I was dilated to five by the time we got there. I didn't have to push long before she came out."

"When did you leave the house?"

"Just before dark. Sorry you had to walk home and then walk to the doctor's house."

Images of the shoot-out on the road flash in Gage's mind. "It's okay." They ride in silence the next few miles until they reach the Reed residence. Gage pulls up close to the front door and her parents climb out to help Holly and the baby into the house before he pulls around the house and parks the truck in the barn. After closing and locking the barn door, he heads for the house. Holly, exhausted and sore, has retreated to the bedroom with Olivia. Gage says good night to his in-laws and retreats down the hall, easing the door open to find Holly sitting on the edge of the bed, staring down at their child.

"Isn't she beautiful, Gage?"

Gage sits down next to Holly and pulls the blanket away from Olivia's face. This is the first time he's seen his daughter in the light. The candles at the doctor's house didn't do her justice. "Yes, she is. She looks just like her mother." He wraps an arm around his wife, as they both stare at the tiny human they created. "Think she's going to have red hair like her mother?"

"I don't know. It's a blessing and a curse. But if she is, we better buy stock in a sunblock company."

Gage chuckles. "We didn't bring the crib. Where's she going to sleep?"

There's a soft knock on the door and Henry, carrying a small bassinet, pushes into the room. "This was

Alyx's and Holly's," he whispers. "We couldn't bear to part with it." Henry places the bassinet in the corner and slips out of the room.

"I guess that answers my question. I can't believe they've kept that for all these years."

"There's no telling what those two have stashed in the attic. Will you hold her while I take a quick shower?"

"How . . . how do I do it?"

Holly laughs. "She's not going to break, Gage." She turns and places Olivia in her husband's arms. "Just make sure you support her head."

Gage positions one of his big paws under Olivia's head. "I wish my dad would wake up so he could see her."

Holly pushes slowly off the bed and turns, placing a hand Gage's cheek. "I don't think your father's going to wake up, sweetheart." She leans in and tenderly kisses Gage on the lips. "We'll take her over to your parents' house in the morning."

Gage nods, tears shimmering in his eyes. "Okay."

Holly gives Gage another kiss before tottering toward the bathroom, bracing against the furniture for support. Gage shoulders away a tear, thinking how one person leaves the world and another arrives. He lifts Olivia to his lips and kisses her cheek and nuzzles his nose against her soft skin. He's in the same position when the lights flash off.

"Gage," Holly shouts from the bathroom, "what happened to the power?"

With the baby held tight to his chest, Gage feels his way in the dark toward the bathroom. "I don't know. Are you okay?"

"Other than the shampoo still in my hair? Yes, I'm okay. Will you go find out what happened to the generator? I need water to finish up."

"What am I supposed to do with Olivia?"

"Hand her off to my mother."

There's a knock on the door and Henry enters with a couple of flashlights. "Are you out of propane?" Gage asks, taking one of the flashlights and clicking it on before placing it on the dresser.

"Not possible. It was eighty percent full the last time I looked. And that was only a couple of days ago."

"Think there's an issue with the generator?"

"Don't know," Henry says. "You mind helping me?"

Gage follows Henry into the living room and hands Olivia off to Susan before he and Henry make their way outside. At the propane tank Henry flips up the lid to look at the gauge. "Goddammit, how could that be?"

"Empty?"

"Yes, but it doesn't make any sense. There's no way the generator burned that much fuel."

"Could it have leaked out?"

"Why would it all of the sudden spring a goddamn leak?"

"I don't know, Henry, but the gas went somewhere."

Henry runs his hands over the fittings that connect to the underground line that feeds the generator. "All the connections feel tight." He scans the flashlight over the pipe going into the ground. "Everything looks good here. You see anything?"

"No," Gage says. He makes his way over to the generator, which is parked up close to the house. He checks the gas pipe connection at the generator and all appears well. With the flashlight, he follows the pipe to where it exits out of the ground. "Henry, I've found the problem."

Henry hurries over. He looks at the ground Gage is highlighting with the flashlight beam. "Are those metal shavings?"

"Yep." Gage focuses the light on a section of the pipe. "And there's your leak."

Henry kicks the ground with his boot. "Son of a bitch. Somebody drilled a hole in the gas line?"

"Looks that way," Gage says. "They must have done it while we were gone."

"But, why?"

"I guess they thought they'd level the playing field."

"I bet it was that cocksucker Ed Yancey. He raised hell about the expansion of the wind farm last year. That bastard could have blown the house up."

"They probably turned the gas off, drilled the hole, and turned it back on. We might never know who did it. And Yancey will deny it. Not much we can do about it now."

"You wait until I see that cocksucker again." Henry mutters a string of curse words. "We now need that turbine up and running as quickly as possible."

CHAPTER 74

Des Moines

McDowell opens his eyes as the first hints of daylight stretch across the landscape. He pushes out of the chair and stands. Either the night was quiet or he slept through another shoot-out. He clicks on his flashlight and smothers the lens. Nope, the Glock is still resting on the table and Melissa and Lauren are snuggled up on the sofa. With the glass gone from the front door, the reception area is chilly. McDowell grabs the pistol and stuffs it into his waistband then slings the shotgun over his shoulder and steps outside to take a piss. It's cold enough that the warm urine produces a cloud of vapor when it hits the grass. He laments the loss of his uniform jacket as he zips up and walks around the corner to check on the fire. A smattering of pale orange embers are glowing and he stokes them before adding more wood. Once the fire is going good, he retraces his steps back inside, rubbing his arms to get the blood moving.

In the reception area, Melissa and Lauren are awake and having a discussion with one of the students. Mc-

Dowell knows the faces, but he hasn't yet attached all the names. Rather than eavesdrop, he begins a search through the offices for some type of jacket. He's on his second office when Lauren steps inside and closes the door.

"Lindsey says Hannah went to the bathroom sometime during the night and has not returned."

"I thought they were supposed to go together?"

"According to Lindsey, Hannah wouldn't allow her to go outside with her. Hannah apparently told her she didn't want anyone watching her taking a crap."

"Maybe she crashed in another office."

"I don't know, but we have to find her."

Melissa, Lauren, and McDowell grab flashlights and fan out through the building. McDowell searches the nicer offices before moving on to the conference room. He shines the beam under the table, in the storage closets, and the small adjoining bathroom. No sign of Hannah. He moves down the corridor, searching offices, restrooms, and closets—anywhere a fourteen-year-old girl might hide. He comes to the end of the corridor and turns back, searching the areas again. Still no sign of Hannah. A tingle of dread prickles his neck. He hurries to the area Lauren and Melissa are searching. "Any sign?"

"No," Lauren says. "The only place we haven't searched is the kitchen."

McDowell reaches back and grabs the pistol, pulling it free. He hands the gun to Lauren. "I'll check the kitchen. I want you to gather the kids in the conference room and keep them there."

"Why? What are you thinking?"

"Nothing good. I'll make a sweep of the kitchen

then I'm headed outside. Do not let any of them out until I give you the all clear."

"Stan, what's going on?" Melissa asks, her face a mask of worry.

"I don't know, but I'm going to find out." McDowell hurries to the kitchen and does a quick sweep before moving to the back door. He unslings the shotgun and steps outside, pausing to listen. The only noise he hears is the rustle of leaves in the early-morning breeze. It's light enough now, and he tucks the flashlight into his pocket, allowing both hands free to handle the shotgun. Veering by the truck he peeks into the cab—no Hannah. Now the tingle is a full-on rush.

Starting from the hood of the truck, he walks a zigzag pattern through the greenbelt, methodically searching the ground. When he reaches the residential street he increases his pace as he hurries up to the next block, scanning both sides of the road. The road dead-ends and McDowell stops and turns a circle, his brain processing what his eyes see. He spots a small park a block over and hurries that way, slowing when he nears. There's a three-person swing set, a slide, and two rotting teeter-totters attached to an iron pole, the wood planks sagging under their own weight. But still no sign of Hannah.

McDowell slowly approaches a small cluster of trees that are dominated by a large white oak, its graceful limbs arching over most of the park. As he fights through the brush, his nose picks up the first hint of trouble—the scent of blood. He pushes into a clearing surrounding the massive trunk. The ground is littered with beer bottles, cigarette butts, and used condoms. He leans forward to peer around the trunk, already knowing what he's going to find. Hannah's body is lying among the refuse of a previous life. McDowell steps around the trunk and kneels down, checking for a pulse as a red-hot rage ignites in his inner core. Hannah's skin is cold to the touch and her jeans and panties are puddled around her ankles. McDowell drops back on his haunches to gather himself.

Could the killer be a part of their group? McDowell lets that thought tumble around his mind for a moment. Not likely, he decides. The students have been together for almost three weeks with no hints of violence. And McDowell hadn't picked up any vibes that evil is lurking in the group over the last few days.

With the smoke-filled skies, it's dark in the underbrush. McDowell clicks on his flashlight and leans forward, examining Hannah's body. Blood has soaked the ground near her vaginal area, but that wouldn't have killed her, McDowell reasons. He pulls up her T-shirt, and working methodically up her body, searches for gunshot or stab wounds and doesn't find any. Her breasts are bruised and covered with bite marks. Moving up to her head and neck area, he finds heavy bruising around the base of her neck with some elongated bruising that stretches nearly all the way around. He sits back on his haunches and sighs. Hannah had been raped and strangled. He picks up Hannah's right hand and finds a hunk of flesh under her middle fingernail. He leans forward to check the left hand and finds more flesh under the nail on her left index finger. Whoever it was, she scratched the bastard good. McDowell takes a moment to pull up Hannah's pants and pushes to his feet, returning to the office building.

The kids are slumped in the chairs surrounding the

conference table. "Gang, if any of you need to go to the bathroom you may. But stay close to the building. Lauren and Melissa, may I speak to you for a moment?"

Lauren and Melissa follow McDowell into one of the other offices. He takes a deep breath and turns to face them. "Hannah is dead."

Lauren sags and has to catch herself on one of the chairs. She shuffles around to the front and sits. "What happened?"

"There's no easy way to say this, but it appears she was raped and strangled."

Melissa shuffles to the other chair and collapses into it, tears streaming down her cheeks. "What are we . . . going to do? How are we going . . . to tell her parents?" She glances up at McDowell. "Who . . . who did it?"

"Unknown. There's a residential area on the other side of the greenbelt. If she was out waving around a flashlight, the killer could have spotted her from over there. The odds of finding the murderer are long and it would be an arduous task that could stretch on for days."

"Can we go to the police?" Lauren asks, wiping the tears from her cheeks.

"I'm not sure a cohesive police unit still exists this deep into the crisis. Most have probably drifted off to rejoin their families. Crime, even one as heinous as this, would be far down their list of worries."

Melissa palms the tears from her cheeks. "So, what should we do?"

The question hangs in the air for a moment.

McDowell pulls the chair from under the desk and

sits. "The way I see it, we have two choices: bury Hannah here, or take her body with us to deliver to her family."

Lauren winces at the mention of Hannah's family. "God, I don't know what we're going to tell her family. She was our responsibility."

"When you planned the trip you had zero chance of predicting the current situation. You two are going well beyond what was ever expected of you," McDowell says. "In the end, Hannah shouldn't have gone outside alone."

Lauren sniffles. "But still. I should have kept a better eye on her."

"You can't watch them twenty-four/seven. At some point they have to take some responsibility," McDowell says. "So, back to the body. I hate to be brusque about the matter, but we need to make a decision. Take her or bury Hannah here?"

Lauren wipes her nose. "Riding around with Hannah's body seems ghoulish, especially with a group of curious teenagers."

"Speaking of the teenagers," Melissa says, pulling a tissue from the box on the desk. "What are we going to tell them?"

"I think we have to tell them the truth," Lauren replies. "Not all the details of how she was killed, only the fact that she was murdered." She glances at McDowell. "If we bury her here, can we do some type of service that would include the students?"

"Of course," McDowell replies. "I need you two to scour the offices for some type of blanket to wrap Hannah's body in. We have a shovel from the sign shop, but it's probably going to take me a couple of hours to dig the grave. We'll bury her in a small neighborhood park three blocks east of here." McDowell pushes out of the chair. "I'll return to lead you back to the grave." He picks up the shotgun and hands it to Lauren. "When the kids are finished using the bathroom, I want all of you to remain indoors. We know there's at least one killer out there." McDowell pauses for a moment to let the statement sink in. "Lauren, you know how to handle that shotgun?"

"Yes. Pump and shoot, right?"

"Yes. And if someone tries to force their way inside, it's shoot first and ask questions later. Can you handle that?"

Lauren nods.

McDowell digs the truck keys out of his pocket and hands them to Lauren. "There are extra shells in the glove box. I'm taking the pistol, but if anything happens to me, you get those kids on board and haul ass."

CHAPTER 75

Hayti

During the night, the mosquitoes drove Zane and Alyx into the cab. Lying side by side on the bench seat, Zane stirs awake and sits up. Who knew mosquitoes could survive a nuclear war? Zane wonders as he pushes open the door and climbs out to empty his bladder. His urine is dark and his usual steady stream is a dribble. The water situation is now critical. He walks over and grabs his still-damp clothing and tugs on his jeans and shirt, envious that Alyx's clothes are dry because she was too busy to wash them out last night. In the daylight, the water looks clear, but with the high number of agricultural fields surrounding the river, there's no telling how much pesticide or fertilizer has been washed into the stream. He bends down and scoops up a handful of water and takes a sniff. The water smells fine and he gives it a taste. There is no chemical taste and no nasty aftertaste. But getting the runs could be a fatal illness in the current climate.

The door squeals and he turns to see Alyx climb down from the cab. She moves around to the front of the truck and squats. Zane chuckles at her modesty. Alyx stands, pulls up her pants, and saunters down to where he's standing. The flip-flops she had on the day they left Fort Meade are now more flop than flip.

"We need to find you some new shoes."

"Sure, we'll pick up a cheap pair at Target when we stop for groceries. Is the water fit to drink?"

"It tastes okay, but I'm not sure we should risk it."

Alyx brushes her hair out of her face. The color is beginning to lighten, transitioning back to her more natural brunette. And the left side of her head that had been shaved close to the skull is filling out. Zane zeros in on her delicate collarbones as they rise and fall with each breath.

"What in the hell are you looking at?" Alyx asks.

"Your collarbones."

"Well, hell. You keep that thing in your pants. We need to worry about finding water."

"With all these fields around here, you'd think we'd find a windmill pumping water."

"Maybe we will now that it's daylight. I don't want to risk getting sick by drinking that water. Besides, we have no idea if it's contaminated with radiation. We need to find an underground source."

"What if we boiled some of this water?" Zane asks.

"Two problems with that. We don't have any way to start a fire or anything to boil the water in. We should have taken some pans and a lighter from that house with the dead couple."

"If I recall correctly, we kind of left in a hurry. But, hey, they start fires all the time on *Survivor*."

Alyx laughs. "I must have missed that season. Were you on the show?"

"Well, no. But how hard can it be?"

Alyx turns and starts walking back to the truck. "C'mon, Mr. Survivor. Let's get the hell out of here. Maybe we'll find one of your windmills."

They climb in the truck and Zane eases the pickup up the hill and makes a right onto the main road. Four miles farther on they come to another small town. Zane skirts around the town and picks up a highway running at a diagonal, leading them toward the southwest. It's more of the same on this side of town—fields for as far as the eye can see with homes spaced miles apart. Zane slows when they pass the houses, hoping to find a place that looks unoccupied. Most of the homes are set close to the road and are dwarfed by the barns and grain silos that sprout up like weeds. The clutter of farming trucks and tractors makes it extremely difficult to determine if a home is vacant or not. A mile farther on, he spots a secluded home that's well off the road and devoid of farm clutter. He slows to a stop.

"See any cars?" Zane asks.

"No, but that doesn't necessarily mean no one's home. Maybe the car died in town and they walked home."

"Hadn't thought of that." Zane gooses the gas, and Old Goldie picks up speed. After another two miles, Zane groans when they pass a sign welcoming them to Arkansas. "Looks like we're back in the land of crazies." In the distance Zane spots what he's been looking for—a windmill. He eases up the road and coasts to a stop at the head of the gravel drive leading to a small home. The drive is vacant and the windmill is positioned off to the side of the house, the blades turning lazily in the morning breeze. A hose runs away from the base of the windmill and ends in a galvanized stock tank on the other side of a barbwire fence. About a hundred yards behind the house is a barn that was in desperate need of repair twenty years ago. "What do you think?"

"I think we don't have a choice."

Zane turns into the driveway and steers around behind the house, putting the truck in park. They take a moment to study the area. No one has charged out of the house, but Zane's hand doesn't stray far from the shifter or the shotgun. "Doesn't look like anyone's home."

"Either that or they're waiting to shoot us when we get out of the truck."

Zane scowls. "You're a pessimist. I can't see any movement through the windows. My bet is the place is vacant."

Alyx begins gathering up the empty water bottles. "How do you want to do this?"

"Do you think I should pull up closer to the windmill?"

"I'd rather the truck remain hidden."

"Okay, I'll cover you with the shotgun while you refill the bottles."

"Sounds like a plan."

They open the doors and spill out of the truck. Zane takes up a position where he can see both the house and the windmill and crosses the shotgun across his chest and waits, sweeping his gaze back and forth. Alyx removes the hose from the stock tank and lets the water run for a few seconds to clear the line. She takes a tentative sip, ponders the taste for a moment, then takes a much longer drink. Once her thirst is quenched she begins filling the bottles. She glances up and shouts, "Zane!"

Zane whirls around and brings the shotgun to bear on an older man exiting the side door of the barn. He's carrying a pistol low to his side and he's limping badly. He raises his free hand in greeting. Not sure of his intentions, Zane keeps the shotgun barrel centered on the man's chest as he approaches. "I'm not gonna hurt ya," the man says.

"How about putting that pistol away, then."

The man shrugs and tucks the pistol into a pocket. "Where you folks from?" The man is dressed in tattered overalls and no shirt, his gray chest hair is peeking over the top of the bib.

The man seems friendly enough and Zane lowers the barrel a few inches.

"We're originally from the Washington, D.C., area."

"I bet that's a real shithole," the man says, coming to a stop ten feet away. "Name's Roger. Roger Webb. Who you be?"

"I'm Zane and the woman filling the water bottles is Alyx. This your place?"

"This here's my castle. Been here goin' on thirty years."

"The house looked unoccupied. I hope you don't mind us taking some of your water."

"You have somethin' to trade?"

Zane's brain replays the images from the roadblock. *And here we are in Arkansas, again.* "The woman, Alyx, is not available."

The man laughs, displaying a mouthful of rotted teeth. "Hell, young un, I ain't been able to get it up since I got Roto-Rootered 'bout twenty years ago."

Zane expels a sigh of relief. "Why are you limping?"

Webb pulls up his pant leg to reveal a nasty pus-filled gash running the length of his calf. "Got hung up on a gotdamn barbwire fence near 'bout a week ago." He turns back toward the barn and waves a hand.

Zane lifts the shotgun, preparing for the worst.

The man laughs again. "It's just my wife. You's a jumpy fellow, ain't you?"

"It pays to be jumpy."

An older, mousy gray–haired woman sticks her head out of the barn for a look before tentatively stepping out. She, too, is dressed in overalls, but unlike her husband, she's wearing an old grimy T-shirt. "That there's Dolores. We been married goin' on 'bout forty years." He glances over his shoulder. "C'mon, hon."

"Anyone else in the barn?" Zane asks.

"Nope, just us. Too damn hot in the house. It's a might cooler in the barn if you don't mind fightin' the skeeters."

Dolores comes to a stop next to her husband. "Hi, ma'am. I'm Zane and my friend at the well is Alyx."

"She's mighty pretty. She belong to you?" Dolores asks.

"That's undecided, ma'am."

"If'n I were you, I'd latch on to that pretty gal while I could."

"I think you're right, ma'am. I have some antibiotics I'll give you, Roger, to clear up that infection in your leg."

"Mighty nice of ya. I'd 'preciate it."

Zane ponders the situation for a moment "You're not going to shoot us, are you, Roger?"

"Why'd I want to shoot ya?"

Zane places the shotgun on the top of the cab as Alyx returns, her outstretched shirt filled with full water bottles. "Alyx, these nice folks are Roger and Dolores Webb."

Alyx nods at the couple. "Nice to meet you two. Thanks for letting us take some water. I'm sorry we didn't ask before taking it."

"Don't worry your pretty noggin 'bout it," Roger says.

Alyx dumps her load into the truck, grabs the remainder of the empty bottles, and returns to the windmill.

"Roger, you hear any news?" Zane asks.

"Nope. Ain't nobody around here knows what the hell's goin' on."

"I think it's the same for everyone," Zane says. "We may never know exactly what happened. Your home is fairly close to the road. Have you had any trouble?"

"Jes one time. I kilt a couple of fellers on the fourth . . . No, that ain't right." Roger turns to his wife. "Hon, what day was't?"

"I think it was day six." She looks at Zane. "I been tryin' to keep track of the days on the calendar we got from the feed store."

Alyx returns with the last of the water bottles and dumps them in the truck.

"You folks hungry?" Dolores asks.

Zane and Alyx share a glance, both wondering if this is too good to be true. "Yes, we are," Alyx says.

"Roger kilt a turkey this mornin'. We got it roasting over the fire. 'Bout done, too."

Zane's mouth is watering. "You don't mind sharing?"

"No, siree. The meat'll spoil before we can finish it. 'Sides, we ain't had no company since this whole mess started."

Zane glances at Alyx again. She nods. "Okay, we'd love some turkey."

"C'mon back to the barn," Roger says.

Zane stares at the shotgun on top of the truck. His usually sharp instincts are muted by hunger. *Take the shotgun, or don't?*

As if reading his mind, Alyx says, "Zane why don't you put the shotgun in the truck and get this nice couple some antibiotics?"

Zane nods. He slides the shogun onto the truck seat and pulls out the bag of medicines. He grabs enough for two courses of antibiotics and shoves the sack back under the seat. He and Alyx walk hand in hand to the barn.

After an hour of visiting and eating their fill, Alyx and Zane say their good-byes. Carrying a bag of leftovers, they climb into the truck and steer back onto the road. Alyx brushes the hair from her face. "I think those two restored my belief that humanity still exists."

"I agree. But we're still a long way from home."

CHAPTER 76

After breakfast for both crews, those on the ballistic missile submarine are back aboard and hard at work. Overnight, radio technicians from both ships worked to restore a rudimentary radio link, allowing the two ships the ability to communicate. But Thompson plans on using it sparingly, if at all. Once the last of the supplies is transferred from the USS *Grant*, Thompson and Garcia say farewell to their friend Murphy, and the lines connecting the two ships are freed. Thompson and Garcia make their way down the main hatch and back to the bridge. After several moments, the last of the sailors are back aboard and the main hatch is sealed.

"Mr. Patterson, set a course for Myrtle Beach," Thompson orders. "Q, take us down to two-zero-zero."

The dive alarm sounds as the dive officer monitors the movement of seawater into the ballast tanks as the submarine slips beneath the surface. "All ahead two-thirds," Thompson orders. "Conn, I want you to match speeds with *Grant* when she's under way."

When Thompson receives confirmation of his orders, he steps over to the navigation station. "Distance to Myrtle Beach?"

Patterson looks up from his computer screen. "Eight hundred ninety-four nautical miles, sir."

The captain does the math in his head. "Somewhere around thirty-eight hours?"

"Yes, sir, if we maintain twenty knots."

"Let's hope *Grant* can run at that speed without burning through too much fuel," Thompson says before turning away. He steps over to Garcia. "Think Murph can maintain twenty knots?"

"It'll be a chore if he's aiming to save fuel."

"Captain," Adams says, "I have a new contact. A surface ship one hundred thirteen miles out."

"One of ours?" Thompson asks.

"No, definitely not one of ours. I'm running the screw signature through the computer."

"Is the propeller signature similar to the previous Russian ship?"

"Negative, Skipper." Adams scrolls through the computer results. "It appears to be a Chinese destroyer, sir."

"Heading?" Thompson asks.

"Current course is eighty degrees, sir."

"So she's headed our way, huh?" the captain mumbles out loud. He looks at Garcia. "Think she spotted us when we were tied up with the *Grant* overnight?"

"I highly doubt it. But *my* main question is—are we at war with China?"

"That's a question we can't answer. Seems strange to have a Chinese ship in the middle of the North Atlantic, though."

"Could be she was stalking the Russian ship," Garcia suggests.

"If she was, the crew was doing a terrible job of it considering they're a day and a half behind." Thompson pauses, thinking. After several moments, he says, "Unless the Chinese have their helicopter in the air. We failed to ask Murphy if his helicopter is operational."

"We can ascend to periscope depth and radio him."

"Call me nervous, but I'm concerned there may be a Chinese sub or two running with that destroyer." Thompson turns to the sonar technician. "Mr. Adams, any other contacts?"

"Negative, Skipper, but we're currently sailing through a convergence zone. Detecting a surface ship is fairly easy—anything else is a crapshoot unless we ascend or descend."

"Roger, keep a close eye on your scope. Q, takes us down to the deepest possible depth."

Lieutenant Commander Quigley confirms the order and the submarine descends. Thompson steps over to the attack center. "Mr. White, load all four tubes," Thompson orders. "Conn, sound the general alarm. Battle stations, torpedo." The Klaxon sounds as the order to man battle stations is piped through the sub. Thompson returns to his spot next to Garcia. "Carlos, I guess the only way we're going to know if we're at war with China is if they fire on Murph's ship. Let's lurk deep until we know what the Chinese intend."

"And if there's a Chinese submarine in the vicinity?"

"I guess we play cat and mouse until we know which side they're on. There's a reason for that Chinese ship to be so far from home. I just wished we knew what it is."

"I hate to rain on your parade, Bull, but how will we know if the *Grant* is under fire? We'll only know if she gets hit or some stray ordnance explodes."

Thompson sighs. "We're going to have to radio Murph, aren't we?"

"Yep. I know that's a dicey proposition, but I'm not seeing an alternative at the moment."

"Let's stay deep for a while. With the *Grant*'s computer glitch on the Aegis Combat System, he'll have to get a hell of a lot closer to the Chinese before anything happens."

"That's not necessarily true for the Chinese, Bull. If their ship is entirely operational, they're nearly within missile range of the *Grant* right now."

CHAPTER 77

Weatherford

The baby was fussy most of the night, and this morning Gage's ass is dragging. With the generator sabotaged, Henry is cooking the remainder of the refrigerated items on the backyard grill. The table is already mounded with food and it looks like brunch at a fancy hotel. They're all hoping the freezer, if they keep the lid closed, will keep the food frozen until they can get one of the turbines running. Gage piles his plate high with steak and eggs and doses everything with hot sauce before taking a seat at the table. Holly is still racked out and Susan is tending to Olivia, who finally fell asleep. Henry comes in and fills his own plate before taking a seat.

Gage forks a piece of steak and asks, "How long do you think it'll take us to rework the rest of the electrical issues?" He pops the steak in his mouth and chews.

"A day, maybe longer," Henry replies before feeding a forkful of eggs into his mouth.

"How are we going to ensure this house receives power?"

"I've got a few rolls of electrical wire that we can run directly to the house, if we need to. It'll be a job to unroll by hand because it's so damn heavy, but one way or another, we'll get power to this house."

"What happens to those who don't receive any power? Some of them will be mad as hell."

"As I said before, if we can restore power to some of the larger buildings people will have a place to go. And if we can get some of the town's wells pumping water, I see no reason for anyone to be angry. I should think that would earn a small token of goodwill, wouldn't it?"

"We can hope, I guess. But we'll need to keep a close eye on the situation and be prepared to take action if needed."

Henry pauses, the fork halfway to his mouth. "You talking gunplay?" he asks, the blood draining from his face.

"If it comes to that, yes. I don't think we have any other options."

Henry lowers the fork and pushes his plate away, his appetite suddenly gone. "Surely, the situation won't escalate to that level."

"It may. And we need to be prepared for that possibility. Maybe come up with a system where those with power take partial responsibility for protecting the turbine."

"First, we have to get it working," Henry says. "We'll figure all the other stuff out later."

Gage polishes off the last of his eggs and stands, carrying his plate to the sink. He's halfway there before he stops and turns. "Damn, I forgot the well's not working. We're going to need water."

"There's a case of bottled water in the garage.

That'll last us a couple of days. Holly's going to need it the most when her milk comes in."

Gage nods. "As of last night she was only producing colostrum. The doctor said it might take a day or two before it happens."

"That sounds about right," Henry says. They file out of the house and climb into the truck. Gage fires it up and drives out to the turbine, where they slog up the tower. Both are drenched in sweat by the time they reach the nacelle. Gage pushes through the hatch and cranks the doors open, taking a moment to study the debris-filled atmosphere overhead. He shakes his head at the madness that happened only days ago. He turns away from the slate-colored sky and starts to work.

Henry is working on the control panel, rearranging switches and other electrical parts. Gage grabs a ratchet and a couple of wrenches and climbs below the floor of the nacelle and starts disconnecting the yaw motors. After unbolting them and tossing them on the floor, he spends some time studying the giant cogged wheel. He steps over and sticks his head through the hatch. "What are we doing to control the yaw?"

Henry looks up. "I thought about that last night. I'm not convinced the turbine head will rotate with the wind without the computer." He bends and pulls a notebook out of his work case and spends a moment studying a chart before digging a compass out of the case. After studying that for a moment he looks up. "We need to lock the hub down at 193.65 degrees." He stands and walks over, passing the compass on to Gage.

"Where's the hub located now?"

"193 degrees."

Gage hands the compass back. "That'll do. I'll run in a couple of bolts to lock her down. How much work do you have left?"

"I'll be through up here soon. I still have to check out the transformer on the trailer. The braking system ready to go?"

"Yes. I finished that up yesterday."

"Good, we'll use your braking system to control the speed. We'll run through a good quantity of brake pads, but we have plenty."

"You see any way we'll be able to start and stop the turbine from below?"

"Unfortunately, no. I hope your braking device will stop it if the wind speed gets too high, but we're not going to know that until it happens. Why? You tired of climbing?"

"That's part of it. The other part is we have no way to forecast the weather. From your house, it'd take me about half an hour to drive over here and climb up the tower. If we get a thunderstorm that pops up, as they have a tendency to do, the turbine could destroy itself before I could get up here to stop it."

"You said it earlier. We're going to need help with this, and not just with security. The ideal situation would be having someone in or near the turbine around the clock. Maybe that same person would be responsible for stopping the turbine in an emergency." Henry takes a swig of water from one of the two bottles they brought from the garage. "Right now, all we're doing is speculating. We won't be able to diagnose all the problems until we get her running."

CHAPTER 78

Des Moines

McDowell pauses digging Hannah Hatcher's grave and mops his brow. It's been a while since he's done any manual labor and his muscles are screaming in protest. The digging was good for the first hour, but two feet down, he hit a ledge of sandstone that he's trying to chip his way through. McDowell lays the shovel aside and grabs his bottle of water. There are a few people out and about, but so far none have approached McDowell to inquire about his activities. He guzzles half the water and reseats the cap and scans the neighborhood again. On the opposite corner he spots a man walking the sidewalk who turns away when McDowell looks in his direction. *Did I see him earlier?* He watches as the man turns a corner and walks out of view.

McDowell probes a blister on his right palm, thinking, *I did see him earlier, when I was returning to the office building after finding Hannah's body. Or is it a different guy wearing a similar coat to this guy?* McDowell reaches behind his back and touches the

Glock to make sure it's still there. With no definitive answers, he sighs and picks up the shovel.

A half an hour later, McDowell has only chipped away a few inches of rock and dirt. He pauses to stretch his back and glances up to see the same man walking down the sidewalk in the opposite direction. *If the guy's wondering what I'm doing, why doesn't he walk over here and ask?* McDowell ponders that question for a moment while he probes another blister on his left palm. It's the size of a quarter and filled with fluid. He glances back toward the man. He's too far away to discern many physical features, other than the man is tall and lanky. McDowell mulls the situation over and a thought charges to the forefront of his mind: *unless he already knows what I'm doing.* McDowell climbs out of the hole, thinking, *It won't hurt to talk to him, would it?*

McDowell waits for the man to walk out of view, before hurrying across the street. He sidles up to a large elm tree and peeks around the edge of the enormous trunk. The man is almost to the next intersection. McDowell waits a moment and looks again just as the man glances over his shoulder. Cursing, McDowell ducks back behind the tree. The next time he looks, the man is gone. "Damn it," McDowell mutters. He steps out from behind the tree and hurries up the sidewalk. The neighborhood has a blue-collar feel to it. Most of the homes are older and many are in desperate need of fresh paint. They're small by today's standards, and many of the homeowners have converted their garages into additional living spaces. As McDowell closes in on the next intersection, he slows, glancing to his left.

The man didn't go that way. Using the cover of a tall wooden fence he shuffles forward and glances around the corner to the right. The man is in the middle of the block, still walking west. McDowell waits. After another moment or two, he leans forward for another peek.

The man is walking up the driveway of a home six houses down. McDowell marks the location—a white Ford pickup in the drive—and pulls back behind the fence. He counts to twenty then slips around the corner. He squares his shoulders and strolls down the sidewalk like any neighbor would do. When he reaches the home with the white pickup, he turns up the drive. A large maple tree obscures most of the house and McDowell steps into the deep shade. Two square windows are positioned on either side of a front door that looks out over the weedy front lawn. McDowell slips over to the side of the house and eases toward the door. He pauses to glance through the closest window. The interior is dark, but not dark enough to conceal the trash scattered across what was once white carpet. McDowell ducks down below the window and crab-walks toward the front door. He kneels and pulls out the Glock, checking to make sure a round is seated.

McDowell reaches up to test the doorknob and finds it unlocked. He pauses for a deep breath and stands. In one swift move, he twists the knob and launches into the house, the Glock up and ready to fire. The man, seated in an easy chair, lunges forward, reaching for a pistol on the coffee table. McDowell takes two long strides and stomps on the man's hand, pinning it to the table. He swats the short-barreled revolver to the floor and takes a step back, clicking on his flashlight and sweeping the beam across the man's face. "How did you get those scratches on your cheeks?"

"Clearing brush. What the hell is it to you, and why the fuck are you in my house?"

McDowell ignores the questions. "Those scratches look pretty fresh. You were clearing brush yesterday, and what? You just happened to scratch both sides of your face?"

"Fuck you. Get out of my house."

"Hannah."

"What? Who the hell's Hannah?"

"Hannah is the name of the girl you raped and strangled last night."

The man tries to lunge out of the chair again and McDowell fires, punching a hole in the man's forehead. He slumps back into the chair and McDowell tucks the Glock into the waistband at his back, turns, and walks back through the front door.

Back at the office building, McDowell takes the shotgun from Lauren. "We'll go to the park as a group. Once there, you and Melissa can get Hannah wrapped up and then we'll carry her to the grave."

Lauren nods. Her eyes are red rimmed and her cheeks are damp.

"How'd they take the news?" McDowell asks in a low voice.

"Not well. There were some hysterics from the girls, but they've since calmed down. The boys are stoic. I think half of them were in love with Hannah." Lauren sniffles and McDowell gives her shoulder a squeeze.

He rounds up the group, leads them out of the building, the shotgun slung over his shoulder. At the park, Melissa and Lauren, with tears streaming down their faces, roll Hannah onto the blanket and wrap her up. Once they finish, McDowell and Melissa carry the body to the grave and lower Hannah into her final resting place. Now everyone is weeping. In halting, broken voices, the students each take a turn to say something about Hannah. When they finish, Melissa recites a Bible verse from memory and everyone takes a turn on the shovel. McDowell finishes shoveling the dirt while the kids search for something to mark the grave. They return, each carrying a small rock. Taking turns, they each lay a stone at the head of the grave and the group walks solemnly back to the truck. Working silently, Lauren, Melissa, and McDowell load everything up and McDowell climbs behind the wheel. They won't get far today with probably only four hours of daylight left. But anywhere is better than here.

CHAPTER 79

North Atlantic

With the Chinese ship still a good distance out, Captain Thompson orders a slow ascent to periscope depth. The sonar technician hasn't spotted any subsurface contacts, but that's not much consolation—submarines are damn hard to detect. As the sub levels off, Thompson grabs a radio handset from overhead then hesitates. Any radio broadcast will pinpoint their position. But there are too many unanswered questions. He clicks the button and says, "Thompson to Murphy. Over."

"I'm here, Bull," Captain Wayne Murphy replies. "We've got eyes on the Chinese destroyer."

"Have you deployed your towed array sonar?"

"Yep. She's a mile off our stern. Haven't picked up anything yet, but we're locked and loaded."

"Any hint of the Chinese intentions?"

"Negative. Her course remains the same. She's headed our way. Let's just hope they don't know you're lurking below."

A clock is ticking in Thompson's head. Every second on the radio only furthers the chances of discovery. "Any choppers up?"

"No. Ours is operational and she's on deck, ready to go if needed."

"Good. Detonate a depth charge at fifty feet if the Chinese turn hostile."

"What do you want me to do if the towed array detects a sub?"

"Kill it. Thompson out." The captain hangs up the handset. "Dive, emergency deep." The nose of the sub immediately sinks as the sub descends at a steep angle. "All ahead full."

The mood on the bridge is tense. Not knowing if the oncoming ship is friend or foe adds another layer of anxiety. "Mr. Adams, any changes in course for the Chinese ship?" Thompson asks.

"Negative, Skipper. Course and speed remain the same," Adams replies.

Thompson glances at Garcia. "What's your gut telling you, Carlos?"

"It's telling me Murph is in for some type of confrontation. What type is yet to be determined. The Chinese know where the *Grant* is and haven't taken any measures to avoid her. It could be as simple as a meet and greet—"

"I have a subsurface contact, Captain," Adams says in a tight voice.

Thompson steps over to the sonar station. "Distance and type?"

"Unknown on both, Skipper. Signal is intermittent."

"Course?"

"Also unknown," Adams answers.

"Keep tracking," Thompson orders. "I want that submarine and its position identified yesterday."

"Aye, aye, Skipper."

Thompson walks over to the chart table and punches up the sonar display. He's far from an expert, but he's seen enough sonar images over his career to be, at minimum, competent. The only blips visible are those of the two surface ships. Thompson glances up from the monitor. "Quartermaster, pull up all known contacts with Chinese submarines on the ship's computer." The order is affirmed and Thompson asks another member of the sonar team to compare the results from the computer to the recorded image of the recent subsurface contact.

Thompson returns to his position on the bridge. "I wish like hell we knew their intentions, Carlos. We could spend days screwing around with that sub."

"What if things turn hostile?"

"I know what we're not going to do. Torpedoes stay in their tubes until we identify this other sub. Murph can handle the Chinese destroyer."

Sonar Technician Adams swivels his chair around, his face pinched with concern. "Captain, I mark a detonation two miles off our stern."

"Depth?" Thompson asks.

"Fifty feet, sir."

CHAPTER 80

On the outskirts of Searcy, Zane pulls the truck up close to a newer pickup with out-of-state tags and steps from the cab. Alyx rolls out on her side, the shotgun in her hands. Zane crams the hose into the truck's gas tank.

"Hold off, Zane," Alyx whispers.

Zane glances up and Alyx points toward the interior of the truck. He shuffles forward and peers inside. Two people are seated on the front seat, the cause of death readily apparent by the bullet holes punched in their foreheads. Zane turns to Alyx. "They were executed," Zane whispers.

"Thanks, Captain Obvious. Let's get the hell out of here."

"We need fuel."

"We'll get it elsewhere."

Zane nods and tosses the hose in the back, hurrying back around to his side of the truck. A little farther down the highway, he spots an exit leading to downtown Searcy. "Think we'll have better luck looking for gas in town?"

"I'd rather stay on the highway. Seeing that murdered couple gives me the heebie-jeebies."

"We don't know if people from town were responsible for the killing."

Alyx turns in the seat to check behind them. "And I don't want to find out."

Zane glances at the gas gauge. "I don't want to push it much farther." After traveling another quarter mile, Zane slows, easing up on a late-model sedan with Tennessee tags. Inside the car is another dead couple, the interior buzzing with flies. "The killers must have been working in pairs," Zane says. "Probably came up from behind the car."

"I understand protecting what's yours, but these executions are just senseless murders."

Zane takes a moment to survey the area. Across the highway is a run-down hotel with people milling around in the parking lot. None appear to be too interested in the truck—yet. On the other side of the highway is a strip mall containing a mix of cheap clothing stores and a furniture rental outfit. The glass façades are smashed and clothing is strewn across the parking lot. "Can you stand watch while I siphon some gas?"

"Can we please get past this town?"

"We're running on fumes now. I'd feel a hell of a lot more comfortable with a gallon or two in our tank. Won't take but four or five minutes."

Alyx sighs, grabs the shotgun, and pushes her door open.

Zane steps out. "Keep an eye on that hotel."

Alyx nods as she takes up a position at the front of the truck. Zane grabs the hose and moves around to the other side and starts cursing because the fuel door has to be opened from the inside. He takes a deep breath and holds it as he sneaks his arm through the shattered window and pops the latch. He steps away, exhales, and starts the process of siphoning gas.

"Zane," Alyx says softly, stepping closer. "Two people are walking up the on-ramp about a quarter mile behind us."

Zane turns. From this distance it's hard to ascertain much about the pair, but what's not hard to distinguish are the two rifles riding on their shoulders. They don't appear to be in a hurry, a fact that prickles the hairs at the nape of Zane's neck. "Alyx, check our front," he says quietly, keeping an eye on the two coming up behind them.

The shotgun roars and Zane whips around to see another pair of individuals duck behind a stalled car, only thirty yards ahead. He yanks the hose out, tosses it into the bed, and steps forward to take the shotgun from Alyx. "Take the wheel," he says, backpedaling toward the passenger side. He sticks a hand through the window and blindly fumbles for more shotgun shells, his eyes focused on the dead sedan ahead. Alyx races around the truck and scrambles into the driver's seat. Zane glances back to see the two people running in their direction. They're seconds away from being pinned down by crossfire. His fingers light on the carton of shells and he grabs a handful and quickly reloads the shotgun. The two behind are still a good distance away so Zane turns his focus to the pair ahead.

Talking out of the side of his mouth he says, "Ease the pickup forward, Alyx. About walking speed. And keep your head down."

The truck eases forward and Zane walks with it, his gaze centered on the sedan ahead. The shotgun is braced against his shoulder, his right eye sighted down the barrel as he slowly walks forward. With only a few shotgun shells remaining, he can ill afford to waste any. A man peeks up behind the trunk, but Zane holds his fire, his mind clicking through scenarios. Zane's eyes drift toward the front of the car just as a man pops up by the hood, a rifle braced to his shoulder. Zane swings the shotgun and fires the right barrel. Rather than see if his shot hit the mark, he shifts the gun toward the rear of the car. Just as he thought, that man pops up, a pistol in his hand. Zane fires and quickly cracks the breech to reload.

A red smear is visible on the hood of the car. At that distance the buckshot would have spread a couple of feet, meaning the man is injured, but likely not dead. Zane hastens his pace. They need to get the hell out of here before the two behind them start firing. He lopes around the front of the pickup for protection. Alyx matches his speed as he walks sideways, the shotgun centered on his target. He takes a quick glance toward the rear. Those two are now less than a hundred yards away. They stop and raise their rifles, but there's little Zane can do. They're well beyond shotgun range. He turns his focus back to the stalled car, knowing the two behind will need time to catch their breath before being able to hit anything smaller than a barn. The man near the trunk lurches to his feet, his injured left arm tucked tight to his body. Zane fires and the double-aught buckshot rips through the man's midsection.

As shots ring out behind them, Zane dives into the bed of the truck, pounding on the cab. Alyx floors it, and Old Goldie takes off like a spooked deer. On the outskirts of town, Alyx pulls up to a rusted-out farm truck and Zane siphons some gas. He climbs back into the cab, smelling like gasoline. "We need to either avoid people trying to kill us, or find some more ammo."

"How many shells are left?"

"Three."

CHAPTER 81

Off the coast of Kitty Hawk

Brad Dixon awakens and, finding himself alone, tosses off the blanket and jumps to his feet, grabbing for the rifle. He'd made Nicole sleep topside while he stood guard. As thoughts of her harming Tanner bombard his mind, he cocks the rifle and steps over to the hatch, nearly colliding with Nicole coming up from below. She's carrying two steaming mugs of coffee and passes one to Brad. He eases the hammer down and takes the offered mug.

"Sorry. I had to use the restroom and put the coffee on to brew while I was down there." She walks to the back and plops down on the seat. "That's the last of the coffee."

"We'll reuse the grounds for a day or two," Brad says, taking a seat behind the wheel.

"You might want to brush up on your guarding skills."

Brad's cheeks pink up and he takes a sip of coffee to hide it.

"I'm just saying," Nicole says. "You were snoring, by the way."

Brad fires up the engine and steers the boat closer to shore. When he's satisfied with the location, he kills the engine and drops an anchor off the stern. He stows the rifle, well out of Nicole's reach, and picks up the fishing pole. He ties on a different lure and casts it over the stern and into the water.

"Your son seems sad," Nicole says.

"With good reason. He lost his mother and sister only days ago."

Nicole blows the steam rising from her cup and takes another sip. "And you lost a wife and daughter."

"Yep." Brad works the lure using short tugs on the fishing pole. He lets the lure drift for a moment and takes a pull from his coffee cup.

"Do you want to talk about it?" Nicole asks.

"Nope." Brad places his coffee cup aside and returns to the fishing pole. He reels in the lure and recasts. After five more casts and no hits, he switches to the lure he caught the black sea bass on yesterday morning.

Nicole sets her coffee on the rail and stands and stretches. "Do you have a final destination in mind?"

"Someplace that hasn't been bombed to shit."

"Are you always this pleasant in the mornings?" Nicole bends over and touches her palms to the deck. She glances up, her head cocked sideways. "No, let me rephrase. Are you always unpleasant?"

Brad's cheeks pink up again. "No, not always. Only when people try to steal our boat.'"

Nicole stands, places her hands on her hips, and

leans to the left. "I wasn't, nor am I currently, trying to steal your boat." Nicole returns to center and arches her back before stretching her arms over her head.

"Could have fooled me," Brad says.

Nicole returns to center and sighs. "I'll never convince you, will I?"

"Never is a very long time. Your stay aboard won't be quite that long."

Nicole changes the subject. "You're reeling the line in too fast. Mind if I give it a try?"

Brad hands her the fishing rig. "Fish aren't biting, but knock yourself out." He sits and retrieves his coffee, watching her.

She reels in the lure, digs through the tackle box, and pulls out a heavy sinker, which she attaches to the line two feet in front of the lure. With that accomplished, she cuts off the lure and installs a double hook. She pulls a plastic squid from the tackle box and slides it on to conceal the hooks. "It'd be better with live bait, but let's see what this does." Nicole casts the lure out and once it hits the water, allows the lure to sink to the bottom. Bobbing the pole up and down, Nicole slowly cranks the reel. Within minutes she gets a hit and yanks on the pole to set the hook. She glances over her shoulder. "Would you mind grabbing the net?"

Brad scowls as he stands and pulls the net from the gunwale and moves to the stern. When the fish is within reach, he nets it and pulls it aboard. "Looks like you snagged a flounder. And a big one at that."

Nicole smiles.

Brad unhooks the fish and Nicole casts out again. She quits after catching four more good-sized flounder.

"What were you doing different than me?" Brad asks.

"If I told you my secret you wouldn't have any reason to keep me around." Nicole smiles. "It's all in how you work the pole, no pun intended." She attaches a stringer to the extra fish and tosses them in the water.

Brad sets to work fileting the flounder while Nicole works on a second cup of coffee. Watching Brad butcher the job, she stands, takes the knife from his hand, and pushes him out of the way. He leans over the side to rinse his hands before heading below to fire up the stove. Tanner wakes up when the fish hits the pan. Brad glances up to see Nicole standing at the hatch, watching. "Am I cooking it wrong, too?"

Nicole smiles. "Smells good to me." She turns to look at Tanner. "Good morning, Tanner."

"Morning, ma'am," he says before ducking into the head.

Once the fish is cooked, Brad plates three equal portions and carries them topside. "Never thought I'd be eating fish for breakfast," Tanner mumbles, digging in.

Brad swallows the food in his mouth and says, "We need to eat fish when we can and save the canned stuff for bad-weather days." He turns to Nicole. "Where did you learn to fish, Nicole?"

Nicole takes notice of his first use of her name. "I grew up around Chesapeake Bay. My dad would take my brother and me out fishing every weekend until I hit high school and decided it wasn't cool anymore. I haven't fished in years, but I guess I retained some of what he taught us."

"How did you catch this flounder?" Brad asks around a mouthful of fish.

"I was drift-fishing the bottom where the flounder live."

Brad puts his fork down. "That's what I was doing."

Nicole holds up a finger. "No, not exactly. You were dragging the bait through the mud. I put the sinker on there to keep the lure off the bottom." She takes a bite and turns to Tanner. "What grade would you be going into?"

"Eighth." Tanner sighs. "And it was going to be the first year for me to start on the basketball team."

"I can see why. You're a tall young man. I bet you can bury the three at will."

Tanner smiles. Brad notices because it's the first time Tanner has smiled since boarding the boat. "I can. They don't call me Deadeye Dixon for nothing."

All three laugh. "Who calls you that?" Brad asks.

"Will and Trent. Most of the time they're razzing me, but I can hit the three more often than not."

"Are you good at getting boards?" Nicole asks.

"That's not the best part of my game. I get pushed around a little bit in the paint. Sometimes I forget to box out." He glances up at his father. "Think I'll ever get to play basketball again?"

"Absolutely," Brad says with more conviction than he feels. "We'll find a place to park this boat eventually."

"I'd like that," Tanner says, finishing up his fish. He rinses his plate and ducks below to retrieve his book before returning.

"What are you reading?" Nicole asks.

"Something we were going to read this semester in English lit." He turns the book around to show her the cover.

"Bradbury, one of my favorites," Nicole says.

"You've read *Fahrenheit 451*?" Tanner asks, as if asking Nicole if she has walked on the moon.

"Of course. I've read most all of Bradbury's works, some more than a few times. How do you like it?"

"It's . . . well, I guess, strange. I just started it yesterday, so I haven't gotten very far."

"*Strange* is a good way to describe some of his work, but the man was a genius. I'd love to discuss the novel when you get a little deeper into the story."

Nicole sees Tanner glance at his father to gauge his reaction before he says, "I'd love that. Dad's not much of a reader and it would be nice to discuss a book sometimes."

Brad stands and rinses his plate before hoisting the anchor. He unfurls the mainsail and sets the trim. They bypass two docks before heading out to open water.

CHAPTER 82

North Atlantic

The USS *New York* is parked at a depth of 800 feet, while a battle rages overhead. Petty Officer Adams, the sonar technician, has noted numerous detonations but no one on the sub knows who's winning the battle between the USS *Grant* and the Chinese destroyer. The sub crew's focus is on other matters: another submarine is lurking the depths. The assumption is she's Chinese, but that has yet to be confirmed. The one thing the crew *is* certain of—they're at war with the People's Republic of China.

"All ahead one-third," Captain Thompson orders. "Conn, steer us on a lazy S to see if we can pick up the other submarine."

His orders are confirmed and Thompson leans back in his chair, waiting. The ballistic missile submarine is designed for a single purpose—to sail the world's oceans in silence until ordered to launch its deadly cadre of nuclear missiles. Other U.S. Navy submarines, such as the Virginia-class attack subs, are built and designed to hunt and kill the enemy above or below the surface of the world's oceans. But the *New York* is no slouch when it comes to stealth or technology.

Midway through their maneuver, Adams announces, "Contact, Skipper. Signal remains faint. Bearing is two-niner-zero and contact is five miles out at a depth of five-nine-zero."

Captain Thompson stands. "Mr. Patterson, plot a course." He turns to Adams. "Enough for an ID?"

"Negative, sir."

"Damn," Thompson mutters. "Carlos, any chance the other sub could be a friendly?"

"I highly doubt it, Bull. I don't know—"

"Torpedo in the water," Adams says, his voice high, strained.

"Target?" Thompson barks.

"Running for the *Grant*, sir."

"Mark the launch point."

"Done, sir," Adams replies.

"I guess that answers one question," Thompson says to Garcia. "The next question is, where did she go after launching? My guess is deep, but I don't have a feel for which direction."

"If she doesn't know we're here, maybe she didn't stray far."

"Two more fish in the water," Adams reports.

"On course for the *Grant*?" Thompson asks.

"Affirmative, sir."

"Did she shoot from the same location?"

"Negative, Skipper. Bearing is now two-six-zero. Depth is seven-two-zero."

Thompson looks at Garcia. "You're right. She descended but didn't stray far from the original launch point."

"Mr. Adams, distance to the enemy sub?" Thompson asks.

"Four miles and closing, sir."

Thompson crosses his arms. "Conn, maintain course and speed." He glances at Garcia. "I want to be in that sub's back pocket before we launch our torpedoes."

"Makes sense," Garcia says. "Take away their reaction time. How close do you want to be?"

"As close as we can get. Anywhere within a mile should do it." Thompson pivots toward the sonar station. "Mr. Adams, distance to target?"

"Trying to reacquire, sir. Could be she ascended into the convergence zone."

Thompson thumbs the sweat from his brow. "Find her quick, Mr. Adams."

"Aye, aye, Skipper."

Thompson steps over to the attack center. "Mr. White, tubes loaded?"

"They are, Skipper," Weapons Officer David White says.

"How long to produce a firing solution when we reacquire the target?"

"Seconds, sir," White says.

"That may be all the time we have. Flood the tubes and stand by," Thompson says before returning to his place on the bridge. Thoughts of what Murphy might be encountering attempt to invade his brain, but he quickly builds a mental wall—there will be plenty of time for that later. "Mr. Adams?"

"I've got her, sir. She's running full out at a depth of six-zero-zero."

"Course?" Thompson asks.

"She's on an eighty-degree course, three miles out.

If she maintains current course, she'll pass within a half a mile of our bow."

"Any hints if they've discovered our presence?"

"Negative, sir. I see no evasive maneuvers."

"Status of the surface ships, Mr. Adams?"

"All screws are still turning for both ships. The USS *Grant* is six miles off our stern, running on a 360-degree course. The Chinese destroyer is ten miles off our bow and running on a 180-degree course."

"Maybe both ships are having targeting issues," Garcia says.

"Could be. Sounds like they're lining up for an old-fashioned naval battle," Thompson replies.

Silence descends on the bridge. Thompson mops his face with his uniform sleeve and reclasps his hands behind his back. Garcia shuffles his feet wider to provide a more stable base.

"Enemy sub two miles and closing," Adams says in a hushed voice.

"Conn, all stop," Thompson orders.

One of the young sailors piloting the sub dries his palms on his thighs and returns his hands to the controls. Thompson unclasps his hands and crosses his arms. Garcia repositions his feet and rakes a hand through his thinning hair. A blast wave from the battle overhead reverberates across the hull. Adams, the sonar technician, turns a knob to fine-tune the growing image on his screen.

"One-point-five miles and closing," Adams says in a near whisper.

"Thank you, Mr. Adams," Thompson says. A small smile forms on Thompson's lips at the performance of his crew. All appear to be calm and steady, but Thompson knows their insides are tied up in knots, much like his own.

"One mile and closing," Adams says.

"Same course?" Thompson asks, his voice low and clear.

Adams nods.

Thompson steps over to the attack center. "David, we're going to let her in close. Stand by." Thompson watches the target on the screen for a moment. "Conn, stand by right full rudder." Thompson cranks his head left, then right, in an attempt to reduce the strain in his neck. Garcia quietly shuffles over to the navigation table for a peek at the sonar.

Adams clears his throat. "Sixteen hundred yards and closing."

Thompson bends down to talk quietly to White. "Do you have the firing solution?"

"Yes, sir," White says, his eyes never leaving the control panel in front of him. A thin man, White's hands appear steady at the controls.

"Well done. Stand by."

"Fourteen hundred yards," Adams says.

Thompson calculates the distances in his head. If they're correct, the enemy sub will pass within three hundred yards of their bow.

"Mr. Adams, have they detected our presence?"

"Negative, sir. Twelve hundred yards."

Thompson inhales a deep breath and releases it. A trickle of sweat runs down his back. He repositions his stance for the upcoming dive.

"One thousand yards to port, three hundred yards off our bow," Adams says in a soft voice.

Thompson waits. The seconds tick by in absolute silence.

"Eight hundred yards," Adams says.

Thompson leans over and whispers, "Mr. White, fire tubes one and two."

White punches the button for tube one then tube two, and the boat shudders as the torpedoes explode from their tubes. "Fish away," White says.

"Hard left rudder," Thompson barks. "Emergency deep."

As the nose of the sub tilts down at a steep angle, Thompson orders a report on the torpedoes.

"They're tracking, sir," White says.

Those on the bridge are holding their breath. After an agonizing wait that feels like hours, White shouts, "Contact." A collective sigh escapes from the crew as the blast waves from the two massive explosions rock the sub.

"Status?" Thompson asks.

"Multiple sonar signatures, Captain," Adams says. "Target destroyed."

Those words elicit a subdued cheer from those on the bridge. Yes, the torpedoes found their target, but the crew of Chinese submarine were sailors doing their jobs, a point that hits a little too close to home for the crew of the USS *New York*.

"Mr. Patterson, plot a course for that Chinese destroyer."

CHAPTER 83

Weatherford

Rather than climb up and down the turbine's tower, Gage stays topside as Henry works below after climbing down following lunch. All of the electrical work is completed—or so they hope. They won't know for sure until Gage releases the brake and the blades start spinning. Gage grabs a large crowbar and stuffs some wrenches into the pouch on his tool belt before climbing into the hub. During normal operation, the computer controls blade pitch and the position of the turbine head relative to the wind. But now it's as far from normal as anyone ever thought possible a couple of weeks ago.

When the turbine was taken off-line, the blade pitch was set to an acceptable angle and now Gage's job is to make sure it stays that way. The electric motors are fried and the stench of burned plastic and melted wire still lingers within the confined space. Gage reaches back through the hub and grabs a handful of metal plates. Ideally he would weld the plates in place—a twenty-minute job pre-doomsday—but that's out the window now with no electricity. Now he'll have to go through the laborious process of bolting the metal plates in place. He pulls a wrench from his pouch and starts working.

It's not long before he's dripping sweat. Add the fact that he's working in tight quarters and the job is downright miserable. The wrench slips off a nut, ripping the skin from Gage's knuckle. He mutters a string of curse words that goes on for a good minute. After wrapping a rag around his hand, he retrieves the offending wrench and continues working. After a couple of hours, he finishes bolting the last plate onto to the last blade and climbs out of the hub, arching his back to stretch out the kink in his lower spine. He lifts his wet shirt away from his torso, allowing the breeze to sneak in while mopping his face with a rag. He steps over to the side of the nacelle and shouts down to Henry, "How's it looking?"

Henry looks up and shouts, "Looks good. Give me a few more minutes and we'll give her a try."

"Okay," Gage shouts, unhooking his tool belt and letting it drop to the floor as he reaches for a clean rag. He sits, wiping the grease and grime from his hands. A loose flap of skin is dangling over his middle knuckle and he rips it off. A trickle of fresh blood sprouts and he wraps a clean rag around his hand and pushes to his feet to retrieve a bottle of water. Gage takes a long pull from the bottle and returns to his seat. A few minutes later, Henry shouts something he can't hear and he stands and walks over to the side. "What?" he shouts.

Henry cups his hands around his mouth and shouts, "Release the brake."

Gage glances up to see two people turning up the

road to the turbine, rifles slung over their shoulders. The turbine is situated on a gravel drive about two hundred yards from the main road with nothing but plowed fields for as far as the eye can see. The pair is too far away to identify so Gage doesn't know if they're friend or foe, but if they're looking for trouble, Henry and the truck will be impossible to miss.

Gage doesn't want to shout down to Henry and give away his position or reveal the fact that there's more than one person around. But he has no idea if Henry has seen them. With the shotgun still in the truck, there's no way Gage can get to it before the pair arrives. He grabs a wrench from the tool belt on the floor and chucks it toward the truck. Two seconds later, the wrench clangs off the hood, and Henry snaps his head up. Gage waves a hand toward the road. Henry turns that way, drops his tools, and hurries for the truck as the two coming up the road brace their rifles to their shoulders. Shots ring out as Gage clambers through the hatch and grabs the ladder.

Trying to hit every other rung with his feet, Gage's descent is herky-jerky. More shots ring out and it's all rifle fire. When Gage touches down on the upper platform, the shotgun comes to life. The booms from the 12-gauge shells reverberate up the tower, but they're a comfort to Gage knowing that Henry is still alive. Gage swings around to the lower ladder and continues the descent. More shots ring out, a quick succession of rifle fire, answered by the booming blasts from the shotgun. Gage is trying to keep count of the number of shots fired from the shotgun and almost loses his balance. He turns his focus back to the ladder. The shotgun barks twice more before an eerie silence settles in.

Gage scampers down the last twenty feet and takes a peek out the door. No one is waiting to kill him so he eases out the door and works his way around the tower and nearly trips over Henry, who's crumpled at the base. Gage squats down for a closer look. Henry's eyes are open, but his breath is ragged. "Are you hit?"

"Right arm. They rushed the truck. Had to take cover behind the tower."

"And the two men?"

"Dead, I hope."

"Are you sure?"

"No."

Gage pries the shotgun from Henry's hands. "Any ammo left?"

"Left pants pocket. Had to grab what I could."

Gage wedges his hand into Henry's pocket and retrieves three shells. "I'll be back in a sec."

Henry nods as Gage feeds the shells into the gun and racks one into the chamber. He takes a step forward and peers around the tower. One of the assailants is lying by the front tire, but there's no sign of the second one. Gage hunches over and runs for the front of the truck. He slides along the nose to check on the first man. No need to feel for a pulse—his midsection is shredded. Gage turns and eases back the other way, turning around the right fender. Carefully, he creeps toward the rear. At the edge of the tailgate, he pauses for a deep breath, tucks the shotgun tight to his shoulder, and swings around the rear of the truck.

The second man is lying in a pool of blood a foot from the gravel driveway. Gage steps forward, kicks the rifle out of reach, and bends down for a closer look. The man's left shoulder looks as if it has been run through a meat grinder and his chest is fluttering up and down with each breath. Gage squats down on his haunches. "Why did you attack us?"

"Truck," the man whispers.

"You risked your life for a pickup?"

The man can do little more than nod.

"In the current climate, you know your odds of survival are slim to none, right?"

Another nod.

"I can walk away and let you bleed out or do you a favor."

"Favor," the man mutters.

Gage stands and moves ten feet away. He braces the stock to his shoulder and fires one round at the man's chest. Gage turns away from the gory scene and returns to his father-in-law. He helps Henry to his feet and guides him to the truck. Henry doesn't ask about the final shot. Gage helps him into the cab and rotates him so that he's facing the open door. Gently, Gage lifts Henry's sleeve for a look at the wound. "Looks like the bullet went through clean. We need to clean up the wound and see if there are any fragments of material inside. Might be best to wait until we get back to the house. You're going to live but your bicep is going to hurt like hell for a while."

"About what I figured. Thought I was a better shot than that."

"It's different when someone's shooting back at you. Not that I would know a whole lot about that." Gage helps Henry get situated and climbs behind the wheel. He fires up the truck and makes a big looping turn around the bodies before steering toward the drive.

CHAPTER 84

Now about fifteen miles northeast of Little Rock, Arkansas, Zane is eager to get back on 1-40 and away from these one-stoplight towns. He glances at the gas gauge and the needle is hovering near empty. He exits off Highway 67 to avoid a traffic jam of dead autos and makes a slow drive through town. They pass a looted Sonic Drive-In, and Alyx moans. "Wouldn't a cherry limeade just hit the spot?"

"Thanks for the reminder. We need gas."

"Dream crasher." Alyx's voice sounds odd, a result of her still-swollen nose.

They pass a retirement home on one corner with a funeral home just opposite. "Must have saved on travel expenses," Alyx says. "Hell, they could have just walked a gurney across the street and hauled the dead back without ever firing an engine."

"You're morbid. Although, their business would be booming now if they were open."

"And who's morbid?"

They ride in silence for the next block, passing a couple of homegrown restaurants that dot small towns all across the country. Never large enough for the big chains, the locals made do with what they had, no matter the food quality. Zane makes a turn and they bypass a Walmart and a run-down shanty called a flea market. There are a few people out, but they appear to be paying little mind to the pickup motoring down the road. At the next intersection they find the high school and Zane steers into the lot. It appears the school was already in session when doomsday arrived. The lot is littered with autos, a veritable smorgasbord of vehicles to choose from to meet their gasoline needs.

"See anyone around?" Zane asks.

Alyx cranes her neck to look. "Nope. But make it quick."

"That's not what you said last night."

Alyx shows him her middle finger.

Zane pulls up to a newer Ford truck and puts the transmission in park. He climbs out and grabs the hose as Alyx steps out with the shotgun. He sets to work and, miracle of miracles, he gets the gas flowing with the first suck from his mouth. Despite the persistent haze, temps are in the midseventies and, in the distance, there's a smattering of birdcalls. Old Goldie has a twenty-gallon gas tank and it takes a while for gravity to do its work. Zane plucks the bag of leftover turkey from the cab and walks over to Alyx, offering her some. "Eat up. It'll be spoiled soon."

Alyx props the shotgun against the hood of the truck and grabs a handful of turkey. "How's the leg?"

"It's sore. Could have been much worse if we hadn't run into your friend Sarah. How's the nose?"

"Tender." Alyx feeds another piece of turkey into her mouth.

"How far from Little Rock to Weatherford?" Zane asks between bites.

"Six hours on a normal day. Now, probably twice that or longer. But given the luck we've had so far, it could be days."

"I feel like we've been traveling for months. I'm ready for somewhere where we can hunker down."

"At least we're not walking."

"There is that. Old Goldie might be ugly, but she saved our ass." Zane grabs another piece of turkey and offers more to Alyx, who declines. "Tank ought to be about full." He walks back to check the gas gauge. "Good to go, Alyx." He pulls the hose out, tosses it into the bed, and secures the gas cap.

Cruising back through town toward the highway, Zane spots a sign for a gunsmith. He slows and pulls into the lot of a '60s-era strip mall. The place hasn't been updated since the day it was built, and the shake shingle facade is more tar paper than shingle. He spots the store in the far corner and eases the truck that direction. Someone, the owner presumably, has piled up sandbags to block entrance to the store. Sitting on top of the sandbags is a monster gun resting on bipod legs.

"This guy's not screwing around," Zane says, easing the pickup to a stop in front of the store.

"That thing looks like a cannon. What the hell is it?"

"It is a Barrett .50 caliber long-range sniper rifle. About as deadly as any hand-carried weapon there is, other than an RPG."

"Why would someone, a civilian especially, need something like that?" Alyx asks.

"Probably come in pretty handy about now." Zane leans over and pulls out the sack of meds, grabbing a bottle of antibiotics. "Keep that shotgun handy."

"What are we doing?"

"Trying to get some more ammo for said shotgun."

"And if the guy decides to shoot you with that monster gun?"

"I guess you'll have to scrape up my insides from the parking lot."

"Comforting thought. Do we need more ammo that desperately?"

"The luck we've been having? Absolutely. We've still got a long way to go." Zane stuffs the pill bottle down his front pocket and exits the truck, his hands held high. He works around the nose of the pickup and approaches the store. At ten feet away, a heavily bearded face pops up behind the Barrett.

"What the hell you want?" the man says, peering through the rifle's scope.

"I want to barter for a couple of boxes of 12-gauge shotgun shells."

"What do you have?" The man eyes Alyx, and Zane's hoping this man doesn't mean he wants her.

"Medicine."

"I've got more ibuprofen than I could use in a lifetime."

"Do you have any antibiotics?" Zane asks.

"That I don't have. How much you got?"

"I have a bottle of Augmentin, enough for a ten-day course."

The man ponders for a moment. "That might get you one box of shells."

Zane thinks of their tradable items and hits on an

idea. "How about a couple of handfuls of turkey, cooked fresh this morning?"

This time the man doesn't hesitate. "You got yourself a deal." The man steps out from behind the rifle. Only his head is visible and it's mostly hair. But judging from the height of the sandbags, he's either tall or standing on a step stool. "How do you want to work this?"

"I'm a man of my word," Zane says.

"Yeah, well, fuck that. I'll grab the shells and we'll do the exchange on top of the sandbags."

"I need to grab the turkey from the truck."

"Go ahead. Try anything funny and I'll splatter your insides all over that ugly-ass pickup."

With his hands still high in the air, Zane steps off the curb, grabs the turkey from Alyx's outstretched hand, and returns. He passes it across, and the man opens the bag and takes a sniff. One carton of shells appears on top of the sandbags. Zane picks it up and opens the lid to make sure he's not getting a box of ball bearings.

"I'm a man of my word, too," the man says around a mouthful of turkey. "It's a damn shame that no one trusts anybody anymore."

Zane digs the pill bottle out of his pocket and places it on top of the sandbags. Another box of shells appears, but this time Zane doesn't open the lid. "You in the military?"

"Yep. Four tours in the sandbox. You?"

"One."

"Hoorah," the man says. "Probably ain't no military left now."

"You're probably right. How long have you been holed up in there?"

"Since day one. Got a pretty good supply of water and grub. Wife left during the third tour. Just me now."

Zane scans the Barrett. "Had to fire that thing?"

"Only once. I guess word spread."

"I bet. Nice doing business with you, soldier," Zane says.

"Back at ya. You be safe out there."

"Will do." Zane turns and heads back to the truck. He waves before climbing inside.

"That was a bonding moment," Alyx says.

"Hell, he's not a bad guy. He's in the same boat we're in."

"Yeah, but he has a bigger gun in his boat."

Zane smiles and steers back to the main road. A mile farther on he spots an on-ramp and pulls back onto the highway.

CHAPTER 85

North Atlantic

With the Chinese submarine destroyed, the USS *New York* is stalking the Chinese destroyer that is now ten miles off their bow. The distance is well within torpedo range yet Captain Thompson, much as he did with the Chinese sub, is holding fire until they close the distance. Cruising at a depth of 600 feet, the sub is running at full speed, hoping to sink the enemy destroyer before the USS *Grant* suffers further damage. Thompson is itching to talk with Murphy to find out exactly what his status is. Situations such as this are one of the negatives of submarine life—you're enclosed in a metal tube with no windows, and situational awareness of the surrounding environment is limited to an array of computer-controlled sensors. Thompson decides to scratch the itch. "Q, slow ascent to periscope depth."

"Aye, aye, Captain," Quigley replies.

The nose of the sub tilts up slightly and Thompson steps over to the sonar station. "Mr. Adams, what's the status of the two surface ships?"

"*Grant* is five miles off our bow. The enemy destroyer is ten miles from our position and seven miles from *Grant*'s location. Sir, *Grant* is currently turning only one screw."

"Could be she's saving fuel." Saying it doesn't necessarily mean Thompson believes it. He steps back over to his command post. "Q, steepen the ascent."

The nose of the sub tilts up on a steeper angle and those standing lean forward to compensate. Thompson looks at Garcia. "Carlos, make sure we're locked and loaded. Flood the tubes. The Chinese destroyer knows we're here now."

Garcia steps over to the attack center and relays the captain's orders.

"Captain, we're at periscope depth," Quigley reports.

"Periscope up. Comms, get me Captain Murphy." Thompson steps over and catches the handles of the periscope as it ascends. He positions his face in the eyecups and walks a 360-degree circle. In the far distance is the Chinese destroyer, smoke billowing from the deck. He turns the scope and centers it on the USS *Grant*. There is visible damage but she appears to be watertight.

"Captain, fish in the water," Adams says.

"Course and distance."

"She's headed our way, sir. Ten miles out and closing."

"Thank you, Mr. Adams. Keep tracking her."

"Skipper, I have Captain Murphy on the radio," the radio technician says.

Thompson grabs a radio handset from above. "Murph, you there?"

"I'm here, Bull. Good shooting down there."

"Thanks. What's your status?"

"We've sustained some damage, but nothing we can't handle. Still having issues with the goddamn targeting computer. We hit the Chinese with a couple of missiles, but she's still afloat. We're currently turning one screw to conserve fuel."

"You tracking the torpedo she just launched?"

"Torpedo nine miles and closing," Adams says.

"Yep, Bull. We'll handle that one. Can you get close and launch a few torpedoes of your own?"

"Working on it, Murph."

"Another fish in the water, Skipper," Adams says. "Same course, ten miles and closing."

"Murph, they launched another torpedo."

"We're tracking it. We'll handle any that come your way."

"Roger. See you on the other side. Thompson out." He clicks the radio handset back in place. "Dive, take us down to four-zero-zero. All ahead full." As his orders are carried out, he turns to the sonar tech. "Mr. Adams, status of the torpedoes?"

"Torpedo one is seven miles out and closing at sixty knots. Fish two is at eight miles."

"Thank you," Thompson says.

Seconds later, Adams says, "Detonation, Skipper. Enemy torpedo one destroyed."

As the blast wave from the first explosion washes over the hull, Adams announces another detonation. "Enemy torpedo two destroyed."

The second blast wave hits and Thompson steps over to the sonar station. "Distance to enemy destroyer?"

"Eight miles, Skipper," Adams says.

"Thank you, Mr. Adams." Thompson wipes a hand across his brow and flicks away the sweat that had accumulated there.

"Two enemy torpedoes in the water," Adams says. "They're targeting the *Grant*, sir."

"Roger," Thompson says, turning to Garcia. "We're going with the same game plan we used for their sub. Hopefully they've lost us for the moment. Might be one reason they're back to targeting *Grant* again."

"Unless they're baiting a trap," Garcia says.

Thompson scowls. "Don't jinx us, Carlos." Thompson turns to the sonar station. "Distance to target?"

"Six miles, sir."

Thompson walks over to the navigation area. "Mr. Patterson, I want to slip in behind her."

Patterson confirms the order, and the boat makes a slow turn to the right.

"Mr. Adams, target's speed?"

"She's turning fifteen knots, Skipper."

"Any indication she's towing her sonar?"

"Negative."

"Good. Mr. Patterson, let me know when we're within a mile of target," Thompson says to the navigator.

After six minutes of running in silence the target is now one mile out. Thompson steps over to the attack center. "Mr. White, you have the firing solution?"

"Yes, Skipper," White replies.

"Fire tubes one and two and stand by three and four."

"Firing tubes one and two," White says.

The sub shudders as the torpedoes are shot out of their tubes.

"Fish away," White says. "One mile to target."

The bridge is silent. With the enemy ship moving away from them at fifteen knots, it'll take better than a minute for the torpedoes to reach their target.

"Fifteen hundred yards to target," White says.

"Roger," Thompson replies. "Conn, left ten-degrees rudder."

White, the weapons officer, fine-tunes the resolution on his video screen. "One thousand yards to target."

Thompson nods and crosses his arms. There are currently twelve people on the bridge and it's quiet enough that Thompson can hear his own heartbeat. He removes his cap, mops his brow, and puts the hat back on. His hand drifts down to his face, where he rubs the stubble on his chin.

Moments later, White says, "Two hundred yards." Then seconds later, "Direct hit, sir. Both torpedoes."

This time the cheer on the bridge is not muted. Once the shouts and high fives have died down, Thompson orders the sub to periscope depth. Minutes later the sub levels off and Thompson orders both periscopes up. He takes one and Garcia the other, both walking a circular path until the Chinese destroyer comes into view. The captain triggers the video camera. "Punch periscope one up on the video system," he orders. When the image of the destroyed enemy ship appears on-screen, the crew's cheer can be heard all across the boat.

CHAPTER 86

Weatherford

Gunshot victims are a rare occurrence in a small town like Weatherford, and Susan was shocked to find her husband with just that. After berating her husband with a few choice words, she is now tending to the wound while Gage and Holly share a private moment with Olivia in their bedroom.

"What happened to the two men who attacked you?" Holly asks. She pulls up her top and settles the baby against her breast.

Gage spends a moment considering how to frame his answer then says, "They didn't make it. Let's just leave it at that." Gage gently rubs a hand across the fine hairs on his daughter's head. "Is your milk in?"

"No."

"Are we worried about that?" Gage asks, tentatively.

"Not yet. The doctor said Olivia should get enough colostrum to satisfy her for a day or two." She readjusts the baby's position and uses her free hand to put

Olivia's mouth on her nipple. "How much danger were you two in?"

"Well, it's never a real good thing to have people shooting at you. I was up in the tower, so your dad got the worst of it. It was mostly over by the time I made it to the bottom."

"Mostly?"

Gage turns his gaze to his daughter, refusing to look his wife in the eyes. Holly still doesn't know about his encounter with the Marston family killers. "It was over. I just had to get your dad to the pickup." Gage pushes up off the bed and stands. "I need to run back out there and tidy up."

Holly scowls. "What do you mean, 'tidy up'?"

Gage ignores her question. "Can we run over to my parents' when I get back?"

Holly moves the baby to the opposite breast. "Yeah, but how long are you going to be gone? How's the work on the wind turbine going?"

"Not more than an hour or two, hopefully. As far as the turbine goes, we'll know more tomorrow. But it's looking good. Hopefully we'll have the water well pumping soon. I need a bath."

"I noticed," Holly says, playfully pinching her nose.

"I don't think any of us are a bed of roses. How's the pain?"

"It's tender as hell down there and you'll be lucky to ever venture into that territory again."

Gage smiles. "I'm going to need to venture down there if we're going to have more babies." He leans down and kisses Holly on the forehead. "I'll probably be fighting *you* off in a few weeks."

Holly gives his arm a small pinch and bats her eyelashes. "Maybe."

Gage laughs. "I'll be back in a bit." He exits the bedroom and pauses in the kitchen to check on Henry. "How's the wound look, Susan?"

The bottle of bourbon is sitting on the table, a half-empty glass next to it. Several candles are burning, creating a mix of smells—lavender, vanilla bean, sugar cookies, pumpkin pie—that permeate the room, all courtesy of Bath & Body Works. Susan, equipped with a headlamp, is operating. "It's pretty clean. I pulled out a couple of threads and did my best to disinfect the area. All that's left is to bandage him up."

"I'm here, you know." Henry says, a slight slur in his voice. "Feels like someone ran a hot poker through my arm, Gage."

"How's the medicine going down?" Gage asks.

"It takes the edge off. I'll know more after the next glass."

Gage smiles. "I'm going to run out to the turbine and do some tidying up."

"Want me to come with?" Henry asks.

"No," Susan and Gage say in near unison. Susan begins wrapping a bandage around her husband's arm. "You're gonna sit your butt on the sofa and finish your bourbon."

"Yes, ma'am." Henry replies, reaching for his drink with his good arm.

Gage ducks into the utility room and grabs a flashlight. It's not dark yet, but it will be in a couple of hours and he has no idea how long his task is going to take. He steps outside and heads to the barn for a rope and a shovel, before firing up the pickup.

Minutes later, turning down the road to the turbine, he slows, scanning for other threats. He's still shocked that two people attacked them just to steal the truck. But when people are desperate, rational thinking goes out the window, Gage surmises. Not seeing anyone, he eases down the gravel drive.

When he nears the first body, he whips the truck around and backs it up. He climbs out and spends a few moments deciphering the best way to approach the issue of body disposal. Neither man is small and Gage estimates that each weighs north of two hundred pounds. Lifting them into the pickup is going to be a chore. Not to mention the worry over the bodily fluids that continue to ooze from both. Gage thinks, briefly, of burying them where they lie but it probably wouldn't be long before a pack of hungry dogs came along and dug them up. And digging in the hard clay would consume too much time. He makes his decision and lashes the rope around the ankle of the first man and ties it off on the trailer hitch. He climbs back in the truck and drags the first body over to the second. After tying on the second body, he slides behind the wheel, wondering what to do now.

There aren't any trees or brush piles, only plowed fields in the entire 640-acre section. Dragging the bodies down the road to another piece of property is out of the question. Knowing the fields won't be worked anytime soon, he drops the truck into gear and steers for the plowed field ahead. When he's a good distance away from the turbine and somewhat centered in the field, he climbs out and unties the rope, tossing it into the back.

Back on the road, he stops by the Reed home to pick

up Holly and Olivia before working their way to the other side of town. Gage pulls into the drive of his boyhood home and climbs out to help Holly and Olivia out of the cab. Gage pauses to take a long, calming breath before approaching the front door. His mother steps out of the house, her eyes red and her cheeks damp. Gage knows his father is gone.

"When?" Gage asks.

"This morning." Ginny moves aside to allow them in the house and she gets her first glance at her grandchild. She takes the baby from Holly and nuzzles her nose against her soft cheeks. "Aren't you beautiful . . ." She glances at Holly. "Which name did you two pick?"

"Olivia," Holly replies.

Ginny turns back to the baby. "You're beautiful, Olivia. Welcome to the world."

Gage steps tentatively into the living room. Raymond Larson is lying on the bed, the sheet pulled up to his chin. Gage shuffles over to the side of the bed and places a hand on his father's forehead. The skin is cool to the touch and Gage's hand drifts up where he fingers the last remaining tufts of his father's silvery hair.

His mother steps up beside him and places a hand on Gage's back, the other still cradling Olivia. "We wanted you to have a chance to say good-bye, son. I'm sorry he won't get to meet this beautiful little girl."

"Did he ever wake up?" Gage asks, wiping a tear from the corner of his eye.

"No."

Gage nods. "Was he in pain?"

"No. We had some leftover Oxycontin from his shoulder surgery last year. I've been crushing them up and mixing them with a little water to spoon into his mouth. He drifted away peacefully this morning."

Gage turns away. "I'll get Garrett and we'll dig the grave."

"It's already done. Your brother's been working on it for the past couple of days."

"Where?" Gage asks.

"Under that big oak tree by the barn."

Gage wipes away a tear. "That was his favorite place."

"I know, honey," Ginny says, stroking her free hand across Gage's broad shoulders.

"He used to come in out of the field, grab a couple of cold beers from the fridge, and sit out there until dinner. It's perfect."

"That's what we thought, too. I'll get him fixed up if you want to go round up Garrett, Juliet, and the kids."

Gage turns to take one final look at his father, as Holly shuffles over and puts a hand around his waist. "He's gone too soon, babe," Gage mutters, tears now streaming down his cheeks.

"I know. I'm sorry, Gage." Holly takes her husband's hand and threads her fingers through his. "Come on, we'll walk down to your brother's house." Holly leads Gage away from the bed.

At the door, Holly takes Olivia from Ginny and snuggles the baby against her chest. They step outside and walk toward Garrett's house, two hundred yards away. The home is a well-kept three-bedroom rancher with a detached two-car garage that Garrett and Juliet built soon after their wedding. Gage hears a screen door slam and looks up to see his brother and the girls coming their way. Gage and Holly move into the shade of the old oak tree to await their arrival. Both Emma and Elizabeth are in pigtails and the braids sway back and forth with each step they take.

When they arrive, Garrett steps up and gives his brother a hug before moving on to Holly. The girls squeal at the sight of Olivia as Gage steps over to give Juliet a hug. Together, they amble back to the house.

"I would have helped you dig the grave," Gage tells Garrett when they're out of earshot.

"I'm bored out of my mind. Gave me something to do," Garrett replies.

"Any of the tractors running?"

"Nope. I guess the fields will lie fallow. I've got six hundred acres of corn in the south field and nothing to harvest it with."

"Probably not fit to eat, anyway," Gage says. "I don't think I'd want to risk it."

Garrett sighs. "I know." He glances at the kids ahead and lowers his voice. "It scares the hell out of me. I got two young mouths to feed."

"And I now have one of my own. A lot of open country. I guess we'll go back to hunting."

Garrett steals another quick glance at his family. "I went out to scout a couple of days ago. Everything I found was dead."

"They can't all be dead, Garrett. There have to be pockets of wildlife that are still alive."

"We'll have to find them if there are. Any of your cattle survive?"

"Nope. I herded them all up into the barn and even that didn't help."

Once they reach the house, Holly, Juliet, and the girls take seats at the picnic table while Gage and Garrett duck into the house. Their father is bound up in the sheet. Gage takes the head and Garrett the feet as they carry Raymond Larson out of the family home for the last time. Ginny follows them and joins the girls and, as dusk descends, the family procession makes their way to the grave amid a shower of tears. The boys, aided by ropes, lower their father into the ground, and each family member takes a turn on the shovel, the white sheet gradually disappearing beneath the red Oklahoma clay.

CHAPTER 87

Off the coast of Hatteras, North Carolina

The Outer Banks are a boomerang-shaped series of barrier islands that stretch for two hundred miles along the coast of North Carolina. The islands vary in size—some narrow enough to be measured with a tape measure while others widen to a mile or more—and Brad is now tacking the *EmmaSophia* toward Hatteras, one of the larger islands.

As the veiled sun drifts lower on the horizon, Brad works the wheel as his mind works through a quandary. There has been no further discussion of Nicole's status aboard ship and Brad is now conflicted. Yes, he and Emma had hit a rough patch in their marriage recently—the second time in two years—but is it sacrilegious to now have another, different woman on board the *EmmaSophia*? he wonders. Especially so soon after the death of his wife and daughter? He sighs and tries to push the thoughts from his mind.

About a half mile from shore, he drops the mainsail and tosses the anchor overboard. They'll stay here and fish before moving out to deeper water to bed down.

On shore, a hodgepodge of tents and shelters built from scavenged material stretch to the horizon. Cooking fires are scattered among the shelters, creating a smoky haze that lingers now that the wind has died. Brad stands and stretches. "Nicole, work your magic with the fishing pole, please," he says. He turns to watch as she moves comfortably around the boat in a pair of Tanner's shorts and one of his T-shirts.

"Any particular species of fish I should be baiting for?" Nicole asks. "What's your palate craving?"

"Food," Brad answers. "I guess we'll eat whatever you can catch."

"I'm going to rig it for yellowfin tuna and see if I can get any bites. I've never fished the Outer Banks before, so it's going to be hit or miss."

"I could go for tuna," Brad offers.

Once Nicole has her pole rigged up, she tosses the lure toward the deeper water. "I can't make any guarantees. We'll see what happens."

Brad notices her gnawing her bottom lip as she works the lure through the water. His gaze drifts lower to her legs and bare feet. "Where are your shoes?" Brad asks.

Nicole glances over her shoulder. "Lost them when you made me jump back in the water."

"Oh." Brad looks down at his feet as if searching for a lost valuable.

Nicole yanks on the pole. "Got something. Not sure what. Brad, will you grab the net?"

"I'm on it."

Tanner ventures up on deck, his dark, wavy hair matted with sleep.

"You fall asleep?" Brad asks.

"Yeah. What's going on up here?"

"Nicole is about to land another fish. Luckiest fisher-person I've ever seen."

"I don't think *luck* is the right word, Dad. She could probably teach you a thing or two."

Brad scowls at this son before turning back to the water. As the fish draws closer, Brad leans over the rail and scoops up the fish, placing the net on the deck. Nicole bends over to work the hook out.

"What kind is it?" Brad asks.

Nicole blows the hair out of her face. "A mackerel. If Tanner's not too fond of fish, we should probably throw it back. It has a distinct fishy taste."

"Throw it back," Tanner says.

Nicole grabs a pair of pliers and jiggles the hook out of the fish's mouth and Brad tosses it overboard. He looks up to see a dead powerboat coming their way, two makeshift paddles rowing on either side of the boat. Brad grabs the rifle and jacks a shell into the chamber. When the boat cuts the distance in half, Brad orders them to stop. A tall man with a large round belly works his way toward the bow of his boat. He looks to be in his midsixties and is outfitted with paisley swimming trunks and a stained white T-shirt.

"Hi, neighbor. I was hoping you'd give me a ride," the man says with a wave of his hand.

Holding the rifle down by his leg, Brad says, "I'm sorry, we're anchored for the night. Out of fuel?"

"Yes. Ran out this morning and this boat is a real bitch to paddle."

"I bet it is," Brad says. He scans the cockpit area of the forty-eight-foot Sea Ray and spots the tops of two other heads, but all he can see is hair. Brad's gaze flicks back and forth between the man and cockpit. "That your boat?"

"Yep. Bought it new two years ago."

The boat most likely cost north of four hundred grand when the man bought it and now it's as worthless as a partially inflated inner tube. "You alone?"

"Yep, just me. My wife didn't make it out of D.C."

"You two get down," Brad whispers out of the corner of his mouth. Nicole and Tanner slowly duck below the rail and hunker down on the deck as Brad repositions his feet, his eyes never wavering from the man and his boat. "Now, sir, that can't be true. I saw two sets of hands rowing."

"You must be mistaken," the man says. "I'm the only one aboard."

"I hate to call a man a liar to his face, but you, sir, are a lia—"

The man makes a sudden move for something behind his back and a pistol is just clearing the man's swimsuit when Brad tucks the rifle to his shoulder and fires. At this range, and being on unstable footing, the large bullet knocks the man off his feet. Brad quickly levers another shell and pivots toward the cockpit area as Nicole screams and claps her hands over her ears. Two other men pop up, pistols extended over the top of the cabin. Brad fires again, hitting the man on the left before he can fire a shot. The second man fires, and Brad can feel the pressure wave of the bullet whizzing by his ear. He levers another shell and fires, but the man ducks down behind the cabin at the last second. Brad squats down until only his head and the rifle are exposed. "Tanner, reach under the helm's seat and hand me some more ammo."

Tanner crawls across the deck, lifts the seat, and grabs a box of cartridges, sliding them over to his father. With his eyes glued to the Sea Ray's cockpit, Brad blindly feeds more shells into the magazine. When the rifle is fully loaded, he scans the rest of the enemy boat. If the man ducks into the cabin, he could possibly pop up in the forward hatch. Brad's eyes flick back to the cockpit and he spots a hand easing out from behind the cabin. He waits to see if the man's going to fire blind or take a peek. Sighting in on the hand, Brad eases the barrel up and left to line up with the side of the cockpit. Seconds later the man sticks his head up and Brad drills him in the nose. Before the man's pistol can hit the water, Brad orders Tanner to pull the anchor and raise the mainsail. The cabin on the Sea Ray is large enough to easily hold ten or fifteen people, and the question drilling through Brad's brain is: Are there more? He keeps the rifle tucked tight to his shoulder.

Tanner gets the mainsail partially up and a gust of wind hits, pushing their boat closer to the dead power-boat. "Screw the sail, Tanner," Brad says in a low, urgent voice. "Fire up the engine."

Tanner twists the key and the engine purrs to life. He cuts the wheel hard to the left and the *EmmaSophia* turns away. They're a half a mile away before Brad lowers the rifle.

Nicole climbs up on the rear seat, her face ashen. "What the hell just happened?"

Brad feeds another cartridge into the rifle. "Welcome to life in the new world."

CHAPTER 88

Near Little Rock, Arkansas

In three hours, Zane and Alyx have covered, at most, ten miles, due to the number of scorched vehicles and the mountains of debris that litter the roadway. Whatever lies ahead was bombed to hell. Zane curses and steers off the shoulder to bypass a looted semi. Once back on the road, he thumbs the sweat from his brow and cuts the wheel to the right to veer around the charred remnants of a mobile home. Wildfires continue to smolder in the distance, leaving behind a funky stench that's difficult to describe.

"What the hell did they bomb?" Zane asks. "The Clinton Library?"

"No, probably something more strategic. My bet is the Little Rock Air Force Base."

"Who flies out of there?"

Alyx brushes the hair out of her eyes. "One of the airlift wings. Can't remember which one, but it's one of the largest fleets of C-130s in the world."

"Bastards," Zane mutters as he slows to avoid running into the tail section of a large aircraft sitting in the middle of the road.

"It's getting too dark to see," Alyx says. "I've seen better headlights on a riding lawn mower."

Zane steers around the scorched frame of a midsize sedan. "At least the headlights work. But, you're right, we're tempting fate, but I'd really like to get back to I-40 before we stop. At least we'll feel like we accomplished something today."

"You're driving." Alyx pulls her legs up beneath her and focuses her gaze on the road ahead, pointing out objects for Zane. Finally, they reach the outskirts of what was once a small city. The place is identifiable as a city only by the sprawl of streets—everything else is gone, either burned up or blown apart by the succession of pressure waves from the nuclear bombs. In the failing light, the scene is eerie, making the hair stand at the nape of Zane's neck. It reminds him of the images he's seen of Hiroshima or Nagasaki. He shudders at the thought and taps the brakes, bringing the pickup to a stop. Ahead of them the highway is jammed with overturned vehicles scorched down to their metal frames. "No telling how many bombs they dropped on this place, whatever this place was."

"I think it was Jacksonville. Although it was called the Little Rock Air Force Base, it was actually located on the outskirts of Jacksonville. That's about all I remember about it."

"The people around here never had a chance. I bet most were vaporized within milliseconds."

"I don't want to think about it," Alyx says. "We need to get the hell out of here. Probably still a major hot zone."

Zane turns the truck around and they backtrack on Highway 67 until they're clear of the major destruction. "Getting back to I-40 is out for tonight." Zane slows and steers down the highway embankment, picking up the feeder road heading back the way they came. Finding a place to bed down is difficult because the wildfires have burned every structure and every tree within sight. "Think there's anybody left alive to worry about?"

"Could be someone migrating through the area. I'd feel safer if we could find a place to hide."

Zane waves at the scoured earth. "I'm open for suggestions."

"Keep driving. We'll find something."

Zane gooses the gas. Two miles down the road he spots a promising location and pulls into the parking lot. "What do you think?"

Alyx uncrosses her legs. "Perfect."

The gate is hanging askew, and Zane eases the pickup into the lot. The charred automobiles are arranged in evenly spaced rows and stacked three or four high. Zane drives to the back of the salvage yard and parks at the end of one of the rows. He puts the transmission in park and kills the engine and the lights.

In the darkness, Alyx says, "You take me to all the best places."

CHAPTER 89

North Atlantic

Captain Rex "Bull" Thompson glances at his watch and pulls a radio set from overhead. "Thompson to Murphy. Over."

Seconds later, Murphy answers, "I'm here, Bull. I'm thinking of changing your nickname to Ace. You smoked that Chinese destroyer."

"We aim to please. Anything on your radar?"

"Negative. Blow your ballast tanks. It's burger night aboard the USS *Grant*."

"See you in a few," Thompson says. He clicks the handset back into the holder. "Mr. Adams, position of the *Grant*?"

"A half a mile off our bow, Skipper."

"Roger. Thank you. Q, take us up."

Once on the surface, the two ships go through the same docking procedures as before. Thompson and Garcia make their way up the gangway and bump fists with Murphy, who leads them back to the officers' wardroom. Thompson and Garcia sit, while Murphy retrieves the bottle of bourbon. Murph grabs three mugs and carries the booze over to the table, taking a seat in his usual chair.

"How do you think we ended up on the wrong side with China, Murph?" Garcia asks.

"Hell if I know. They shot the shit out of my helicopter. I guess we're lucky the damn thing didn't explode."

Thompson leans forward in his chair. "Were they targeting the chopper?"

"I don't know the answer to that, Bull. I was up to my ass blowing up torpedoes and firing missiles. Why?"

"Can you call someone to find out?"

"Sure. What's going on in that noggin of yours?"

"Nothing good."

Murphy shrugs and picks up a ship's phone to contact the bridge. After a few moments of conversation, he says, "Punch it up on the officers' wardroom's screen." He hangs up and picks up a remote to click on the video monitor. "We had all the cameras running. You guys want to eat before we wade through the video?"

Although Thompson's stomach is grumbling, he knows this could be important. "Let's watch first."

"Okay." Murphy switches the inputs on the monitor and fast-forwards through the video. "Where do you want me to stop?"

"At your first interaction with them."

"Should be coming up. They were coming toward our bow and we made a jog to starboard to widen our firing stance. If that piece of shit Aegis system hadn't crapped out we would've taken her much earlier." When the Chinese destroyer comes into view, Murphy mashes the play button. They watch for a few minutes with very little happening on-screen. "Remember, at this point we didn't know if the destroyer was friend or foe."

"I remember," Thompson says. He scoots to the edge of his seat. "Fast forward to the first shots, Murph."

Murphy fast-forwards until they see a puff of smoke from the deck of the Chinese destroyer. Murphy slows the video to normal speed. "Their first shot was an antiship missile that we obliterated with the Gatling gun."

Seconds later on the video there are multiple puffs of smoke coming off the deck of the enemy ship. She, too, is firing her Gatling gun.

"Are the cameras synced?" Thompson asks.

"You bet your ass they are," Murphy says. "The shipboard computers are working fine."

"Will you punch up the rear-deck camera?" Thompson asks.

Murphy punches more buttons on the remote and the view switches to the rear deck of the *Grant*. He rewinds the video and hits play. On-screen the helicopter shudders as the 20-mm rounds from the Chinese shred the fuselage.

"I'll be damned," Garcia says.

Thompson leans back in his chair. "Their first shot was a missile they knew you could defeat. But then they go after the chopper on the next barrage."

"Why?" Murphy asks.

Thompson sags against the chair back. "At this point in the battle, they knew a submarine was lurking below after we torpedoed their sub. Their odds of survival went from fifty-fifty to a much lower number. I think they took out your helicopter as insurance in case they didn't make it."

Murphy leans forward in his chair. "Insurance for what?"

Thompson takes a sip of bourbon. "To keep you from discovering other Chinese ships in the area."

Murphy sags back in his chair. "Well, shit." He chugs his drink and refills his cup. "We're damn near running on fumes now."

"Where are you on fuel?" Garcia asks.

Murphy sighs. "Less than twenty percent. Enough to maybe make the Virgin Islands, but not if we have to fight our way there. And that'll be running only one screw." Murphy punches off the monitor with disgust.

All three men chug the shots of bourbon and sit, thinking. After a few minutes of silence Thompson says, "Think there's any place left along the eastern seaboard to refuel?"

"Not from what I saw. Certainly not Norfolk," Murphy replies.

"What about a Coast Guard station?" Garcia asks. "Surely, they couldn't have targeted every one of those. There have to be twenty or thirty along the East Coast alone."

"Maybe," Thompson says. "You'd have to cut that number in half now because anywhere north of Virginia will be toast. Might get lucky with one in the Carolinas. What do you think, Murph?"

"Maybe, if they have the type of fuel we need. We're headed that way anyhow. Might get lucky. If—and that's a big if—we don't encounter more Chinese ships before we get there."

Thompson leans forward and props his forearms on

the table. "Fuel is not an issue for us. And we still have a good supply of torpedoes. Murph, how about you make a quick run for the Hatteras area and we'll follow along at a slower pace to protect your tail?"

"A quick run just ain't happening, Bull."

"I think we're about five hundred miles off the East Coast. Run at best possible speed, then. If you can make twenty knots that'll put you in the vicinity of Nags Head in about in about twenty-five hours," Thompson says. "Any of those ships in Norfolk still upright?"

"A couple of them were the last time we were there. No telling now. Why?"

"As a last resort you could pump some fuel from those sinking ships. You've got pumps on board, right?"

"Yes. And that might work. Norfolk is in the general vicinity, too."

Thompson slaps the table. "Okay, we have a plan. We'll run at periscope depth for a while so we can remain in radio contact. I say we eat and get on with the mission."

"I don't know if I have much of an appetite now," Garcia says.

Murphy stands and places his hands on Garcia's thin shoulders and gives them a squeeze. "Shit, Carlos, a man's got to eat. It could be days—or never—before we run into any more Chinese ships."

Garcia pushes up from his chair. "I sure as hell hope you're right."

CHAPTER 90

Kansas City, Missouri

Although they got off to a late start after the burial of Hannah Hatcher, they've made good progress. Now approaching Kansas City from the north, they're on the hunt, again, for somewhere to bed down for the night. McDowell glances at the fuel gauge. "We need diesel, and I'd like to fill up before dark. That'll allow us to get a quick start in the morning."

Lauren brushes her dark hair out of her face. "So what are we looking for?"

"I found a hose back at the sign shop that connects to a tanker truck. That would be the quickest way, but I also have a piece of garden hose if we need to siphon from another vehicle."

"I'll keep an eye out. How come Kansas City is relatively intact and Des Moines wasn't?"

"Des Moines had that big National Guard base close to the city. Missouri really only has one large military installation, Whiteman Air Force Base. It's located in the middle of nowhere, southeast, but mostly east, of Kansas City. It's a big base and the permanent home for our B-2 bomber, making them top-five in target value. No telling how many nukes they targeted at that base." McDowell spots a tanker truck in the distance and speeds up. "Also, Kansas City is not a big population center and probably wouldn't merit a direct attack. In a nutshell, they were extremely lucky."

"I don't think *lucky* is the word I'd choose," Lauren says.

McDowell shrugs. "They're still upright and walking. Some of them will make it out of this." He pulls the truck up close to the tanker. "Will you cover with the shotgun?"

Lauren grabs the shotgun and climbs out of the truck. McDowell steps out and walks around the back, telling the students they can get down to stretch their legs for a few moments. He unlashes the hose from the side of the bed rails and grabs his bucket of tools. Using a large pair of pliers, he uncaps the four external valves on the tanker. Working down the line, he cracks the first gate valve open just a hair and finds gasoline. The second valve offers the same, but when he cracks open the third valve he finds diesel. He clamps on the hose and unscrews the lid of their truck's fuel tank. McDowell steps over and cracks the valve open and a steady stream of diesel pours out. He fills the truck's tank and refills all the spare containers. "See anyone?" McDowell asks Lauren.

"I see some people walking but they don't appear threatening."

"They're all threats until proven otherwise."

"Duly noted," Lauren replies, offering a mock salute.

McDowell finishes up and wipes his hands on one

of the leftover rags. He glances down and notices the rag came from Hannah's dress. Remorse fills his heart. Not remorse for the man he shot, but remorse for a life snuffed out entirely too young. And worse, it happened on his watch. McDowell folds the rag and slips it into his back pocket as a reminder. As the kids reload, he takes a moment to study their surroundings in the failing light.

Two big-box home improvement stores are situated on opposite sides of the highway—too wide open, and too close to the highway for an overnight stay. After last night, McDowell is eager to find a secluded place, even if it means sleeping outside. He climbs behind the wheel and starts the truck, slipping the transmission into gear. At the next exit he pulls off the highway, and travels west on 152. They pass a looted Walmart, a plundered strip center, and a golf course before breaking into open country. The light is fading quickly and they have only minutes to find a spot before full dark settles in.

Lauren points to the left. "There's a big open field and what looks like a small creek."

"Perfect." McDowell turns onto a side road and searches for a gate into the property. "Do you think the kids will mind sleeping outdoors?"

"We're not going to give them a choice. After last night, the more secluded, the better."

"Agreed." McDowell spots a dirt road and turns onto it, following it until they come to the creek. He puts the truck in neutral and steps out for a quick look. There's a line of trees that'll shield them from view if someone approaches along the road, and a thicket of trees snuggled up to the creek to the west that will obscure their movements from that side. He walks out into the grass to check the ground for firmness. Getting the truck stuck now could well be a fatal mistake. The ground feels firm and he returns to the truck and steers off the road, nudging the truck into a dense copse of trees. He kills the engine and climbs out of the cab, slinging the shotgun over his shoulder. "Hey, gang, gather as much wood as you can before it gets too dark. I don't want a bunch of flashlights waving around."

The kids fan out and McDowell picks up a handful of smaller twigs. With some leftover paper from last night, he grabs the lighter and starts work on the fire. Lauren returns, her arms loaded down with wood. She dumps it in a pile and brushes the hair from her face. "Think we're safe here?"

McDowell glances up, the orange-yellow flames lighting his face. "I sure as hell hope so. We'll rotate guard shifts just in case."

The students wander in and dump their wood on the pile Lauren started. McDowell puts on more wood as Melissa and the kids unload the food and water. Lauren returns to the truck and retrieves their meager supply of cooking gear. Once the fire builds up a layer of coals, McDowell places the pot in the coals for their dinner to warm. From the looks of it, they're having some type of soup. It actually smells better than it looks.

Once everyone has eaten, McDowell banks the fire as the students work out their sleeping arrangements. The girls snuggle up next to the fire while the boys opt for a place under the truck. McDowell takes the first watch and Lauren and Melissa lie down beside the girls. McDowell unslings the shotgun and leans up against the pile of wood, the Glock in his lap. It's not long before the girls fall asleep, their collective breathing falling into a natural rhythm. McDowell can hear the boys whispering to one another, but that too soon fades away. McDowell is left to stare at the flames.

Sometime later, Lauren stirs awake and takes over guard duty. McDowell adds more wood to the fire before stretching out on the ground. It takes him a while to fall asleep, the images from the day playing like a movie in his mind. He thinks briefly of the man he killed then decides the man shouldn't merit much thought after what he'd done. He got what was coming to him. McDowell shifts positions, trying to get comfortable. Eventually the images fade and he falls asleep.

But sleep doesn't last long. He feels Lauren's hot breath in his ear as she whispers, "Wake up, Stan."

McDowell sits up. "What?" he whispers.

"I heard something. Sounded like people whispering."

CHAPTER 91

Weatherford

Back at Holly's parents' house for the night, Gage and Holly are getting ready for bed. Still without power, they share a dampened cloth to wipe the grime from their faces and arms. Gage lifts Olivia to his face and kisses her tiny forehead. "I wish you could have met your grandpa," he whispers to her. "He was a good man."

"Yes, he was," Holly says, wrapping an arm around her husband's waist. They stand together in silence for a few minutes, staring at the tiny child they both created.

"I think she has my father's chin," Gage says.

"I think you're right." Holly gently brushes a fly-away of Olivia's hair from her forehead. "It's your chin, too."

As if knowing that she is currently the center of attention, Olivia opens her tiny mouth and belts out a cry.

"Is she hungry?" Gage asks.

Holly removes Olivia from Gage's hands and snuggles her against her chest. "Yes. I don't know what we're going to do if my milk doesn't come in soon."

Gage's brow wrinkles with concern. "Do you think it has anything to do with radiation exposure?"

Holly sits on the edge of the bed and pulls up her shirt, positioning the baby's mouth on her nipple. "I don't think so, Gage. We were underground for an entire week. According to a few of the pregnancy books I read, some first-time mothers experience a delay in milk production."

Gage is on the verge of asking a what-if-it-doesn't? question before his brain takes over and clamps his mouth closed. He wanders out of the bedroom with his mind spinning through possible future scenarios, none of them good. He makes a mental note to pay a visit to Holly's doctor in the morning to inquire about any leftover infant formula the doctor may have. If she doesn't have any, Gage may be forced into going door-to-door in search of breast milk.

As Gage's worry deepens, he shuffles into the living room. Susan has a half a dozen candles burning, the weak light casting shadows along the far wall as she putters around in the kitchen. Henry is sitting in his favorite recliner, his feet up.

"How's the arm, Henry?" Gage asks, sinking into the sofa.

"Other than the fact it feels like a hot coal is embedded under my skin, it's good. Could have been much worse." He repositions himself in the chair and winces. He glances up to make sure Susan is out of earshot and lowers his voice. "What did you do with the bodies?"

"I drug them into the middle of the field and left them there. Burying them would have taken the better part of the day; time I don't have."

"They didn't deserve a proper burial," Henry says,

rubbing a hand across the bandage on his right arm. "I'm sorry about your dad, Gage. He was a man of few words and a hard man to get to know, but that's not necessarily a negative. He was a damn good man who could work circles around men half his age."

Gage smiles. "He worked from daylight to dark most every day of his life. I always thought he'd die out in the field doing what he loved doing."

"We don't get to choose how or when we die, Gage. The only thing we know for certain is that we *will* die. From what you told me, him being unconscious the last few days is a blessing in the end." Henry repositions himself in his chair and falls silent.

Gage is eager to change the subject. "How much longer before the turbine is up and running?"

"My injury is a setback. There's no way I can climb the tower, but I don't think much else needs to be done topside. You can handle the problems up there. I figure half a day to finish with the step-up transformer. My hope is we have the turbine up and running by the end of the day tomorrow."

Gage nods and pushes up out of the sofa. He says good night to Susan and Henry and returns to the bedroom. Holly is asleep in the bed, the baby cuddled up next to her bare breast. Gently, Gage lifts Olivia and carries her to the bassinet, snuggling her down in the blankets. He strips off his clothes, clicks off the flashlight, and climbs into bed. Staring into the darkness, sleep proves elusive as he wonders what calamity will befall them tomorrow.

CHAPTER 92

Kansas City

McDowell is now fully awake, a sudden dump of adrenaline pumping through his system. In the darkness he feels for Lauren's hands and fits the Glock into her right palm. He leans forward and whispers, "Which direction?"

"Back toward the road," Lauren whispers. "I think."

McDowell grimaces at how loud the whispers sound in the stillness of the night. He extends a hand, searching for Lauren's face. He finds it, slips his hand around her head and pulls her forward, placing his mouth next to her ear. In the faintest of voices he asks, "How many?"

"Don't know," Lauren whispers. Her hot breath in his ear sends a shiver down his spine.

"Sit tight. Make them think we're still sleeping. If shooting starts, herd the kids up under the truck. The pistol is locked and loaded. Okay?" With his hands still on her neck, he can feel her head nod. McDowell gives her neck a squeeze and pushes quietly to his feet, reaching for the shotgun. The darkness is absolute—

the only hints of light coming from the dying embers of the fire. Working slowly, McDowell shuffles out into the darkness. He calls up a mental picture of the area and uses the position of the truck and the fire to get his bearings. If he's correct, the dirt road leading to the property is in front of him. He pauses to listen. The only sound is the faint rattle of cottonwood leaves from the large trees lining the creek.

McDowell angles toward the left, one hand extended in front of him, the shotgun riding against his right leg. With the bandolier of shotgun shells wrapped around the lower stock and the five shells already loaded in the shotgun, he has fifteen rounds of ammo. And no idea the number of people he's facing. He feels his way toward a large oak tree and snuggles up to the trunk, his eyes searching forward for any hints of movement—a futile attempt because he can't see his hand two inches in front of his face. He'll have to wait for someone to make a mistake. After a few minutes with no hints of noise, he's wondering if Lauren had been hearing things.

Seconds later, a twig snaps.

McDowell knows now, she wasn't. He brings the shotgun up and rests the barrel against the tree trunk, the stock seated against his shoulder and his index finger stroking the trigger. Listening, he hears feet shuffling through the leaves out in front of him. But there's still no indication of how many are coming. McDowell clicks off the safety and waits.

Someone stumbles to the far left and curse words zing around inside McDowell's head. The tree trunk is now a liability, limiting his field of fire. Carefully, he shuffles forward three steps, but the last step is costly because his foot hits a limb that snaps loudly. He stands frozen as the shuffling of feet stops. McDowell holds his breath, the shotgun up and ready.

A voice to his right says, "All we want is some food."

McDowell swings the barrel to the right, locking in on the voice.

Silence descends in the darkness as McDowell plots his moves in his mind: *Take the one on the right and shuffle hard left? I know there's at least one on the left. How many in the middle?*

"I know you're here," the voice on the right says. "We'll make you a deal. We'll split the food down the middle. Half for you and half for us."

McDowell remains silent. He lets his legs relax a little to keep from cramping up.

Finally, after what feels like an eternity, the voice on the right speaks again. "Or we can take it all."

McDowell remains silent. Dealing with the unknown, especially when weapons are involved, ratchets the tension up to an unbelievable level. Only those who have been to war have ever experienced the sensation. And McDowell's been to war.

"I don't know who you are," the man on the right says, "but, pardner, you're seriously outgunned."

Either the man's boasting or McDowell is in for the fight of his life. Either way, it's seconds from happening.

"You had your—"

McDowell pulls the trigger. The shotgun barks and he spins to his left and drops to his haunches, the barrel swinging left. A pistol fires from the left, kicking up dirt where McDowell had been standing. McDowell targets the flash and fires again, flame shooting from the barrel and lighting the night. In the brief flash, McDowell spots two people moving forward from the middle. McDowell pivots the shotgun and fires off two quick shots. He jumps to his feet and lunges to the left, needing to draw their fire away from the campsite. A limb slaps him in the face, bringing tears to his eyes. He grabs the limb and follows it to the trunk, where he squats down and feeds more shells into the shotgun.

After several more seconds of silence, McDowell hears the shuffle of feet, but this time they're moving away. McDowell waits for the footsteps to fade before standing. Using the dying coals of the fire as a beacon, he makes his way back toward the campsite. He stops when he comes within earshot and says in a low voice, "Lauren it's me."

He hears a sigh of relief in the distance and makes his way toward Lauren. The fire casts some light and McDowell can just make out the students crawling out from underneath the truck like babies scampering away from the mother spider. Once they're huddled up, McDowell whispers a series of orders. Within minutes, the truck is loaded up and everyone is aboard. Melissa reluctantly climbs behind the wheel as McDowell takes up a position in the back, the shotgun tight to his shoulder and extended over the top of the cab.

With no working headlights, Jonathon is ducked down beside the cab with a flashlight, which he clicks off and on every few seconds. After several stops and starts that nearly send everyone tumbling out the back, Melissa gets the truck turned around and pointed in the right direction. She eases out on the clutch and the truck stutters forward before finding a rhythm. She shifts to second as McDowell keeps a watchful eye on their left flank. He has no idea about the status of the four people he shot, nor does he care. Getting away safely is the only thing that matters now. Melissa has to swerve to avoid hitting a tree, and the kids tumble across the bed. Shots ring out and McDowell orders the students on their bellies. He swings the shotgun left and fires off three well-spaced rounds, hoping to drive the enemy to cover. Finally, mercifully, they reach the main road.

Melissa turns left and Jonathon lights the flashlight, shining the beam along the hard-packed earth stretched out before them. A mile down the road, Melissa stops the truck and they make a rapid transition. Melissa climbs into the back to take over flashlight duties while McDowell climbs behind the wheel. He eases out on the clutch as Melissa moves to the middle rear of the cab and stands, the flashlight extended in her hand. The light stretches only about twenty feet beyond the hood, and the going is slow, but at least they're moving.

CHAPTER 93

Russellville, Arkansas

A new day provided a turn of luck. Early this morning, Zane and Alyx had backtracked to Highway 89 and took it west to pick up I-40 coming out of Little Rock. Now approaching midday, they're facing their first hiccup of the day. Passing through Russellville, the highway makes a steady ascent up a slight ridge to a summit that overlooks a once-tree-filled valley and a small lake now spewing steam. The only thing that suggests the valley was once covered with trees are the scorched tree stumps that stretch on for miles. Zane slows the truck to a stop. "What the hell is that?"

Alyx leans forward in the seat for a better look out the windshield. "That is, or was, I should say, Arkansas Nuclear One."

Zane turns to look at Alyx. "They bombed a nuclear power plant?"

Alyx shrugs. "Why not? If you're going to launch nuclear weapons, targeting nuclear power plants is a no-brainer. What the bombs don't get the melting cores will. They'll spew radiation unchecked for years. Call it an added bonus or, from their perspective, *good* collateral damage."

The fires swept across the highway, cutting a wide swath through the rolling foothills to the north. In the far distance, smoke continues to rise from the surface. Zane returns his gaze to the road to see a group of people cresting the next ridge and shuffling in their direction. It's a large group, probably twenty or more, and several are dragging makeshift travois. Zane reaches for the shotgun, and Alyx reaches out a hand to stop him.

"Don't, Zane. There are too many of them. Besides, it looks like a consortium of families. I count five little ones."

"That doesn't make them any less dangerous. As a matter of fact, it makes them far more dangerous."

"I'm not sensing any hostility."

"Hell, they're still a quarter of a mile away. Are you gifted with long-range ESP?"

"Look at their body language, Zane. They can see us and yet there has been little response. I'd like to talk to them. Find out what's over the next ridge past the power plant." Alyx bends down and pulls their stash of meds out from beneath the seat. She pulls out one of the large bottles of antibiotics and stuffs the sack back under the seat.

When the group is closer Zane can begin to distinguish physical features. It appears there are ten or eleven women, eleven children of varying ages, and eight males. One of the males, a short, burly man with a wiry beard, appears to be leading the group. Several of the others are pushing a shopping carts loaded with their supplies. Alyx gasps. "Look at their faces, Zane. Those are fresh radiation burns."

At fifty feet the group comes to a halt, the leader walking forward. He stops near Zane's open window, his face a blistered mess. A pack is tied to his back and the handle of an older revolver peeks over the waistband of the man's jeans. Zane takes the antibiotics from Alyx and sticks his arm out the window. "A peace offering."

The man steps forward and takes the bottle. "Thank you."

"We're Zane and Alyx."

The man nods. "I'm Robert. My wife, Alice, is the one with the red bandanna. Two of the little ones are ours."

"Where are you coming from, Robert?"

"Originally from Dallas. At least most of us. We picked up a straggler here and there. We barely made it out alive. They bombed the hell out of the city. What about you?"

"We started out at Fort Meade, Maryland. We're on our way to Weatherford, Oklahoma, where Alyx's family lives. How far east are you planning on going?"

"Hoping to make Memphis. My wife has some family there."

"We passed through Memphis. It's still relatively intact. How's it look out west?"

"We were traveling along a more southerly route until we got to what used to be Shreveport. Made a jog north and picked up I-40 in Fort Smith. It's relatively clear to there."

There's a lull in the conversation until the man sighs

and says, "We screwed up. We camped the last two days down in a valley about a mile down the road. We were trying to let the little ones get their legs underneath them. I saw the smoke, but hell, we see smoke all day, every day. Had no idea about the nuclear power plant here. Guess we got a pretty good dose of radiation. Don't know how much, but enough to blister up." Robert sighs again. "Guess we'll know more in the next couple of weeks."

"I don't know if the antibiotics will help with the radiation, but that's all we have to offer. I'm sorry," Alyx says.

"I don't know, either, but I appreciate it. I'm sure we'll find a use for them."

There's another lull in the conversation. What do you tell a man who is likely going to die within weeks or maybe even days? "Safe travels to you, Robert, and to the rest of the group," Zane says.

"Same to you, Zane." He nods at Alyx. "Nice to meet you."

"Same to you." A tear forms in the corner of Alyx's eye and drifts down her cheek as Zane drops the truck in gear and eases down the road.

Once clear of the group, Zane feeds the engine more gas and cranks up the window. "We need to move quickly through this area."

Alyx nods and wipes her cheeks.

Decaying bodies line the highway and the stench of rotting meat fills the cab. Zane consciously breathes through his mouth as he swerves around the debris, trying to hurry through the hot zone. When they've covered ten miles, he slows to a more manageable speed. "Think we're clear?"

"Yes."

Those are the first words Alyx has spoken since encountering Robert and his group.

She turns in her seat, pulling her left leg beneath her. "Maybe we should have given them the pickup."

"No. They'll all be dead inside a month." Zane reaches over and takes her hand. "What happened to them is terrible, but there are similar situations happening all over the world."

"Did you see those poor children?"

Zane gives Alyx's hand a squeeze. "I saw them. There's nothing that can be done for them."

Alyx lays her head against the seat back. "What a horrible world we're living in."

They ride in silence for many miles. Zane glances over to see if Alyx had fallen asleep, but her eyes are wide open. "You have to let it go, Alyx. Otherwise it'll eat you up. Think how glad your family will be to see you."

Alyx tucks a strand of hair behind her ear and turns to look at Zane. "You know what they'll really be excited about?"

"I think having a daughter return from the edge of the world would be at the top of any parent's wish list."

Alyx slides across the seat and snuggles up next to Zane. "Oh, they'll be happy to see me, but they'll be even more delighted I've finally found a man I want to spend the rest of my life with."

CHAPTER 94

North Atlantic

After six hours of sleep, Thompson is back on the bridge of the USS *New York*. During the night, the ballistic missile submarine has covered nearly 400 miles and is now submerged at a depth of 400 feet, a hundred miles off the coast of Virginia and North Carolina. Although the top-end speed of the sub is classified, they sailed a little north of 25 knots all night long. The top speed of the destroyer USS *Grant* is also classified, but they are currently fifty miles closer. Captain Murphy, knowing they didn't have enough fuel to make it to the Virgin Islands, dropped the hammer in an all-or-nothing gamble.

Thompson turns to his sonar technician, Mike Adams, who had also just come on shift. "What's the *Grant*'s current speed?"

"She dropped back to one screw, Skipper. She's currently turning thirteen knots."

"Probably running on fumes," Thompson mutters. He walks over to the navigation table and pulls up the chart for the North Carolina coast. Although Murphy is going to Norfolk to see if any of the disabled ships are still floating, Thompson has a sneaking suspicion he'll come up empty. Using a mouse he zooms in on the North Carolina coast, searching for nearby Coast Guard stations.

On the other side of the bridge, two blips suddenly appear on the screen Adams is manning. "Sir, I'm tracking two contacts."

Thompson steps over. "Where?"

"They're rounding Cape Lookout, sir."

"Ours?"

"Negative, sir. Screw signature suggests Chinese in origin."

"Goddammit," Thompson says. "Where the hell did they come from, Mr. Adams?"

"I picked them up the moment they engaged their propellers, sir. Could be they were lying in wait."

Thompson snatches a microphone from overhead and keys the trigger. "XO Garcia to the bridge." He clicks the handset in place and turns to the helm. "Conn, sound the general alarm—battle stations, torpedo."

As his orders are carried out and the Klaxon sounds signaling the general alarm, he steps back over to the chart table and pulls up the chart for the Cape Lookout area. Situated on the lower end of the Outer Banks, the point creates a natural hiding place within Lookout Bight. The shoreline of the bay consists of a series of unpopulated islands, away from prying eyes. "Those bastards," Thompson mutters. "Mr. Adams, current course of the Chinese ships?"

"They are currently one mile off the coast and are turning to a heading of thirty degrees, Skipper." Adams's voice is high, tight.

"Distance from the *Grant*?"

"Fifty miles and closing at thirty knots."

Thompson does the math in his head. He glances up when Garcia climbs through the hatch.

"What's up, Bull?"

"Nothing good. Mr. Adams, *Grant*'s current course?"

"They are turning to starboard, Captain. I'll have the new course in a moment."

"Still turning one screw?"

"Yes," Adams replies.

Thompson turns to Garcia. "Two Chinese ships must have been hiding around the Cape Lookout area."

"Goddammit," Garcia mutters, running a hand across the top of his head. "You think they're guarding our coastline?"

"From what? I think most of our navy is toast."

"They're here for a reason, Bull. Could be they're on mop-up duty, picking off any stragglers trying to make it home."

"What gives them that right? The United States is sovereign territory."

"Different ball game now. We may have given up that right when we, as a nation, launched nuclear weapons." Garcia steps around the table to look at the chart for Cape Lookout. "Damn, they had the perfect hiding place, didn't they?"

"Yes. Do you recall which targeting package was inserted in our missiles?"

"Not precisely. But I can pull it up on the ship's computer."

"Do that."

"Captain," Adams says in a louder-than-normal voice, "The USS *Grant* is dead in the water."

"Roger, Mr. Adams. Mr. Patterson, plot an intersecting course for those two Chinese ships."

"Aye, aye, Skipper," Patterson replies.

Thompson turns back to Garcia. "Damn it, Murph's a sitting duck, and we're in a very precarious position with those two enemy ships in the mix."

Garcia looks up from the monitor. "I know what you were hunting for with the targeting package question. And, no, none of our missiles were targeted at China or other Chinese interests."

"About what I figured. And you can bet your ass every missile in the Russian arsenal was pointed at an American target. Who's left who would have targeted the Chinese?"

"India and Pakistan no doubt targeted each other. The French or British, maybe?" Garcia says.

"Maybe," Thompson says. "China may be the only superpower left on the planet." Thompson removes his cap and wipes his brow.

Garcia pushes to his feet. "How are we going to handle the two Chinese ships?"

"Very delicately."

CHAPTER 95

Off the coast of Hatteras

After yesterday's shoot-out with those on the disabled powerboat, Brad motored the *EmmaSophia* a mile offshore and dropped anchor. Too dark to fish, they had opened two cans of soup and heated it on the small propane stove, though neither Nicole nor Brad had much of an appetite. This morning, Brad has the main-sail up, but the boat remains stationary, the canvas limp. He steps over to the helm and clicks on the key. The needle on the fuel gauge ticks up a notch just above empty and Brad sighs. Maybe a couple of gallons of fuel remain, which they'll need to maneuver around a marina, if they ever find one. They're now at the mercy of Mother Nature.

Nicole, carrying two cups of weak coffee, walks up the stairs. She's wearing a pair of Tanner's jeans, the waist cinched tight with a piece of rope and the cuffs rolled up, and one of Brad's old college sweatshirts that's so big the neck hangs off one of her bare shoulders. She steps over and hands Brad a mug.

"Thank you," Brad says. He glances down at her

bare feet and feels a pang of regret for causing her to lose her shoes. "Are your feet cold?"

"No, I'm good. But thanks for loaning me the sweatshirt."

"You're welcome. Tanner still asleep?"

"Yep. I don't know how with all the noise I made."

"He could sleep through a hurricane."

Nicole smiles. "I wish I could sleep like that. I've always been a light sleeper."

Brad moseys to the back of the boat and takes a seat. Nicole follows and takes a seat at the helm, their knees nearly touching. She glances up at the listless sail. "I could make a really rude joke about my ex-husband."

Brad smiles. "I bet. Hopefully the breeze will pick up." He takes a sip of coffee and stretches his legs out. "How long were you married?"

"Nine years." Nicole blows across the surface of her cup and takes a tiny sip. "First five were great. It wasn't until we thought about starting a family that things began to fall apart."

"Did he not want children?"

"No. We both wanted children, but I had a difficult time getting pregnant." Nicole takes another sip of coffee. "We had fertility issues. We went through four rounds of fertility treatments, including three in-vitro procedures." She puts the coffee cup to her lips and pauses. "I suffered three miscarriages, all in the first trimester." She takes a drink and lowers her cup. "We rode an emotional roller coaster for three long years and it took a toll." She stares off into the distance for a moment. "We had an amicable parting three years ago and he moved to Norfolk to work for the government."

"Neither of you remarried?"

"Me, no. He, his name is Tom, remarried a year after the divorce." She turns and places her coffee cup on the helm. When she turns back around, tears are shimmering in her eyes. "He and his new wife had a baby boy last year."

Brad wants to lean forward and wrap her in his arms, but he remains where he is. "I'm sorry you had to go through all of that."

Nicole shrugs. "That's life." She wipes her eyes and stands. "How about I catch us some breakfast?"

"Sounds like a plan."

The boat shudders as Tanner lumbers up the steps. He stops where he's standing and points. "Dad, look."

Brad and Nicole swivel around to see two enormous warships a mile off their stern and moving rapidly north. Brad grabs the binoculars for a closer look.

Tanner strides across the deck, eager for an up-close look. "Are they ours, Dad?"

Brad twists the focus knob and zeros in on the nearest ship. His shoulders sag when he spots the red flag with yellow stars. "No, not ours, Tanner. They're Chinese." Dejected, he hands the binoculars to Tanner.

"Why would the Chinese be in our waters?" Nicole asks.

Brad shrugs. "We have no idea what has happened in the rest of the world. I don't know if we're still at war, or even who the enemies are. But those ships here can't be good."

Tanner lowers the binoculars. "Where do you think they're going?"

"No idea, but they're in a hurry to get there." He glances up at the limp sail. "We need to get the hell out of her—"

His last words are clipped when the two ships unleash a series of missiles. They stand in awe as the deadly weapons race higher in the sky, the plumes of smoke hanging in the still air.

Once the initial noise dies down, Brad mutters, "Those assholes. I bet they're shooting at one of our ships."

Tanner turns around, his face pale. "Dad, we need to get out of here."

Brad points at the drooping canvas. "Believe me, I know, Tanner. If I start the engine, we'll get maybe a half a mile. With weapons like those, a half a mile's not going to buy us much."

They turn as the two ships launch another barrage of missiles, the flames from the rocket motors streaking across the leaden sky.

CHAPTER 96

Gage ties a tether to one of Henry's deer rifles and begins to climb. He's running on fumes after Olivia kept him and Holly up most of the night. Unbeknownst to Holly, Gage is planning on a trip to the doctor's house as soon as they finish up here. Sweat begins to drip in his face and he pauses to mop his brow. After what happened last time, the deer rifle and a box of cartridges are going to remain topside for the duration. However long that might be.

After fifteen minutes of climbing, Gage reaches up, slides the hatch open, and climbs into the nacelle. He pulls the deer rifle up and unclips it, setting it aside. Sweat is running down his arms and dripping from the tips of his fingers as he cranks the doors open. The doors fold out much like the lid on a carton, and a cool breeze enters, spurring a rash of goose bumps along his forearms and neck. Gage steps over to the side for a moment to catch his breath. Looking out over the landscape, he can just make out the two bodies in the center of the field. It appears they've been tugged around during the night, probably by local dogs that survived the radiation fallout by being inside with their owners. Now, with food in short supply, most people are more concerned with feeding themselves, leaving the dogs to fend for themselves. Gage surmises that it won't be long before those same dogs end up in someone's stew pot. He shivers at the thought and turns away.

With a majority of the work completed up here, Gage is on hand to start the turbine and troubleshoot any problems that arise, while Henry finishes working on the step-up transformer below. Working one-armed, Henry's pace of work has slowed considerably. Gage meanders to the other side, where he has a view of town. He's good with the mechanical aspects of the job, but only has a vague understanding of how electricity works. According to Henry, the wind turbine has an output of 690 volts, and through a process of magnetic induction, that voltage steps up through the transformer to a higher output of 34.5 kilovolts. Normally that would be increased further through other transformers before being released on the grid. But that was before. If they get lucky, some of those other transformers will be operational and higher voltages will be produced, providing more power to more people. Or not. They won't know until they start the turbine.

Gage scans the roads, searching for threats. A few people are out, looking like ants moving around an anthill from up here, but no one is within two miles of the road approaching the wind turbine. Gage steps over and grabs the deer rifle and puts the scope to his eye for a closer look—anything to keep his mind off his hungry baby girl. He scans several barns within the closest one-mile section, looking to see if any of the local livestock survived, but the barns and fields are barren. He scans farther out and finds more of the same. Disheartened, he lowers the rifle and props it against the wall. He shuffles around the equipment to make sure all is in order and spends a few more minutes puttering around before sitting.

As feared, thoughts of Olivia crowd into his mind. *What happens if Holly's doctor has no formula? Go door-to-door begging? But how far am I willing to go to get my hands on some?* Gage sighs and pushes to his feet. *Would I kill for it?* He rolls that thought around in his mind for a moment and decides he's not a cold-blooded killer. He steps over to the side and shouts down to Henry, "How much longer?"

Henry looks up and shouts, "Soon."

Gage groans and turns, checking the equipment again. He crawls into the nose to double-check his work on the blade pitch system. Everything is as he left it. It'll be something he'll have to keep an eye on due to the tremendous stresses placed on the blades while rotating. He wriggles back out and picks up the deer rifle again. Moving to the other side, he scopes the doctor's neighborhood. The last time he visited it was at night and he wasn't paying much attention to his whereabouts. Scanning up and down the streets, he pinpoints the doctor's house based on the white Volvo parked in the driveway. He studies the area for a moment to familiarize himself and, once he's imprinted the neighborhood layout in his mind, he sets the deer rifle aside. He hears a shout and leans over to look at Henry.

"Release the brake," Henry shouts.

"Okay," Gage shouts back. He steps over to the

braking system, crosses his fingers, and frees the turbine. Nothing happens, and Gage experiences several
moments of plummeting distress. But then a gust of
wind hits and the turbine inches around.

"C'mon, baby," Gage shouts.

The giant blades make one slow revolution and
stop. Cursing, Gage looks over the braking system.
There's nothing to prevent the turbine from spinning. Another gust of wind hits and the blades make another slow
turn. This time it doesn't stop. One revolution. Two revo-
lutions. The turbine is now spinning. Gage leans over the
side to look at Henry. The equipment makes it impossible
to hear what he's shouting. Henry, realizing Gage can't
hear a thing, raises his left thumb high in the air. Relief
floods through Gage and a large smile forms on his
face.

But then he remembers the situation at home, and
the smile fades.

CHAPTER 97

100 miles off the coast of North Carolina

Captain Thompson is kicking himself for allowing the USS *Grant* a fifty-mile cushion. With two Chinese ships sailing at full speed for the dead-in-the-water destroyer, there's little the crew of the ballistic missile sub can do. He turns to the helm. "Conn, current speed?"

"Skipper, we're turning twenty-four knots," the helmsman answers.

Thompson removes his cap and wipes his brow. "Thank you." If they really pushed it, they might get another three or four knots, but they'd also run the risk of creating propeller cavitation. An outcome no one wants because the air bubbles can be detected by sonar and any possibility of creating noise in the presence of two enemy ships might prove fatal.

Thompson runs the torpedo numbers in his head. The sub won't be in firing range anytime soon. Thompson glances over at the sonar station. "Mr. Adams, position of the Chinese destroyers?"

"They're stationary at the moment, Skipper."

Thompson glances at Garcia. "Why are they stationary?"

Garcia turns toward the sonar station. "Mr. Adams, distance between *Grant* and the Chinese destroyers?"

"Forty-seven miles, sir."

Garcia winces and turns to look at Thompson. "There's your answer, Bull."

Thompson hangs his head. "Hell, the Chinese can sit out there and fire missiles at will."

Garcia nods. "And with the glitch on Murph's Aegis system, the *Grant* might well be shooting in the dark."

Brad, Tanner, and Nicole startle when the Chinese ships launch another barrage of missiles. The *Emma-Sophia* is only a mile and a half from the massive warships as they begin to slow. Brad glances up at the listless sail and groans. Without warning, some type of automatic gun begins firing and they all clap their hands over their ears. Moments later, an enormous explosion occurs somewhere overhead and a blast wave arrives seconds later, nearly sweeping Nicole off her feet. She grabs the wheel and screams as shrapnel begins peppering the water around them. The gun falls silent and Brad ushers Tanner and Nicole down into the cabin as another round of missiles streaks through the sky.

Brad closes the door and walks unsteadily down the steps.

"Dad, someone's shooting back. Think it's one of ours?" Tanner asks.

Brad slumps down next to Nicole. "Don't know,

Tanner. I hope not. I don't see how another ship could survive a barrage like that."

Thompson moves to the chart table for a visual on the location of the three ships. He braces his hands against the table and blows out a shaky breath. "Murph doesn't stand a chance, Carlos."

"He still has a lot of fire—"

"Captain," Adams says in a flat voice, "I count multiple detonations at the *Grant*'s current position."

Thompson's shoulders sag and he mutters, "Those cocksuckers." He glances at the sonar tech. "Is she still afloat?"

"Yes, she . . ." Adams pauses for a moment. "Sir, I count six more detonations."

Thompson marches over to the attack center, his face red, the veins pulsing in his forehead. "David, I want firing solutions on those ships as soon as you have them."

"Aye, aye, Skipper," White says.

Garcia glances at the bridge crew crowded into the small space and steps over close to Thompson. In a low voice he says, "Bull, can we chat in the officers' wardroom?"

Thompson turns, prepared to rip into Garcia, but his tirade dies when he sees the look of concern on Garcia's face. "Okay, Carlos." He turns to Lieutenant Commander Thomas Quigley. "Q, you're officer of the deck."

The two men make their way down one level and move forward to the wardroom in silence. Thompson yanks open the door and collapses into the chair at the head of the table. Garcia eases the door closed and calmly takes a chair opposite the captain, waiting. Thompson rakes his hands across his face, then leans forward in his chair, propping his elbows on his knees and burying his face in his hands. "Murph's gone, Carlos."

"I know, Bull."

A heavy silence settles over the room. Thompson sobs and Garcia reaches out to put a hand on his friend's shoulder. After several moments, Thompson sniffles and exhales a long, slow breath. He wipes his eyes and leans back in his chair. "You think it's a suicide mission, right?"

"Yes. One ship we could handle. But as soon as we fire a torpedo, the other ship will be on us like stink on shit."

"So we let them go? After they just killed over three hundred of our fellow sailors?"

"That's our only option, Bull. We can't bring that crew back. You're responsible for the crew on *this* boat and trying to take out those Chinese warships would put the crew at grave risk."

"Not if we slip up behind one and kill it and then dive deep for a day or two. They don't know we're here. The element of surprise is a huge factor in our favor."

"They'll know as soon as we fire the first torpedo. Then the second ship will deploy their towed sonar and go hunting."

"I want these sonsabitches, Carlos. And who's to say there won't be other U.S. Navy ships out there who will try to come home and get ambushed by these bastards?" Thompson wipes a stray tear from his cheek. "We sink the first ship and wait as long as needed to torpedo the second."

"I don't know, Bull. It's dicey."

"Not if we play our cards right." Thompson takes off his cap and tosses it on the table.

Garcia leans forward and looks Thompson in the eyes. "How much of this is revenge?"

Thompson crosses his arms. "I'm not going to lie—a bunch. But if we don't take out those ships, we'll never be able to surface and search for family members."

"How many family members do you think are still alive on the mainland?"

"Don't know," Thompson snaps. He pauses, takes a deep breath, and tries to get a handle on his emotions. "But even one is worth the effort, isn't it? And"—Thompson stabs his finger on the table—"it turns my stomach to think the Chinese are controlling our coastline."

Garcia ponders the situation for a few moments. "What time frame are you thinking?"

"We get one now, today, and worry about the other one tomorrow or the next day." Thompson pulls a computer keyboard over and, after entering his credentials, pulls up a chart for the area. "Perfect."

Garcia points at the screen. "You thinking about nestling down in that trough?"

"Yep. Hell, we get close enough we might get lucky and get both in the first go-round. That would allow us to surface and search for survivors from the *Grant*. If not, we dive deep and hide out for a day. Then go hunting again. We still might get lucky and pick up a few survivors." Thompson picks up his cap and places it back on his head. "What do you think, Carlos?"

Garcia runs his hand across the top of his head. "It's going to take us a while to get within effective torpedo range."

"Even better. It'll give them a chance to let their guards down."

CHAPTER 98

Zane and Alyx high-five when they pass the WEL-COME TO OKLAHOMA sign. The last couple of hours have been somber after encountering the group of families who will probably be dead by the end of the month. And the persistent grayness of the ash-filled skies only adds to the somberness. But the sign, and knowing they're nearing the end of a physically and emotionally exhausting journey, lightens the mood. Zane glances down at the gas gauge and starts scanning for a suitable host. He eases Old Goldie up next to a battered farm truck and climbs from the cab. Alyx, shotgun in hand, slides out on the passenger side and takes up her usual position near the front of the truck.

Gage unscrews the two gas caps and inserts the hose into the farm truck's gas tank. After several attempts and a mouthful of gasoline, he finally gets the fuel to flow.

"You'd think you would eventually get better at that," Alyx says. "Lord knows you've had plenty of practice."

Zane salutes her with his middle finger. "You're

welcome to take over." He hawks a mouthful of phlegm and spits it out on the pavement. "I'm hoping we'll get enough fuel that I won't have to do that again anytime soon. I've swallowed enough gasoline I'm probably flammable."

Alyx chuckles. "You haven't caught fire yet." Alyx scans the area behind them and tenses up. "Zane, two people are coming up on our six."

Zane turns to look. It appears to be a young couple and they're about two hundred yards away. "Where'd they come from?"

"Don't know. Just spotted them."

Zane eases over, takes the shotgun, and moves to the cab, where he pulls the box of shotgun shells closer to the passenger window. "We should leave before they get here."

"I'm hungry, Zane. Maybe they have some food we could trade for. We haven't had anything to eat since we had that turkey early yesterday."

"We'll be at your parents' house by the end of the day."

"What's it going to hurt, Zane? You've got a shot-gun in your hands."

"I just think it's an unnecessary risk."

"They're almost here. If they don't have any food, we'll head on down the road."

Zane shakes his head. "Why do you have to be so damn stubborn?"

"I'm not stubborn. Just determined."

The couple stops when they're ten feet away, and Zane's already picking up a bad vibe from the man. He appears to be in his midtwenties and has broad shoulders and narrow hips. She appears to be of similar age and she's attractive, with long, dark hair, large, dark eyes, and a well-proportioned body. Probably homecoming queen back in her day, Zane guesses. Although attractive, there's something off about her. She appears timid, almost frightened.

The young man is holding his hands up, about chest high. He's wearing jeans, heavy boots, and a pullover shirt. "I'm Chad and this is Lori. Do I need to be worried about the shotgun?"

Zane widens his stance. "Depends."

"On what?" Chad asks. Either the young man is cocky as hell or he was born with a permanent smirk on his face.

"Your behavior. I'm Zane and my friend is Alyx. You guys from around here?"

Chad lowers his hands. "Naw, I'm just passin' through. Originally from Wichita Falls. Found an abandoned house and decided to hole up for a while."

Zane nods. Lori, the young woman, begins to visibly tremble. "You both from Wichita Falls?"

"Lori's local. We hooked up a couple of days ago."

Alyx steps around the truck and takes a position next to Zane. "Willingly?"

"Of course." He glances at the girl. "Right, Lori?"

Lori offers a timid nod and clutches her hands together. Upon closer inspection, she appears younger than Zane originally thought, maybe late teens, at best. She's dressed in jeans, sneakers, and a long-sleeved T-shirt. Zane can see the remnants of a faint bruise edging beyond the collar of her shirt.

"See. We're good."

"You two out for a stroll and just happened upon us?" Alyx asks.

"No, I spotted your truck when you rolled in. Thought maybe we could do some trading."

Alyx takes a moment to study the situation. She glances up at Zane to see him clenching his jaw. "We're willing to trade some meds for food."

"What kind of meds? Oxy?"

Alyx brushes a strand of hair from her face. "No, antibiotics."

Chad takes two steps forward and leans in. "You'll have to do better than that, if you want something to eat."

Zane takes a half step to the left, putting himself between Alyx and Chad. "That's all we have. Take it or leave it."

"You a hard-ass?" Chad asks, turning to eyeball Zane.

"Only when I need to be."

Chad smiles. "Don't you have something else to barter with?" He turns to Alyx. "Alyx? That your name?"

"Yes," Alyx answers.

Chad switches his gaze back to Zane. "You willing to turn her out?"

Instead of answering, Zane smashes the stock of the shotgun into Chad's face, and he drops where he's standing as Lori sinks to her knees. Alyx hurries over and helps the girl up as Chad rolls over and gets up to his hands and knees. Lori breaks free of Alyx's grip and runs over and starts kicking Chad in the ribs and head until he collapses back to the ground. Alyx wraps an arm around Lori and pulls her off. "What's going on?"

Tears are streaming down Lori's cheeks. "That bastard . . . that bastard tied me . . . up . . . and . . . and tortured my . . . my parents to . . . death. He . . . made . . . me . . . watch."

Alyx pulls her close and wraps both arms around her, whispering in her ear. "It's okay, Lori. It's over now."

Lori sniffles. "And . . . he . . . raped me . . . repeatedly."

Zane, the veins pulsing in his forehead, reaches down and pulls Chad up by the collar of his shirt. "Get up, you piece of shit."

Once Chad is up and standing, Zane and Alyx exchange a quick glance.

"Start walking," Zane orders.

"She's lying," Chad shouts.

"You're the damn liar," Lori screams, spittle flying into the air. "You murdered my parents."

"Walk," Zane orders again. He lifts a foot and kicks Chad in the ass.

Chad stumbles forward and regains his balance.

Lori stomps a foot and screams, "You can't let him go! He'll just come back."

Alyx gently places a hand on either side of Lori's head. "Shh, it's going to be okay." Alyx gently turns her head, forcing Lori to look at her. "I promise."

The shotgun roars and both women jump. Lori whirls around to see Chad lying in the middle of the road, his blood already pooling around him. She sinks to her knees again, and Alyx kneels next to her. "It's over, Lori. He can't hurt you anymore."

Lori nods and continues to sob. Alyx helps her to her feet and Zane drops the tailgate. Alyx steers Lori over and gently helps her into a sitting position. Alyx sits next to the young woman and hugs her as she sobs,

Lori's entire body trembling. Eventually, the trembling subsides and the tears slow. Lori wipes her nose with the back of her hand.

"Do you have other family in town to stay with?" Alyx asks.

Lori nods. "An aunt and . . . uncle."

"Do you think you can make your way there by yourself?"

Lori nods again. "Yes."

When she's ready, Alyx helps her up while Zane shuffles over to the cab and grabs a new shotgun shell and reloads. Lori is tentative at first, but a glance at Chad's body strengthens her resolve. Zane can see her squaring her shoulders and her steps become more determined. Once she disappears down the highway embankment, Zane and Alyx return to the truck and climb in.

"Any remorse?" Alyx asks.

"Not a bit."

CHAPTER 99

The flashlight-for-headlights gig lasted only so long. The high number of expired vehicles on the highway made the going treacherous. After several harrowing miles, McDowell turned off the highway and cruised slowly along the access road and spotted a new-car dealership. He turned into the lot and parked behind the building among a slew of other vehicles. He and the rest of the crew bedded down in the service waiting area. After only three short hours of sleep, McDowell climbs back behind the wheel at daybreak. Two days of gunplay have left him strung out. It's Lauren's turn in the cab while Melissa serves her shift in the back with the group of cranky teenagers.

Lauren wraps a strand of her dark hair around her index finger. "How far to Oklahoma City?"

"On a good day, maybe three and a half hours. Today, who knows? Things will probably get gummed up when we reach Wichita."

"Another military base?" Lauren asks.

"Yes, McConnell Air Force Base. They're a big refueling outfit that was probably high on the target list."

"Have you been to every Air Force base there is?"

McDowell smiles. "Not all of them, but a bunch. I spent twenty years in the Air Force. They like to move people around."

"Did you attend the Air Force Academy?"

"Nope, but I ended up selling my soul to the Air Force anyway. I went to Texas A&M on a ROTC scholarship. Graduated from there and went on active duty."

Lauren turns in her seat and leans against the door. "Did you like the Air Force?"

"Mostly. They taught me how to fly, which allowed me, in retirement, to climb behind the wheel of a civilian airliner."

"What was the worst part of being in the Air Force?"

McDowell glances at Lauren. "Dropping bombs on people." He turns his gaze back to the road.

"Which war?"

"Dubya Bush's. Iraq. I flew a bunch of sorties during the opening days. I'm just thankful I punched out shortly after."

"They ever try to recall you, later in the war?"

"They tried, but I had my twenty in and a steady job."

"Can they compel a person to return to active duty?"

"Yes, until you're five years past retirement. I made it by the skin of my teeth, before they did the big buildup in Afghanistan. Hell, mostly now they fly drones. Some pilot sitting at Creech, out in Nevada, can control a plane on the other side of the world. Or could, I should say. Won't be much flying anything for the foreseeable future. What about you? Did you always want to be a teacher?"

"Yes. I think it's a calling. I know it's damn sure not for the money. There are far more good days than bad." She nods toward the back. "This is a critical time in their lives. Middle school is a turning point in a child's life. They transition from childish behaviors, or at least most do, into young adults. It's a very impressionable age and it's rewarding to see a child blossom before your eyes."

"You're a better person than me, dealing with those kids. I think I would pull my hair out if I had to spend every day in the classroom with them."

"There are days when I feel the same, but overall it's the perfect job for me. Like I said, it's a calling." Lauren turns back in her seat, kicks off her shoes, and props her feet on the dash.

McDowell slows to steer around a group of expired semis. The truck bumps over to the shoulder and he slowly navigates around the bottleneck, pulling back on the road when clear.

"Why are you going back to Dallas?"

McDowell glances over. "Don't really know. Don't know where else I'd go."

Lauren lets the silence linger for a moment, before turning to look at McDowell. "Come to Lubbock with us."

McDowell mulls that statement over for a while. "And do what?"

Lauren shrugs. "I have my own home. I thought, maybe, you . . . you could live with me."

"Oh," McDowell says.

They travel in silence for the next mile or two, Mc-

Dowell's brain zinging with unasked questions. Finally, he stumbles upon a safe one. "As roommates?"

Lauren grabs a strand of hair and twirls it around her index finger. "Or more."

Well, hell. What does she mean by that? "Well . . uh . . . you do realize I'm nearly twice your age?"

Lauren releases that strand of hair and grabs another. "Who cares?"

"Huh," McDowell mutters. "We've only known each other for a few days."

"Again, who cares?" She turns to look at him. "Don' get hung up on the age issue, Stan, or the length of time we've known one another. They're only numbers that don't really mean a damn thing."

"O . . . kay." He switches lanes to avoid a pickup his mind spinning. He steals a peek at Lauren, who's still twirling her hair. He turns back to the road.

Lauren glances over. "No pressure, Stan. Just a possibility."

McDowell switches hands on the steering wheel "Can I think about it?"

Lauren laughs. "Of course. I'm thinking of my own future, too, and I want all possible options on the table And one of those options, I hope, is you coming to Lubbock."

McDowell's face flushes red, and Lauren laughs again. "Stan, you're blushing."

"Well, hell, it's a lot to take in."

An hour later, nearing Wichita, McDowell's prediction proves true. Wichita is gone. A few concrete buildings remain, the rest scoured from the earth. From the looks of it, not one living thing remains. The highway leading into downtown is clogged with the burned-out husks, some large, some small—all unidentifiable. Before they get in too deep, McDowell slows the truck to a stop to allow everyone a chance to stretch their legs and answer the call of nature.

McDowell exits and walks behind a charred auto to take a piss, his mind still turning with thoughts about Lauren and how all that would work. *At fifty-six, I might have twenty years of good living left, maybe twenty-five if I'm lucky. Dad made it to seventy-four before succumbing to cancer and Mom made it to seventy-eight before Alzheimer's took her. Okay, not twenty-five, but a good twenty, surely. Not knowing Lauren's exact age, but assuming she's in her late twenties, she could end up being a widow before her fiftieth birthday.* He zips his pants and returns to the truck. Once everyone is loaded up, McDowell resumes his place behind the wheel and is somewhat relieved to find Melissa parked in the passenger seat. "We need to find another road that bypasses what was the downtown area."

Melissa tucks her legs under her. "I bet there's a loop around the city. All fairly large cities have some type of highway loop to funnel the commuters into and away from the city."

"I wonder what happens if we stay on this highway?"

"Guess we won't know unless you try."

"Good point." McDowell steers over to the far shoulder to get around the roadblock and is feeling good about his choice until they top a ridge to see the highway in front of them gone.

"Hell, I forgot the Air Force base was down in this area."

"Where was it?" Melissa asks.

McDowell points out the window. "See those big craters in what used to be a runway?"

Melissa sits up to look through the window. "Jeez, it looks like a meteorite hit."

"Pretty much what it was, only worse." McDowell makes a U-turn and backtracks north. After twenty minutes of turning, backtracking, and missed exits, he finally reaches a highway that leads south.

Melissa turns to look at him. "Do you have any idea where we're going?"

McDowell shakes his head. "Not really. I'm kind of playing it by ear."

"Well, I assume since you're a pilot you have a pretty good sense of direction."

"Oh, I do. But everything looks a little different on the ground."

Melissa chuckles.

A mile farther on, they come to a highway running west again and McDowell takes it. It looks to be the highway he's looking for, and it must have been a popular route, judging from the number of scorched auto frames. The going is slow as he weaves across the three-lane highway, making good use of the extra-wide shoulder.

Melissa uncrosses her legs and stretches. "How many people do you think lived in Wichita?"

"I don't know for sure, but I'd estimate it's north of three hundred thousand."

"And they all died?"

"Most likely. Many of them would have been vaporized instantaneously, judging by the size of those craters."

"And the rest of them?"

"Some would have died in the resulting pressure wave, especially if they were inside a building that wasn't constructed out of concrete. What the blast and pressure wave didn't get, the resulting firestorm would have."

Melissa looks ahead at the long string of incinerated vehicles stretching out ahead of them. "Do you think these cars were occupied when bombs hit?"

McDowell turns to glance at Melissa. "Yes."

Melissa shudders. "And this is just one city."

"Yes. We'll never know the exact number of those killed in the initial attack. And since then, a good number of people would have succumbed to their injuries or are currently suffering radiation exposure that could linger for a month or more."

Melissa swivels in her seat, pulling her left leg under her. "How many of us do you think are left?"

"Lauren and I had this discussion. We have no idea the state of affairs in other countries. But when we were running scenarios at Global Strike Command, many of the results suggested two thirds of the world population wouldn't survive the first week."

"That's unbelievable. Do you know how large that number would be?"

"Yes, I do know."

They ride in silence for several miles, each consumed with their own thoughts. The highway eventually curves back to the east and McDowell mutters a string of curses and slows the truck to a stop. The loop road has led them to a spot that's maybe a half mile from their original position before they were forced to turn back.

Melissa scoots to the edge of the seat. "Where did the highway go?"

"It got bombed to hell when they were nuking the Air Force base." McDowell sighs. He spins the wheel and backtracks to the next exit. After driving west for about three miles, McDowell cuts back south, then east, and returns to I-35 south. An hour later they zip across the Oklahoma state line.

"It'll be dark in a few hours," Melissa says. "And we haven't had much luck with our previous nighttime arrangements."

"The last few nights have been a nightmare. I'm hoping tonight we can drop in on an old friend."

CHAPTER 100

After getting the all clear from Henry, Gage starts the arduous process of climbing back down the tower. When he reaches the bottom, he ducks through the door and locks it behind him, before making his way over to Henry. "Is the transformer working?"

Henry glances up, a smile on his face. "Yes. On the out-feed side I'm measuring a consistent 34.5 thousand volts."

"And what happens from here?"

"Well, if any of the other step-up transformers on the grid are operational, they'll up the voltages significantly to provide more power to more places."

"How are we going to know who has power?" Gage asks.

Henry closes the access door on the transformer. "We'll know when it gets dark." Out of habit, Henry moves his right arm to pick up his tools and mutters a few choice curse words. "Why'd the bastards have to shoot me in the right arm? Ever try to work left-handed when you've been using your right for sixty-eight years?"

Gage gathers up the tools. "You're damn lucky you can move anything. A couple of inches to your left and we wouldn't be having this conversation."

Henry sighs. "I suppose you're right."

They make their way to the truck and pause to watch the turbine in action before climbing in. Gage repositions the shotgun and fires up the pickup. When they pull into the drive of the Reed home, Henry shouts, "Hot damn."

"What?" Gage asks.

"Look at the kitchen window."

Gage stops the truck and stares at the window. When you've spent your entire life seeing something everyone took for granted, it takes a few moments for Gage's mind to interpret the image. Then it does. The light above the kitchen sink is on. "I'll be damned—we've got power."

"Yes, we do."

Gage pulls the truck around behind the house and stops. "I need to run an errand, Henry. I'll be back in a bit."

Henry reaches across his body with his left hand and opens the door. "Where are you going?"

"To see if my mom and brother have power." Sounds like a sensible lie to Gage's ears.

"If not, invite them out here. If we can't make room in the house, the barn's heated. We'll make it work."

"I'll tell them." Henry exits and Gage turns the truck around in the wide gravel area fronting the barn and eases back by the house, picking up the road into town. After a few minutes of driving, he steers into the doctor's neighborhood and winds through the neighborhood streets until finding the white Volvo. He pulls in behind it, puts the truck in park, and kills the engine. After a long look at the shotgun, he exits the cab empty-handed.

Gage climbs the steps and he raps his knuckles on the door. He hears footsteps and the same man, holding the same gun, opens the door.

"Yes?"

"Is Dr. Samia here?"

The man eyes Gage for a moment. "You were here the other night, correct?"

"Yes, sir. I'm Holly's husband."

The man nods and moves aside. The interior of the house is dim, but there's enough light to see most of the front room. The place is tidy, a stack of magazines precisely arranged on a wooden coffee table, and two wing chairs flanking a large leather sofa. On the far wall hangs a large flat-screen television—all things he didn't see the night Holly gave birth.

"She's in the kitchen," the man says.

Gage nods and steps deeper into the house and finds Eliana Samia seated at the kitchen table, surrounded by a pile of books and a half-dozen lit candles.

She glances up and stands. "Gage, is Holly having complications?"

"No, ma'am, she's fine. It's the baby we're worried about."

Dr. Samia waves to a chair and Gage sits as she returns to her spot. "Tell me what is going on."

"Doc, Holly's milk still hasn't come in. The baby cries all the time. I was hoping you might have some infant formula."

"I don't, Gage. I'm in charge of the mother and baby until birth. After that, the pediatrician is responsible for the baby's health. The only items I have are several bottles of prenatal vitamins." She puts a finger to her lips. "I don't remember who you and Holly selected for a pediatrician."

"We chose Dr. Abbasi."

Samia visibly winces at the name. "I'm sorry to tell you, Gage, Dr. Abbasi was killed on the second day when a group of thugs broke into the hospital."

Gage's shoulders slump. "Maybe he kept some formula at his house. Do you know where he lived?"

"His home, I believe, was in Oklahoma City. He would come out here three to four days a week. His wife is a tenured professor at the University of Oklahoma, so they were forced to choose who would do the bulk of the commuting."

"What about other pediatricians? I'm desperate, Doc."

"Gage, I believe Holly will soon begin producing milk. You need to be patient."

"When, Doc? And what do we do in the meantime?"

"Let nature take its course. You might supplement the baby's feedings with a bottle of warmed broth. Do you have any broth at home?"

Gage nods, "Yeah, I think so."

Samia stands. "Babies are resilient little creatures, Gage. Closely monitor the baby's weight for the next day or two and supplement Holly's feedings with the broth."

Disheartened, Gage pushes out of the chair and stands. "And if the baby is losing weight?"

"Two or three ounces shouldn't be an issue."

"And if it's more?"

"Let us not go there, Gage. See how she does over the next twenty-four hours."

"Will you tell me where another pediatrician might live?"

Samia walks toward the front door, Gage following behind. She stops near the open door and turns. "I do not believe it is my position to involve others. Give it time, Gage."

Gage nods and brushes past. He's working hard to tamp down his growing anger as he climbs back in the truck. "I'll find out one way or another," he mumbles as he backs out of the drive.

CHAPTER 101

After a good morning of sailing, the breeze gradually diminished in the early afternoon and the *Emma-Sophia* is now slowly drifting south toward Cape Lookout. Brad climbs on top of the cabin to examine the hull for damage from the flaming shrapnel. He scrambles across the top of the cabin and inspects the furled jib for burns or gashes. Nothing is apparent, but he won't know for sure until they unfurl it. He works his way back along the perimeter and discovers a couple of pockmarks in the hull. He kneels down for a closer look. It appears the shrapnel chipped the paint and did no permanent damage. Brad sighs with relief and stands.

Nicole is at the stern, drift-fishing after swapping the sweatshirt for a T-shirt. Tanner is curled up on the side bench, his nose buried in Bradbury's *Fahrenheit 451*. To look at them you wouldn't know they had witnessed a naval battle that put their lives in jeopardy only hours ago. Brad steps down into the cockpit and resumes his place behind the wheel.

Nicole, sitting sideways in the seat, reels in her line to make sure the lure is still attached. It is and she recasts, letting the boat's wake pull the lure farther out. She swivels around. "Where do you think the Chinese went?"

"South, is all we know," Brad says. "My bet is we encounter them again."

Tanner dog-ears a page and closes the book. "Dad, who's in charge?"

"Of what?" Brad asks.

"Well, I guess the world."

"No way to know, Tanner."

"Is it the Chinese?"

"No doubt they have a hand in it. But we don't know what's happened in our own country, much less the rest of the world." He turns to Nicole. "What do you think?"

"I think it doesn't really matter. What's left to take charge of? A group of devastated countries with more problems than anyone could ever imagine?"

Tanner brushes the hair out of his eyes. "We studied China last year in social studies. I know they have to import a lot of natural resources to keep up with demand. What if they take over our country for the oil?"

"Hadn't really thought about that, Tanner," Brad says. "If that's true, their presence here, now, would add some legitimacy to that idea."

Nicole tucks her legs beneath her, the fishing pole still in her hands. "And we have no way of stopping them, if that is indeed their intent."

Brad turns where he can see both Nicole and Tanner. "Some of our military assets must have survived. Someone was shooting at those Chinese warships."

"Could have been Russians, for all we know," Nicole says. "Either way, there is little doubt the other ship was destroyed or they would have continued their pursuit." Nicole feels a tug on the line and jumps to her feet and looks back over her shoulder. "Even if some of our military assets survived, who's left to command them?" She tugs the pole up and reels on the downswing, over and over again.

Brad finds himself admiring the strain of her shoulder muscles beneath the T-shirt and is not quite sure how he feels about it.

"Tanner, will you grab the net?" Nicole asks.

Tanner stands, grabs the net, and steps to the back of the boat.

Brad watches as they work together. At the beginning of the trip, Tanner had been withdrawn and depressed. But since Nicole came aboard he's gradually returned to his normal self. It could be he simply emerged from his period of grieving or, more likely, Nicole has played an important role in his recovery—maybe for both Tanner and himself.

"Scoop it, Tanner," Nicole says.

Tanner bends over the rail and nets the fish, pulling it aboard. He reaches into the net to pull the fish out, and Nicole puts a hand on his arm. "Better let me do it, Tanner. It's a bluefish with razor-sharp teeth."

"I can handle it," Tanner says. He digs into the net and grabs the fish by the gills. "It's heavy." He pulls the fish out and holds it up.

"Maybe fifteen pounds," Nicole says. "Time for a feast."

Thoughts of the Chinese taking over the world fade from conversation as Nicole teaches Tanner how to clean the fish and Brad lights the propane stove. Once the catch is cooked, each carries a plateful topside. Brad disappears back inside and returns with a bottle of chardonnay—one of four on board—and three glasses. He pulls the cork, pours, and passes out the drinks. Tanner takes a sip and scrunches his nose. "Is this supposed to be good?"

He sets the glass aside, Brad and Nicole chuckling.

"It's an acquired taste, son."

"Yeah, if you say so. I'll stick to water for now."

They finish their feast, and Tanner and Nicole rinse the plates off the stern. Tanner's statement had struck a nerve. Brad sneaks downstairs and pulls up a hatch in the floor. He's been hesitant to look, knowing the news won't be good. He grabs a flashlight from a drawer and kneels down. His heart sinks when he sees the freshwater tank nearly empty.

CHAPTER 102

Edmond, Oklahoma

Stan McDowell is still mulling over Lauren Thomas's proposition when he sees a sign announcing: EDMOND NEXT SIX EXITS. Having flown in and out of Oklahoma City numerous times, he knows Edmond is a suburb just north of the state capital. By McDowell's reckoning, he has about ten miles to make a shit-or-get-off-the-pot decision. He had told Lauren and Melissa he would travel with them to the Texas state line before going their separate ways, but really, Oklahoma City is the point where the decision needs to be made. From here, it's a straight shot south to Dallas on I-35, or a straight shot west to Amarillo on I-40, then on south to Lubbock. McDowell switches hands on the steering wheel and sighs.

They pass a giant cross that's nestled up close to the highway then a string of businesses situated on a hill overlooking the interstate. All have been looted, with the unwanted or unneeded items thrown across the parking lot. McDowell glances at Lauren, who had moved back inside at their last stop. "I wonder why they didn't leave the things no one wanted inside the store." He points out the window. "See, look at all those tires bunched up in a pile. Who needs tires?"

Lauren slips off her shoes and pulls her legs under her, sitting cross-legged. "Those stores have probably been searched a dozen times or more since all this happened. Maybe someone thought they could use a few tires for something and carried them outside and realized how pointless they were. Or, maybe there are dozens of people camped out inside the Walmart and they needed the space." Lauren smiles. "We could stop and try to solve the tire dilemma."

"I think we'll pass." McDowell eyes the gas gauge. "Although, we're going to need to stop somewhere soon to refuel." McDowell's gaze flicks to the rearview mirror out of habit, something he's done continuously throughout the journey. Every other time the result has been the same—nothing behind them except a static image of areas they've already passed. This time it's different. "Looks like we have some company."

Lauren swivels her head for a look. "Where did they come from?"

"No idea, but it's smart when you think about it." McDowell zeros in on the semi in the rearview. "Looks like an old Peterbilt or Kenworth, but the tanker looks to be of a more recent vintage. Must be nice for them, not having to search for fuel all the time. But, jeez, would you look at that truck. It looks like it's been through a demolition derby." The front end of the semi is battered, with both front fenders hanging on by a thread.

"Should we be concerned? My mind is flashing on images from one of those stupid *Mad Max* movies."

McDowell chuckles. "Not a *Mad Max* fan?"

"No. Can't say I made it past the five-minute mark on any of them. Seriously, Stan, should we be worried?"

McDowell glances over to see her face pinched with worry. "I don't think so. They have as much right to the road as we do."

"That's all well and good, but where did they come from? Have you seen that truck before?"

McDowell's eyes dart to the rearview to see the truck inching closer. "No." A tingle of dread flickers at the base of McDowell's neck. "We're not a threat to them."

"No, we're not, but you're thinking about the situation from the wrong angle."

"What?" Then it hits him. "Oh shit." His eyes drift down to the gas gauge and a pit forms in his stomach. "We should have refueled earlier."

"How far can we go on what we have?"

McDowell sighs. "Not far enough." He glances at the side mirror. The truck has dropped back a bit, now maybe a hundred feet behind them. He turns his gaze to the front and spots a truck stop coming up on the right. The lot is littered with semis, including a couple of tankers. One of the smart things they did before departing the sign shop back in Minnesota was to break out the back window. McDowell glances over his shoulder and shouts, "Hold on!" He waits until the last possible second, then whips onto the exit ramp. Both he and Lauren exhale a sigh of relief when the semi zooms past.

McDowell slows and steers onto the access road, turning into the truck stop parking lot. He eases the truck up to one of the tankers, puts the transmission into neutral, and stomps on the parking brake. He peers through the back opening. "Everyone, sit tight." He turns to Lauren. "Keep that shotgun handy."

Lauren pulls the shotgun onto her lap. "Hurry, Stan."

"Why don't you climb out, just in case?"

Lauren nods and opens her door as McDowell exits. He quickly unlashes the hose and hurries over to the tanker. He spins off all the caps and cracks open the valves in search of diesel. Just as before, he finds it on the third attempt. After clamping on the hose, he nudges the valve open and carries the other end over to the truck's tank, where he cranks off the cap and holds the hose, allowing the diesel to dribble into the tank. He looks up at Lauren. "This is too slow. Will you crank the valve open an little more?"

"How?"

"Follow the hose. Just turn the handle a quarter of a turn."

Lauren nods and hurries over to the tanker.

Jonathon stands and looks over the railing. "Mr. McDowell, I really need to pee."

McDowell groans. "Okay, Jonathon. Step off and pee, but don't wander off."

Jonathon jumps off the back, setting off a round of "Me, too's" from the other students.

McDowell groans again. "I promise we'll stop soon. Please try to hold it a little longer."

"How come Jonathon gets to pee?" someone asks.

McDowell snaps and shouts, "Enough!" He then

lowers his voice. "Did you see the semi that was following us? I don't think they have good intentions."

That sobers the students and they quiet down.

"Stan!" Lauren shouts.

McDowell looks up to see the semi turning off the overpass, heading in their direction.

"Shut it off," he shouts. He turns and races over to Lauren as she's closing the valve and takes the shotgun from her hands. "Unclamp the hose and tie it back on, then climb in the truck. We're getting the hell out of here."

He cracks the chamber to make sure a shell is seated and waits for Lauren to finish up. He catches movement out of the corner of his eye and turns. Jonathon is on the far side of the lot, a good two hundred yards away. He curses, then shouts, "Jonathon!"

CHAPTER 103

Weatherford

Still desperate for baby formula, Gage drives out to the Walmart on the other side of the highway and pulls into the lot. He gags when he gets a whiff of the decomposing bodies. It seems as though every fly in the state of Oklahoma has made this parking lot home. Even from this distance he can see a writhing, wiggling mass of maggots feeding on the bodies. Gage gags again and looks beyond the bodies to see the store's facade blackened by fire. Gage gooses the gas and exits the parking lot and is passing under the highway when he's struck with a sudden thought.

He whips a U-turn and drives up the exit ramp, pulling up close to the first car for a look inside. What he's looking for is not there. He eases up close to an old farm truck, knowing the probabilities are unlikely and finds he's correct. He passes one semi, then another. The possibilities of finding what he's looking for in a semi are slim to none. Gage spots a sedan with Ohio plates, pulls up next to it, and finds what he's looking for—a child's car seat.

He climbs out, tries the door handle, and curses. "Who locks a dead car?" He grumbles as he returns to the truck. He grabs a hammer from the back and steps over to the sedan and smashes the driver's side glass. After unlocking the door, he searches the car for formula and ends up finding a balled-up dirty diaper under the driver's seat. After tossing the diaper back in the car, he returns to the truck for his crowbar. Sliding behind the rear of the sedan, he jams the crowbar beneath the trunk lid and presses down. The lid pops, but the trunk is empty.

Gage pauses to refine his strategy. *If a person is stranded with a small child, what's the one thing they'll never leave behind?* Of course the answer is as clear as a bell when Gage thinks about it. They'll leave a purse, or a piece of luggage, but never the food, in this case formula, that would be critical for a child's survival. Gage tosses the hammer and the crowbar in the back and climbs back behind the wheel. *Unless they're on a long, extended trip and packed more formula than they could carry, hoping they could return to their stash at a later date.* Easing down the highway, he scans vehicles, searching for car seats and out-of-state tags.

Gage ransacks six more cars—all empty. He mulls the situation further. *Who'd pack a bunch of formula knowing you could always stop at the next Target, the next Walmart, or the next grocery store? No one, unless they kept a large reserve at home, maybe bought at a two-for-one special. And how many times have you seen a two-for-one on anything someone might really need?* Gage sighs. He could spend all of today and the next, and on, and on, tearing into cars and not finding a thing other than items no one needs in today's world. Crestfallen, he climbs back behind the wheel.

Gage pulls into the drive of the Reed home and parks behind the house. The lights in the house are still on and the instant he walks through the back door, he cringes. Susan is holding a crying Olivia and pacing around the room, patting her granddaughter's back.

"Has she been crying all day?" Gage asks.

"Not *all* day. Just most of it," Susan replies. She makes a halfhearted attempt at a smile.

"I went over to Dr. Samia's to see if she had any baby formula."

Susan's eyes widen with hope. "Did she?"

"Unfortunately, no. She said she was only responsible for the child until the moment of birth, when Dr. Abbasi was supposed to take over."

Susan switches positions, snuggling Olivia to her chest. "Did you try his house?"

"He's dead. Killed at the hospital. And she thought he lived somewhere in Oklahoma City. Dr. Samia suggested filling a bottle with warm broth."

"Already tried. She won't take it."

Gage hangs his head. "Do you want me to take her?"

"No, I'll hold her. You can console Holly. She's in the bedroom."

Gage nods and trudges down the hall. He eases the door open and finds the room dark. Thinking Holly might be asleep, he starts to pull the door closed and hears a sniffle. "Holly?"

This time it's a sob. Gage clicks on the light to see his wife on the bed, a pillow over her head. He walks over and lies down beside her.

"Where . . . where . . . did . . . you go?" she asks, between sobs.

Gage wraps an arm around his wife and pulls her closer. "I went over to Dr. Samia's to see if she had any formula."

"She didn't . . . did . . . she?"

"No."

Holly lifts the pillow off her head. "Maybe Dr. Abbasi has some?"

Gage is hesitant to tell her the truth in her fragile state of mind. "Doc says he lived in Oklahoma City."

Holly drops the pillow back on her head and sobs.

"We'll get through this, babe."

The sobs stop and Holly flashes immediately to anger. She throws the pillow to the floor. "How? You going to start producing milk in your breasts?" She sits up and scoots back, sagging against the headboard.

"Dr. Samia seemed confident your milk will come in."

"Yeah, well, she's not here, is she?"

Gage pulls himself to a sitting position and leans back against the headboard. Holly refuses to look at him. "Are you producing any milk?" he asks in a soft, calm tone.

She shakes her head side to side like a dog with a snake. "Not enough!"

Gage knows another question will push her over the edge. Instead, he reaches out to take her hand and she yanks it away. "I even went looking through the cars on the highway. I don't know what else to do, Holly."

Holly swipes a tear away with the back of her hand and exhales a long, shaky breath. "Gage, our baby is going to die and I can't do a damn thing about it."

Gage scoots closer and tentatively reaches out for her hand again. This time she allows him to take it. "She's not going to die, Holly. If I have to drive across the state looking for formula, that's what I'm going to do."

Holly, staring straight ahead, says, "You better start driving."

Gage nods, pushes off the bed, and steps out into the hall, pulling the door closed behind him. Olivia is still crying and Susan is still walking.

"Where's Henry?"

Susan glances up. "In the barn. How's Holly?"

"Not good," Gage mutters as he walks down the hallway to Henry's study. After entering the combination he pops the door on the gun safe and grabs one of Henry's pistols and a box of ammo before relocking the door. Gage heads for the door and strides across the yard, entering the barn. "Henry, you know everybody in town. You have to know where another pediatrician lives."

Henry is puttering around with something on the workbench. He pauses to think. "We haven't been to a pediatrician since the girls were small. But, I think old Dr. Stone is still around."

"Where does he live?"

"Uh-uh, Gage. If you're going, I'm going."

"Load up." Gage turns and heads for the pickup.

CHAPTER 104

Shawnee, Oklahoma

"We should be coming up on a highway that'll take us back north," Alyx says, peering out the windshield.

"Why do we want to go north?" Zane asks. "I thought you said I-40 ran right past Weatherford."

"It does. But it also runs right by Tinker Air Force Base."

"Damn."

"I agree. We need to head north and pick up the turnpike, which feeds into I-35. From there, we can pick up I-40 again, bypassing the entire mess at Tinker."

Zane shakes his head. "That's miles out of the way."

"We have no other choice. Right now, we're about thirty miles east of the base. We're not going to get much closer and Highway 177 feeds right into the turnpike. Otherwise we'll be chasing our tail trying to navigate the back roads."

Although not particularly happy with the decision, Zane takes the exit when they come to it. He navigates around a clump of cars at the exit before hitting open road. The area is mostly rolling farmland that's interspersed with an occasional house. Most of the homes are postage-stamp size compared to the barns and farming equipment that surrounds them. Trucks of all shapes and sizes are parked haphazardly around the yards and there's an assortment of tractors that range, sizewise, from a notch above a riding lawn mower to hulking behemoths that are taller than most of the home's rooflines. Toss in an occasional combine here and there, along with all the tractor implements needed to run a farm, and Zane bets the final tally has to be in the millions of dollars.

"How do they afford those monster tractors?"

"It's the great American way. They're mortgaged to the hilt."

"I guess they won't have to worry about making payments for a while. Your dad have any tractors?"

"Of course. You can't have a farm and not have a tractor. It's tiny compared to most of these."

Zane glances at Alyx and smiles. "Do you put on your Daisy Dukes and drive the tractor around the pasture?"

"Does that turn you on?"

"Yeah, a little."

Alyx laughs. "During the summers when I was home from college, I'd help Dad bale the hay, but I sure as hell wasn't wearing a pair of short shorts. The mosquitoes would eat you alive, and what they didn't get, the wasps and bees would. Sorry to burst your bubble, but most of the time I was wearing jeans and a long-sleeved shirt."

Zane smiles. "That's kind of sexy, too. Were you wearing a cowboy hat?"

Alyx bats her eyelashes. "Nope, a ball cap."

They hit the turnpike at Wellston and follow it west, back toward Oklahoma City.

"So your dad designs wind farms?" Zane asks.

"Yep. Got his engineering degree from Texas A&M and went to work for an energy company that was just starting a wind division."

"Your mom and dad meet in college?"

Alyx nods. "Their junior year, and married after both graduated. What about your parents?"

Zane grows silent. After several moments he says, "My parents died when I was eight years old."

Alyx gasps. "I'm so sorry, Zane. What happened?"

"My father had a business meeting in Frankfurt. He did something in banking, but I don't know exactly what. We were living in Brooklyn, and my sister and I were out of school for Christmas break. We were all, the entire family, going to spend the week of Christmas at my grandparents' house out on Long Island. At the last minute, Mom decided to join my dad on the trip. A second honeymoon, they said, although it was supposed to be a relatively short trip—three or four days. They were supposed to be back home four days before Christmas. My grandparents drove into the city to pick us up and that was the last time we ever saw our parents."

Alyx edges closer and puts a hand on his arm. "How did they die?"

Zane stares at the road ahead for a few minutes before turning to look at Alyx. "Ever hear of Pan Am Flight 103?"

"Oh my God. They were aboard that plane when it went down over Lockerbie, Scotland?"

"Yes. December 21, 1988. And it didn't go down; it was blown up by two Libyan nationals. My parents were on their way back from Frankfurt."

Alyx sits in silence, processing the news. After several moments, she asks, "And your grandparents raised you and your sister?"

"They did, even though it was hard for them to feed themselves much less two extra mouths."

"I thought Gaddafi paid some type of compensation."

"Not until 2008. My father had a life insurance policy that my grandparents put away for our education. They were both gone by the time the Libyans ponied up any money. The families were supposed to receive eight million dollars, but by the time the attorneys were through, we received a little over two million dollars. I'd trade every cent if it would bring my parents back." Zane pauses to stare out the windshield for a few moments. "Anyway, my sister and I divided the money equally. I donated my portion to the 9/11 memorial."

"And your sister?"

"Jennifer. Her name's Jennifer. She donated some and kept some."

"Younger or older?"

"Younger by three years. She's thirty-three now and lives in Monterey with her husband and two kids."

Alyx pauses to wonder what it would be like to lose both parents at eight years old, and can't even fathom the idea. "And that's why you went into intelligence?"

"Yes. After college I joined the army after assurances

they would place me with an intelligence unit. I served five years of active duty, most of it overseas in the Middle East, and punched out and went to work for the government."

"How long before you ended up at the National Security Agency?"

Zane glances at Alyx. "Not long. I'm good at what I do."

Alyx scoots across the seat until their bodies are touching. "What was your degree in?"

"Undergrad in computer engineering and a master's in computer architecture, both from Columbia."

"Wow. That's impressive, and here you had me fooled, playing dumb all along."

Zane smiles. "I had to see if you had the chops. What about you?"

Alyx playfully punches him in the arm. "Undergrad in computer engineering and a master's with a primary focus on distributed and networked systems, both from Vanderbilt."

"Very impressive. How did you end up at the NSA?"

"I spent a year working toward a Ph.D., and said screw it. With my résumé, it wasn't hard to get a job. Hell, they were begging people with computer science degrees to come to work for them." Alyx tucks a flyaway of hair behind her ear. "I thought about going out to Silicon Valley and striking it rich, but I've never been motivated by money."

Zane slows to veer around a collection of cars. "What *does* motivate you?"

"Catching the bad guys. I want to be the smartest person on any network I'm operating on."

"So what do we do now? We may never have a working computer network during our lifetime."

Alyx sighs. "I'll—no *we'll*—help my dad rebuild the wind farm."

"Do you think he has a turbine up and running by now?"

"I wouldn't be surprised. Plus, he has my brother-in-law, Gage, to help him. They're both very resourceful."

"We can hope." Zane's eyes dart to the gas gauge. "We'll need to get gas soon."

"We're almost to I-35. There's a big amusement park there and I'm sure the lot is full of abandoned cars."

Zane glances at the gas gauge again. "We could stop anywhere along here to siphon some gasoline."

"Let's wait if we can. I feel like we have some momentum for the first time in days. And I'd like to stretch my legs for a few minutes. The place is somewhat secluded and I'd feel safer."

"How far?"

"From here, maybe five miles. It's the first exit off I-35 once we leave the turnpike."

"We can make that."

A few minutes later he takes the exit for I-35 south and Alyx points out the exit to the amusement park. Zane threads the truck through three lanes of dead cars and pulls off the highway.

"Next left," Alyx says scanning the surroundings. "Oh shit. Stop, Zane."

Zane brakes to a stop. "What?"

Alyx points. "The truck stop."

"Damn it. It's not our fight, Alyx."

"They're kids, Zane. And a bunch of them."

Zane groans but relents, and they spend a momen studying the layout. There's a flatbed truck parked nex to a tanker, which is wedged in by another semi tha looks as if it had been in a demolition derby. The mos distressing matter are the two large men standing at the edge of the group, their pistols up and ready to fire. An older gentleman is leaning against the flatbed, his shir covered by what appears to be blood. Zane counts sixteer younger people, probably teenagers, and two womer who look to be older, but not old enough to be parents to any of the kids.

One of the men holding a pistol steps forward and grabs one of the female teenagers by the hair and begins dragging her toward the cab of the battered semi.

"Bastard," Zane mutters as he crosses the intersection and pulls in behind a ransacked McDonald's. He kills the engine, crams his pockets full of ammo, grabs the shotgun, and slips out the door. "You stay here, Alyx."

"I can—"

Zane cuts her off with the wave of his hand. He leans through the window and lowers his voice. "I know you want to help, but let me clear the area first. I can't be worried about you."

Alyx scowls for a moment, then nods.

Using the building as cover, Zane works his way forward and peeks around the corner. There's a cluster of vehicles in front of him that will allow him to move freely. He races up a short incline and ducks in behind a truck. After quickly working through the jam, he sidles up next to an older sedan and kneels down for a look. A large grouping of feet is visible beneath the ad-

acent tanker, meaning the bad guys are positioned at
three o'clock. Not knowing how much time he has left,
he slips around the back of the sedan and sidles up next
to the tanker. Zane kneels down for a closer look. The
kids, and the two older women, are just in front of him.
One of the men is standing to the right, his pistol covering the group. The other man is still trying to get the
young girl into the cab of their truck. Yanking on her
hair, he turns the girl around and slaps her in the face.
The girl sags to her knees.

"Get your ass in the truck," the man shouts.

Zane has seen all he needs to see. He tamps down
the rage that's building in his gut like a roaring fire and
steps carefully to the front of the big rig, easing around
the nose. Now he has a clear field of fire—except for
the man with his hands on the girl. Zane calculates the
firing order in his brain. *Shoot the closest man and
hope the other turns around and steps clear of the girl?
Or will the man have the presence of mind to grab the
girl to use as a hostage?* All unanswerable questions,
but Zane can feel the time ticking down.

Suddenly the unexpected happens. The girl fighting
to stay out of the truck switches tactics. Instead of
fighting, she lets her body go slack and she slips from
the man's grasp. Zane fires the right barrel and the man
drops to the ground as if a sinkhole had opened up beneath him. Zane swings the barrel to the closest man
and fires before the man can even turn, shredding the
man's upper body with the double-aught buckshot.
The man turns a quarter turn and face-plants on the asphalt. Zane cracks the breech and reloads as he moves
out from behind the truck, his hand up. "Don't move
yet," he shouts.

He steps over the closest man and doesn't even pause before moving on to the second. The young girl still on the ground, is weeping and trembling. "It's okay," Zane says in a soft voice. "It's all over." With the shotgun still aimed at the second man, he steps in for a closer look. The man is facedown, but the rapidly spreading pool of blood tells Zane all he needs to know. He removes his finger from the trigger and helps the young woman up. "What's your name?"

"A . . . Amanda," she says between sobs.

Zane puts his arm around her. "It's all over, Amanda. That was a very brave thing you did."

Amanda nods and wipes at her tears. "Only . . . thing . . . I . . . could think . . . of."

"It was perfect, Amanda."

Zane leads Amanda back and retrieves the pistol before rejoining the group. Alyx makes an appearance and starts working on the injured man. Zane takes a moment to study the crowd and shakes his head. He turns to the stouter of the two women. "You want to fill me in?"

"It's a long story but thank you for saving us." She reaches a hand out. "I'm Melissa."

Zane takes it. "Zane, and my friend over there is Alyx. How did you end up with a group of teenagers?"

"We were on an international flight when everything hit. Apparently we were far enough to the north to avoid the EMPs. We finally found a place to land at Minneapolis–Saint—"

Alyx shrieks and Zane is instantly on high alert. Then he hears her laugh, and he relaxes a little. "Hold that story for a sec, Melissa," he says before making his way over to Alyx and the older gentleman.

Alyx looks up, grinning from ear to ear. "Zane, I'd like you to meet Stan McDowell, an old college friend of my father's."

Zane glances around, searching for the cameras, then turns back and cocks his head to the side. "Do what?"

The man, his face now free of blood, looks up and smiles. "It's a small world."

"You're telling me," Zane mutters.

CHAPTER 105

Slowly, the USS *New York* is working closer to the two Chinese destroyers who are back in their hideout in the waters of Lookout Bight. Positioned five miles off the coast, the submarine is submerged in 400 feet of water, traveling along a deep depression in the sea floor. Thompson steps over to the sonar station. "Mr. Adams, where are they?"

"According to my chart, Skipper, it appears they're tucked in behind the point of Cape Lookout. I'm not detecting any prop wash, but I am picking up three distinct engine noises."

"Probably running their gen—wait, did you say three different engines?"

"I did, Skipper. By my reckoning, there are three ships out there, not two."

"Damn it," Thompson mumbles. He steps over to the chart table, and Garcia walks over to join him.

"Three ships, Carlos? Another destroyer?"

"Could be, but I'd lean toward a supply ship or a fuel tanker. They're a long way from home with zero resources available to draw on. And those destroyers are refueling somewhere."

"A tanker, huh? Makes sense and it doesn't change our plan of attack. We sink the two Chinese destroyers and the tanker will be easy pickings." Thompson clicks on the computer mouse and brings up a depth chart for the Cape Lookout area. "The bottom begins to rise fairly significantly about a mile and a half out from shore. We won't be able to get as close as I'd like."

"If they're anchored, our torpedoes will hit before they have time to respond, even if we shoot from three miles out," Garcia says.

"But would they be anchored so close to the shoreline of a hostile country? I wouldn't. It could be the tanker is anchored and the other ships are tied up. Hell of a lot easier to slip some ropes than waiting for the anchor to be hoisted aboard."

"That makes sense, but there's a hell of a lot we don't know, Bull."

Thompson glances at the digital clock. "It'll be dark before we're in position. We'll ascend to periscope depth for a quick look."

Garcia points at the monitor. "I spot one more possible issue."

"What's that?"

"Look at the depths. If they're positioned where we think they are, they'll only sink about twenty feet, leaving a good portion of the superstructure above the waterline. Any survivors will be able to swim to shore."

"*That* is not our problem. Good luck to 'em." Thompson steps over to the attack center. "Mr. White, locked and loaded?"

"Almost, Skipper," White replies. "The target picture is somewhat muddy, sir. We would prefer visual confirmation of their positions."

"You'll have your visual as soon as it's dark. Flood all tubes. I want your crew ready for a rapid reload."

"Four fish are loaded, Skipper." He triggers the radio handset draped around his neck. "Attack center to torpedo room. Flood all tubes. Repeat, flood all tubes." White looks up from his control board. "We'll be ready for a quick reload, Skipper."

Thompson gives his shoulder a squeeze. "Notify when you have final firing solution after visual confirmation." Thompson turns and walks back to his place on the bridge "Mr. Patterson, where are we?"

"We're three miles from the targets, Skipper. Should be at your specified location in a little over three minutes," Patterson, the navigator, says.

"Thank you. Q, take us up to two hundred."

The nose of the sub tilts upward as Thompson walks sideways toward his chair. He sits and removes his cap to wipe the sweat from his forehead. "Conn, slow to one-third."

His order is repeated and those inside can feel the sub slow. The crew on the bridge is tense, yet focused. Chatter is nonexistent and the only audible sounds are the nervous breaths from the crew. The sub levels off and, after a few moments of maneuvering, Patterson announces they are ten seconds from the specified position. A clock starts ticking in Thompson's head. The moment they fire, they give away their position. His plan is to target the two warships with two torpedoes each, and haul ass, coming back later for the tanker.

"Conn, all stop," Thompson orders. "Q, slow ascent to periscope depth."

As the sub drifts upward, Thompson stands and waits for the sub to level off. Once it does he orders the periscope up. He steps over and catches the handles as they rise from the floor. With a flick of his finger, he switches the scope's view to night vision and positions his eyes on the scope. He walks a circle, getting his bearings. After triggering the periscope camera, Thompson zeros in on the Chinese ships and curses. The two warships are stacked one against the other with the broadside of the nearest ship facing outward. They are positioned about 500 yards from shore and the tanker is anchored a hundred yards to the south. He spins around, searching for nearby ships and spots a sailboat anchored a mile offshore, opposite of Cape Lookout Lighthouse. He nudges the scope toward shore and finds the beach lined by a shantytown of pop-up structures, but nothing within a thousand yards of the three enemy ships. They should be safe from collateral damage, Thompson thinks as he steps away from the scope. "Scope down," he orders in a low voice. "Q, slow descent to one-five-zero."

He walks over to the attack center. "You see the video?"

"We're studying it now, Skipper," White says. "Not an ideal situation, but doable. I assume we're coming back for the tanker."

"You assume correctly. Will you be able to, at minimum, disable the ship tucked behind the first one?"

"We're aiming to sink both, Skipper. Give me thirty seconds to refine the firing solution."

Thompson looks over at the bridge. "Conn, stand by, flank speed, hard left rudder," he says in a low, clear voice.

He receives a nod for his answer.

White looks up. "We're ready, Skipper."

"Fire all tubes."

CHAPTER 106

Near Cape Lookout Lighthouse

The wind conditions improved during the afternoon and the *EmmaSophia* made good time until the wind died, along with the light. Like all previous evenings, the gray sky made it dark early and Brad dropped anchor opposite the Cape Lookout Lighthouse, a mile offshore. It had been, though, a good day for fishing. Nicole bagged four extra fish that are tied to a stringer off the stern. Now Brad, Nicole, and Tanner are situated around the cabin table, polishing off a portion of the day's catch and being serenaded by the hiss of the propane lantern hanging from a hook in the ceiling

Brad gathers up the dirty dishes and stands. His right foot is on the first step of the ladder when the first explosion rips through the night. The plates slip through his hands and crash onto the floor, sending shards of pottery skittering in every direction. Before the mishap can register in his mind, another massive explosion erupts just as the blast wave from the first races across the water and slams into the boat. Nicole shouts, but she's drowned out by a third thudding explosion, followed closely by a fourth. "Grab something and hold on," Brad shouts as the aftereffects from the second explosion batter the boat, keeling her hard to starboard. Brad neglected to latch the spice cabinet closed and bottles of spices rain down like leaves in autumn.

As the boat begins to settle back in the water, the concussive blast wave from the last two explosions plows into the boat, pushing her hard over to starboard again. Brad's hand slips off the handrail and he goes tumbling head over ass, banging his head on the table base before thudding into the far bulkhead. He lies in a heap, but before the pain can register in his brain, the propane lantern flies off the hook and shatters against the far wall, igniting a curtain. Brad pushes to his feet and stumbles forward as the curtain blooms with fire. He yanks it from the wall and singes the hair on his arms as he balls it up, trying to smother the flames. His efforts prove fruitless and he lurches toward the ladder, tossing the flaming curtain through the hatch and wobbling after it. Stumbling and fumbling upward, he belly flops onto the deck and scrambles to his feet. As the boat begins to settle, he grabs the flaming curtain and tosses it overboard.

Brad sucks in a lungful of air and bends over, his hands on his knees, trying to regain his breath after it was crushed from his lungs when he slammed into the bulkhead. Nicole and Tanner scramble up the ladder and onto the deck as the boat finally comes to rest. After several deep breaths, Brad stands on shaking legs and grabs the rail for support. Back to the south, it looks and sounds as if hell has surfaced on earth as the roaring wall of flames shoots skyward, accompanied by the agonizing screams of those engulfed in the fire.

Nicole turns away from the ghastly scene and clicks on a flashlight, pulling Brad close. "You're bleeding." She shines the light across his upper torso before moving to his head. "You have a nasty scalp laceration. Probably needs stiches, but you'll live."

"Thanks, Doc. I'll stop in at the next urgent care cent—"

His words are clipped by another enormous explosion. They scramble to find a handhold as the giant wave races across the sea and slams into the boat. Again the boat keels over and just when it feels like the boat is going to overturn, the wave passes and the *EmmaSophia* settles back in the water. It takes a few moments before the three can regain their footing.

"What was that, Dad?" Tanner asks.

Brad shuffles unsteadily toward the back and sinks onto the vinyl bench. "That, Tanner, was payback." He walks his fingers up his skull, searching gently for the wound and groaning when he finds it. "And before you ask, I don't know who."

"I bet it was one of ours," Tanner says.

"Or the Russians, or the Iraqis, or the Turks, or whoever is left in this godforsaken world," Brad says, his voice laced with pain. "Let's just be grateful the Chinese were on the receiving end this time."

Nicole sits down next to Brad. She pulls his probing fingers away from their exploration. "You're going to get it infected if you don't stop."

"It hurts."

"I know it hurts. But digging your dirty fingers in it isn't going to help. Do you have rubbing alcohol and bandages?"

"There's a first aid kit in the bottom drawer, left of the sink."

Nicole releases his hand and climbs down the ladder, returning moments later with a small mesh pack and a bottle of alcohol. "Tanner, will you hold the flashlight while I patch up your father?"

Tanner reluctantly turns away from the carnage and grabs the flashlight, clicking it on. "I still think it was one of ours."

"It could be. I don't see any other surface—ssshh-hhiiiittt," Brad shouts, jerking his head away from Nicole's hand. "You could have warned me."

"It's done now." Using a patch of gauze, she delicately cleans the wound on Brad's head. "You were saying?"

Brad scowls at Nicole. "I was saying, we haven't seen any other surface ships. And we didn't see any telltale signs of incoming missiles. That leads me to believe a submarine attacked the enemy ships. If that's the case, we may never know—"

His words are drowned out by another massive explosion.

Chapter 107

1.5 miles off the tip of Cape Lookout

"Fire tube two," Captain Thompson orders. The sub shudders as the second torpedo explodes away from the submarine and tracks toward the Chinese tanker.

"One minute to target," Weapons Officer White says as the blast wave from the first explosion ripples across the submarine.

Thompson is standing in the middle of the attack center. "Mr. White, load tubes three and four and stand by." Thompson lifts his cap, wipes his brow with the back of his hand, and resettles the cap on his head. Immediately after firing the initial salvo, the USS *New York* ran hard and deep for two minutes before slowing. With no return fire, the sub made a long, looping turn and began sneaking into position, a mile north and another mile east from their original firing location.

"Mr. Adams, anything from the two destroyers?"

"A few subsequent explosions, Skipper."

"Damage estimates from the first torpedo?" Thompson asks.

"I can confirm detonation on target, sir."

"Thank you. We'll go up for a peek after the second torpedo detonates."

"Ten seconds, Skipper," White says.

The crew waits in silence. Seconds later there's an explosion, followed by a much larger explosion.

"We hit their fuel storage, Skipper," Adams says.

Those on the bridge offer a muted cheer before the sub is rocked by a succession of blast waves, the second one actually rocking the boat from side to side. "Q, take us to periscope depth," Thompson orders as he steps over to the chart table.

Garcia walks over to join him. "Good shooting, Bull."

"Not me. It's our crew." Thompson pulls up a map of the area and widens the view. "How many torpedoes still in inventory?"

"Eight. Hopefully we'll get to hang on to them for a while."

"You and me both, Carlos. I'm weary, you're weary, and the crew's weary. We need a game plan."

"What are the odds we run into more Chinese ships?"

Thompson sits. "Fifty-fifty, maybe. This group was positioned well. It allowed them to roam up and down the eastern seaboard, at least the parts that still exist. Could be there might be another pod off the coast of southern Florida, but I find that unlikely. Most of Florida would have been obliterated."

"So the odds are better than fifty-fifty," Garcia says, taking a seat next to Thompson.

"Maybe. But we don't know who else may be lurking out there. If it looks good through the periscope, I think we should sail offshore a couple miles and surface to let the crew stretch their legs and get some fresh air. I don't want to risk resurfacing until we're a mile off the coast of the Virgin Islands."

"What about searching for survivors from the *Grant*?"

Thompson winces and glances at the clock. "Any survivors would have been in the water for hours now, not to mention the hours it would take for us to return to their position. It rips my guts out, but I don't think there's anything we can do."

Garcia nods. "I concur. And Myrtle Beach?"

Thompson sighs and lets the question linger for a few moments. Finally, he says, "I won't put the crew at risk. I'll find my way back if I can. I'm hoping if they're still alive, they've assimilated with other families. Or that's what I choose to believe."

Once the sub levels off, Thompson stands and orders the periscope up. He waits for it to ascend and positions his eyes in the eyecups and triggers the video camera. With the ensuing fires there's no need for night vision. He walks a circle, getting an overall impression of the situation. The tanker is nothing but a ball of fire and the two destroyers look as if a giant had cleaved them with an ax. Both are entirely destroyed and partially submerged, their bows and sterns pointing skyward at a thirty-degree angle. "Comms, put the periscope feed on the video monitors." He magnifies the image until the three destroyed ships fill the entire frame, and steps over to one of the monitors on the bridge. The cameras are high-definition and the image is as clear as if seeing it through the naked eye, maybe better.

There are Chinese sailors in the water and he wonders, briefly, what will happen to them. Nothing good, he surmises, turning away from the monitor and stepping back to the periscope, curious about the sailboat he'd seen earlier. After clicking the periscope camera off, he positions the periscope on the sailboat and dials the magnification to the max. Technology is an amazing thing. Although the boat is nearly a mile away, the roaring fires produce enough light to read the facial expressions of those onboard. On deck are three people—a man, a woman, and a younger person, probably a teenager. He feels the pang of loss watching the three interact like a normal family. After observing their interactions for a few more moments, he nudges the scope to the right, trying to discover the boat's name. All he can see from this angle is the word *Emma*.

"Scope down," Thompson orders. "Mr. Patterson, nudge us out to sea another mile or two and we'll bring her to the surface. Carlos, put a topside security team together."

CHAPTER 108

Down in the galley, Brad ducks into the head to check his wound in the mirror. There's nothing much to see other that a large wad of gauze held in place by a piece of tape. He exits and grabs another bottle of wine and pulls the cork. After retrieving two glasses, he makes his way up to the deck, where he pours a glass and hands it to Nicole. "Medicinal purposes," Brad says, pouring a good amount into his glass.

Nicole clinks glasses with him. "For both of us. I think my nerves are shot. Tanner, you want some?"

"Uh, no," Tanner replies without turning, his gaze focused on the mayhem near the shore.

Brad sinks onto the seat and Nicole sits down beside him, the distant flames casting an orange light across the deck. "Think that's the end of it?" Nicole asks.

"I sure as hell hope so."

They sip their wine in silence for a few moments before Nicole says, "What's the ultimate goal, Brad?"

Brad shrugs. "I'm hoping we can make it to Key

West, where we could anchor offshore for a while. If not there, we'll work our way down to the Bahamas. There has to be a place in the world that hasn't been bombed to hell."

"You keep saying *we*. Do you mean you and Tanner?"

Brad glances at the burning ships for a moment before turning to face Nicole. "No, *we* means all three of us. That is, if you want to tag along with us."

"I would like that very much," Nicole says.

"Good," Brad replies.

Seconds later they hear a splash, which is followed moments later by a large swell that rocks the boat. Brad hands his wineglass to Nicole. "Will you hold that for a sec?" He stands and grabs the binoculars off the helm, stepping to the back of the boat. It felt like the swell started off their stern, and he puts the binoculars to his eyes and scans the ocean surface. On the first pass he doesn't see anything so he returns to his starting point and tries again, scanning very slowly. He stops midway and rolls the focus knob. "I'll be damned," he mutters when he sees a very large silhouette just visible in the flickering light. He marks the location in his mind and lowers the binocs. "Tanner, pull the anchor."

He hurries back to the helm. "Nicole, will you grab a couple of flashlights from below?"

"What's going on?" Nicole asks.

"Maybe an answer to a prayer."

Nicole offers a bewildered look before ducking down the hatch to the galley.

Brad clicks the key to check the fuel gauge again.

The needle hasn't changed—it's still hovering near the empty mark. "Screw it," he mutters, twisting the key and firing up the engine.

As soon as Tanner has the anchor aboard, Brad shouts, "Hold on," and gooses the throttle. He turns the wheel until the bow is pointed out to sea and looks through the binoculars again and adjusts his course.

Nicole climbs the stairs and returns to the deck. "What do you want me to do with the flashlights?"

"Just hold on to them for a second."

He puts the binoculars to his eyes and makes a slight course adjustment. After running at full speed for a few moments, the engine begins to sputter and Brad eases up on the throttle. He shouts into the wind, "Tanner, come stand back here with us."

Tanner scampers across the deck and climbs down into the cockpit, taking a position next to his father. "What are we doing, Dad?"

"You'll see in just a moment."

Tanner and Nicole share a confused glance.

Brad stands on his tiptoes to look over the top of the boat. "Nicole, turn on the flashlights and hand one to Tanner. I want you to point them up at our faces."

Nicole glances at Tanner and both shrug. They click on the lights and turn them so the beams wash upward across their faces. Brad eases back on the throttle, nudges the wheel to the left, and holds course. A minute later, a light as bright as the sun hits them in the face. All three raise their arms to shield their eyes.

A loudspeaker clicks on and a voice says: "You are approaching a U.S. naval vessel and are hereby ordered to change course."

"What the hell, Dad," Tanner says. "Are you crazy?"

"Maybe," Brad says. He nudges the throttle forward.

The voice over the loudspeaker is booming when it says: "We will not issue a second warning. Change course immediately or we will fire on your vessel."

Brad pulls the throttle to neutral and cups his hands around his mouth. "We are American citizens. I would like to speak to the captain." They're close enough now to see a row of sailors on the deck of the submarine—a row of rifles pointed in their direction.

This time when the loudspeaker sounds, it's a different voice. "What is the name of your boat?"

"The *EmmaSophia*," Brad shouts.

Almost instantly the bright light is switched off, but it'll be a while before Brad's night vision returns. He hears something thud against the bow of the boat and he scrambles forward, searching. He feels around the deck and finds a thick, heavy rope.

"Tie it off to your boat," the same voice says, this time from nearby and not over the loudspeaker.

Brad ties the rope to one of the cleats on the bow, and the boat begins to move forward, bumping up against something hard.

Flashlights kick on, revealing two men standing on a deck about eight feet above the sailboat. Both men are smiling. "I'm Captain Rex Thompson and this is my executive officer, Carlos Garcia. Sorry you were caught in the middle of our little war."

"I don't think *little* begins to describe it," Brad says before introducing himself, then Tanner and Nicole.

"Mind if we come aboard?" the captain asks.

"Please," Brad says.

The sub crew tosses down a net ladder and tie lines to the two officers' harnesses and they climb down the net onto the deck of the sailboat one after the other. The captain frees his harness. "Just a little insurance in case we miss a step." He steps across the deck and steps down into the cockpit, followed by Garcia. Brad steps forward and offers his hand. After a round of handshakes they all take a seat.

"Would you two like a glass of wine?" Nicole asks, clicking on a couple of flashlights.

"We would love a glass of wine," Garcia says without checking with his boss. Nicole ducks below and returns with two more glasses and another bottle from the stash. She fills them and passes them across.

"Looks like you suffered a nasty bump on the head," Thompson says. "You get rocked around a little?"

"Again, *little* doesn't begin to describe it," Brad answers.

"Want my medics to check you over?" Thompson asks. "That's the least we can do."

Brad waves his hand. "No, I'm fine. But I do have a request."

Thompson takes a sip of wine and smacks his lips. "Shoot."

"You have a desalination plant aboard, correct?"

"We have a lot of things aboard that I can't divulge, Brad."

Brad's shoulders slump.

"But the desalination plant isn't one of them." Thompson laughs and takes another sip of wine.

Garcia puts a radio to his lips and orders a hose lowered to the *EmmaSophia*.

"Water's about the *only* thing we do have to offer," Garcia says. "Glad we can accommodate you."

"Are you out of food?" Tanner asks.

"Not out, but we're close. We'll make it stretch for a few more days."

"Speaking of food, can you two stay for dinner?" Nicole asks. "We have some fresh black sea bass."

Thompson and Garcia share a glance before Thompson says, "Black sea bass sounds wonderful."

Nicole pulls the cork on the new bottle and refills the four glasses.

Brad thanks her, picks up his glass, and takes a sip. "We were about a mile away when those Chinese ships launched a barrage of missiles."

Thompson squirms in his seat as Garcia answers. "They took out one of our destroyers, the USS *Grant*." Garcia pauses, swirling the wine around in his glass. "The captain was one of our good friends. We'd been sailing together for a couple of days, but were out of range when they attacked." He glances at the fires in the distance and says, "I think their shooting days are over."

"I'll say. I'm very sorry for your loss," Brad says. He tilts his wineglass and lets the wine fill his mouth, savoring the taste on his tongue before swallowing. "You said *one of*—are there more of our ships out there?"

"Not that we've found," Thompson says, his voice subdued. "But you'd have to think some survived."

"Have you had radio contact with anyone?" Brad asks.

"No," Garcia says. "We established a sight-line radio link to talk to the *Grant*, but that's it."

Nicole places her wineglass on the helm. "Tanner, will you help me with the fish?"

"Sure," Tanner says. They step to the stern and pull the fish aboard. Tanner helps Nicole clean and fillet them while Brad ducks down into the galley to fire up the stove.

Garcia appears in the hatch with the hose. "Where's your freshwater tank?"

Brad kneels and lifts a hatch then steps up and takes the hose from Garcia and feeds it into the tank. After another radio call from Garcia, a stream of clean water jets out the end of the hose. "Give me a shout when she's full," Garcia says.

"Will do," Brad says. "Enjoy the wine." He pulls a large pan down and places it on the stove to heat and bends down to pick up a handful of spice containers. "That's tomorrow's project," he mutters. Tanner arrives with the fillets and Brad places them in the pan as his son returns topside to rinse his hands. Once the fish is cooked he fills the plates with heaping portions and Nicole helps him carry them topside. "Dig in," Brad says, taking a seat next to Nicole.

They eat at a leisurely pace, interspersing the food with pleasant conversation. There is no talk of war, or the dead, or the future. Most of the conversation is centered on recent adventures or past experiences of life before doomsday. Above them, sailors stroll along the deck of the submarine and the muted conversations or occasional laughter drift down to the *EmmaSophia*.

Brad occasionally checks the water level of the tank, and on the next trip discovers the tank full. Garcia radios the boat and the water is turned off and the hose retrieved.

"How long are you going to stay surfaced?" Tanner asks.

"We'll slip under the water before daylight," Thompson says. "On a normal deployment we never surface. Too many eyes in the sky."

"How long's a deployment?" Tanner asks.

"Usually seventy days—some missions stretch to ninety days."

"And you're under the water the whole time?" Tanner asks.

"Yep, we only surface when we return to port."

"I don't think I would like that," Tanner says.

Garcia laughs. "Some people can't handle it, but you do get used to it. Hey, Tanner, you want a look inside the boat?"

Tanner scoots forward on the bench. "Yes. I'd love to." He glances at his father. "Dad?"

"Fine with me. But keep your hands off the buttons."

They all laugh, something they've done very little of since it all began. Garcia makes a radio call and leads Tanner to the bow of the sailboat, where he straps him into a harness. "Now the hard part, Tanner. You have to climb the net."

It's a struggle for Tanner the first few times, but he eventually gets the hang of it and scampers up the net. After another hour or so of conversation and with the wine bottles empty, Thompson and Garcia push to their feet as Tanner returns as excited as Brad has seen him in a very long time.

"How was it, son?"

"It's awesome. Everything's computerized and the

bridge looks like the control room of the Starship *Enterprise*. And they let me look through the periscope."

"So you ready to sign up?" Brad asks.

"Uh, no. It was okay, knowing I could climb out the hatch anytime I wanted. But I get the willies thinking about being in there for days."

Thompson and Garcia laugh. Garcia says, "Once you're on mission, you don't really think about being underwater."

Tanner thanks them and eagerly shakes their hands.

"Where are you headed?" Nicole asks the captain.

"Probably the U.S. Virgin Islands. We'll see where we end up. What about you?"

"We were hoping to dock or anchor at Key West," Brad answers.

Thompson shakes his head. "Key West is a no-go. There's a big naval air base on Boca Chica Key, about four miles north of Key West. I have no doubt it was hit, and hit hard."

"If not there, then where?" Brad asks.

"That's a tough one to answer, Brad. There are some very large military installations in the Carolinas, Georgia, and Florida. Your best bet is probably the Bahamas."

"I guess that's where we're headed," Brad says. "Good luck to you in your journey."

"May I have a word, Brad?" Thompson asks.

"Certainly," Brad replies.

Thompson takes Brad by the elbow and leads him to the back of the boat. He pulls a folded piece of paper from his back pocket and hands it to Brad.

Brad looks down to see three names and Thompson's last name, along with an address, written on the outside.

"My family was vacationing around Myrtle Beach when everything happened. If you pass that way on your travels, I'd appreciate it if you could pass on this letter to one of the locals. Maybe it'll eventually find its way to my family. They were staying at the Bayshore Resort."

"Of course, Captain. I'd be happy to."

Thompson pats Brad on the shoulder. "Thank you." He turns and gives Nicole a hug and, after another round of good-byes, both officers pull on their harnesses and Thompson says, "Brad, you can stay tied up for the night. I'll send someone from the crew to untie your boat before we depart."

"Thank you," Brad says.

Thompson shouts up to the deck and the two men climb the net with assistance from the crew above. Brad rinses the plates as Nicole gathers up the wineglasses. Once everything is clean and stowed away, they bed down for the night. For the first time since their journey began, they can sleep peacefully, knowing they're safe.

CHAPTER 109

With darkness only a few hours away, and with the kids' growing curiosity with the two dead bodies on the ground, it was decided the explanations could wait. Now on I-40, east of Oklahoma City, Zane and Alyx are at the head of their small caravan, the flatbed truck following closely behind.

"They did a number on Oklahoma City," Alyx says.

"You knew it was going to be that way. Tinker was probably pretty high up the food chain when it came to selecting targets. They probably dropped six or seven nukes on it and the blast waves and firestorms ate up the rest of the city." Zane squirms in the seat, trying to get comfortable. "What's the deal with this Stan guy?"

Alyx smiles. "Who would have ever thought? The odds of running into him there have to be astronomical."

"We've established the unlikely nature of his appearance but who is he to you?"

"I told you, a friend of my dad's. Actually, they were more than friends. They were fraternity brothers at Texas A&M. He'd drop in on us occasionally over the years. Mom and Dad would run down to Dallas a couple times a year and spend the weekend doing who knows what with Stan and his wife, or ex-wife, I should say."

"How did he get hooked up with that group?"

"He didn't have time to tell me the entire story. A large group of travelers were stranded at the Minneapolis–Saint Paul airport. He said some of the international flights survived and the closest place they could find to land was there in Minnesota. The students were on their way home after spending some time overseas with one of those student ambassador groups. They're all from the Lubbock area, and from what I understand the situation at the airport was degrading, or they were running out of food. I'm not sure. Like I said, he didn't have time to provide details, but somehow they got together and decided to strike out for Texas."

"I assume the two adult women are chaperones?"

"Yeah, I think so. What a nightmare for them. Can you imagine?"

Zane slows to steer around a looted semi. "No, I can't and don't really want to. Being responsible for a bunch of kids that don't belong to you in this environment—jeez, it almost gives me a headache thinking about it. They deserve some type of humanitarian award. But back to the situation—what I find astonishing is that Stan is headed the same place we are."

"Just for a day or two. It does make sense when you think about it. Weatherford sits along I-40, and that same highway runs straight into Amarillo. From there it's a short jog south to Lubbock. I don't know if you've ever been to Lubbock, Texas, but there's no easy way to get there. The easiest way from here is the Amarillo route."

McDowell is back behind the wheel and he's back on the fence in regard to the decisions he must make. He can still get to Dallas by dropping south out of Weatherford and heading through Wichita Falls and on into Dallas—a rugged journey on foot, but doable. *But for what? In all likelihood, Dallas no longer exists.* He steals a glimpse of Lauren as she stares out the side window.

Melissa had tried to enter the cab back at the truck stop, but Lauren had nudged her away and whispered something in Melissa's ear. Now Lauren is in the cab and Melissa's in the back. He'd almost prefer Melissa be up front so he didn't have to think about it. He found it impossible to tell Alyx that he was thinking of going to Lubbock with a woman half his age, so when she asked, he told her the matter was undecided. Hell, he might be better off hanging around Weatherford. Find an abandoned house and settle in. Knowing Henry, he'll probably have the lights on in no time.

He steals another glance at Lauren. This time she catches him. She smiles. "You know, I can actually talk, too."

McDowell blushes. "I know that. I'm just trying to figure out what I should say."

"Do you want to discuss the pros and cons of coming to Lubbock with me?"

McDowell shrugs. "Already did that in my head— several times."

"And?"

"There's a lot to like about it on my part. But I'm concerned you haven't thoroughly thought out the situation." He glances at Lauren. "That's not a knock on you, but I don't want you to make an impulsive decision you'll regret later."

She turns in her seat so that she's facing McDowell. "There's nothing impulsive about my decision, Stan. I'm not suggesting we chain ourselves together until the end of time, but I do feel a connection between you and me that I would like to explore further. Like I said, no strings attached. We play it by ear and see what happens."

McDowell nods. "Okay."

"Okay? Does that mean you're going to think about it some more?"

McDowell glances at Lauren. "No, okay means we'll give it a try and see what happens."

Lauren nods and smiles. "Good. You made the right decision. Why was it so hard for you?"

"I still get hung up on the age issue. I don't want you spoon-feeding me before you even hit menopause."

Lauren laughs. "Quit worrying about the future, Stan. Let's just worry about the here and now. Deal?"

McDowell nods. "Deal."

They travel the next few miles in peaceful silence until McDowell glances over to see Lauren's face pinched with worry. "What's wrong? Changing your mind?"

She sighs. "Not at all. I'm worried about what to tell Hannah's parents."

"Only one thing you can tell them. The truth."

"But I was responsible for her. And you don't know her father. He'll spend every dime of his substantial fortune to make sure I pay for the death of his daughter."

"How? There was nothing criminal on our part about what happened, only on the part of the man who raped and murdered her."

"What if her father takes me to court?"

"There won't be any courts for the foreseeable future and even if there were there are no grounds for a lawsuit. Hannah was just at the wrong place at the wrong time."

"But I was responsible for making sure that didn't happen."

"Lauren, no one could have predicted what happened. I think you've done a tremendous job in the worst possible conditions anyone could ever imagine. Look in the back. There are sixteen other kids who are here because of you and Melissa."

"You don't know Alexander Hatcher. He's a vengeful, spiteful, hateful egomaniac. Believe me when I say, he'll find a way to punish me."

"You're right, I don't know this man, but I know his type. You let me worry about Alexander Hatcher."

They pass a sign signaling the Weatherford exit one mile ahead.

Lauren grabs a strand of hair and curls it around her index finger. "And what about the person responsible for her murder? How do we know he won't do it again?"

McDowell glances at Lauren. "That is one thing you won't ever have to worry about."

* * *

Zane takes the Weatherford exit, the off-ramp dumping them onto Washington Avenue.

"Turn right," Alyx says.

Zane does as instructed. They pass a couple of looted restaurants before entering a residential area. Washington Avenue is lined with a row of small ranch homes, many in need of paint or repair and, instead of curtains, most of the windows are covered with sheets or cardboard. Older-model autos are parked in the driveways, many with mismatched wheels or missing hubcaps.

Zane arches his brow. "This is home, huh?"

"Hey, every town has some undesirable neighborhoods. But there's not a lot of wealth in these small towns. For many it's a hardscrabble existence, doing what needs doing and little else. Besides, I was only here for a few summers."

"You excited to see your family?"

"Of course, and I'm really looking forward to being in one place longer than twenty-four hours." Alyx glances forward. "Stay on this road as it takes us out of town. I'll tell you where to turn."

Zane nods. They enter another residential area, this one a step up from the previous one. The yards are well tended, the cars a little newer, the homes a little larger. After another mile, the neighborhoods fade, giving way to a wide expanse of farmland. Here the homes are few and far between, separated by fields of row crops like soybeans or corn, interspersed with idle fields waiting the next planting.

Alyx scoots to the edge of her seat. "Make the next right. We're not far now." She looks back to make sure Stan's truck is still following and finds it is. She has mixed feelings about Stan's group trailing them to her parents' home—most of them selfish. Her homecoming will be short-lived and there will be no quiet time with her family, time she was hoping to use to assimilate Zane into the family. But it is what it is. "The next road to the left is their driveway."

Zane nods. "Looks like a nice spread." He glances over at Alyx and smiles. "Where's your dad keep the tractor?"

Alyx laughs. "In the barn. There's a small apartment on the second floor inside the barn and that's probably where we'll be staying. If you play your cards right, we might have a little midnight hanky-panky involving the tractor."

Zane grins and glances out the side window. "Hey, it just registered with me that some of the homes have lights on."

"I bet Dad and Gage got some of the turbines working. That means we'll have water and other creature comforts we haven't had for a long time."

Zane turns into the drive. "I'll settle for a bed."

"That, too," Alyx says. She's tapping the dash with her hand and pumping her right leg. "Do me a favor, Zane. Will you hold off the others until I have a chance to see my family?"

"Absolutely. He wheels into the circle drive and kills the engine. Alyx kicks her door open and races toward the house. She takes a deep breath then twists the knob and barges into the house. "I'm home," she shouts. The initial response is not what she was expecting, and Alyx's gaze sweeps the room. Her sister is sitting on the couch, cradling a screaming infant and crying, while their mother looks on, her face a mask of

worry. After overcoming her initial surprise, Alyx
mother stands from her chair and hurries across th
room, wrapping her older daughter in an embrac
"What's going on?" Alyx whispers to her mother.

"Holly's milk hasn't come in and we have nothin
to feed the baby. Been going on most of two days. You
father and Gage are out looking for baby formula."

Alyx kisses her mother on the cheek. "Hold on
She turns, sticks her head out the door, and shout
"Zane, bring the baby formula."

"You have formula?" Susan Reed asks, her eyes i
big as Frisbees.

"Yes. We got some from Sarah—never mind, it's
long story that's going to have to wait."

"And Zane?"

"*Not* a long story—he's the one."

Zane enters, carrying two cases of infant formula
"Where do you want them, Ms. Reed?"

"It's Susan, and on the kitchen counter." She an
Alyx follow Zane into the kitchen as Holly pushes u
from the sofa and hurries over, the baby still wailing.

"You must be Holly," Zane says, leaning forward t
grab a clean bottle from the windowsill over the sink
He twists off the nipple, adds water to the bottle, an
adds a scoop of powdered formula.

"I'm Zane." He screws on the nipple and shakes
up before handing the bottle to Holly. "Alyx says yo
haven't yet decided on a name for your baby."

Alyx sidesteps her mother and wraps an arm aroun
Zane's waist.

Holly inserts the nipple into the baby's mouth, an
the sudden quiet is a welcome relief. "Olivia, Zane
Her name is Olivia."

"A beautiful name, for a beautiful little girl."

"Thank you," Holly says. "I hope my sister keeps you around for a while."

"Me, too," Zane replies, glancing at Alyx. "You tell your mother yet?"

"Wha—no. Mom, we're not the only ones to show up on your doorstep today."

Susan's eyes open wider. "What do you mean?"

"Look out the window."

Susan strides to the window, glances out, and gasps. "Is that Stan?"

Alyx and Zane join her at the window. "Yes," Alyx says, "and believe me, that's *another* long story."

CHAPTER 110

Weatherford

Gage is seething. They've been to two different neighborhoods and Henry still can't recall exactly where Dr. Stone lives.

Henry glances at Gage. "It's not my fault, Gage. I bet I haven't seen Dr. Stone in five years or more."

Gage white-knuckles the steering wheel.

"Let's try that new neighborhood north of town. Now that I think about it, I recall him telling me that he and Harriet had moved out there."

Gage wants to yell, *Why didn't you think of that sooner?* but doesn't. Clenching his jaw, he steers onto North Washington Avenue, mashing the gas. He jerks the wheel to veer around a dead truck then jerks the wheel back, the tires on the old truck barking.

Henry rubs his injured arm. "We're not going to be a damn bit of good to anyone if we're dead."

Gage glances over at his father-in-law and eases up on the gas. "We really don't have time to be driving all over town."

"She's my only grandchild, Gage. We're all on the same team, here."

Gage exhales a long breath. "I know. I just feel so damn helpless."

"I know and I feel the same. The only thing we can do is find that baby some formula."

They ride in silence for a few moments, passing another neighborhood, then the high school, before Gage turns into the new addition. "Do you know which street?" Gage asks.

"No. Drive around a bit. Now that we're here, I think we came to a Christmas party at his house several years ago. I'll know it when I see it."

Gage stifles his sigh and drives down one street, turns, and drives up another.

Henry scoots to the edge of his seat and leans forward. "I think we're getting close. I remember he had a big oak tree in the front yard."

Gage makes a right turn at the end and pulls down another street.

"There it is," Henry says, pointing.

Gage's heart plummets. He pulls into the drive of a fairly large home, a FOR SALE sign staked in the middle of the yard. "Goddammit," Gage mutters.

"I'm sorry, Gage. I had no idea."

Gage slams the truck into park. "Now what?"

Henry scoots back in his seat.

"Know any other pediatricians?"

Henry shakes his head. "Have you tried the hospital?"

"No." Gage reverses out of drive and returns to the main road. After a couple of miles he pulls into the parking lot fronting the hospital and eases up to the front door. The glass is shattered, the fragments scattered all around the entry area. Gage puts the truck in park and grabs the pistol off the seat.

"Want me to come with you?"

Gage pushes open the door and climbs out, grabbing a flashlight from the door pocket. "No. You stay with the truck. Somebody steals it we'll really be screwed."

Henry nods and pulls the shotgun closer.

Gage steps through the shattered door and clicks on the flashlight. The corridor is littered with desks, beds, chairs, dead bodies, and trash. Gage pulls his shirt up over his nose and takes it a room at a time, trying to tamp down his growing nausea while flinging open cabinet doors and searching for infant formula. The hospital is a reflection of the town; neither is very large. Gage darts down another corridor. The door to the hospital pharmacy is hanging on by a hinge, and he ducks inside. Nothing but empty shelves—not even a box of hemorrhoid cream. He returns to the corridor and continues to search. After ten minutes, he's covered the entire hospital. Nothing. He hurries back to the truck and climbs in.

"I've been thinking, Gage. I have an old phonebook back at the house. We can use it to find another pediatrician."

Gage drops the truck in gear. "About the only plan we have left."

They skirt the edge of town and Gage turns onto Main Street, which transitions into Highway 54 outside of town. They cover the next three miles in silence. He makes a right then a left into the drive and brakes hard.

"Who the hell is that?" Henry asks.

Gage eases off the brake, steering around an old flatbed truck and a gold rusted-out pickup. "Keep that shotgun handy."

Gage parks, grabs the pistol, and steps out. Henry piles out the other side, the shotgun up and ready for action. "What do you want to do?" Gage whispers.

Henry glances toward the barn. It doesn't appear anyone is out there. "You go for the door and I'll cover you."

Gage eases up next to the house. The windows are covered by curtains, but he can hear voices, and a lot of them. *Are we being raided by a gang of killers?* He inches closer to the door, waving Henry to the other side, where he'll have a clear field of fire if someone steps out. Gage puts a hand on the doorknob and takes a deep breath. He plays the scenario in his mind based on what he'd seen on *Law & Order.* They always go in low, so Gage squats down, turns the knob, and pushes the door open. He pivots inside, the pistol an extension of his arm. It takes him a moment to process what his eyes see, and then his brain kicks in—it's Alyx holding Olivia. He points the gun toward the ceiling and stands. He ducks his head outside and calls Henry toward the house. "You're not going to need the shotgun."

Henry looks at him, bewildered. Gage steps aside, and Henry nearly sags to his knees at the sight of his older daughter.

ONE
WEEK
LATER

CHAPTER 111

After weeks underground, the ayatollah is looking forward to a little fresh air—and some time away from his bickering wives. Buried deep, the bunker has been sealed since the first shot. The last contact the ayatollah had with the outside world was confirmation from General Mohammadi that the attack was under way. The ayatollah stops on the stairs and adjusts his turban. As the mastermind, and the first to initiate talks with the North Koreans, he's now ready to receive the well-deserved adoration from his people.

After a furious argument with his security detail this morning, he will be stepping into the light alone. He climbs to the next landing and pauses to catch his breath. Members of his security detail did, for the first time, venture outside earlier in the day. They returned grim faced but had little to report. What the ayatollah doesn't know is that they were reluctant to tell their leader the truth. The last security guard to report bad news had been shot on sight. The ayatollah looks up to see one more flight of stairs. The light spreads down the shaft, warming the leader's face. He smiles and continues to climb. On the next-to-last step, well out of view of his people, he pauses to straighten his turban again. He takes a deep, calming breath, spreads his arms wide to welcome his flock, and ascends the final step.

His arms drop to his sides when he sees the utter devastation around him. The stench of rotting bodies is nearly overwhelming, and he puts a hand over his mouth and nose to keep from gagging. Slowly, he turns a circle. His beautiful palace, furnished to his exacting tastes, had occupied the space over his bunker. It is now rubble—as is all of Tehran. He stops turning when he spots a man in a tattered military uniform digging through a pile of stones. The man looks up, stands, and approaches, dragging his left leg.

It takes a while for the man to cover the distance, but the ayatollah waits patiently for him to arrive. When the man is within four feet he stops, and rather than defer to the Iranian leader, he stands tall.

The ayatollah is somewhat taken aback by the man's brazenness. "What is your name, my son?"

"My name is Saman Rezaei. And I'm not your son."

The ayatollah shuffles back a step. He looks at the insignia on the man's uniform, but he'd never really learned to differentiate the symbols of the lower ranks. "Where are you posted?"

"I was stationed at the Semnan Missile and Space Center."

"Why aren't you with your unit?"

"There is no more unit. It took me six days to dig out of the rubble. I am the only survivor." Rezaei limps forward a step. "Do you know what it is like to spend six days underground? Not in a bunker where you're well fed and surrounded by your family, but six days, digging and scraping, no food and no water, and not knowing if you are going to live or die?"

The ayatollah glances around to see if any of his security detail had followed him up despite his orders not to do so. But the Iranian leader remains alone. He straightens his robe and squares his shoulders before turning back to Rezaei. "I'm proud of your service to our great country."

"Your great country no longer exists." Rezaei limps forward another step, the distance between them now narrowed to arm's length. "I spent more than a week making the journey to this city. And even then I had to wait."

"What were you waiting for, my son?"

Rezaei slowly reaches behind and pulls out his service pistol. "For the sniveling dog who started all this to show his face." Rezaei raises the pistol and fires, punching a hole in the ayatollah's forehead. As the Iranian leader crumples to ground, Rezaei calmly tucks the pistol behind his back and turns, limping back through the rubble.

CHAPTER 112

Charlotte Amalie, Saint Thomas, U.S. Virgin Islands

"Steady as she goes," Thompson tells the helmsman, Roy Wisdom, who's standing next to him on the sail. "The last thing we need to do is wreck the boat after everything we've been through." They surfaced at the mouth of the bay and are now maneuvering toward the Havensight Point pier on the east side of the bay.

"Yes, sir," Wisdom replies.

Spread out before them is Charlotte Amalie, the capital city of the U.S. Virgin Islands. Located on Saint Thomas, the irregular-shaped bay is surrounded by a string of heavily forested, low-rise mountains with homes perched at various levels before spilling down to the bay. The town itself is situated on the floor of the valley and spreads the width of the bay, the red tile roofs in stark contrast to the luscious greenery that slopes upward behind the town. It's a spectacular sight, especially after everything the crew of the USS *New York* has endured.

Two large cruise ships are tied up at the pier and, from the looks of them, are still functioning—at least partially. Towels and swimsuits are draped over balcony railings to dry, and people are milling about on deck. A group has formed at the stern of the nearest cruise ship, watching the *New York* approach.

The Havensight Point pier juts out into the bay nearly a thousand feet, and that's exactly where Thompson is planning to dock the boat. "Mr. Wisdom, I want the sail lined up on the edge of the pier."

"Aye, aye, Skipper," Wisdom replies as he works the controls from the upper bridge. "Sure wished we had a tug, sir."

"You and me both. But we don't. Take her slow and steady."

The sub is two hundred yards from the pier when Wisdom idles the engines. The forward momentum allows them to coast the rest of the distance. Sailors from the crew jump onto the pier to handle the dock lines. Thompson climbs down the conning tower and returns to the bridge. He and Garcia are outfitted in their dress uniforms. The next item on their list is a meeting with the territorial governor who resides in the Government House, located in the center of town.

"You sure you don't want a security detail on deck?" Garcia asks.

"I'm sure." He turns to Lieutenant Commander Quigley. "Q, make sure the security team is assembled and ready to go just in case. But keep them below deck for now."

Garcia and Thompson make their way to the forward hatch and climb up to the deck. The crew has secured the gangway and they walk down to the pier—their first contact with solid ground in almost four months. Along the pier is a collection of restaurants and stores, many of them open. The aroma of grilling burgers makes Thompson's mouth water.

"What are they doing for money?" Garcia asks.

Thompson shrugs. "Maybe it's a barter economy."

"Wonder what I'd have to give up for a burger and a beer?"

"Don't know. But I bet we find out later."

The two cruise ships are enormous, towering over the pier. People are coming and going up the gangways, in various states of dress, as if they were on a normal vacation. Some of the crew members from the ships are hanging out on the pier, and Thompson is tempted to stop and talk to them to get the lay of the land. But he doesn't. Best to make an official appearance first. At the end of the pier they find a line of bicycle cabs and they climb into the one at the head of the line and tell the driver their destination.

People are out and about as if it were any normal day. The journey to Government House is short and the driver pulls up to the front steps. Garcia pays the tab and they don their caps and climb the red-carpeted steps toward the front door, bracing for the unknown. The building is a white three-story structure with wide expansive balconies on the first and second floors. An ornate iron balustrade runs the length of both balconies and each section is separated by a row of stately round columns. The double doors open inward when Garcia and Thompson arrive. They remove their hats and step inside.

A butler leads them to an ornate office and a large black man moves from behind the desk, a smile on his face and his hand outstretched. Garcia and Thompson relax.

"I'm Territorial Governor Charles Knapp. Welcome to Saint Thomas." He shakes their hands and offers Thompson and Garcia chairs. After working his way back around his desk, he sits. "Not very many people on the island have ever seen a submarine."

"Not very many people, period, have ever seen a submarine," Thompson says. "We kind of like it that way."

Knapp laughs. "I suppose that's right." He steeples his fingers and leans back in his chair. "I assume you're looking for safe harbor."

"Yes, and more importantly, a place to live," Thompson replies.

"We'll find a way to accommodate you and your crew."

Thompson's shoulders sag with relief. "Thank you," Thompson says, "We were beginning to think we'd never find a place to call home."

"We saw a lot of businesses and restaurants open. Are you operating a barter economy?" Garcia asks.

"No, it's a cash economy."

Garcia scoots to the edge of the seat. "The crew, ourselves included, has very little ready cash available."

"Not to worry," Knapp says. "We're running everything through the island banks. I'm willing to allocate twenty-five hundred dollars for each enlisted crew member and five thousand for you and your officers.

The local government is also willing to provide free room and board for the first three months to allow your men time to find employment on the island."

Thompson and Garcia share a surprised glance before Thompson turns back to Knapp. "What's the catch?"

Knapp laughs. "No catch. We are a United States territory and you are members of the United States Navy. Did you think we were going to throw you to the wolves?"

"We didn't really know what to expect," Thompson says, thinking back to Ponta Delgada. "But we were bracing for the worst. Where will you house my men?"

"There are numerous unoccupied vacation rentals. Housing won't be a problem."

"And jobs?" Garcia asks.

"There are jobs available. You and your officers will be prized for your expertise. Most likely you'll find employment within the island government."

Thompson leans back in his chair. "That's very generous, Governor Knapp. I'm not necessarily a skeptic, but, sir, I keep waiting for the other shoe to drop."

Knapp laughs, his expansive belly jiggling. "I assure you, Captain, there are no more shoes, dropping or otherwise. The local government met as soon as we heard what had happened and developed this plan. We knew it was only a matter of time before one or more Navy ships arrived."

"What about the sub?" Thompson asks.

"We'll place a guard at the pier, though I don't know what anyone would want with it. I assume the nuclear missiles are no longer on board?"

"Correct," Thompson answers.

Knapp nods.

"Have you heard anything from the mainland?" Garcia asks.

"Nothing," Knapp replies. "Rumor has it—and it's only rumor and we may never know precisely what happened—that a couple of the Russian ballistic missile submarines were lurking off the eastern seaboard when everything started. You're the expert. How long do you think it would take their missiles to strike the D.C. area?"

"Not long. It depends on their exact location, but certainly within minutes. Maybe ten, possibly fifteen, if they were lucky."

Knapp nods and leans forward in his chair. "That's about what I thought. It will take a day or two for my staff to sort out the living arrangements, but I'll have the money delivered to you at the submarine within the hour. I trust you'll take responsibility for distributing each share?"

"Of course," Thompson says. "And, thank you."

"You're very welcome. I would take great pleasure if you and your officers would join me tonight for dinner."

Thompson and Garcia stand. "We'd love to," Thompson says.

Knapp stands and works his way around the desk. "Seven okay with you?"

Thompson shakes the governor's hand. "Perfect."

Knapp walks them to the door and Garcia and Thompson take their leave. After they step outside and don their hats, Garcia drapes an arm across his friend's shoulders. "Beers and burgers on me."

CHAPTER 113

Near Myrtle Beach, South Carolina

When you rely on Mother Nature to provide propulsion there are good days and bad days. Brad doesn't know how far they've traveled over the last week because of the lack of identifiable landmarks along the shore, but he estimates they've covered about fifty miles. Yesterday, they rounded Bald Head Island and picked up a consistent breeze they rode all day long. And today's been much of the same, and they're now approaching the Myrtle Beach area, at least according to the atlas Brad keeps on the boat.

Brad trims the mainsail and the boat picks up speed. He glances at the map in his lap then glances toward shore. One area that's surrounded on three sides by water is the most intact area they've seen during the past week. But just to the south of that little enclave it's a continuation of the same—denuded ground dotted with occasional tree stumps. Tanner and Nicole are snuggled under a blanket on the port side, reading. Brad looks at the map again and swivels his gaze toward shore. He spots a pier jutting out into the bay and,